The Widows of Braxton County

Also by Jess McConkey

Love Lies Bleeding

The Widows of Braxton County

JESS McCONKEY

WILLIAM MORROW
An Imprint of HarperCollins*Publishers*

P.S.™ is a trademark of HarperCollins Publishers.

THE WIDOWS OF BRAXTON COUNTY. Copyright © 2013 by Shirley Damsgaard. All rights reserved. Printed in the United States of America. No part of this book may be used or reproduced in any manner whatsoever without written permission except in the case of brief quotations embodied in critical articles and reviews. For information address HarperCollins Publishers, 10 East 53rd Street, New York, NY 10022.

HarperCollins books may be purchased for educational, business, or sales promotional use. For information please write: Special Markets Department, HarperCollins Publishers, 10 East 53rd Street, New York, NY 10022.

FIRST EDITION

Designed by Diahann Sturge

Library of Congress Cataloging-in-Publication Data has been applied for.

ISBN 978-0-06-218826-7

13 14 15 16 17 18   OV/RRD   10 9 8 7 6 5 4 3 2 1

To my mother, Rosey Damsgaard Davis.
You were liberated before it was fashionable and
your example gave me the courage to pursue my dreams.
Thanks for setting boundaries, but never limitations.

The Widows of Braxton County

Chapter 1

Summer 1890, the Krause Homestead, Braxton County, Iowa

Hannah Krause drew the back of her hand over her eyes and, careful of the squeaking bedsprings, slowly rolled onto her side. Her tongue felt thick and coated. She longed for a drink of water, but getting out of bed might disturb her sleeping husband, Jacob. She swallowed hard. It was never a good idea to wake Jacob. As she brought her knees up and tucked her hands beneath her pillow, she heard the clock in the parlor strike eleven. She'd slept less than two hours. Unbelievably weary after supper, it had taken twice her normal time to mix the bread dough for tomorrow's baking. It had been past nine before she'd finally gone to bed. Jacob had complained of an upset stomach and retired before her. She gave a soft snort in the dark thinking of it. Too lazy and too full of the home-brewed beer that he'd shared with his son, Joseph, he'd plopped down on her side of the bed. When she'd finally gone to bed, she'd been forced to crawl over the footboard. She turned her head slightly and looked at the mound lying next to her. At least he wasn't snoring.

Turning back, she gazed at the old lace curtains. They stirred lightly as the breeze floating through the open window carried the scent of wild petunias. Unfortunately, it also carried the scent of Jacob's hog lot.

Hannah's nose wrinkled. If she shut the window, the air inside the bedroom would be stifling. Closing her eyes, she tried to remember the scents of home—apple blossoms in the spring; wild honeysuckle growing around her family's wide front porch; her mother's roses. Even the musty, muddy odor of the Mississippi River would be preferable to the stench that surrounded her on this God-forsaken farm, stuck out in the middle of the prairie. An unbroken stretch of rolling hills and flatlands where the wind blew without end and winter brought snow so deep, she'd be locked inside for days; with summers so hot that not even the shade of the big maple tree in the front yard brought relief.

She thought of home and the hills of eastern Iowa. Her life there had included neighbors to visit, ice cream socials in the summer, sledding parties in the winter. And her books. She couldn't remember the last time she'd been allowed to read a novel. Jacob didn't hold with her reading anything except the Bible.

A tear slipped down the side of her cheek. This wasn't the life she'd wanted. It had been ten years, but her father's reaction to her pleading still hurt. It had been nothing more than harmless flirting. Why hadn't he believed her? Why had he forced Jacob on her? The gossip would've eventually died away once they'd learned it had no basis. Her hand beneath her pillow clenched into a fist. If her father had known what kind of a man Jacob truly was, would he have accepted Jacob's offer to marry her? She should've fled when she had the chance. Run off to the city. A life working in a sweatshop wouldn't have been any worse than the one she had.

She sniffed. "Stop it," she whispered to herself. "No use crying over spilt milk."

What had the minister said when she'd asked for his help? A woman's place is to submit to her husband and that she should count her blessings? Her hand came out from beneath the pillow and touched the bruise on the side of her face as she glanced again at the still form of her husband. Slowly, she edged her body down toward the bottom of the bed. She had to get out of this room—get away from him, if only for a few stolen moments. That alone would be a blessing.

Hannah eased off the bed and, throwing her heavy braid over her shoulder, quickly shoved her arms into the sleeves of her cotton wrapper. She belted it as she crept from the room.

As she crossed the threshold into the kitchen, she closed the door softly. Pressing her back against it, she let out a long breath. She did have a blessing in her life, and he lay sleeping upstairs in the back bedroom.

She headed into the dining room and lit one of the kerosene lamps sitting on the sideboard. Her shadow bobbed and weaved across the walls as she silently made her way through the farmhouse and up the stairs into her son's room. She went to the side of the bed and stood for a moment, staring down at him.

He lay on his back, his arms and legs spread wide across the lumpy mattress. Even in the faint light, Hannah saw the spattering of freckles across his nose.

"My precious boy," she murmured as she bent to cover his legs with the thin sheet.

The boy stirred and his blue eyes opened. "Mama?"

Hannah's heart seized with love, and with a smile, she sat down next to her son. "You kicked off your covers again."

"Ahh, Mama. I'm not a baby—I'm nine years old. You don't have to check on me in the middle of the night," he grumbled, rolling toward her.

She brushed his blond hair away from his forehead. "I know, but I like checking on you, Willie."

"Pa was really happy tonight, wasn't he?" Willie asked, his voice hopeful.

Hannah turned her face to hide her scowl. Jacob did seem lighthearted tonight, but she doubted the change was permanent. It was more likely thanks to the beer and his plan to win a seat as a county supervisor. He and Joseph had talked of nothing else all evening.

She forced a smile. "Your pa had a good day and he's looking forward to the Fourth of July celebration."

His eyes suddenly widened. "It's only two days away," he whispered, his excitement lighting his face.

"I know."

"Pa's going to take us to town for the fireworks."

Without thinking, her hand started toward her face. She let it fall. "I don't think so."

"But Joseph said we were going."

Her lips tightened at the mention of her stepson. "Joseph was wrong. We're staying here."

"But he's going with Pa."

"Yes, but you and I aren't." She saw the frown crease his face. "It's business," she said quickly. "You heard your father's plans tonight—he's running for supervisor this fall, and he's going to town to persuade people to vote for him. He'll be too busy to look after us."

"Why's he taking Joseph, then?"

"Joseph is a grown man and doesn't need looking after. Besides," she said with a quick poke to his ribs, "we'll have fun just the two of us."

One eye narrowed skeptically. "Yeah?"

"Yes," she said in a firm voice. "We're going to have fried chicken, and I'm saving some cream back after milking tomorrow to make ice cream."

"Ice cream—"

She leaned down and whispered in his ear. "*And . . .* I've got some firecrackers."

Willie jerked up in bed "Fire—"

Hannah's finger across his lips stopped him. "Shh. Your father doesn't know about them. It's our secret."

"But—"

"I used some of the egg money, and you know what your father would say."

"You were spending his money frivo— frivat—" He stumbled on the word.

"'Frivolously.' And, yes, that's right. That's exactly what he'd say."

She looked away from Willie so he wouldn't see the anger in her eyes. She was the one who cleaned out the henhouse, the one who fed and watered those nasty squawking birds, and the one who got pecked when gathering the eggs. It was only right that she should be entitled to some of the profit—especially if it meant making Willie happy.

"You'll keep our secret, won't you?" she asked, taking his hand in hers.

He nodded.

"That's my boy," she said, leaning in and placing a kiss on his forehead. Then she stood. "Now it's time for you to go back to sleep."

"Will you wind up my music box?" he asked with a sly grin.

"Do you promise to go right to sleep?" she asked indulgently.

He broke into a wide grin and nodded.

Hannah wound the box and the reedy sounds of "When Johnny Comes Marching Home" filled the room.

After Willie had scooted down in his bed, Hannah fussed with his sheet, then brushed his hair back one more time. "I love you."

"Love you, too, Mama," he said with a grin.

With a lighter heart, Hannah left her son's room and quietly stole down the stairs and toward the room she shared with Jacob. She was reaching for the doorknob when she heard it. *Tap, tap, tap* from the kitchen.

Raising the lamp, she hurried through the parlor and dining room. After rounding the corner, she noticed that the kitchen door stood wide open, while the screen door, moved by the breeze, gently knocked against the door frame.

Puzzled, her eyes scanned the room. She'd shut it before she'd gone to bed, and the house had been peaceful as she crept up to Willie's room.

Nothing appeared to have been disturbed. The dough still

sat rising on the back of the cookstove and the dishes were where she'd left them drying on the rack. Her attention flew to the door of the pantry. The egg money. She placed the lamp on the table and hurried into the pantry. Moving aside the sack of sugar sitting on the top shelf, she groped until her fingers felt the old tin coffee can. She pulled it down and, hugging it to her chest, raced to the kitchen table. Bright coins rolled across its scarred surface as she dumped the can and quickly began to count the money. When finished, she gave a long sigh. No, it was all there.

As she slid the money back into the can, her eyes roamed the kitchen. Maybe Jacob had risen and left the house to check the livestock. There had been a coyote bothering the chickens last week. After setting the lamp on the table, she stepped out onto the front porch.

The smell of the hog lot was stronger out here, Hannah thought as her eyes roamed the yard. The cabin where her stepson slept was dark. Joseph had drunk as much as his father, and she imagined he had fallen into a stupor similar to Jacob's once he'd reached his bed.

Her attention focused on the apple orchard. No shadows moved beneath the trees, nor were there any lurking near the barn or chicken house.

With a shake of her head, she entered the house and spied Willie peeking around the door from the dining room into the kitchen. In the dim light, the boy's face looked pale and his eyes were wide.

"Willie," she chided, "you were supposed to stay in bed."

"I heard something," he whispered.

"It's fine. Just the screen door tapping." She gave him a stern look. "You scoot back up to bed, and I'd better not hear another peep out of you."

He ran to her and threw his arms around her waist in a tight hug before doing as he was told.

As she watched her son go, a small smile played across her face while the love for her boy filled her.

She grabbed the lamp and headed to the bedroom. If Jacob were still in bed, he could get up and check the rest of the house. That door *had* been shut, and she didn't care if getting startled out of a sound sleep did make him angry. He had a responsibility to protect Willie.

"Jacob," she called sharply while she flung the door open and held the lamp high, "I think someone's—"

As the clock struck midnight, Hannah screamed.

Jacob lay on his side, with his face turned toward the window—blood red sheets tangled around his legs, and a knife protruded from his back.

Chapter 2

Summer 2012, Braxton County, Iowa

Kate Krause admired the shiny gold band on the third finger of her left hand. She felt the silly grin spread across her face as she watched the way the late morning light, shining through the car window, glinted off the simple ring. Dropping her hand to her lap, her attention moved to her husband as he drove down the thin ribbon of blacktop. His dark blond hair lay tousled across his forehead and she longed to touch it, but knew Joe wouldn't appreciate the distraction. Such a strong profile—such a strong man. A man a woman could lean on. A man without the Peter Pan syndrome who expected her to take care of him.

A bubble of joy tickled around her heart. She was so lucky. Thank God she'd responded to his "wink" on that online dating site. Who knew that one, innocuous beginning would lead to the sensitive e-mails, the thought-provoking conversations, and, most of all, to a man who took the time to know her better than she knew herself. They'd lived hundreds of miles apart, yet they'd found each other against the odds. True soul mates.

She gave a little sigh of contentment and snuggled back in her seat. Her childhood memories would fade and she'd at last have the home she'd always longed for. Her grin slipped and she looked down at her wedding band again.

Joe's hand suddenly covered hers. "You're worried about your grandmother," he stated.

She turned toward him with a grimace. "I'm sorry she was so rude to you after the ceremony."

"Don't be," he replied with a light squeeze. "Your grandmother raised you. It's got to be hard for her to watch you marry a man she barely knows, then see you move to a new home so far away."

Kate turned toward the window. Right, a new home that didn't include her grandmother. No more listening to the endless complaints. No more putting her life on hold for the sake of her grandmother's. And most of all, she'd never have to hear the daily reminders of how her grandparents had taken her in after her widowed mother had died. She wouldn't be relying on the charity of others. She'd have her own home—her own place.

"You're right," she said with a glance at Joe. "I think she thought I'd stay single for the rest of my life."

He shot her a quick look, taking in her dark brown hair and eyes. "Then she should be happy for you—and she will be, once she meets her first great-grandchild," he said with a wink as he gave her stomach a light caress.

Kate hugged her middle as if to protect the new life growing inside. Not bloody likely. She recalled her grandmother's words when she'd announced her news—

"Pregnant! Of all the stupid . . ."

Wincing at the memory, her attention stole back to her new husband. She hadn't told him about her grandmother's reaction. Based on his childhood stories, Joe had grown up in a home where children were treasured. He wouldn't understand. Her grandmother didn't like sharing the attention. A baby would be competition and make it impossible for Kate to come running whenever she called. Again she kept her thoughts to herself and nodded. "Tell me more about my new home," she said, changing the subject.

Joe's laughter echoed in the car. "Kate, for the hundredth time—it's nothing special—just an old farmhouse built in the 1870s."

She released her seat belt and scooted next to him, cuddling her shoulder against his arm. "Yeah, but—"

He suddenly leaned away.

Hurt, Kate lifted her face. "What's wrong?"

"You shouldn't unbuckle your seat belt," he replied, a stern note creeping into his voice.

At his reprimand, she returned to her place by the passenger's window and buckled up. He reached out and patted her leg.

"I'm sorry if I sounded gruff," he said with a sideways glance. "I take my new job as your husband seriously, and part of that job is keeping you safe."

Of course . . . how silly of her not to think of that. And how silly not to be strapped in when riding in a vehicle hurtling sixty miles an hour down the road. It wasn't just her life he wanted to keep safe. He wanted to protect their child, too. Her face brightened. "Back to your farm— Your great-great-grandfather was one of the first settlers of Braxton County, wasn't he?"

He grinned at her persistence and shook his head. "Yes. Jacob. He came to Iowa in the 1870s with his first wife and baby son."

"The baby was your great-grandfather."

"Um-hmm. Joseph. He inherited all the land when his dad died, and we've been there ever since."

Kate stared ahead at the ribbon of road stretching before them. Joe's life had been so different from hers. While her friends had had parents and siblings, all she'd had were her grandparents. She lifted her shoulder in a shrug. None of that mattered now. Finally, she belonged to a family with roots stretching back to the 1870s. Her child would have a heritage that he could be proud of.

The scene passing outside the car window caught her attention as Joe slowed his speed. They were entering a small town whose skyline was dominated by grain elevators. This must be Dutton. She watched eagerly while they traveled down the main drag, noting the small library, the post office, City Hall with one police cruiser parked in front, and finally the shops—many of which held large "for sale" signs in their front windows. Only a couple of the businesses appeared to have any customers. One was a store with the words *Krause Hardware* written in big letters across the front of the building.

She turned excitedly to Joe. "Does your family own that, too?"

"No," he replied in a terse voice.

Confused, Kate looked back at the store they'd already passed. "But I thought— It's the same last name."

"I guess I should've explained." His grip on the steering wheel tightened. "The owner is a distant cousin, but his branch of the family has never claimed mine." He gave her a quick look. "Their prices are too high, and we *never* do business there. If we need anything, we go to Flint Rapids."

"Oh—well . . ." her voice trailed away as she squirmed uncomfortably in her seat.

Joe's grip on the wheel eased. "It's an old feud and has nothing to do with us." He grinned at her. "You're going to be too busy raising our child and I'm too busy farming to worry about ancient history." With a nod of his head, he motioned toward one of the buildings. "And speaking of children . . . that's Dr. Adams's office. He's just a GP, but he's been delivering babies around these parts for years. I want you to make an appointment with him and get started on your prenatal care as soon as possible."

Kate grimaced. "I don't like doctors."

"I know, sweetheart," he replied gently, "but you haven't seen one yet and we want to make sure everything's okay, don't we?"

"Of course, but I'd rather use a midwife," she answered stiffly.

"Kate, I imagine the closest midwife is in Flint Rapids and I want someone in Dutton. Dr. Adams will be fine."

"I'm not going to let him pump me full of synthetic substances," she shot back, not hiding the stubborn tone in her voice. "I'm sticking with my organic vitamins."

He sighed. "I understand your love of all things natural, but you'll need to do what the doctor thinks is best."

"Like my mother did?"

"Oh, sweetie," Joe said, reaching out and clasping her hand. "It must've been hard losing your mother when you were only a teenager, but your mother's doctor was a quack."

"A quack who caused her death." Her lips settled in a bitter line. "He wouldn't listen to her . . . dismissed her complaints as hormonal," she replied, making quotes in the air. "If he had paid attention to her symptoms, they might have caught the cancer in time."

"And he paid the price, didn't he? You received a nice settlement."

"You mean my *grandparents* received a settlement, and it didn't make up for losing my mom."

He released her hand. "Kate, I'm sorry about what happened to your mom, but it's in the past and you can't let it affect our future," he said, his tone short. "Your health and that of the baby are important. I don't want a midwife handling your care."

Kate rubbed her hand across her forehead. "But I don't trust doctors."

"You trust me, don't you?"

"Of course."

"Then trust me to make the right decision for you."

She let her hand fall to her lap and studied his profile once again. It was hard. For so long she'd been on her own—responsible not only for her own life but for that of her grandmother. She wasn't accustomed to anyone wanting to care for her, for a change—someone who wanted to share her burdens. Hadn't he been overjoyed when he'd learned of her pregnancy and insisted they get married sooner rather than later? She needed to learn how to rely on her husband.

Turning toward him, she smiled. "I'm sorry. I do trust you, and if you think Dr. Adams is the best choice"—she hesitated and swallowed hard—"then that's good enough for me."

A broad grin crossed his face. "That's my girl."

Kate fell silent as they left Dutton and continued to head north on the county road. Soon the small town was replaced by field after field of crops growing in the hot summer sun. They drove by a few farmsteads, but mostly the landscape was nothing but flat land with an occasional rise. The only other buildings Kate saw were long, narrow sheds; and as they drove by, she caught the distinct odor of manure. Crinkling her nose, she tapped the window.

"What are those?"

"Hog confinements." Joe glanced out his window. "They hold maybe seven to eight thousand hogs."

Kate waved a hand in front of her nose. "No wonder it smells."

"But, honey, hogs are mortgage payers." Joe shot her a grin. "And that stink is the smell of money."

She didn't care if hogs were moneymakers. She couldn't imagine breathing that odor day in and day out. "Are there any near your farm?"

"No—not any big operations." He gave her thigh an affection-ate squeeze. "Don't worry, city girl. Our hog lots are away from the house."

She continued to watch the landscape until Joe nudged her arm.

"There. Up the road," he said as he turned off onto a gravel road. "That's my farm."

In the distance, a large white farmhouse sat on a slight rise, and Kate felt her excitement kick in. At last, she'd see where she intended to spend the rest of her life.

Joe slowed and made a turn onto a long driveway leading up the rise. Closer now, the two-story house was even bigger than it had appeared in the distance. It was surrounded by maple trees and had long windows shaded by lace curtains. A wide porch wrapped around two sides. The house looked solid, like something that had withstood the test of time. A delighted smile played across Kate's face as the car came to a stop.

"Here we are," he said, shutting off the car and leaning over to give her a quick kiss. "Welcome to your new home. I know you'll be happy here."

Home. A thrill ran through her as she glanced back at the house and was surprised to see one of the lace curtains flick to the side.

"Joe," she said, turning back to him, "there's someone at the window."

"Umm . . . I didn't expect—" He broke off suddenly and his cheeks flushed as he pulled the keys and opened his door. "I'll explain inside."

Kate's attention returned to the house. *Explain inside?* Her mind flew to what that explanation might be. She'd heard about how neighborly farm families were, and she wondered if Joe hadn't planned a little surprise for her by inviting all of his neighbors by in order to welcome his new bride. How sweet, she thought, smiling over at him. Their wedding had been at the courthouse with her friend Lindsay acting as her witness, and a deputy was drafted into the role for Joe's witness. Kate's lip curled. The only "guest" had been her grandmother. It hadn't exactly been her dream wedding, but they hadn't had the time to plan a large ceremony and reception. Now he was trying to make it up to her.

When Joe got out and retrieved their luggage from the trunk, she flipped the visor down and quickly fluffed her short brown hair. She wished she'd worn a more attractive outfit than a T-shirt and blue jeans. Oh well, she thought, snapping the visor shut, they'll have to accept me as I am.

"Hey," Joe, with his arms full of luggage, hollered from the front porch, "are you going to sit there all day, or do you want to see your new home?"

Laughing, Kate scrambled out of the car and joined him on the porch. She waited for him to set the luggage down and carry her over the threshold—and when he didn't, she took a deep breath and stepped inside, silently preparing herself for the shouts of "surprise."

The small hallway with stairs leading up on her right was empty. Perplexed, she glanced over her shoulder at Joe, who'd followed her through the door and was now stacking the luggage by the stairs.

"Come on," he said, taking her arm and guiding her through a large doorway to her left.

She found herself standing in the living room, or parlor as she supposed it should be called. A large brick fireplace dominated the far wall and its mantel was covered with ornate frames holding pictures of past generations of Krauses. The golden pine floor was partially covered by an area rug. Around the rug sat a couch and two armchairs, definitely Victorian by the looks of them. On all three, the arms and backs were protected with lace doilies. Small tables crowded the room—their surfaces covered with more pictures. *With all the froufrous sitting around, this room had to be a nightmare to clean.*

Her attention moved to the windows. Dark floral drapes with heavy, braided tiebacks hung over the lace curtains Kate had already noticed. All in all, the whole atmosphere was dark and fussy, and Kate felt she'd stepped back in time.

Her eyes narrowed. This would never do. She appreciated history as much as the next person, but there was no way she could imagine herself curling up on that stiff couch to enjoy one of her favorite books. She'd want to keep the same Victorian feel to the room, but make it more comfortable. If the rest of the house looked the same, she had her work cut out for her—turning this museum piece of a house into a home.

An antique music box on one of the end tables caught her eye. She lifted the lid. "When Johnny Comes Marching Home" began to play, but she noticed some of the notes were skipped. Joe quickly joined her and, with a grimace, shut the box, silencing it.

"That's been in the family for a long time," he said, swiftly, "and some of the notes miss. We don't handle it."

"I'm sorry," Kate said, embarrassed. "I didn't mean any harm."

He threw an arm around her shoulder and kissed the top of her head. "It's okay, sweetheart. I acted out of habit." He chuckled. "If you knew the number of times Ma dusted the seat of my pants for doing the same thing, you'd understand my reaction."

Kate smiled up at him.

"Well, what do you think?" Joe asked with his voice full of pride.

"The architecture is lovely," she replied, gauging her words, "but—"

Suddenly, an elderly woman appeared in the doorway leading into the dining room and cut off Kate's words.

"It's about time you got here," the woman said, her voice critical.

"I thought we agreed—" Joe began.

"We'll talk about it later," the old woman said, cutting him off as she looked directly at Kate.

Her gray hair was gathered tightly away from a face webbed

with wrinkles. She wore an apron over her plain housedress and her support stockings were rolled just beneath its hem.

Kate took a step back as she looked into the woman's narrow brown eyes—eyes that were sizing her up. Kate shifted uneasily. From the rigid lines around the woman's mouth, it was apparent that she wasn't impressed with what she saw.

Kate shot her husband a questioning look. He hadn't mentioned a housekeeper, but it only made sense. A man as busy as Joe would need someone to look after his home.

The old woman's gaze shifted from Kate to Joe. "I expected you an hour ago."

Joe exhaled slowly and, taking Kate's arm, pulled her toward the woman. "Sorry, we got a late start." He dropped Kate's arm and leaned in to give the woman a peck on the cheek.

The woman was definitely not his housekeeper.

"Kate," he said, placing his arm around her waist, "I'd like you to meet my mother, Trudy Krause."

Kate's stomach sank. Oh my God, the woman who had been appraising her so closely was her new mother-in-law.

She plastered a smile on her face and took a step forward, holding out her hand. "It's so nice to meet you."

Joe's mother let her fingers brush Kate's hand before crossing her arms over her apron. "Welcome." She turned to Joe. "Come on. Dinner's not getting any warmer while we stand in here flapping our jaws." She pivoted on her heel and marched toward the back of the house.

Looking up at her husband, Kate raised her eyebrows in a silent question.

"Sorry," he whispered, taking her arm and leading her through the dining room. "This wasn't my idea."

Kate paused in the doorway to the kitchen. It looked a little more modern than the parlor, but not much. Faded gray linoleum covered the floor. Glass-fronted white cabinets ringed the room over a pitted gray Formica countertop. Only the stove and refrigerator looked new, and Kate couldn't help noticing that the kitchen lacked both a dishwasher and a microwave.

Mrs. Krause waved a skinny arm toward the table covered with a yellow vinyl tablecloth. Three place settings were laid out. "Sit down and let's eat."

The food she referred to had already been placed on the table. A bowl of mashed potatoes, a platter of fried chicken, and a tureen of what looked like congealed gravy. Two flies inched their way across the plastic, headed for the chicken.

Without warning, Trudy grabbed a fly swatter from the edge of the counter and, with one smack, killed both the flies.

Kate cringed as she watched Trudy fling them off the table with a practiced flip of her wrist.

She cleared her throat and smiled at her mother-in-law. "Mrs. Krause, it was so nice of you to fix us lunch."

"Dinner," Trudy replied in a clipped voice as she placed the fly swatter on the counter and pulled a chair away from the table. "Only city folks have lunch."

"Right," Kate said with a nod and took her place across from Trudy, "dinner, or whatever you want to call it." She gave a nervous laugh. "It was kind of you to come by and prepare it for us."

Trudy snorted and flicked her attention toward Joe, who sat at the head of the table. "Come by? Didn't he tell you? I live here."

Chapter 3

Summer 2012, the Krause family farm, Braxton County, Iowa

"Kate, would you please calm down and let me explain?"

She slammed the dresser drawer in her new bedroom and whirled around to glare at her new husband. "Why didn't you tell me that your mother would be living with us?" she asked, brushing away the angry tears.

"She's not," he replied, shifting his weight on the old double bed.

"Really?" She hugged herself tightly. "That's not the way it looks right now."

Joe hopped off the bed and came to her with swift strides. Placing his hands on her shoulders, he tried to pull her toward him, but she refused to budge. "It's temporary."

Kate took a step back.

"I know this isn't what you expected," he said quickly, "but if you'd let me explain."

Her eyes narrowed. "I'm waiting."

"She wasn't supposed to be here. She was supposed to give me a chance—" He faltered and ran a hand through his hair. "I really thought the situation would be resolved before the wedding."

"How?"

"Ma's name has been on the waiting list at the retirement apartments since the day I decided to ask you to marry me. She was supposed to move last weekend, but there was a problem with the apartment."

"What kind of a problem?"

"The last tenant destroyed the interior. Now the landlord has to replace all the flooring and repaint the walls."

"Really?"

"Yes, really. And it's going to take a month or so to finish it." He traced a cross over his heart. "I swear . . . once it's done, she's moving."

"Why didn't you tell me?" she asked, not softening her rigid stance.

"I didn't want it to be a reason to postpone the wedding."

"So you decided to keep it a secret?"

"Okay, not the smartest decision on my part," he acknowledged. "But I thought once you saw the house and you understood the problem, you'd be okay with this temporary arrangement. She's my mother. I can't kick her out of what's been her home for forty years."

"I get that, but you should've told me before the wedding. I don't like being caught unaware."

"I know and I'm sorry." His lips twisted in a frown. "I never intended for you to be blindsided. Ma was supposed to stay at her friend's until I had a chance to explain."

Kate felt her anger ease at the dejected expression on his face.

"And I was afraid," he continued in a low voice.

"Of what?"

"That even with the baby, you might decide not to marry me."

"Because of your mother?"

"Yes." He looked down at his feet. "Not many women would want to take on a man who's lived with his mother all these years," he answered in a soft voice. "I worried that you might be one of them." Raising his eyes, he searched Kate's face. "I couldn't stand the thought of losing you and the baby."

"You should've trusted me."

Joe brushed a strand of hair away from her ear and leaned in close. "I know . . . this is a terrible way for us to start our new life together." He placed a soft kiss on the crook of her neck. "After meeting your grandmother, I should've been honest with you—"

"What has my grandmother got to do with this?" she asked, jerking away.

Joe stepped back. "Nothing . . . it's just . . . well . . . meeting her and all . . ." He cleared his throat and took a deep breath. "I can tell your grandmother's given you a hard time over the years, but my mother is nothing like her—"

Kate cut him off as she felt her anger spike. "And you think that I would do anything, even if it meant living with your mother, to get away from her?"

He shook his head. "No, that's not what I meant at all, and don't go putting words in my mouth." His face flushed. "I meant it as a compliment. I can see now the sacrifices that you've made for her, and you wouldn't have made them if family didn't matter to you. I should've known you'd accept my mother."

Kate stepped around him, walking to one of the long windows and looking out at the flat fields beyond the front of the house.

Did she? Did she accept his mother? She gave a soft snort. After the lukewarm greeting she'd received, she wasn't sure that Joe's mother was ready to accept *her*. Bowing her head, she rubbed her forehead. She'd spent most of her life placating her grandmother. Would she have to do the same for Joe's mother? If she were honest with herself, Joe was right. She *had* wanted to get away from her grandmother. She wanted her own life. A life that included a husband, a home, and children.

She turned and let her gaze travel the bedroom. She took in the old striped wallpaper, the bed with its carved walnut headboard and chenille bedspread, the washstand that still held an antique pitcher and bowl. Generations of Krauses had been born in this house, and it would be a good place to raise a family. Every marriage had a few bumps . . . maybe not this soon into it . . . but she could either let Joe's lack of honesty spoil her dream or be a good wife and accept his motives.

Her attention settled on her husband, still standing by the dresser while he waited for her to say something. No longer flushed, he looked uncertain, and Kate felt her future hanging in the balance. She made her choice.

Crossing her arms, she studied him. "Your mother *is* taking the apartment as soon as it's finished?"

Joe's face brightened. "Yes. I can't guarantee when that will happen—"

"But it will happen, right?" she asked, cutting him off.

He took a step toward her. "Right. And if you'll just give me time, I promise it will all work out in the end."

Kate felt the tension ease out of her body and she leaned back against the edge of the window. "I'm sorry if I was acting like a child. I just thought it would be you and—"

He quickly moved to where she stood by the window and took her in his arms. "I know, baby, I know," he murmured softly in her ear. "I'm sorry, too. I was wrong. I should've explained about Ma, but if you'll be patient, I promise, I'll make it up to you."

She rested her forehead against his chin. "I do love you, and I want our marriage to be a good one."

He stepped back and held her at arm's length. "It will, baby."

Kate lowered her gaze. "The way I acted—" She hesitated. "I don't think I made a very good impression on your mother."

"Don't worry about it," he replied, lifting her chin. "Ma can be kind of prickly at times, but once she sees what a sweet and gentle woman you are, she'll love you as much as I do." He caressed the side of her face, letting his finger trail down her cheek, stopping at the sensitive spot below her ear. "What do you say we get you settled in, Mrs. Krause? Then"—his eyes strayed to the double bed—"I'll welcome you properly to your new home."

Ignoring the fluttering heat growing inside of her, Kate leaned away from his touch. "But your mother. She's right downstairs." Kate eyed the open old-fashioned heating grate in the floor. "She might hear—"

"Didn't I tell you? . . ." He winked and started to edge toward the bed, pulling her with him. "She's hard of hearing."

Kate lay in bed, content to listen to her husband's even breathing. Stretching her arms over her head, she smiled up at the ceiling. Everything was going to work out. They'd safely navigated the first crisis in their marriage. She curled on her side and stroked her wedding band.

The rest of the day had been perfect. Trudy had made herself scarce while Joe had given Kate a tour of the farm. She'd seen hogs, chickens, cattle, and a few stray barn cats. Joe hadn't seemed fond of the latter and had dismissed her idea of catching one and taming it. She grinned. Well, she'd see about that. She'd never been allowed pets as a child and she'd always wanted a kitten. Surely, he wouldn't mind just one?

On the way to the sprawling machine shed, they'd passed by a massive pristine vegetable garden, the rows straight as soldiers marching in formation. She'd eyed the garden with speculation. Maybe he wouldn't mind if she added a few rows of her favorite herbs.

Joe had pointed out green beans, peppers, tomatoes, and her mouth had watered at the thought of a bacon, lettuce, and tomato sandwich made with her own sun-ripened tomatoes. He informed her that they'd also have homegrown sweet corn, and praised its quality over what had been available to her in the city grocery stores.

He'd shown her an office that any CEO would be proud to call his own. It was located in an enclosed corner of a machine shed used for housing tractors and farm equipment so large that they made the snowmobiles and four-wheelers sitting next to them look like Tinkertoys.

They'd walked by an old cabin, which was the first home Jacob had built on the homestead. She longed to explore it, but Joe dismissed the idea. It was preserved as part of the Krause heritage, but never used. The only residents now were mice and a few pigeons.

On their way back to the house, Kate had spotted two trees in the backyard growing close enough together that she could hang a hammock between them. An image of lazy summer days spent lounging in the shade flitted across her mind as they crossed under the trees' spreading branches—and that image held two towheaded children with Joe's green eyes nestled close to her as she read to them from Dr. Seuss.

Her hand strayed to her lower belly. Kate's stomach fluttered with excitement, but it quickly dampened. Trudy had to be settled in town before the baby came. As it was, the one-bathroom house was going to be crowded enough for three adults without throwing a baby into the mix.

But that didn't mean she couldn't start planning her baby's nursery now. Her gaze traveled to the door and the hallway beyond. The back bedroom would be perfect. She'd love to get out of bed and go look over that room now.

Joe stirred in his sleep and rolled away from her. Why not, she thought with a quick glance at his back. All day he'd stressed that this was her home, and if Trudy's hearing was as poor as Joe claimed, she wouldn't disturb anyone.

Kate slid to the side of the bed and eased her feet onto the floor. Quickly, she stood and crept to the foot of the bed to grab her robe just in case Trudy did catch her wandering the house. It wouldn't do for Joe's mother to get a glimpse of her in the semi-sheer nightgown purchased for the honeymoon that never happened.

She shoved her arms into the sleeves and tiptoed from the room. The hallway was pitch-black.

This is silly, she thought with a shake of her head and turned to go back to bed, but stopped.

A soft sigh came from the back bedroom at the end of the hallway. She cocked her head and listened. The noise sounded like a whisper. Was Trudy upstairs carrying on some kind of conversation with long-gone Krauses? Joe hadn't mentioned anything about his mother's health, but more than once she'd caught her grandmother muttering to shadows in the middle of the night. Maybe Trudy had the same habit?

Whispers again reached her ears. With one hand against the wall to guide her, Kate glided across the hallway, mindful of the creaking boards. When she reached the back bedroom, she turned the knob carefully and slowly swung the door open.

Nothing. The only shapes Kate could make out in the darkness were the numerous boxes that she'd noticed earlier in the day. Closing the door with a faint click, she began to retrace her steps back to her bedroom. She'd reached the door when suddenly the stairs to her right creaked.

Trudy had been upstairs. Disconcerted at the idea of her mother-in-law lurking outside their door while they slept, Kate slipped into the bedroom and headed for the dresser. A penlight was in her top drawer. Using it, she could make her way downstairs and discover what Trudy was doing.

She rummaged around in the darkness until her fingers finally found it. Creeping back out of the room, she flicked it on when she'd reached the hallway and headed down the stairs. As she reached the bottom, she heard rustling coming from the kitchen. If Trudy were awake, maybe this would be a good time for some woman-to-woman bonding. Maybe she could alleviate Trudy's disapproval.

Kate wended her way through the crowded parlor and through the dining room. When she passed the door to Trudy's bedroom, she noticed that it was closed and that the kitchen was dark.

She paused in the kitchen doorway as she shone the tiny light around the room. It was as empty of life as the back bedroom had been. If Trudy had been wandering around, she was safely in bed now.

Half turning, Kate caught a shadow out of the corner of her eye. She whirled around and hit it with her light. She clutched her chest and exhaled.

The back door—it stood partially open and was responsible for the shadow. With a shake of her head, Kate walked over to it. She knew rural areas didn't have the same crime rate as the cities—*but, honestly, not locking the doors at night!* She'd never sleep easy knowing that anyone could walk into their house at any time. She'd talk to Joe about it in the morning.

Her hand reached for the door, but another noise caught her attention. Something moved beyond the trees. Stepping out onto the small back porch, she crossed to the railing. She leaned against it and moved her light in a slow arc across the backyard.

Two glowing eyes stared at her from beneath one of the trees. Startled, her light wavered and she gasped.

At the sound of her voice, the cat turned and scurried off.

Propping her elbows on the railing, Kate shut off her light and stared out into the darkness. Warm humid air, as soft as a lover's touch, caressed her skin. She closed her eyes and took a deep breath. The scent of flowers tickled her nose, but Joe had been wrong. The still night did harbor another odor—the slight smell of the hog lot she'd seen that afternoon.

As she straightened, her lips twisted in irony. So many changes—the sights, the sounds, the different ways. They even used different words for the same meal. Kate felt a flicker of uncertainty. Would she ever fit in? Could she become accustomed to living out in the boonies where the nearest neighbor was a mile away? She wanted to belong. She didn't want to spend the rest of her life being the stranger—the outsider.

She shook her head and tamped down her doubts. Twenty years from now, she'd look back at these worries and laugh. Pushing away from the railing, she turned and made one step before a scream rent the night.

Chapter 4

Summer 1890, the Krause homestead

Joseph Krause lay in bed and looked up at the ceiling of the small cabin. It was the first house his father had built on the property, and he'd moved into it a little over a year ago. He still took all his meals in the big house, and his stepmother was responsible for keeping the cabin neat and tidy. He scoffed at that thought. She barely kept the house passable, let alone the cabin.

He shifted restlessly onto his side, then picked up the small clock sitting on the crate that he used as a nightstand.

Moonlight streaming through the open window illuminated the clock's face while the hour hand slowly clicked toward midnight. In a few minutes it would be a new day—the beginning of a new life.

Rolling to his other side, he watched a cobweb that spanned the open window drift back and forth. Sleep pulled at him, but the restlessness he felt inside wouldn't let it take him under. He threw off the light sheet, jumped out of bed, and began to pace the tiny room.

If the careful plans he and Pa had made worked out, he'd get out of this damn cabin and back to the big house where he belonged. Once Hannah was out of the way and Pa had won the seat on the county board of supervisors, Pa would have to surrender his tightfisted control over the farm and let him make some of the decisions. He could finally step out of the shadow of his father. He'd be treated like a partner, not the hired man.

Joseph jerked to a stop. With the way his life was going to change, he could even start courting a woman. That pretty little redhead he'd spotted sitting with the Turners at church last Sunday would be a good choice. He'd asked a few questions—she was a niece of Mrs. Turner's and there to help her following the birth of the Turners' fifth brat. She was not only easy on the eyes, but well connected. Her daddy was a big farmer over by Montgomery. He rubbed his hands together at the thought. Sure, she probably had plenty of flames, but a sport like him could cut them out. He had all summer to spark her.

He pulled his hand through his hair and resumed his pacing. With Hannah gone, there'd be a scandal, but they could ride it out. Everyone knew what kind of woman she was—always causing trouble, shooting her mouth off instead of staying silent like a dutiful wife should. The blame would be on her, not him and Pa. Willie might be a problem, but Pa would whip him into shape just like he'd done with him when he was a boy. No more of this namby-pamby stuff, clinging to his ma's skirts. *They'd* turn him into a man.

Joseph strode over to the window and looked to the eastern horizon, willing the first rays of sunlight to chase away the moon. He wanted tomorrow to be here.

A woman's scream suddenly echoed through the night.

It couldn't be . . .

Grabbing his pants, he drew them on quickly and shoved his sockless feet into his work boots. He ran to the house, his shoelaces flopping in the dew-soaked grass. Pushing the door open, he saw Hannah sitting in the rocking chair nearest the stove. Willie stood next to her. Using the door frame to steady himself, he stared at her.

"What happened?"

Both Willie and Hannah's eyes turned toward him. In the faint light of the kerosene lamp, their faces were blanched. Hannah raised a trembling hand and pointed toward the room she shared with his pa.

Joseph grabbed the lamp off the table and strode into the bedroom. As he held the lamp high, he saw the knife buried deep in his father's back and sheets soaked with blood. The air seemed to rush from his lungs and rob him of speech. His knees weakened and he started to crumble. He shook himself and took a tentative step toward the bed.

Anger tumbled through him. Taking two quick steps, he approached the bed and, with lips tightened, jerked the knife from his father's back and rolled him over. His pa's eyes were wide, as if death had caught him by surprise. Disgusted, Joseph flung the knife across the room and it clattered to the floor.

He whirled from the room and crossed to where Hannah still sat in the rocking chair. Grabbing her upper arms, he pulled her to her feet.

"What happened?" he yelled, giving her a shake.

Instantly, Willie kicked out at him. "Don't you hurt my ma!"

Brushing the child away, he fixed his gaze on Hannah while she stared at him as if she didn't recognize him. He gave her another shake. Finally, her eyes focused.

"I—I . . . don't know." She gasped.

He let go and began to turn toward Willie, but Hannah snatched his arm.

"He doesn't know anything. He was asleep." Dropping to her knees, she knelt in front of her son and brushed his hair off his forehead. "I need you to go back upstairs," she said in a quiet voice.

"Pa—" Willie's voice caught. "Is he dead?"

"Yes."

Joseph's rage simmered. This wasn't the time for her to coddle the boy. His pa was dead. He wanted answers and he wanted them now.

"What in the hell—"

She stood and cut him off with a wave of her hand. Gently, she pushed Willie toward the stairs. "Do what I told you. I'll be up in a bit and we'll talk."

With a backward glance at his mother, Willie slowly walked to the stairs and did as she had instructed. Once the boy's bare feet had disappeared, Hannah turned to Joseph.

"Ride over to the Thompsons' and get help."

With his hands clenched tightly at his sides, Joseph took a step forward. "Not until you tell me what happened."

She shook her head. "I don't know," she answered, scrubbing her face with her hands. "I was upstairs with Willie when I heard a noise. I came downstairs. The front door was open, and then . . . then I found your pa."

"You think someone came in and killed him?"

She nodded.

He threw his hands in the air. "Everyone respected Pa," he exclaimed. "Who would want to see him dead besides—" He stopped suddenly and stared at her. She'd found her husband dead, yet not a tear ran down her face.

"Did you see anything? Hear anyone outside?"

"No. I already told you . . . I heard a noise, but I didn't see anyone. Whoever did this is long gone." She gave a weary sigh. "Go to the Thompsons'. Have someone there send for the sheriff."

Joseph tromped out of the house, slamming the door behind him. Pausing at the edge of the porch, he turned and glimpsed his stepmother through the window, not moving, standing where he'd left her. She reminded him of a pillar of salt, just like Lot's wife in the Bible.

Bitch—this was all her fault.

Swearing under his breath, he marched down the steps and into the night.

An hour later, when Joseph returned with Martin Thompson and Sheriff Winter, the kitchen was empty.

"In there," he said with a flick of his head toward the dark bedroom. "I'll find Hannah."

Taking two steps at a time, he hurried to the top of the stairs. A faint light shone from beneath the door to Willie's bedroom. Jaw clenched, he flung open the door.

Hannah, fully dressed now, sat calmly at the head of the bed with Willie curled next to her. In her lap lay an open book. In the background, Willie's damn music box played. The rage he'd held in tight rein erupted again. The bitch had been reading fairy stories and listening to music while his pa lay dead.

He slammed the lid on the box shut, then rushed toward the bed. He grabbed the book out of her hands and ripped it apart. "Pa told you to get rid of that," he said, dropping the mangled book and kicking it under the bed. "You're not to turn that boy into a sissy."

"It was a birthday present from my sister," she replied in a flat voice as she drew Willie closer.

Joseph spun on his heel. "Leave the boy. The sheriff's here," he said curtly.

Hannah pulled the covers up to her son's shoulders, stood, then bent and whispered in the child's ear. Without a word, she followed Joseph from the room and down the stairs. When they reached the bottom, they found Sheriff Winter and Martin sitting at the kitchen table waiting for them. Martin, his face pale, mumbled something about needing air and stood abruptly. Moments later the screen door slammed behind him as he hurried out onto the porch. The sheriff then rose and crossed to Hannah.

"Sorry about your loss, Mrs. Krause," he said in a gentle voice while guiding her toward the rocking chair. "Can you explain to me the course of events tonight?"

Joseph paced the room impatiently as Hannah related the same story she'd told him earlier. When she'd finished, he halted at the sheriff's side.

"Well?"

"Well what, Joseph?" Sheriff Winter asked.

"Aren't you going to do something?"

The sheriff shrugged. "Not much to do until the coroner gets here. Then we'll look things over, and ask some more questions . . ." He paused. "I do have one more question for you, Mrs. Krause," he said, crossing to the kitchen table. He picked up the object lying there and held it up.

Dried blood crusted the pointed blade and Joseph shuddered.

"Do you recognize this?" Sheriff Winter asked.

"No," Hannah replied with a shake of her head. "It's not mine."

"Are you sure?"

"Yes, my kitchen knives all have wood handles and that one has a carved silver handle." Rising, she crossed the kitchen to a set of drawers and opened one of them. In a moment, she turned and held up a knife. "This is mine."

Joseph watched her as she gripped the knife tightly and held it aloft. Light glinted off its sharp blade. How many times had he watched her drive that keen point into the carcass of a chicken and split it down the middle? How much easier would it be to thrust a knife with a similar blade into the back of her sleeping husband?

Chapter 5

Summer 2012, the Krause family farm

Kate stumbled out of bed the next morning. Her head felt too big for her body. Instinctively her hand drifted toward her stomach. Lack of sleep was not good for the baby. A frown flitted across her face as her fingers rubbed her lower abdomen. In the last century, people believed scaring a pregnant woman could mark her unborn child, and God knows, she'd been afraid last night. Just thinking about that scream made her heart jump. She'd torn up the stairs and awakened her sleeping husband. A rabbit, he'd murmured into her ear as he pulled her into his arms. *Who knew rabbits screamed?* She shook her head and stood, shoving her arms into her robe. Sleep had eluded her long after Joe's easy breathing filled the room. Every time she closed her eyes, her mind filled with the image of a poor bunny in the grip of a predator. She'd tossed and turned until finally falling asleep in the early hours of the morning.

Tightening the belt on her robe, she squared her shoulders. Buck up, she told herself firmly. This wasn't the city. There'd be a lot of different sights and sounds, and if she wanted to fit in, she needed to learn how to adapt. She couldn't go running to her husband every time she was faced with something strange.

Problem resolved, she made her way out of the bedroom and down the hall. At the top of the stairs, she paused. The smell of fried bacon and fresh coffee drifted up the stairwell and her stomach growled in response. At least there was one advantage to her mother-in-law staying with them . . . Breakfast.

As she approached the kitchen, she heard Joe's chuckle and stopped.

"It was a rabbit, Ma," he said, his voice filled with humor.

Trudy answered in a low voice, but Kate was too far away to make out her words. She took a few steps and stopped.

"Superstition and old family legends," Joe said, the humor gone. "And I don't want you filling Kate's head with a bunch of nonsense."

"I tell you, it's a sign," Trudy replied, her voice louder.

"Don't be silly—"

Kate heard the clatter of something hitting the sink.

"Your grandmother heard that scream, and two months later, she received word that your uncle had been shot down over Vietnam."

A chill tickled the back of Kate's neck.

"Grandma was a flake. She wound up in the nursing home not knowing which way was up," he shot back. "And according to Dad, she never mentioned that old tale until *after* Uncle Fred was killed."

"I don't care what you say. For over one hundred and forty years, people in this family—"

A chair scraped across the kitchen floor.

"Come on, Ma. Do you really believe some rabbit meeting its fate is a harbinger of doom?"

"My boy . . ." Trudy's voice took on a tone Kate had not yet heard her use—soft, gentle, and full of love. "I raised you strong, and you've always made me proud. I couldn't bear it if something happened to you."

"Ah, Ma," Joe replied sheepishly, "I'll be okay. Don't fuss over those silly old stories."

"I can't help it. Your new wife—"

"Hey," Joe cut her off, his voice teasing, "haven't I always told you that you're my best girl?"

Kate felt a stab of jealousy.

"Yes."

"Look, Kate's my wife—and I love her—but you're my mother." The teasing tone was gone and he sounded deadly serious. "You think I'm going to forget everything that you did for me growing up?"

"No."

"You and Kate just try and get along, and everything will be fine. No more talk about that stupid legend, okay?"

Kate strained to hear Trudy's low reply, but she was too far away.

"I've got to get going. When Kate gets up, tell her—"

No, he couldn't leave before she had the chance to see him.

Hurrying into the kitchen, Kate shoved the overheard conversation out of her mind.

"Good morning," she said brightly and quickly crossed to where her husband stood at the counter. She stood on tiptoes and raised her face for a kiss. When Joe bussed the side of her cheek, her smile slipped.

Kate turned and greeted her mother-in-law.

Trudy's eyebrows lifted in response and flicked a hand toward the table. Any softness she might have shown during her conversation with Joe had disappeared. "Have a seat. The bacon's getting cold."

Joe pulled out the chair for Kate and, once she was settled, looked first at his mother, then at Kate.

"I'm going into town," he said, draining the last of his coffee. "I'm meeting Tom, then we're driving over to the Rodman place to see if we can talk some sense into Ed."

"Humph," Trudy snorted, "that'll be the day. He's known all along that fence line was on our land. He's not going to change it now."

Joe's eyes narrowed. "We'll see about that," he said, smacking his cup on the counter. "One way or the other, he's going to move that fence."

Trudy placed a hand on his shoulder. "Be careful, son," she said, her voice tinged with concern. "Ed Rodman's been stubborn and ornery since the day he was born."

"Don't fret, Ma," he said, removing her hand and squeezing it. "Ed's not going to pull anything with the sheriff standing there—"

Kate shot out of her chair. "Wait—what's this about a sheriff?"

"Now see what you did, Ma?" He shook his head. "You've upset Kate." He released his mother's hand and placed his on Kate's shoulder, gently guiding her back to her chair. "Don't you worry your pretty little head about it, sweetheart. I can handle Ed. Once he sees things my way, it'll be fine."

"But—But," she stammered.

He smiled down at her as he patted her head. "I've got to run." He shot a look at his mother. "Don't work her too hard, Ma. Remember what I said and that Kate needs time to adjust."

Trudy crossed her arms over her chest and said nothing.

"See you ladies at dinner." Without a backward glance, he was out the door and gone. A moment later, Kate heard the rumble of a pickup pull down the drive.

Silence hung in the air as Kate stared down at the now-congealed eggs on her plate.

Trudy finally spoke. "You need to eat," she said, pointing at the eggs.

Kate picked up her fork and moved the soggy mess around on her plate. This wasn't how she pictured the first few days of her marriage: rabbits screaming in the night, a disapproving mother-in-law, and a vanishing husband. Tears threatened to fall from the corners of her eyes. Quickly, she brushed them away and forced herself to take a bite of the cold eggs. Their mushiness against her tongue made her stomach roll. She swallowed and pushed her plate away.

"Thanks, Trudy, but I'm really not hungry. Maybe later I'll eat a piece of toast."

Trudy eyed her belly. "Morning sickness, huh?"

Grateful for the excuse, Kate nodded. She stood and, after

picking up her plate, crossed to the garbage can and scraped the eggs into it. Turning, she smiled. "I'll help you with the dishes."

Her mother-in-law waved her away. "I'll do them. Why don't you go back to bed? I heard you up roaming around last night."

Kate's lips quirked into a grin. Roaming was not the way to describe her movements last night. After hearing the rabbit scream, thundering would be more descriptive.

Placing her plate in the sink, Kate turned toward Trudy. "I'm sorry I made so much noise, but the scream that I heard frightened me. Did I wake you?"

Trudy's gaze wandered around the kitchen. "No. I was awake. This house doesn't always promote restful sleep."

Kate drew back at the cryptic remark. "What do you mean?"

"Nothing." She busied herself wiping off the counters and moving dishes over to the sink. "It's an old house. Old houses creak and it can disturb a body, if you let it." She shook the dishrag out over the sink. "I'd just ignore any night sounds, if I were you. It doesn't pay to go wandering around in the dark." She began stacking the dishes, but Kate interrupted her.

"Please, let me help you."

"I think it would be better if you rested," Trudy replied, keeping her back toward Kate.

"No, honestly . . . I want to help. I don't want to spend the day in our bedroom waiting for Joe to come home. I'd be bored out of my mind."

Trudy turned, her eyes narrowing. "You really want to help?"

Joe's remark about them getting along flashed through her mind. *She* wasn't going to be the one responsible for any rift.

"Yes, I'm a part of this family now. I want to do my share."

• • •

Later that night in bed, Kate wished she had taken Trudy's advice. Her ankles were swollen and her body ached in ways she'd never felt before. They'd cooked two big meals and, after each one, cleaned the kitchen until it gleamed. They also weeded the garden; swept and dusted the downstairs; and washed, folded, and ironed two large loads of laundry. Thinking of the latter, Kate grimaced. The woman ironed pillowcases, of all things. Didn't she understand the meaning of permanent press? At supper, she'd caught the gleam in Trudy's eye when she'd asked her if she'd ever "put up" sweet corn. That was Trudy's plan for her tomorrow, and she couldn't wait to see what it entailed. Kate's vision of spending lazy summer days, swinging in a hammock, seemed foolish. There was too much work to be done.

But what Kate regretted most about the last twenty-four hours was the lack of time she'd spent with her new husband. Not counting the time they'd spent sleeping, they'd been together less than three hours, and those hours had included his mother. The only time they'd been alone was in the privacy of their bedroom—and when he'd wanted to make love, she hadn't had the energy.

A bitter tear slipped down the side of her face. She wanted to be a good wife and make Joe happy, but the truth was she didn't know how. If today was any indication, years of nothing but endless work stretched before her.

She dashed the tear away. No, that was unacceptable. She loved her husband and she loved her unborn child. She would create a life in this place and she wouldn't allow it to be measured by the amount of work she accomplished each day. She'd find joy and she'd find happiness.

If Trudy thought to break her and make her feel that she wasn't a fit wife for Joe, Kate would prove her wrong. She'd work harder, longer, faster until Trudy was forced to accept her. She'd had to deal with her grandmother for years, and if now she had to handle her mother-in-law, then so be it.

She would not fail.

Chapter 6

The next two weeks seemed like nothing more than unremitting work as Kate tried to carve out her place in her new family. She had learned to let Trudy handle the cooking. She'd attempted making one meal by herself and the results had been dried-out ham, overdone potatoes, and gravy the consistency of paste.

Joe had laughed and said he hadn't married her for her cooking and to, please, in the future, let his mother teach her how to cook.

She had agreed with everything Trudy said and performed her assigned tasks exactly the way her mother-in-law expected. Finally, she felt Trudy's grudging acceptance.

Joe was also pleased with her. She had acceded to his wishes and seen old Doc Adams, who had pronounced both her and the baby well. And she'd agreed to the prenatal vitamins. To her surprise, her energy level increased.

Another surprise—how much she enjoyed working in Trudy's

garden. There was something about being close to the earth that made her happy. Her arms tanned and strands of dark gold appeared in her brown hair from the hours spent in the sun. It also gave her a bond with her husband. When the rains didn't come and each day was hotter than the last, he grew anxious over the crops wilting in the field and Kate fretted over the garden shriveling in the heat. The shared worries brought them closer.

She established a routine—rising every day before her husband and mother-in-law and using the time to wander the farmstead with coffee cup in hand. Kate was even close to achieving one of the wishes she'd made. On one of her morning strolls, she came across the ugliest cat she'd ever seen. An old yellow tom with golden eyes, he wore the scars of many battles and one ear was missing a piece, yet his lean body spoke of speed and toughness. The cat was a survivor. Fate had dumped him in the middle of nowhere and he'd made the best of it. Kate felt an immediate kinship.

Now every morning she brought him a treat that she'd filched from Trudy's leftovers. At first he'd run, but as the days progressed, he accepted her presence and the treat as long as she stayed by the old maple. Delighted that Trudy and Joe were unaware of her rendezvous with the old tomcat, she adopted him as hers and looked forward to the day when she had finally earned his trust and could touch him.

This morning after clearing the breakfast dishes, Trudy caught her off guard.

"We're going to town," Trudy said abruptly.

"Why?"

"Groceries," Trudy said, folding a dish towel and placing it neatly on the counter. "Joe has decided you've been working too hard and that it's time for you to meet our neighbors. We're having a barbecue on Saturday night."

Kate fought the urge to hug her. "A party!"

"No, a simple barbeque."

"Great," she said, grabbing her cell phone off the kitchen counter.

"What are you doing?" Trudy asked, her voice heavy with suspicion.

"I'm texting my girlfriend Lindsay. It's short notice," she said, her fingers flying across the keyboard, "but maybe she can come up for the party, err, excuse me, *barbecue*, then stay the weekend. It would be wonderful to see—"

Trudy's hand suddenly covered hers. "That's not a good idea."

"Why?"

"This get-together is for the neighbors. We don't want to include a bunch of outsiders."

"But Lindsay is one of my oldest friends," Kate argued.

"And she would be uncomfortable thrust into the middle of a group of strangers."

"No, she wouldn't. Lindsay loves—"

"I said it's not a good idea," she reiterated. "You want to fit in around here, don't you?"

"Yes," Kate mumbled.

"Well then." Trudy gave a satisfied nod. "You need to make new friends and not cling to your old life and old friends. And it would please Joe if you did."

Kate looked down at the half-written text message. There was a certain logic to what Trudy said. If Lindsay did come to the barbecue, Kate would feel obligated to entertain her and, as a result, might neglect the other guests. Reluctantly, she deleted the text.

Trudy smiled, then let her attention wander the kitchen. "We've got a lot of work to do between now and then. This house is filthy."

From behind Trudy's back, Kate rolled her eyes. They dusted and swept every day. Filth wouldn't dare enter Trudy's house.

Trudy's fingers began ticking off the tasks. "Wax the floors; dust upstairs and down; wash windows—" She paused. "We'd better make a few pies in case no one brings any desserts. *And* I'll make potato salad," she added, her lip curling. "Megan Scott will bring hers, but mine's better. Then—"

Kate didn't wait to hear the rest of Trudy's sentence. She ran upstairs and changed into a pair of Capris and a loose cotton shirt. After slipping on sandals, she grabbed the mascara out of her makeup bag and applied a couple of quick swipes to her eyelashes. Studying herself in the mirror, she frowned. How long had it been since she'd worn makeup? With a shake of her head, she twisted her hair into a loose topknot and secured it with bobby pins. One last glance in the mirror and she was out the door and down the stairs, where Trudy stood waiting for her.

She looked Kate up and down. "Why are you all dolled up?"

Kate's hand plucked at her shirt. "I'm not," she replied defensively. "I didn't want to go to the store in my work clothes."

Trudy lifted an eyebrow as she turned on her heel and left Kate standing at the bottom of the stairs. She rushed to follow.

Twenty minutes later, Kate was still following Trudy, pushing the cart up and down the grocery aisle while Trudy picked over the iceberg lettuce, squeezed the bread, and thumped the watermelons.

The back of Kate's neck began to tingle, and she glanced over her shoulder. Two women watched from the end of the frozen food aisle. Their carts close together, their eyes focused on Kate—and avid curiosity was written on their faces. When one of the women lifted her hand and whispered to her companion, Kate quickly turned her attention back to Trudy. But she'd disappeared.

To catch up with her mother-in-law, Kate hurried around the corner of the next aisle and smacked into a cart belonging to an older woman.

"I'm so sorry," Kate apologized as she tried to separate the carts' locked wheels.

Dressed in knee-length denim shorts, a drab green shirt, and scuffed tennis shoes, the stranger turned and smiled. Her face had the color of tanned leather and was webbed with fine lines, but the blue eyes staring at Kate appeared young and lively. Kate guessed her to be Trudy's age, or maybe a little older.

Her smile widened. "That's all right. I shouldn't have left it in the middle of the aisle." As she reached over to help disengage the carts, her focus darted to a spot on Kate's left.

Her eyes narrowed. "Trudy," she said in a clipped voice.

"Rose," Trudy replied stiffly.

Kate's attention bounced back and forth between the two women who continued to size each other up like two gunfighters facing off down the center of Main Street. At any minute she expected one of them to mutter the timeworn line—"This town ain't big enough for the both of us."

To break the building tension, Kate shot out her hand. "Hi, I'm Kate."

The woman, Rose, eyed her hand suspiciously then reluctantly took it in her own.

"Rose Clement," she said with a quick shake before again focusing her attention on Trudy.

"I'm Joe Krause's new—"

"I know who you are," she said, turning toward Kate and studying her. Her lips pursed and she shook her head. "Good luck. You'll need it." With a parting glance at Trudy, Rose yanked on her cart to free the wheels, then quickly pushed the cart down the aisle.

Kate stared after her, stupefied. "Who was that?"

"Rose Clement. Her farm's on the other side of Dutton." Trudy gave a snort. "She's buried two husbands and is looking for another one."

A perplexed look crossed Kate's face. "But she's—"

"Eighty if she's a day," Trudy said, finishing her sentence for her. "And she's been a thorn in the side of this family for each and every one of them."

"Why?"

Trudy grabbed their cart and began to move away. "Never mind. Just stay away from her."

Kate dropped the subject but, on the drive home, wondered what had caused such animosity between Trudy and Rose. It was evident that the hatred was shared. Staring out the window, she reminded herself to ask Joe about the feud the minute they were alone.

When they pulled into the driveway, Kate's heart thumped

with excitement. Joe's pickup sat next to the house. He was home early. As soon as the car came to a stop, she flung open her door and ran off in search of him.

She found him out back, walking toward the fence line that separated the bean field from the yard. One hand held a rifle, with its barrel resting on his shoulder. In his other hand, he carried the carcass of a small animal. Blood matted the striped yellow fur. Kate's sandals slid in the dry grass as she came to a halt. She watched with tears pouring down her face as her husband walked to the fence and flung the body out into the field.

"What have you done!" she screamed at him.

Joe whirled, dropped the rifle, and strode toward her. "Kate—what's wrong?"

"You killed him," she sobbed.

He grabbed her upper arms. "Killed who?"

Her throat clogged and she could barely answer. "My cat!"

He shot a look over his shoulder at the bean field. "That old yellow tom?" He sighed. "I caught him killing Ma's baby chicks."

Kate jerked away from him. "You didn't have to shoot him," she exclaimed.

"Yes, I did," he said in an even voice. "We can't have an animal around killing stock. If he'd stayed in the barn where he belonged—"

Kate's wail cut him off and she fell to her knees. Oh God, it was her fault. If she'd left well enough alone and not lured him closer to the house, he might not have attacked the chickens.

Trudy, hearing the commotion, came running around the corner of the house, a bag of groceries still in her arms.

"What's wrong?" she asked.

"Kate's upset that I shot the old yellow tomcat. I caught him in with the chickens."

Trudy stared down at Kate sobbing in the grass, and with a shake of her head turned on her heel.

"You'd better learn how to control your wife, Joe, before she embarrasses you in public."

Chapter 7

Summer 2012, the Clement family farm

Rose Clement parked her pickup in the shed and, after unloading and putting away her groceries, grabbed a beer out of the refrigerator. She strolled out onto her wide front porch and plopped down on the porch swing. Holding the ice cold can to the side of her face, she looked out over the waving stalks of corn.

My goodness, it was hot and if the rains didn't come soon, the crops would suffer terribly. Already yields were going to be down. She knew the young man who rented her farm ground was worried and was already hinting at leasing at a lower price next year.

She shrugged. She'd probably agree. Her bank account would see her through a couple of bad years, and she had no wish to put the young farmer out of business.

The swing moved slowly back and forth as she gently pushed

with one foot. The same couldn't be said for some of her neighbors. Many were hanging on by a thread, and a failed crop could put them under. Even the Krauses. She frowned, thinking of her encounter with Trudy. She detested that woman, but did she hate her enough to take joy in her son Joe's failure? He'd been a gambler and speculator just like his grandfather, and now it looked as if it was about to catch up with him. If the rumors were true, he could lose everything. If that happened, she hoped she'd find some sympathy for him even if they had always acted like they were above everyone else. That act had never fooled her—she knew the truth.

Rose thought back to the stories her grandmother Essie had told her about the first Joseph Krause and his father, Jacob. And Jacob's wife, Hannah. Essie had only been a child at the time, but she had big ears. Rose always surmised that Essie had noticed things that had failed to be obvious to the adults of that time.

Poor Hannah. According to her grandmother, Jacob had ruled his family with an iron fist and would've run the county the same way if someone hadn't killed him first.

Frowning, she shook her head. Old Jacob's descendants weren't much better. She'd heard how Joe had found his new wife on an online dating site. Rose sniffed. Didn't surprise her— the women around here were smart, and they knew if they took on Joe, they'd get Trudy in the bargain. Already the gossip mill was churning with stories of how Trudy treated the young woman like her personal slave.

The new wife seemed friendly enough and Rose did feel sorry for her, even if she didn't have much sympathy for the rest of them.

She drained her beer and stood, her old bones creaking and popping. Too hot to sit outside any longer and time to push thoughts of the Krauses aside. Whatever happened to Joe and his new wife wasn't her business. Rose opened the door and took one last look at the still green fields.

What had Essie always said? . . . *"The sins of the father . . ."*

Chapter 8

Summer 2012, the Krause family farm

The last thing Kate wanted to do was to attend a party in her honor. For the past two days, the old house had creaked with tension. She still followed Trudy's instructions, but she was done acting bright and shiny for the woman. She couldn't forgive Trudy's lack of empathy toward her over the dead cat.

Joe had tried to make amends. After she'd calmed down, he'd gently explained that the hogs, chickens, and cattle were part of their livelihood and anything that put that at risk had to be eliminated. He also cautioned her against getting attached to any of the animals. Baby calves grew up to be steers that were shipped off to the slaughterhouse. The fluffy baby chicks that had cost the tom his life would one day be Sunday dinner. It was part of life on a working farm and she'd have to learn to accept it.

Kate grimaced at her reflection in the mirror. In a way, she felt sorry for him. In showing compassion to her, he'd driven a wedge between himself and his mother. Yesterday, Kate had overheard a conversation where his mother accused him of coddling his new wife. He was willing to find Kate a kitten and allow her to keep it in the house, but Trudy's response to Joe's plan was swift and to the point. She had no intention of sharing her house with a cat.

Kate, of course, had a remedy for that—move Trudy into the retirement apartments. And as soon as this party was over, she'd insist Joe keep his promise.

Leaning closer to the mirror, she put the finishing touches on her makeup. Not that it would do any good. It was so hot that once she stepped outside, it would melt off her face. She cocked her head to the side. The skin underneath her tan looked pasty, but two quick swipes of her blush fixed it.

"Kate, honey," Joe called up from downstairs, "our guests are here."

By the time the party was in full swing, some of Kate's tension had vanished. She'd never remember all the names she'd heard this evening, but everyone seemed nice. The men had drifted off to one corner of the yard, and Kate caught snatches of their conversation while they discussed the current heat wave, crop prices, and sports. Once or twice she'd heard one of the men mention Ed Rodman, but she was too far away to hear Joe's response.

The women sat clustered in lawn chairs near the back porch and the conversation flowed easily. Trudy hadn't joined them. She flitted back and forth between the house and the yard, picking up plates and replenishing drinks. A couple of times the women had tried to draw her into the group, but she'd de-

clined their overture. When she'd hustled off yet again, one of
the women turned to Kate.

"How do you like Dutton?" she asked.

Kate gave a little shrug. "I really haven't seen much of it—just
the grocery store."

Another one of them spoke up. "We heard about it. You ran
into Rose Clement. What did you think of her? Did—"

"Doris," another woman interrupted, "you shouldn't put her
on the spot."

"Oh, come on, Betty. Kate's living with Trudy. I'm sure she
got an earful about Rose."

Kate squirmed in her chair. "Ah no. Trudy didn't say much."

"That's a first," Doris replied, rolling her eyes. "According to
my mother, Trudy's been feuding with Rose ever since she married into the Krauses."

"I know your mother is Rose's friend, but Kate doesn't need to
hear about that old fight," Betty chided.

"She does if she's going to live with Trudy," Doris argued.

Kate sat forward. "I don't expect to be living with her much
longer. She's planning on moving into the retirement apartments as soon as one's available."

"What do you mean? I heard there's—"

Betty's foot shot out and nudged Doris before she could
complete her sentence. "That'll be nice for you, Kate," she said
smoothly. "My dad always made jokes about too many hens in
the henhouse," she finished with a laugh.

A third woman leaned forward and placed her hand on Kate's
forearm. "You mustn't let Trudy get to you, sweetie. And take
anything you might hear about her with a grain of salt. She's led

a hard life and it's turned her into a hard woman. Ninety percent of the people in Dutton are intimidated by her."

"Rose isn't, Marjorie," Doris interjected, "and that's why Trudy and her don't get along."

Marjorie gave a snort. "I know your family's friends with her, but there *are* those who don't think Rose is all that sweet either."

The questions that had been troubling Kate since meeting Rose came to the surface. These women wanted to gossip, why not make the most of it?

With a quick look over her shoulder to make sure Trudy wasn't nearby, she leaned forward. "I really would like to know why Rose and Trudy don't get along," she said in a low voice.

Doris and Betty exchanged a look, then Betty shrugged.

"Rose has never liked the Krauses," Doris said, scooting closer to Kate. "No one knows exactly why, but it has something to do with the murder—"

Kate drew back. "Murder!"

Doris's glance darted to the side. "Shh, not so loud. Joe and Trudy don't like it when people bring it up." She looked over at Joe before returning her attention to Kate. "Jacob Krause was found murdered in his bed." She pointed over her shoulder. "Right here in this house. Rose's great-grandfather was the sheriff—"

Kate quickly did the math, then held up her hand. "Wait, wasn't Jacob the one who homesteaded this farm?"

Doris nodded.

"That was over a hundred years ago," Kate said, her eyes widening in surprise. "How could that matter now?"

"The Krause family curse," Doris replied calmly.

Kate shook her head in confusion. "I don't understand."

"Doris, I think you'd better leave well enough alone," Betty said sternly.

"No . . . no . . . that's okay," Kate murmured. "I want to hear the story."

"Well," Doris said, settling back into her chair as she warmed to her subject. "On July 2, 1890, someone slipped into the house and killed Jacob. Rose's great-grandfather was the sheriff and the case was never resolved."

"No one was found guilty?"

"Not exactly. Jacob's oldest son accused Rose's great-grandfather of botching the investigation. Shortly afterwards he resigned and moved his family over by Montgomery. According to Rose, those accusations ruined her great-grandfather's life, and it took her family a long time to regain respect."

"How does a family curse play into this?"

"The Krause family won't talk about it, but from what people have pieced together over the years, they've always believed Jacob's restless spirit roams—"

"Whoa . . . wait a second. You're telling me this place is haunted?" Kate shot a nervous glance toward the house.

"Stop it, Doris," Betty said, "you're scaring her."

Kate shook her head. "No, that's okay. I want to hear the rest of the story."

"Not much more to tell . . . because the killer was never brought to justice, they believe his ghost wanders this homestead and any sighting is an omen of bad luck."

Kate glanced toward the old cabin. Was Jacob's spirit there along with the mice and pigeons? She stifled a nervous laugh.

"That's just a bunch of bull," Marjorie interjected.

"But, Marjorie," Doris began, "you've got to admit the Krauses have suffered a lot of tragedy. Fred was killed in Vietnam; two of Joe's great-uncles died in World War Two; another great-uncle was killed in a farming accident. And they haven't exactly prospered. At one time, they were the richest farmers in the neighborhood, but now Joe is barely—"

"Kate," Betty broke in, glaring at Doris, "your glass is empty. Let me fetch you some lemonade."

"I'm fine," Kate muttered, trying to digest all this information about her new family. "I do have one more question—how many people have claimed to see Jacob?"

"Oh, they don't see him," Doris replied. "It's a scream heard at midnight."

The glass fell from Kate's numb fingers.

Kate cornered her mother-in-law later that night after all the guests had left. Joe had gone to bed and they were alone in the kitchen.

"Trudy, I know you resent me—"

"I don't resent you," she sputtered. "I don't know how you could think that."

Kate chose not to remind her of the disapproving stares, the snide remarks, and the way Trudy treated her like a slave. "Okay, but do you agree that we got off to a bad start?"

Trudy's attention shifted away from her. "Maybe."

"Well, I'm sorry for the part I played, but I am a member of this family now and I'm going to be the mother of your grandchild. Don't you think I deserve to know this family's secrets?"

Trudy bristled. "It was that Doris Hill, wasn't it? She never could keep her mouth shut, and her and her mother are thick as thieves with Rose Clement. I figured she'd stir up trouble when Joe wanted to invite them."

"It doesn't make any difference who did the talking. Do you believe this family's cursed?"

Her mother-in-law crumpled into a chair and covered her face with her hands. "Joe doesn't want me talking about it."

"I won't tell him."

Trudy's hands fell away from her face as her eyes grew hard. "I knew you'd bring trouble to this house from the minute Joe told me he planned to marry you," she said in a vehement voice. "Finding you on that damn computer, like the women around here weren't good enough for him. Getting you pregnant. Sneaking off to marry you. I told him then no good could come from it, but he wouldn't listen."

"You didn't answer my question—do you believe there's a family curse?"

"Yes," she exclaimed, "ever since Jacob Krause was found murdered, this family has suffered."

"But every family has problems," Kate argued.

"Not like ours . . . too many deaths . . . too much loss. And now you're here, and I see my son pacing the floor in the middle of the night and worrying about losing this farm."

"I imagine Joe's money problems started way before I came into the picture."

"But if he'd have married Denise Michelson like I told him to do, her daddy would've helped him. He's a banker and got plenty of money."

Kate was shocked. "You wanted your son to marry for money?"

"There's a lot of reasons to get married and love doesn't always have to be one of them. It can come later."

Kate rubbed a tired hand across her forehead. This conversation was going nowhere, but she'd finally learned why Trudy disliked her.

"I've seen my son change since he met you." Trudy's eyes narrowed and she looked Kate up and down. "You're going to destroy him, just like Hannah destroyed Jacob."

"What? Who's Hannah?" Kate asked, confused.

"Hannah was Jacob's second wife and you're just like her. She didn't fit in any better than you do." Trudy wagged a finger at Kate. "Mark my words . . . history is going to repeat itself."

Kate had had enough. She stood tall and glared at her mother-in-law. "I don't care if I'm not the woman you wanted for Joe. I love him and I will make my place here, whether you like it or not," she exclaimed. "This family curse is a bunch of crap and you're crazy to believe in it." She spun on her heel, then called over her shoulder. "History *will not* be repeated. I won't let it."

Halfway up the stairs, Kate heard the old music box begin to play. She paused and her teeth clenched as the tune skipped. Grabbing the stair railing, she stomped up the stairs.

I don't care if the music box *is* an antique. At the first opportunity, that sucker's getting fixed, she thought as she tromped into the bedroom.

Chapter 9

After church, Trudy busied herself frying chicken while Kate mashed the potatoes. As she whipped them into creamy mounds, she thought about last night's conversation. Joe's financial problems worried her, and what was more worrisome, he hadn't bothered to share them with her. Trudy was well aware of them, but they'd kept her in the dark. That's not the type of marriage she wanted.

She stole a glance at Trudy. She'd been colder than usual this morning. Joe had picked up on it and had spent the morning trying to ease the tension by first paying attention to his mother, then to Kate. He'd been back and forth like a tennis ball and Kate felt for him. She wanted to be his partner, but it wasn't fair to force him to choose. He'd spoken very little about his father. Most of his childhood stories had revolved around Trudy. If she'd paid attention going into this marriage, she would've realized how close he and his mother were and would have been better prepared, yet doubted she could have anticipated this.

What a mess. She needed to find a some way to be more to him than just the mother of his children. She wanted to be his partner.

Thoughts were still racing around in her head when Joe slipped up behind her and planted a kiss on her neck. He turned her around and gave her a big smile.

"I've been on the phone with David Turner and we're joining him and his wife, Sandra, for dinner."

"Oh, wow," Kate teased. "I get to dress up two nights in a row."

At the same time, Trudy clapped her hands in delight. "Oh, son, that's wonderful."

He ignored his mother and kissed Kate's forehead. "Have we been keeping you on the farm too much?"

She shook her head. "No, I know work comes first." Her answer pleased her. There—she'd showed him that she took his work seriously.

Joe reached around her and swiped a scoop of the mashed potatoes. After licking off the spoon, he stepped back. "This is work, too. David Turner is the head of Turner Farms and—"

Kate's eyes widened. "You're not thinking of selling, are you?"

"'Course not. Farming's all I know. Turner Farms are pork producers. They lease land and build hog confinements."

"Like the ones I saw on our way here? The ones I smelled?"

Joe's gaze darted away. "Not exactly. This one would hold less than twenty-five hundred head."

"Less than? That sounds like a lot of pigs," Kate exclaimed.

"But," he said quickly, "it wouldn't be near here. We own land over by the Clement place, and that's the land they're interested in leasing."

Out of the corner of her eye, Kate caught Trudy's sly smile.

"So," she said, stepping away from the counter and crossing her arms, "we wouldn't have to put up with the stink, but Rose Clement would? That's not right, Joe."

His eyes narrowed and his jaw clenched. "Would it be right to lose this farm?"

"No, that's not what I meant . . . but everything I've read about those confinements . . . They can pollute the water, damage the air quality—"

He stepped toward her. "You grew up in the city. You don't understand this way of life."

"Maybe not, but I understand protecting the environment, being responsible—"

"You're like the rest of those bleeding hearts," he cut in, his voice growing louder. "I'll do whatever it takes to keep this farm. And this lease is a good deal. I get my cut off the top and don't have to worry about the risk. It'll be a steady income every year."

"But what about Rose and her neighbors? Will it be a good deal for them?" she argued back.

"You don't get it—I don't care about Rose and her neighbors. If they don't like it, they can move."

"But, Joe, there has to be another way—"

He grabbed her upper arm and gave it a shake. "There is no other way, and you either—"

"Joe," Trudy said in a stern voice, cutting him off.

He dropped her arm, but his glare remained constant.

Kate's attention turned to her mother-in-law, then back to her husband. Tears stung the back of her eyelids and her insides crumpled. Spinning on her heel, she fled to the safety of their bedroom.

She was still there three hours later when Joe entered the

bedroom fresh from his shower. Without a word, he strode to their closet and grabbed a dress shirt and pair of pants.

"Joe, I'm—"

"Forget it, Kate. Ma's going with me."

The words cut and the tears threatened to start again.

"But—"

He whirled around and stared at her. "I said to forget it. I'll make up some excuse why you're not with me. It's better this way. The last thing I need is you shooting off your mouth and screwing me out of this opportunity."

"Can't we talk about this?"

"I'm done trying to explain things to you. I'll dress downstairs." He threw his clothes over his arm and headed for the door, then stopped and looked at Kate curled in a ball on their bed. "And while we're gone, I suggest you think about being the kind of wife I need."

Fifteen minutes later over the sounds of her crying, Kate heard the sound of the car pulling out of the driveway.

Kate spent the next few hours alternating between anger and hurt. What chance did her marriage have if they couldn't have a reasonable discussion? How dare he treat her like an idiot? Okay, so maybe she didn't understand the financial stress her husband faced, but it was no reason to fly into a rage. She hated confrontations and wanted to avoid them. Was this her fault? Should she have kept quiet and trusted him to do the right thing? Perhaps that was what he expected of her?

Thoughts chased around in her mind until she was exhausted. Curling on her side, she had begun to drift off to sleep when the sound of heavy footsteps made her sit up in bed. A moment later, Joe came through the door.

"How did the meeting go?" she asked in a thick voice.

"Fine," he replied brusquely as he picked up a pair of sweats and a T-shirt and walked back toward the door.

"I'm sleeping on the couch."

The warmth of the sun on her face woke Kate up the next morning. Memories of yesterday made her heart twist. She'd never seen that side of her husband—withdrawn and hard. She wanted the man who'd courted her so thoughtfully, the one who'd tried to steer an even course between her and her mother-in-law. How could she get him back?

She rolled over onto her back and patted her eyes. Without seeing herself in a mirror, she knew how she looked. Eyes swollen, face puffy, and her hair a tangled mess. Part of her wanted to play the coward and stay in their bedroom, but other than bathroom breaks, she'd been alone in this room for close to twenty-four hours. She had to face her husband and mother-in-law eventually. Might as well do it now. She'd get Joe alone, away from Trudy, and they'd talk. In the middle of the night, she'd come to the conclusion that she'd started the fight yesterday by arguing with him. Today, she'd change her approach. Apologize for questioning his management of the farm, then gently explain how she felt. The kind, sensitive man that she'd fallen in love with would listen as long as she went about it the right way.

She sat up and swung her legs over the edge of the bed and started to stand. Suddenly a sharp cramp doubled her over and she fell back on the bed, clutching her lower abdomen. Kate took a deep breath and the pain eased. Pushing off the bed, she tried to stand again, but another cramp hit her, followed by heaviness in the lower part of her body. She looked down in horror as blood soaked through the bottom half of her night-gown.

"Joe . . . Joe," she screamed.

When he came into the room, she stared at him helplessly as the life of her baby leaked away.

Kate spent the next three days in a haze of medical terms, being poked and prodded by the doctors, and finally suffering through the surgery to remove the rest of the fetal tissue. How had the life she'd carried gone from being a baby to nothing more than a group of cells? It wasn't fair, and the pain of her loss squeezed until she couldn't breathe.

Joe had been wonderful. The angry man she'd faced a few days ago had disappeared, and she had her husband back. In a way, it made it worse. Every time he came near her, the guilt she felt for failing him and losing their child pushed her grief away. She was on a roller coaster of emotion and wished she could get off.

And the neighbors, the women whom she'd met at the barbe-cue, came to call. Loaded with cakes and casseroles, they tried to comfort her, but if she heard the words "it was meant to be" one more time, she'd flee, screaming from the house. She knew they were trying to be kind, but in their kindness they weren't allowing her to mourn.

Lost in her thoughts, Kate didn't notice Trudy standing next to the couch.

"Here," she said, handing Kate a plate, "you need to eat."

Kate turned her head toward the window. "I'm not hungry."

"Eat," she said, brooking no argument and placing it on Kate's lap. Instead of returning to the kitchen, she sat down in one of the armchairs and watched Kate with a pensive expression on her face.

"It gets better, you know," she said abruptly. "You simply need a little time to grieve." She settled back in the chair and slowly rubbed its arms.

Astonished at her insight, Kate stopped midbite and stared at her.

Trudy leaned forward. "Joe was my fourth baby," she said with a sigh.

"You had three miscarriages?"

"Yes, I never made it past the second month with the other three." Her eyes took on a faraway look. "I got so tired of everyone's sympathy and their platitudes. Each time was worse than the last."

Kate placed her sandwich back on her plate. "I'm sorry . . . it must've been hard for you."

"Humph," she said, moving back in the chair. "They wouldn't leave me alone and let me deal with my loss in my own way. Everyone just kept picking at me . . . I hated it."

Kate's heart was broken after one miscarriage. She couldn't imagine the pain Trudy had suffered after three failed preganancies. The hole in her heart getting bigger with each lost child. The bitterness she must've felt.

"How did you live through it?"

She waved Kate's question away. "You just do. I do think about what might have been once in a while, but then I see my son . . . and—" She rose to her feet unexpectedly. "I need to get the dishes done."

"Thank you, Trudy."

"You're welcome. Rest and don't worry. If you're lucky, you'll be blessed someday with a son like Joe."

A soft touch on her arm woke Kate from a sound sleep. Opening her eyes, she saw her husband grinning down at her in the moonlight.

Scooting up in bed, she rubbed her tired eyes. "What's wrong?"

"Shhh," he replied, placing a finger on her lips. "I've got a surprise for you."

Kate's brow wrinkled. "Now?"

"Yes, now," he answered with a chuckle as he tugged her out of bed and handed her a robe. "Come on."

They snuck down the stairs and through the house like a couple of little kids up past their bedtime. When they reached the kitchen, Joe handed her a dish towel.

"Cover your eyes," he instructed in a whisper.

"Joe—"

"Hey, don't spoil it," he chided.

Reluctantly, Kate held the towel over her eyes and let him lead her out of the house.

"Where are we going?"

"You'll see."

"Don't let me trip and fall," she warned.

"Never, sweetheart, never," he responded and placed a warm kiss on her temple.

A quiver shot through her. This could be fun, she thought as the dew-covered grass tickled her bare feet.

Abruptly Joe stopped. "Okay, you can look now."

Kate dropped the towel and her eyes widened in amazement.

A blanket, circled with lighted candles, lay spread out beneath one of the apple trees. On it sat a bottle of wine, two glasses, and a basket.

"A picnic." Kate gave a little squeal and threw herself in her husband's arms. "This is wonderful," she murmured, then kissed him deeply.

After a few moments, Joe drew away, his eyes dark. "If we keep this up, we're going to wind up back in the house," he said with a playful slap to Kate's bottom.

"Okay," she said and, after stepping over the candles, settled onto the blanket.

Joe joined her and opened the picnic basket to withdraw a plate of cheese, summer sausage, and grapes. He filled a small plate and handed it to her. "Sorry, I'm not much of a cook, so this was all I could come up with."

Kate laughed, remembering the disastrous meal she had prepared. "Neither am I."

"You'll learn," he said, opening the wine and pouring a glass for her.

Kate took a sip and let the fruity liquid slide down her throat. "Mmm, this is good." Her gazed traveled the romantic setting. "This reminds me of the night you proposed."

Joe poured a glass of wine for himself, then leaned back against the tree. "But that meal was a little fancier."

"Foie gras, wild rice, Cornish hen—"

"I thought they were just little chickens," he interrupted with a grin.

"Joe . . . it was wonderful," she said with a half-smile. "It was one of the most romantic things you've ever done for me."

"We haven't had much time for romance lately, have we?"

"You've been busy."

"I'll make it up to you, I promise."

Kate laid a hand on his knee. "I know."

He rested the back of his head on the trunk of the tree. "God, I was nervous that night. I was so afraid you'd think the only reason I wanted to marry you was—" He stopped.

"Because of the baby?" she asked, finishing for him.

"Yes." He picked up her hand and, raising it to his lips, kissed her wrist. "I do love you, you know."

She nodded. "I love you, too."

Suddenly feeling shy, Kate looked around the orchard. "I've tried to imagine you playing here as a child—climbing trees, snitching apples." She nibbled on her cheese. "You never say much about your childhood, but I've shared everything about mine."

"Yours was more interesting," he said with a shrug. "My memories are mostly about working with my father. He had me driving a tractor as soon as my legs were long enough to reach the pedals."

"You never say much about him. Why?"

Joe sat forward and drew his knees up to his chest. "He was a hard man," he said thoughtfully. "I guess maybe that's why soft words don't come easy to me. I never heard them much when I was a kid."

Kate looked at him with surprise. "But your e-mails were always so expressive."

He gave a rueful laugh. "It's one thing sitting at a computer, typing out a bunch of words. It's different when a pretty woman is right next to you, looking at you. Maybe that's what I should do . . . leave little love notes lying around the house for you to find." He winked at her. "Just don't let Ma find them first, okay?"

Remembering his passionate e-mails brought the blood to Kate's cheeks. Joe might have trouble expressing himself in person, but his messages had been very specific. Some were enough to scorch her eyeballs, she thought with a smile. No, it wouldn't do for Trudy to read them. Another thought occurred to her and she lost her smile. Though she was reluctant to ruin the moment, she still felt a need to ask the question.

"Do you think we rushed into this?" she asked in a hesitant voice.

"Our marriage?" He leaned forward. "You're not having regrets, are you?"

"No," she reassured him, "but it did happen awfully fast. The e-mails, your weekend trips to Des Moines, then the baby." She pressed her fingertips to her eyelids. "Should we have taken things a little slower?"

Taking her wrists, he pulled her hands away from her face and looked at her intently. "Baby, I was half in love with you before I ever met you." He gathered her in his arms. "Then the first time I saw you—" He paused. "I didn't stand a chance. You were pretty, smart, funny . . . I never thought anyone like you could fall for a guy like me." He drew back. "Being with you makes me a better man."

Kate looked up at him. "You're pretty special just as you are."

"Ahh no, I'm not," he teased, "I'm just a dumb farmer."

She arched an eyebrow. "I hardly think that. You have to be intelligent to run a place like this."

"I love you." He hugged her close. "Our son will run this farm someday."

"Joe—" Kate began, then jerking away.

"Don't say it," he said and pulled her against him. "We'll have another child." He released her abruptly and knelt in front of her. "I have an idea. If we have a good yield this year and the markets stay firm, what do you think of taking a cruise this winter? Maybe to the Caribbean? I can get away then."

She flung her arms around his neck. "That would be great," she exclaimed. "But I thought money was tight."

"Don't worry about it. I'll figure out a way to pay for it."

Kate smiled as visions of warm nights, moonlit skies, and the soft ocean waves filled her brain.

Joe leaned forward and drew a finger down her cheek. "Who knows? Spending that much time together is bound to have results," he said, wiggling his eyebrows.

Kate felt as if she were wrapped in a soft glow. Maybe it was the wine, or maybe it was Joe's promises. Whichever one, she didn't care as she collapsed happily into the arms of her husband.

Chapter 10

Early fall 2012, the Krause family farm

The hope Kate held for establishing a bond with her mother-in-law after Trudy's revelations withered and died. The more attention Joe paid to Kate, the more Trudy's resentment simmered. Within a few short weeks, the snubs had returned. Joe's attitude shifted. The night in the orchard was forgotten as the strife seemed to drive him away. He spent less and less time with both women. Kate fretted, but felt powerless to resolve the situation. It took all of her strength to finally make the phone call that she'd been avoiding.

Her grandmother picked up on the second ring.

"Hi, Gran," Kate said with forced brightness.

"Well, you're still alive." The snarky tone made Kate's jaw clench. "I haven't heard from you in so long that I was beginning to wonder."

"Um . . . sorry. I've been under the weather."

"Really, Kate, is that an excuse to ignore me?"

"I lost the baby," Kate blurted out.

Silence met her confession.

"Are you still there?" Kate finally asked.

"I'm here."

"Aren't you going to say something?" Kate crossed her fingers and made a wish for kindness.

"What do you want me to say?"

Kate uncrossed her fingers. "That you're sorry for my loss?"

"I knew no good would come of this. Didn't I tell you not to expect children at your age?"

Kate's grip on the phone tightened. "I'm not that old . . . Dr. Adams said that I can still have children," she said defensively.

"And we both know that doctors aren't always right."

The veiled reference to her mother's illness and death shook Kate's confidence. What if Dr. Adams was wrong and there'd be no other pregnancies? What would that do to her marriage?

Her grandmother continued. "I think your wisest choice would be to realize your mistake and come home where you belong. You can't handle the life you've chosen."

"I love my husband."

"You barely know your husband," her grandmother replied swiftly. "You married in a rush and now this. It's a sign that it's not meant to be."

Gran's words reminded Kate of her first morning in her new home and the conversation she'd overheard between Joe and Trudy. She shoved the thought away.

"I don't believe in signs," Kate answered stubbornly.

"Maybe you should."

"Give it up, Gran. I'm staying with Joe."

"You're just like your mother."

Here we go. Kate ground her teeth and waited for the tirade she'd heard a hundred times.

"She wouldn't listen to me either, and look where it got her. Married to a worthless man who was dumb enough to get himself killed and leave her alone with a baby to support."

"My father wasn't worthless and it wasn't his fault he died," Kate said in a small voice. "It was an industrial accident."

"Right. And your mother could've been set for life if she'd done what I told her and sued that company." Her grandmother sniffed. "But, oh no, she had to do it her way and wound up with nothing."

Kate drew a weary hand across her forehead. "There's no point in dredging up the past. I need to focus on my future, and my future is with Joe."

Her grandmother switched tactics.

"What about me? What about my future?" she asked in a whiny voice that set Kate's nerves on edge. "The doctors are worried about my heart, and my arthritis is so bad I can hardly get up in the morning." She gave a long-suffering sigh. "We were the ones who took you in after your mother died, and this is the way you repay me?"

The guilt Kate had suffered since childhood began to creep in. She shoved it away.

"I'm sorry that you're not feeling well, but your home health-care aides are there to help you."

"Them?" she sniffed. "I don't trust them to clean my bathroom floor. *I know* they're stealing from me."

Kate stifled a groan. The malpractice settlement they'd won after her mother's death had disappeared. Spent long ago on worthless crap. And unless the aides had an abnormal desire for plastic figurines of Elvis, her grandmother didn't have anything worth taking.

Her grandmother's voice weakened. "I guess if you won't help me, I can go to the county home. God knows, I can't afford to go to somewhere nice." She sighed again. "I'll at least get fed three times a day. Never mind that all their food smells like cooked cabbage."

"Gran, you're not going to the county home," Kate said, exasperated.

"Why?" Her voice sounded brighter. "Am I going to move in with you?"

Kate almost dropped the phone. Her grandmother and Trudy in the same house? No way. Her life wouldn't be worth living.

"Sorry, Gran, my cell phone is dying and I didn't hear that last part," she said in a rush. "I'll call back later."

Kate hit the end button and chucked the phone onto the couch. Scrubbing her face with her hands, she shuddered.

Would she never be free of mean old ladies?

Two days later, Kate felt the house pressing in on her. Joe had been withdrawing even more and new lines of worry etched his forehead. The more she tried to be a partner, the more short-tempered he became. Now she had to deal, not only with Trudy's resentment, but with Joe's coldness, too. Was he falling out of love with her because she'd failed to give him a much anticipated child? She had to prove to him that she had value.

She found Trudy out in the garden picking green beans.

"Where's Joe?"

"In his office," she said without looking up. "Where did you expect him to be?"

Kate ignored her short remark and hurried off to find Joe. He was sitting at his desk, staring at the computer screen. Frown lines snaked across his face and Kate longed to wipe them away.

"Hi," she said, trying to capture his attention.

He stayed focused on the screen. "Is dinner ready?"

"No." She sauntered over next to him and leaned against the desk. "I've something that I'd like to discuss."

He groaned. "I'm not taking you to Flint Rapids."

"That's not what I wanted to discuss." She took a deep breath and let it out slowly. "I know you're worried about the farm and I've an idea that might help."

Pushing away from the desk, he tilted back in his chair. "You have an extra forty thousand lying around?"

"No." Her gaze dropped to the floor. "I turned my savings over to you when we got married."

He reached out and squeezed her knee. "I know and I appreciate it. I was teasing." Smiling, he rocked back in his chair. "So, what's your idea?"

"Umm . . . well I've always been good at handling money and I thought maybe I could help you with a budget and investments—"

Joe rocketed out of his chair and Kate slid off the desk. "Who's been talking to you? You think you know more about the markets than I do?"

She backed up. "No . . . no, that's not what I meant at all. My savings came from the investments I'd made, and I did fairly well."

"That doesn't make you an expert on farming."

"I never said it did," she tried to keep her voice reasonable. "I know I don't know much about money when it comes to farm management, but I could learn."

"No, you can't. It takes years. You think you can waltz in here and tell me what to do?" He took an angry step away from the desk.

"I don't want to *tell* you anything—I want to help you," she pleaded.

He kicked his chair across the room. "I don't need your help. Go back to the house where you belong."

Kate whirled to hide her hurt and hurried to the house. Slamming the back door, she studied the key rack hanging next to it.

"Which keys are for the car?"

"The set with the red tag," Trudy answered from across the kitchen.

She grabbed them and started out the door.

"Hey, that's Joe's car," Trudy called out.

"And I'm his wife, in case you didn't notice," Kate said, picking up her purse from the counter and hurrying out the door.

She didn't calm down until she was almost in Dutton. Reason had set in once her temper cooled. She let out a long, shaky breath and thought how she had handled it all wrong. When she walked into the office, it was obvious that Joe was troubled. But instead of waiting for a better time, she'd steamrolled ahead and made the situation worse. When would she learn to pick her moments?

Another thought struck her. Joe never talked about the miscarriage. She had been so wrapped up in her grief that she'd been oblivious to his. After promising herself to be more understanding, she began looking for a spot to turn around and head home when a sign caught her eye.

KRAUSE HARDWARE.

In spite of her resolution to be more patient, her defiance still simmered. After parking the car, Kate got out and strolled into the store. A little bell from above the door jingled.

Long aisles stretched to the back of the store and the air smelled of turpentine and fertilizer. Hoes, rakes, and other yard implements hung along one aisle while another held cans of paint, racks of brushes, and sandpaper. A sales clerk, a tall dark man, stood behind the counter, waiting on a customer. The clerk wore a navy shirt with KRAUSE HARDWARE embroidered on the pocket.

"Here you go, Ed," he said, handing the customer a gallon of paint and a couple of stir sticks. "If this isn't enough, give us a call and we'll have it ready and waiting for you."

The customer gave a curt nod and with an "excuse me" to Kate, headed out the door.

After watching the man exit the store, Kate looked back at the clerk and tried to think of a reason for wandering into the store.

The excuse fled her brain as she found herself staring into the same green eyes as her husband's.

Chapter 11

Early fall 2012, Dutton

Kate's breath hitched and the man smiled.

"It's the eyes, right? Strange twist of the old DNA, isn't it," he said as he held out his hand. "Hi, I'm Will, and you must be Kate."

At a loss for words, she shook his hand.

"It's nice to meet you . . . unexpected, but nice."

Where was the animosity Will's side of the family supposedly felt? It wasn't apparent in the smiling man who stood in front of her.

"Ahh . . . nice to meet you, too."

His eyes twinkled. "I've heard a lot about you."

"I hope it was good," she replied.

Will laughed. "Around here one never knows, do they? But it was. Doris Hill had nothing but kind words to say about you." His face sobered. "I'm sorry to hear about your loss."

Kate cocked her head and studied him. No "it was meant to be," but a simple acknowledgment of her grief. She instantly liked him in spite of the feud with her husband.

"Is there something in particular you need?" He leaned in, and in a conspiratorial voice, whispered, "If you do buy something, get rid of the sack before you get home. Joe wouldn't let anything with 'Krause Hardware' on it in the house."

Kate smirked. "I *have* been told not to shop here."

"I'm sure you have," he said and gave a low chuckle. "You must be a bit of a rebel."

She drew back. "Who me?" Kate thought of the many ways that she'd tried to please both Joe and his mother. "No . . . no, not at all." She shifted nervously. "Maybe I should go."

Will held up a hand. "No, please let me show you the store. I think this is the second time in our history that one of the 'other Krauses' has had the gumption to come inside. This is a momentous occasion, let's celebrate it with a cup of coffee," he finished with a grin.

"Okay," she said with a shrug as she followed Will down one of the aisles. "Exactly how are you and Joe related?"

Will glanced over his shoulder. "Have you heard about old Jacob yet?"

"The one found murdered?"

"That would be the one." He winked. "And," he said, deepening his voice, "he who is the herald of misfortune and who will not rest until his killer's found."

"Got ya," she said and stole a look out of the corner of her eye. "Do you believe in that family curse?"

"No. Jacob was my great-great-grandfather, too, and I can't say my family has suffered an unusual amount of trouble . . ." He paused. "No offense intended, but I think some of the Krauses invented that story to explain their bad luck when it was actually their greed backfiring on them."

Suddenly Kate felt disloyal standing here with Joe's cousin. "You know . . . I think I'll pass on that coffee. I'd—"

"Wait. I'm sorry. I shouldn't have made that remark about greed." He motioned for them to continue to the back of the store. "Let me explain how we're related. Joe and I share Jacob as an ancestor, but Joe is descended from Joseph, Jacob's oldest son, and I'm a descendant of Willie, the second son and the one Jacob had with his second wife, Hannah."

"So both you and Joe are named after your great-grandfathers?"

"Yeah. Weird isn't it?"

"Are you, also, going to explain how Joe's great-grandfather cheated yours out of his inheritance, Will?"

Kate pivoted to see Rose Clement standing at the end of the aisle.

"I'd better go." She looked down at the floor. "This was a bad idea."

"Hold on." His attention turned to Rose. "You're bringing up ancient history, Rose. What happened back then doesn't matter."

"Yes, it does," she replied, joining them. "The past always matters, especially when you get to be my age." She focused on Kate. "If there's a family curse, it's because of Joseph. He lied, cheated, and spoiled several lives, including that of his little brother."

"No," Will objected. "He didn't ruin Willie's. According to my family, Willie had a long and happy life."

Rose eyed him skeptically. "Maybe Willie did overcome

the misfortune of his early years, but it was no thanks to his brother."

"Rose . . . stop." He glanced at Kate, then at Rose. "You're talking about Kate's new family."

"Right." She pointed at Kate. "And her husband is just as sneaky as the first Joseph."

Will stepped in front of Kate. "You've gone too far, Rose."

"So has her husband." She peeked around Will at Kate. "Haven't you heard Joe Krause is leasing the land next to mine for a hog confinement?"

"I've heard rumors, but that doesn't mean he'll do it," Will replied.

"Are the rumors true?" she asked Kate.

"I don't know," she mumbled, not meeting Rose's stare as she edged away. Finally looking up, she found Rose's eyes drilling into hers.

"Your mother-in-law has made some enemies over the years, but it's nothing compared to how this town is going to react if your husband proceeds with his plan."

After delivering her parting shot, Rose marched out of the store, leaving Kate and Will standing there in silence.

Will was the first to break it. "I'm sorry, Kate," he said, his face red. "Rose really is a nice lady, but if what she says is true, it's going to hurt her financially."

"How?"

"Like most people around here, her assets are tied up in her farm and she's worked hard managing it ever since her husband died." He frowned. "If a hog confinement is built near her place, her property values will drop. She'd have a hard time finding a buyer if she ever decided to sell. Hog lots stink and the flies are terrible. Who'd want to live under those conditions?"

"Was she right about the town's reaction?" Kate asked softly, sympathizing with Rose's predicament.

Will shrugged and didn't answer.

Kate drove home, still boggled over the situation between Rose and her husband. Her dream of belonging was in danger of crashing. She hadn't lived in Braxton County long, but it was long enough to appreciate how far people's memories stretched. My God, they were still gossiping about something that had happened over a hundred years ago. Joe's actions would stigmatize not only her, Trudy, and Joe, but also her future children. She couldn't let that happen. She had to make him see reason.

As she pulled into the driveway, she noticed a strange pickup sitting back by the machine shed. Upon exiting the car, she heard voices raised in anger. Following the voices, she rounded the corner of the house to see her husband squaring off with a stranger dressed in bib overalls and wearing a green cap.

"I've tried to be reasonable, Ed, but if you won't move that fence line, then I'll have to take legal action."

The other man, Ed, snorted. "From what I hear, you ain't got the money for no lawyers."

Joe answered him with a smirk. "If you don't take care of it, I will. I'll hire a bulldozer to push that son of a bitching fence back over the property line." He crossed his arms over his chest. "Then I'll send you the bill."

Ed's face turned red and he took a step forward. "That'll cost me thousands," he screamed. "Damn it—it's two fuckin' feet over the line!"

Joe turned with a shrug and began to walk away. "Suit yourself. Either you move it and save yourself some money, or I'm calling in a dozer."

"Everyone in town knows what you're doing," Ed yelled after him. "And they're all sick of you and your family trying to ride roughshod over this community." He stopped and spit on the ground. "You're no better than your daddy or old Jacob."

Joe lurched around to face him. "Get the hell off my land!"

Ed wheeled toward where Kate stood and stomped right by her without looking her way. A minute later his pickup peeled out of the driveway.

No . . . no, she couldn't let this happen. She had to help Joe find a way out of this mess without losing respect.

"Joe," she said after following him into the office.

"Not now, Kate," he said in a rough voice.

"We need to talk," she persisted.

She jumped at the sudden sound of his hand slamming the desk.

"I said not now," he growled between clenched teeth.

Shoving her fear to the side, she cautiously went up to him and placed her hand on his arm. "Joe," she said gently, "calm down."

He glared at her and she dropped her hand.

"You can't do this. Think of the repercussions. There has to be another solution. What's two—"

"It's two feet of *my* land." A vein on the side of his neck began to throb. "I can do whatever I want."

"I have to live here, too, Joe. And I want to raise my children here. Do you want everyone in this community to hate us?"

"What I want," he replied, his voice dripping with sarcasm,

"is a wife who knows her place and quits meddling in things that don't concern her."

Kate's anger chased away her fear. "Meddling? That's what you call it?" she fumed. "It's nice to know that giving you all of my money and turning myself into your mother's personal slave—"

Before she could react, Joe's hand lashed out and struck the side of her face. Shocked, Kate backed away, nursing her cheek.

His anger deflated and he held out his open palm. "Oh God, Kate . . . I'm sorry . . . I didn't mean—"

Kate didn't wait to hear the rest. She twisted away from him and ran.

Chapter 12

Summer 1890, the Krause homestead

Hannah sat quietly in the corner of her kitchen, rocking slowly back and forth. The body of her husband lay in the bedroom while two doctors examined his mortal remains. Occasionally, soft voices would drift into the kitchen from behind the closed door—too faint for Hannah to hear their words.

The undertaker, with his cooling board, was on his way. Once the doctors were finished and the inquest had been held later this afternoon, he'd begin preparing Jacob for his burial. Some of the men had already rearranged the furniture in the parlor. Jacob's coffin would remain in that room until the day of the funeral, then Jacob would take his last journey and join his first wife in the family's burial plot.

She looked toward the dining room. Sheriff Winter, Charles Walker, the county attorney, and Dr. Arthur Morgan, the county coroner, sat gathered around the table. Their faces were somber, and a couple of times, Hannah had caught them watching her.

From out of the window, she could see the rest of the neighborhood men, who'd been drifting in all morning, gathered over by the barn. Children, Willie included, played marbles nearby. She was thankful for that. At least Willie was engaged with his friends and not in the house with his dead father.

The womenfolk from the surrounding farms had taken over her kitchen and flitted back and forth, offering the men coffee and sandwiches. How anyone could eat with a body in the next room was beyond her. Thinking about it made the bile rise in her throat.

Her mouth twisted in a frown. Some of these women, like Fannie Thompson, Martin's wife, were her friends. But not Grace Rosenthal and Bessie Schwab—they'd come to satisfy their curiosity. She watched in disgust as Bessie ran her finger along Hannah's plate shelf. Holding her dusty hand out to Grace, Hannah saw her eyebrows lift in disapproval.

She turned her head back toward the window. She didn't care. They'd always thought she was a shoddy housekeeper and now they had proof.

Her attention wandered to the apple orchard beyond the barn. Since she was now a widow and could hold property, the farm would probably come to her. Joseph wouldn't like that. He'd want her gone, but she had to think of Willie's future. She gave a soft snort. How ironic. This place had never been anything other than a symbol of Jacob's success, and he'd always delighted in holding it over their less-than-successful neighbors. To her, it was only a roof over her head and a place to raise her son. The house and the farm had meant nothing—and now the homestead might belong to her.

Her thoughts were suddenly interrupted by Fannie's hand on her shoulder.

"Hannah," she said quietly, "Reverend Green is in the parlor."

Hannah scowled. After the first time Jacob had raised his hand to her, she'd gone to the reverend for help. Instead, he'd quoted platitudes and lectured her on her wifely duty of providing comfort to her husband. When he moved on to chiding her about airing her family problems to outsiders, she'd left disheartened and never went back.

Her stomach tightened in panic, and her eyes sought an escape.

Fannie squeezed her shoulder. "You have to see him."

"No, I don't." She shot out of the chair as quiet fell over the kitchen.

"Hush," Fannie hissed, her eyes darting over her shoulder to where Grace and Bessie stood listening. She stepped in front of Hannah, blocking the two women's view. "Do you want them telling the neighborhood that you're hysterical?"

Hannah took a deep breath. "No, but I'm not talking to Reverend Green." Her gaze traveled the room. "I can't stand this, Fannie . . . I've got to be by myself. Tell Reverend Green that I'm outside praying for Jacob's soul."

With her head down, Hannah left the kitchen and hurried outside. She didn't stop until she reached the apple orchard.

A soft, hot breeze whispered through the trees, and free of the oppressive house, Hannah closed her eyes and inhaled the scent of ripening apples. She had no intention of praying for

Jacob. She didn't care if the weight of Jacob's sins bound him to this earth forever. He'd earned it.

A delicious sense of freedom bubbled inside of her. She never had to deal with Jacob's anger again. Tossing her head back, she spread her arms and spun in a circle, just like she'd done as a child.

A voice stopped her midspin.

"I want to talk to you," Joseph said from the edge of the orchard.

Hannah dropped her arms and folded them primly at her waist. "If it's about the funeral, we'll talk after the inquest."

"It's about the farm," he replied, walking toward her.

"Now's not the time."

"Yes, it is." His lips tightened with determination.

"It's not seemly," she insisted.

"Neither is spinning around like a kid." He grabbed her arm and began to pull her deeper into the orchard.

She jerked away and skidded to a stop. "You will *not* touch me."

Joseph held up his hands and stepped back. He smirked. "Pa had a will—" He paused dramatically. "It names me as Willie's guardian."

She gripped her stomach while her breath left her in a hiss. "No."

Joseph's smirk became a smile. "Yes. Pa didn't think you were a good influence. He wanted Willie to grow to be a man."

"A man," Hannah said, dropping her arms to her sides, "who sees no harm in using his fists to settle disagreements?" She straightened and lifted her chin. "I won't let you."

"You can't stop me. Children belong to their fathers, not their mothers."

"His father's dead, so Willie belongs to me."

Joseph gave a nasty laugh. "After reading Pa's will, a court might not agree, especially after they hear about your 'unnatural attachment' to your son."

"You're mad," she exclaimed. "There's nothing 'unnatural' about a mother caring for her son."

"That's not what the neighbors think."

"I don't care what they think."

"You will when they testify against you in court." He lifted an eyebrow. "Remember the scene you caused at the school board meeting after Miss Rosenthal had punished Willie at school? You wanted the woman fired."

"His punishment was too severe," she said indignantly. "He was whispering and she had the gall to whack him on the side of his head with a book."

"I don't think that's the way Miss Rosenthal would tell it on the witness stand." Joseph shook his head slowly. "You've always been a troublemaker, Hannah. Refusing to be a proper wife, shooting your mouth off about things that don't concern you." He snickered. "You have enemies, and they'll all stand against you in court."

"We'll see about that. My brother-in-law is an important man, and he'll stop you from taking Willie."

Joseph sobered. "Now, Hannah, I never said I wanted Willie." He stroked his chin. "I want my own family and he would be in the way—"

"Get to the point, Joseph."

Sticking his hands in his pockets, he leaned against an apple tree and studied Hannah. "I might be willing to let you have Willie if you let me have the farm."

"Impossible. Willie deserves his share of this land," she said in a sweeping motion. "It's his birthright, too."

Joseph exploded. "His birthright? What has that kid ever done around here?" He shoved away from the tree. "He's been mollycoddled since the day he was born and has never done a lick of work."

"He's a boy," Hannah said quietly.

"I was a boy once, too, and nobody ever stopped Pa working me half to death," he answered, his voice full of bitterness.

"I tried, Joseph—when I first married your pa—and I got the worst beating of my life . . ." Her voice trailed away as she pressed her fingers to her forehead.

"But then Willie came along and he was more important." He puffed out his chest. "I probably should thank you for not interfering—Pa was hard, but it made me strong."

Sadness for the little boy who'd got lost in his father's violence tugged at her.

"Oh, Joseph, I know it was hard losing your mother and—"

He shook a finger in her face. "Don't you speak of my mother," he said in a threatening voice. "She was a *lady*."

"I'm sure she was," Hannah said, trying to calm his anger, "I only meant that I'm sorry—"

"I don't need your pity," he yelled. A malicious look stole over his face. "You're the one to be pitied. Pa was making plans to divorce you—"

"What?"

"That's right." He chuckled. "He didn't want you and your ways spoiling his chances in the election. He was taking you back to your mother's house and dumping you like a bucket of slop—" Stopping, he watched Hannah's reaction. "He was going to tell everyone you'd run off."

His words hit Hannah like one of Jacob's blows.

"You know what that means, don't you?" He swaggered toward her. "You never would've seen your precious son again."

The abuse hadn't been enough for Jacob. He'd planned on stealing her only reason for living. Cold rage enveloped her and she faced Joseph with a freezing glare.

"Then I'm glad he's dead."

Chapter 13

Hannah walked back and forth across Willie's room, her black silk dress rustling with every step and her boots clicking on the plank floor. She stopped and tugged at the scratchy crepe collar. This was her best dress and she hated it. Jacob had purchased it for her when her father had passed five years ago, and had spent more on it than he had on all her other clothes combined. Scowling, she continued her pacing. He hadn't wanted her to show up at her father's funeral looking like a poor relation, so he'd parted with the money for the dress. Now she'd have to wear the damn thing for the next year.

She mopped her face with a black-edged handkerchief. Between the stench of mothballs emanating from the dress and the heat, she felt faint. She had to have some air and strode to the window.

"Hannah, you can't," Fannie called from across the room.

"I can't breathe," Hannah replied, pulling back the curtains and rolling up the shade. She grasped the window and threw it open. Fresh air blew into the room and Hannah closed her eyes, inhaling deeply. When she opened them, she noticed the men standing in the shade of the old oak tree.

Clarence Schwab looked up and saw Hannah. Disdain crossed his face.

Fannie tugged her away from the window, then pulled down the shade. "You have to keep them closed out of respect for Jacob," she chided. After leading her to a chair in the corner, she motioned for her to sit down. "This pacing isn't doing you any good."

Hannah sank into the chair and bowed her head. "This inquest is taking hours. It's obvious what killed Jacob—a knife."

Fannie knelt next to the chair and placed a hand on Hannah's knee. "But they need to learn the events that led up to his death."

Hannah's head shot up. "I don't like them questioning Willie."

"They must. Willie was in the house last night, too."

"He's only a child."

"But he might have heard something." Fannie patted her knee and rose. "Once you're finished testifying, they'll return him to you."

"And until then," Hannah sniffed, "Grace Rosenthal is with him. She's as harsh as her daughter."

"Willie's fine, Hannah. You mustn't worry."

Hannah stood and crossed to Willie's dresser. She picked up the music box that her sister, Ida, had sent him for Christmas and ran her hand over the smooth finish. Mindful of Sheriff Winter's warning not to discuss the investigation, and with Abe

Engel standing in the hallway guarding the door, Hannah lowered her voice.

"What do you think about the men who Charles Walker," she said, referring to the county attorney, "picked to serve on the jury?"

Fannie shot a look over her shoulder at the door, then crossed to Hannah. "Harry Rosenthal will use it to show how important he is," Fannie whispered, "but Martin and Walter Bauer will keep him in line. They'll want to find the truth."

"I've already told them the truth," Hannah cried.

"Shh," Fannie said, placing a finger on her lips, "Abe might hear you."

"But—"

A knock on the door cut her off.

"They're ready for you now, Mrs. Krause," Abe called from the hallway.

Hannah carefully placed the music box back on the dresser, smoothed her skirt, and left the room.

With the drapes and blinds drawn, the light in the dining room was subdued and shadows clung to the corners, but Hannah saw each of the men gathered around the table clearly. Martin, Walter, and Harry sat in a row with Dr. Morgan at the end. Martin and Walter both leaned forward with their arms resting on the table. Their faces wore the same somber and determined expression.

Harry leaned back in his chair with arms folded over his large stomach. His expression was anything but somber. As he watched Hannah, his eyes glinted with skepticism and he appeared ready to dismiss whatever she had to say.

Hannah looked down at her hands clutched tightly in her lap and prayed for this to be over.

She looked up at Charles Walker, standing in front of her, and steeled herself for his questioning. Slowly and calmly, she repeated her movements of the previous night.

Yes, they'd had supper, then Joseph and his father had spent the evening talking while she straightened the kitchen and prepared to do the baking. Yes, she'd retired to bed after Jacob. Yes, she'd gone to Willie's room. No, she hadn't noticed anything unusual on her way up the stairs. Yes, she'd spent time with Willie then returned to the kitchen. Yes, the back door had been open. No, nothing had been missing.

"And it was at that time you discovered Mr. Krause?"

"Yes."

"What happened next?"

"I really don't remember—I think I screamed, then Willie came running into the room."

The attorney picked up a sheaf of papers lying on the table and glanced at them. "Your stepson, Joseph Krause, testified that he found you sitting in the kitchen."

"Yes—yes," Hannah stammered, trying to remember how she and Willie came to be in the kitchen. "I didn't want Willie to see his father."

"After Joseph arrived, you sent Willie upstairs and Joseph for Sheriff Winter?"

She nodded and inhaled deeply. Thank God this was about over.

"Were you aware of Mr. Krause's disagreement with Peter Ziegler?" he asked, catching her off guard.

"Ah no."

"So you weren't aware that Mr. Ziegler questioned your husband's friendship with his widowed sister, Minnie Voigt?"

"What!" Hannah's mouth dropped in shock. "Are you implying—"

"I'm not implying anything, Mrs. Krause," he said hastily as he looked at the paper again. "Did you and Mr. Krause ever have disagreements?"

A sudden movement from the far corner of the dining room caught Hannah's attention as Reverend Green stepped out. Her attention darted to Charles Walker, then back to Reverend Green.

"You didn't answer my question, Mrs. Krause," the county attorney insisted. "Did you and your husband have problems?"

"Occasionally," she replied in a low voice.

"I'm sorry, Mrs. Krause. I didn't hear you."

Hannah lifted her chin. "Yes."

"Did he ever strike you?"

"Yes."

"Willie? Did he ever strike Willie?"

"No."

"So you were the one who bore the brunt of your husband's temper . . ." He paused. "Did you ever fear for your life?"

She stared at the attorney defiantly. "No, Jacob knew he'd be punished if he killed me."

"But he wouldn't be punished for striking you?"

"Not unless I made a fuss." Her attention traveled to Reverend Green. "And I was encouraged not to do that."

He scratched his head. "Let me understand your situation, Mrs. Krause. You willingly accepted your husband's treatment?"

"I didn't have much choice in the matter," she replied quietly.

At her words, the attorney's attention stole to the knife lying on the table in front of Walter. His thoughts were as clear as if he'd spoken them aloud.

"I—I—" Hannah gasped.

"Did you know of his plan to divorce you?"

Joseph had told them about his father's intent. Hannah fought to regain her composure. She turned to Dr. Morgan. "May I please have a glass of water?"

Reverend Green hurried from the room and returned a moment later. He handed her the glass, and she took it without meeting his eyes. She took several sips, then placed the glass on a small table next to her chair before returning her attention to the county attorney.

"I never discussed divorce with my husband." She met his stare head-on. "The first I heard of it was today, and I only have my stepson's word that it was something my husband was considering." She looked pointedly at the knife. "I've never seen that knife before and I *did not* kill my husband," she declared firmly.

"You want us to assume that your stepson might be mistaken concerning your husband's plans?" Charles Walker lifted an eyebrow. "Might we, also, assume that he was mistaken," he said and glanced down at the paper, "when you made the statement—I quote—'then I'm glad he's dead'?"

Chapter 14

Early fall 2012, the Krause family farm

Trudy turned as Kate flew into the house. "What's wrong?" she asked, startled by Kate's haste.

"Leave me alone," Kate cried as she hurried past her. Not stopping until she reached the second floor, she started toward her bedroom but then changed her mind. Hurrying down the hallway, she headed for the back bedroom.

Boxes of Christmas decorations, old books, and family photographs sat stacked along the wall. The bed, covered with an old chenille bedspread, had stacks of clothes wrapped tightly in clear plastic. After shoving the clothes aside, Kate sank down on the old mattress, making the bedsprings creak loudly.

Trembling, she laid a palm on her injured cheek. He'd struck her . . . Hot tears began a path down her face. Her knight in shining armor had bullied her. She pulled a shaking hand through her hair while she sobbed, her shoulders shook. Did he leave a mark? A cold cloth would feel good on her still-stinging cheek, but that would mean facing Trudy again. Better to stay here.

Kate tilted sideways onto the bed and drew her legs into a fetal position. She should pack her clothes and get out. But where would she go? She'd given up her apartment when she'd married Joe. That left her grandmother's, and hell would freeze over before she gave that woman the satisfaction of saying "I told you so." She didn't even have a girlfriend to call. She'd been so involved with Joe and their courtship that she'd let all her friendships slide. Lindsay's friendship had been the only one she'd maintained; but since Trudy's lecture about letting go of her old life, she hadn't talked to Lindsay all summer. Now it was too late. She was too embarrassed to suddenly call her now for emotional support.

Bitter tears ran down her face while self-pity kicked in. She didn't deserve this. She'd tried to be a good person, and where was the payoff? A dead mother, a lost baby, an angry husband, and a mean mother-in-law.

She heard the sound of footsteps and raised her head. *Joe coming to apologize?* Part of her wanted this—wanted him to take her in his arms and swear he'd never hurt her again. But the other part of her was too angry to listen to him. How dare he raise his hand to her?

The footsteps faded.

Her grandmother's voice carped in her mind: *"Your fault . . . you never could do anything right."*

She drove the words from her head. She had promised her-self after their last fight to do better at picking the right time to broach a difficult subject. It had been stupid of her to confront him when she knew he was furious with that neighbor. She should've known better.

Kate looked longingly at the window. God, it was hot in here and the air was stifling. She wanted to open the blinds and window—let a fresh breeze blow through the room—but her legs were too heavy to move. Too much effort to cross the room, she thought, wiping the crusted tears and dried sweat off her face.

Again she heard footsteps, and a moment later, Trudy appeared in the doorway.

"What's going on? Joe just took off in his pickup."

Kate rolled over, putting her back toward Trudy. "I don't want to talk about it."

Trudy came around the bed and gawked at her. "That man's my son and your husband. Anything—"

"*My* husband? He's not *acting* like it," Kate exclaimed.

"Like that, is it?" Trudy scowled. "Another fight. What are you trying to do? Destroy him?"

Kate shot up in bed. "Of course not."

"The Krause men have always been high-strung," she replied, crossing her arms, "and—"

"*That's* what you call these rages?" Kate butted in. "Acting high-strung?"

Trudy continued, ignoring Kate's question. "Joe works hard. He needs a stress-free home life."

"So this is my fault?"

"If you'd quit pushing at him, he might treat you better."

"That's bullshit," Kate blurted out.

"Didn't you question his business deal with David Turner?"

Kate stiffened. "I have a right to try and understand the family's business. *And* a right to an opinion."

Trudy's brow lifted. "No, you don't. Joe runs this farm and his opinion is the only one that counts. The sooner you realize that, the better off you'll be." She swung away from the bed and tromped from the room.

"Of all the ridiculous things," Kate muttered to herself, fuming. "I'm supposed to suck it up and take it?"

"*Do you love your husband?*" asked a little voice inside her head.

After throwing herself back onto the pillow, she stared up at the tiny cracks webbing the old plaster ceiling. Yesterday she wouldn't have questioned it. She scooted down in the bed and curled onto her side. She'd had such dreams—belonging to a community, raising a baby, living in a happy home. Now those dreams had turned to dross.

She tucked her hand under the pillow. No life, no job, and after giving Joe her savings to use on the farm, no money. All she had was her marriage.

Her head began to pound, and she closed her eyes. As she drifted off to sleep, she felt a roughened hand smooth the hair away from her forehead.

In the twilight state between waking and dreaming, she was comforted.

When Kate woke up a couple of hours later, the blinds had been raised and the window was open. A light breeze ruffled the curtains.

She took a sharp breath and rolled over onto her back. Flopping her arm over her eyes, she exhaled slowly. Sooner or later she had to face Joe. Maybe Trudy was right—she was pushing him, whether she meant to or not. At first, his anger hadn't been directed at her, but she hadn't backed off, even when he'd told her not to press.

Kate swung her legs over the side of the bed and sat up. Joe had been so kind and loving after the miscarriage, and that man had to still be inside of him. She needed to face him.

When she reached the kitchen, she found Joe standing against the counter. He looked quickly away.

"Where's your mother?" she asked.

"I asked her to spend the night at her friend's," he replied, not meeting Kate's eyes. "I figured we needed to talk in private." He let out a long breath as he raised his attention to Kate. "Are you going to leave me?"

"I don't want to," she answered in a hushed voice, "but I'm not going to allow you to hit me again."

He took a step forward. "I won't—I swear—I don't know what got into me."

Kate held up her hand as the house seemed to close around her. "Let's go for a walk."

Together they went out into the yard and headed for the old apple orchard. As they walked, only a couple of feet separated them, but Kate felt a gaping distance between them. They stopped under a tree and Joe faced her.

"Kate," he shook his head, "I'm ashamed of what I did. I should've never taken my anger out on you."

"You're right," she said coldly. "I'm not your whipping post."

"Of course not," he declared vehemently. "I was angry and I let my temper get the best of me." He held out his hands, palms up. "I've been under so much stress that I just lost it." He placed his hand over his heart. "I swear it will never happen again."

Kate eyed him skeptically. He seemed sincere, but could she trust him? Lines of worry crisscrossed his forehead and his eyes were red as if he'd been crying. Maybe his reaction had shocked him as much as it had her.

He slowly moved forward. "You're everything I've ever wanted and I don't want to lose you," he pleaded in a soft voice. "I'm not a man to beg, but I'm begging you for another chance."

To watch him humble himself this way broke the wall around Kate's heart, and she ran to him. Catching her in his arms, he hung on tight while his ragged breath brushed against her ear.

"I'm sorry . . . I'm sorry," he kept repeating.

Kate took a step back, reaching up to cup his cheek. He took her hand and placed a light kiss in the center of her palm. Wrapping his arm around her waist, he led her back to the house.

Kate was so relieved at their reconciliation that she failed to notice the pale light winking in and out from inside the old cabin.

The next morning, Kate raised her arms above her head and stretched. The last twenty-four hours had been an emotional roller coaster; she'd gone from misery to bliss. Her reconciliation with Joe had put their relationship on a higher level, and she finally felt at one with her husband. She had faith it wouldn't happen again. Her smile widened. And the makeup sex wasn't bad either.

She'd cuddled in her husband's arms and, together, they'd planned their future. They'd even engaged in a little midnight snack fest in the kitchen . . . clothing optional . . . something they never could've done with Trudy in the house.

She sobered. If her marriage was to survive, she had to get Trudy into her own place. But how? Thinking back on her arguments with Joe, Kate realized that Trudy always seemed to be at the heart of them. Last night had been wonderful, but she knew that their bond was tenuous. She needed to approach Joe with caution when it came to his mother.

Standing and grabbing her robe, she wrenched it on. Trudy's influence was not positive, in fact, the woman wore negativity like a shroud, and it seeped through every room in the house. She had to go.

First things first—she needed a car. She'd sold hers right before the wedding and now missed not having the freedom of her own wheels.

Coming into the kitchen, she noticed Joe had already made coffee. She crossed to him, and throwing her arms around his neck, gave him a lingering kiss.

Pulling back, she smiled up at him. "Good morning."

"Mornin' yourself," he answered, moving in for another kiss, then resting his forehead against Kate's. "That was nice."

"I agree," she answered as she stroked his cheek. Stepping away from her husband, she backed toward the refrigerator. "What would you like for breakfast?"

"It's fine. I had cereal."

"But that's not enough."

He waved her concern away. "Ma will be home by noon and she'll make a big dinner. I'll be okay until then."

Kate's happiness slipped. She grabbed a cup from the cupboard and poured her coffee. With her back to him, she carefully picked the words she'd use to explain her plan. She had to make sure she didn't make it sound as if she lacked faith in him.

"Um, Joe," she said, facing him and leaning back against the counter. "I've been thinking—"

"That's not good," he said with a chuckle.

"No, seriously—ah—um, I need to get out of the house more often."

"Why?"

She shrugged. "I've lived here now for a couple of months, but barely know anyone."

"So you want to join Ma's church group?"

Kate shuddered. The last thing she wanted to do was socialize with Trudy and her friends.

"Ah . . . no," she said with hesitation. "I'd like to get a job. Nothing full-time," she continued swiftly, "just something to get me out of the house a couple of days a week."

He snorted. "You want to sling hash over at the Four Corners Café?"

"No," she answered with a lift of her chin. "I am a certified public accountant."

He took a sip of his coffee before commenting. "Won't do you much good around here. Jobs are pretty scarce."

"Maybe I could work for a local attorney?"

He drained his coffee and placed the cup on the counter. "Sure. Give it a try, but nobody will hire you."

"Umm"—she paused—"one last thing. I need a car."

"Huh?" He looked at her with surprise. "We've got a car and a pickup."

Kate crossed her arms over her chest. "But I always feel like I need permission to use them."

"We don't have the money for a new car—"

"But it doesn't have to be new," she interrupted. "All I need is something to get me back and forth to town."

"Kate," he said in a condescending voice, "do you know what the roads around here are like in the winter? There are drifts as high as your waist. If you drove an old junker, I'd be spending all my time pulling you out of the ditch with the tractor." He shook his head again. "We don't have the money." He tilted his head, studying her. "Tell you what . . . you get a job, then figure out how to pay for a car, and I'll go along with it."

"Seriously?" she squealed, throwing her arms around his neck.

"Sure," he answered with a smirk. "Why not?" He glanced over her shoulder at the clock. "Daylight's burning, so I need to get going." He planted a kiss on the top of her head and turned to leave.

"I'm driving into town to look for a job as soon as your mother gets back," she called after him.

"Fine by me," he said with a wave and another chuckle.

Kate narrowed her eyes as she watched him leave. He didn't think she could do it. She'd show him.

Chapter 15

Early fall 2012, Dutton

By early afternoon, Kate was ready to concede defeat. She'd been to the only attorney in town, the local accountant, and even the lumberyard. The only business other than the Four Corners Café that she hadn't visited was Krause Hardware. Joe and Trudy would have a stroke if she applied there. Hmm, Trudy . . . *No,* she chided herself. *Stop right there. Wishing ill only brings it home.* And it wasn't that she didn't want Trudy in her life, she just didn't want her in her home.

Standing on the sidewalk, she eyed the store. According to the sticker on the front door, Will was a member of the Chamber of Commerce. She couldn't work for him, but she could ask him if he knew of any job openings. Mind made up, she entered the store.

"Hey," Will called from behind the counter, "you really are

a rebel. Twice now you've had the guts to come through that door."

Kate blushed. "No, I'm not."

After stepping around the counter, he crossed over to her. "What can I do for you?"

"Find me a job."

His eyebrows shot up. "You want a job here—"

"No, no," she said quickly, "let me rephrase that. Do you know of any businesses who are hiring?"

A look of disbelief crossed his face. "Joe's going to let you work? That'll be a first. The women on that side of the family usually aren't let off the farm."

"Joe's not like that," she declared hotly.

"Whatever you say," he replied, sounding unconvinced. He tapped his chin. "Well, we've already decided that you can't work here—"

"Are you going to help me or not," Kate snapped.

"Okay, I'll knock it off. It's just . . . never mind." He thought for a moment, then snapped his fingers. "How about a job as a receptionist?"

Kate nodded eagerly. "That would be good. It would give me a chance to get to know people in the community."

"Doc Adams. I heard he's looking for a part-time receptionist. The pay probably isn't much—"

Kate thought of how she distrusted doctors, but during her miscarriage, Doc Adams had been more than kind and she liked him.

"I don't need much," she broke in, "and the job would get me out of the house."

"And away from Trudy?"

She flashed him a stern look and he held up both hands in surrender.

"Okay, okay, no more 'Krause cracks.'" He glanced out the window. "If you get a job, she's going to let you use the car?"

"Um—no. That's next on my list . . . getting my own. I don't need anything fancy. Just as long as it can get me to work and back."

"I've got a friend over in Flint Rapids who owns a body shop. He buys old cars and fixes them up on the side. He might have something for you."

Kate glanced away in embarrassment before returning her attention to Will. "I don't have much money."

His eyes narrowed. "Joe won't buy you one?"

"No," she replied with a shake of her head.

"Do you have good credit?"

"Excellent credit."

"Not a problem, then. With a little down, my friend will take payments."

"Really?" Kate asked, her voice excited. She thought of her mother's diamond earrings. She never wore them and they might bring enough. "Is there a pawnshop in Flint Rapids?"

Will grinned. "What are you going to hock? One of Trudy's precious Krause family heirlooms?"

"Of course not," she answered. "I have a pair of diamond earrings that belonged to my mother."

"Hey." His face tightened with concern. "You shouldn't have to do that."

Kate shrugged and kept silent.

"Tell you what," he said, leaning in, "if you get the job at Doc's, I'll loan you the down payment."

"No," she said hotly, "I couldn't do that."

"Why not? I'll hold the earrings as collateral. Same thing as going to a pawnbroker, only my interest is a lot cheaper," he said with a wink.

Will's offer unsettled her. If she did accept, then she wouldn't have to worry about the earrings being sold before she had a chance to buy them back.

He looked down at his watch, then back at Kate. "Tell you what—I'm leaving early today. You go apply at Doc's, and if you get the job, I'll meet you at the body shop in Flint Rapids and we'll see what we can do about getting you a car."

"You're kidding me," she sputtered. "If Joe ever found out I went to Flint Rapids with you, he'd—"

"Don't finish that thought," he said, his face suddenly serious. "That side of the family isn't known for their understanding nature." He stole a look over her shoulder. "I won't tell anyone if you don't."

"Are you suggesting that I lie to my husband?"

"Not lie, just omit certain facts. If he asks, tell him you got a loan on the earrings, which is the truth. He doesn't need to know where the money came from."

"And if he *does* ask me where I got it?"

Will gave her a sheepish smile. "Then I guess you lie."

"What if someone sees us?"

"No one from Flint Rapids will even notice. Contrary to what Trudy might have you believe, Krause influence doesn't extend that far."

Kate was torn. She wanted a job and the freedom having a car would provide. And she didn't want to lose her mother's earrings to a pawnbroker.

She cocked her head and watched Will with a dubious look on her face. "Why are you helping me? You barely know me."

He brushed it away with a lift of his brow. "If you think I'm trying to get back at Joe, you're wrong," he assured her with a smile. "I've always been a sucker for the underdog, and living in the same house with Trudy—"

"Puts me at a disadvantage," she said, finishing for him.

He laughed. "That's a diplomatic way to phrase it."

"You're right. She rules that house, which is why—"

"You want something of your own," he stated. "Look, I'm not out to cause any trouble. The plain truth is I don't like Trudy, but I do like you. She's always been a bully, and if this stops her from pushing you around, then I'm all for it."

Taking her arm, he guided her toward the door. "Honest," he said, smiling down at her, "my motives are pure."

Kate turned and stuck out her hand. "Then you've got a deal."

Kate danced up the front porch steps. She'd done it. She had a job and a car, thanks to Will. Okay, the job was only three days a week and she'd bring home less than two hundred dollars, but for twenty-four hours each week, she'd feel useful. And with her talent for investing, she was sure she could turn what was left out of her paycheck into a respectable amount, given enough time. She grinned broadly, imagining the look of surprise on Joe's face when she'd someday wave her bank book under his nose. That would show him she had value.

She stopped with her hand on the door. And her "new" car? An old dinged-up Jeep, not the best vehicle she'd ever owned, but at least it was hers. Will's friend was bringing it out later this evening after work.

Running into the kitchen, she skidded around the corner.

"Where's Joe?"

Trudy glared at her over her shoulder. "You missed dinner. What kept you?"

"My business in town took longer than expected."

"What kind of business could you possibly have?" she sniffed.

"Never mind," Kate replied as she snagged a carrot out of the refrigerator. "Do you need any help with supper?"

"It's all ready. *I* stayed home where I belong instead of gallivanting all over the country."

Kate ignored her, then spent the next couple of hours while she waited for Joe going through her closet, picking out clothes to wear to work.

Finally, she heard Joe's pickup coming up the driveway and took off down the stairs. Before she had time to announce her success, two vehicles pulled in and parked behind Joe's truck.

"My Jeep," she squealed, hurrying past Joe and over to the vehicles.

By the time Joe and Trudy joined her, Kate had the keys and was running her hand lovingly over the pitted hood.

"What in the hell is that?" Joe asked, pointing toward the Jeep.

"My new car—well, not new—but isn't it great?" Kate babbled.

He watched her with apprehension. "Where did you get the money?"

"Don't worry," she said, forcing a laugh and not meeting his gaze, "I didn't clean out any bank accounts. I used my mom's diamond earrings for a down payment."

"You hocked them."

Since it wasn't really a question, Kate ignored him and opened the driver's side door. "The body might not be the best, but the interior's clean. And the mechanic said the engine was in tiptop shape." She turned and smiled at her husband. "It also has four-wheel drive, so you won't be pulling me out of any drifts this winter."

"Kate," he scolded, "I said you could buy a car if and when you got a job."

Her eyes sparkled. "But I did. And it's not slinging hash," she teased. "I'm going to work three days a week as a receptionist for Doc Adams." She took a deep breath before continuing, "I'll be answering the phones, setting up appointments, helping with the billing. Doc said—"

She stopped, catching the look that passed between Joe and his mother.

"I don't care what Doc said." Joe spun on his heel and started toward the house. "You're not going to do it," he called over his shoulder.

"Yes, I am."

"What?" He turned and advanced toward her.

"I'm going to work at Doc's," she said, a mutinous expression settling over her face.

Joe grabbed her wrist. "No, you're not."

Kate winced in pain. "Joe."

He quickly released her. "Sorry," he mumbled. "You caught me off guard. I didn't mean—"

"You thought I'd fail, didn't you," she spit out.

Joe didn't answer.

"Just what I figured." She pushed past him and stomped off to the house.

Chapter 16

Summer 1890, Braxton County, Iowa

While Minnie Voigt squeaked out the final verse of "Shall We Gather at the River" at his father's graveside, Joseph Krause prayed for this day to be finished. His head pounded from the jug of whiskey he'd drunk last night as he sat with his pa's coffin. He rubbed his nose and tried to forget how the beeswax candles and floral tributes had failed to mask the scent of decay. The smell still lingered on his skin, on his clothes, and in his hair. No amount of scrubbing seemed to get rid of it.

He watched a tear leak from the corner of Minnie's eye as she hit the last note. She'd miss Pa. According to her brother, Peter, she'd "gathered at the river" plenty of times with his father. Jumping Jehoshaphat, that had been some fight—it had taken all of his strength to pull Pa off Peter after he'd confronted Pa about Minnie. It was a miracle Hannah hadn't heard the tussle from the house and come out to investigate. Knowing Hannah, she'd have made a big fuss and hurt Pa's chances in the election. Another reason why they needed her gone before November.

Joseph tilted forward and stared at the ground. None of that mattered now. All that was left of his larger-than-life pa lay in that pine box. His father was gone and Hannah was still here. His chest ached at the thought of it, and he sat up straight. It wasn't fair.

He heard a sob and looked out of the corner of his eye at Hannah's sister, Ida, sitting between her husband and Hannah. She hadn't made the sound. She wept delicately into a lace-trimmed handkerchief. A slight sneer twisted his lips. Her, with her fancy clothes and fancy husband. They'd arrived yesterday by train, and she'd taken over the house, ordering everyone around while Hannah "rested." She'd never liked Pa, and he knew the tears she wept now were for show.

After hearing it again, his attention turned toward Hannah. She sat rigid in her widow weeds with a heavy veil obscuring her face. No signs of grief from her.

He leaned slightly forward and spied Willie, tucked against his mother's side. The child's shoulders shook as he cried unashamedly. Joseph sat back with satisfaction. At least someone other than him and Minnie felt the pain of Pa's passing. Maybe he had more in common with Willie than he thought.

After the funeral, Joseph separated himself from the men standing out by the barn and walked over to the fence separating the hay field from the yard. He placed a foot on the bottom rail and looked out over the freshly cut alfalfa. He took a deep breath and let its sweet smell finally chase the odor of death away. Life went on, and this field would need to be baled before the next rain. He'd talk to Abe Engel later about bringing his baling machine over.

"Sorry about your loss," a voice said from behind him.

Joseph twisted his head and saw Louis Dunlap, Hannah's brother-in-law, standing a few feet away. One look at Louis's expensive suit, and Joseph suddenly felt ragged. His jaw tightened.

"Terrible thing about your father," Louis said as he approached and brushed a speck of dust from his fine coat.

"Yup."

"Do you know . . . Does the sheriff have any suspects?"

Joseph hid a sneer. Just as he thought. Ida had sent her husband out to pump him for information.

"The sheriff doesn't share his thoughts with me," Joseph replied.

"You must be anxious to find your father's killer."

"I want to see justice done." Joseph spit on the ground near Louis's shiny shoes and was pleased to see the man jerk. "Pa won't rest easy otherwise."

Louis joined him at the fence and mimicked Joseph's stance by placing his foot on the bottom rail. He acted uncertain where to put his arms, then with a frown, he finally rested them on the dusty top rail.

"Not that I know much about farming," Louis began, looking out over the field, "but this is a nice place."

"Yup."

"So"—he hesitated—"how much is it worth?"

His pa wasn't even cold in the grave, and Hannah's family was worried about money. Not that he wasn't, but the farm was his and he had a right to be concerned.

"Enough."

Louis pulled at his tight shirt collar. "Ida said something about your father leaving a will?"

Joseph shrugged. "You'd have to ask an attorney about that."

"But Ida said that you told Hannah—"

Joseph cut him off. "You know how women are at times like this." His gaze traveled to a hawk making lazy circles in the sky above them. "They don't hear things right. I might have said *maybe* there was a will."

Louis looked confused. "If there was a will, do you know how the property was divided?"

"Not for certain."

"But I thought—" He waved his hand and stood straight. "Never mind. Ida is concerned about what kind of arrangements your father made for Hannah and Willie's future," he finished emphatically.

Joseph took in the land he'd sweated and worked over since he was old enough to hold a hoe, then judged his words carefully before he answered. Best to pretend to be friendly and let Louis show his hand first.

"Well, Louis," he said, dropping his foot as he carefully observed him, "I don't rightly know what those might be. Depends on whether or not Pa left a will."

Louis frowned. "I believe regardless of whether there's a will or not, the widow has rights to any property."

He gave Louis a hard look as his temper rose. "If you think I'm staying on as my stepmother's hired man, think again."

"Wait," Louis replied, holding up his hand, "I didn't say you should. Once we find out where everyone stands, maybe a monetary remuneration could be given to Hannah and the boy in place of actual property."

"Buy 'em out?" he asked in a shrewd voice.

Louis exhaled slowly. "Yes. That way Hannah will be able to provide for Willie."

Ahh, so Ida wasn't the only one worried about her sister. Louis was afraid that he might get saddled with Hannah and her son, he thought to himself.

Joseph held out his hand. "Whatever you think, Louis. I want to see them get what's fair."

Chapter 17

Fall 2012, Dutton

"You look tired, sweetie," Doris Hill said sympathetically.

Kate gave her new friend a wry look. Since she started working for Doc Adams last month, she and Doris had been meeting for lunch at the Four Corners Café every Wednesday. It was nice to be able to talk to someone other than Trudy or Joe.

"I am," Kate replied.

"Is the job too much?"

"Oh no," she responded passionately. "I love my job."

"Home?"

She hated airing her problems in public and took a couple of minutes to gaze around the room before answering. Taking in the worn linoleum, the red vinyl stools at the counter, and ceiling tile yellowed with years of grease, she thought how to answer Doris. She spotted two of Doc's patients at a table not far from them, gobbling down pieces of the café's homemade pie. And no matter what Trudy might say about it, the crust was as flaky as hers.

Trudy, she thought with a frown. She'd not made the last month easy. Not only did Kate have to listen to her constant digs as well as learning the ropes at Doc's, she always had a list of things that could only be done with Kate's help. They'd cleaned out the attic, hauled forty years' worth of newspapers to the burn barrel, and cleared the basement. Kate gave a shudder. One of the basement jobs had been dumping jars of tomatoes that had failed to seal. One whiff of the stinky, rotten goop and she'd almost lost it. She hadn't missed the gleam in Trudy's eye as she watched Kate haul the wretched bucket up the stairs.

"Well?" asked Doris, calling Kate's attention back to her question.

Quickly, Kate gave her a rundown of the last month. When she finished, she smiled wryly. "I sound whiny, don't I?"

Anger lit Doris's face. "Absolutely not," she exclaimed, drumming her fingers on the table. "She's trying to make you quit, you know. Have you talked to Joe about his mother working you to death?"

"Ahh, no—" She stopped. "There are two topics that are off limits: his mother and the farm."

Doris gave a quick glance around the room, then leaned forward. "He, well, he hasn't hurt you, has he?"

"Doris," Kate hissed.

"I know—I'm sorry—it's none of my business and I shouldn't pry. It's just the Krause men have a reputation of being 'hard.'"

"Joe's family?"

Doris nodded. "His dad, grandfather, and great-grandfather," she answered, keeping her voice down. "Then there's old Jacob . . . I heard a meaner man never drew breath."

Kate sat back. "You mean the ghost?"

"Yeah, have you seen him?"

A shiver crept up her back as she remembered the day Joe had struck her. The blinds and the window had been closed when she'd gone to sleep, yet when she'd awakened they'd been open. Then there was the feeling of someone stroking her hair and the sense of comfort. She gave a quick shake of her head. *Impossible.*

"No, I don't believe in ghosts or family curses," she said swiftly.

Doris clicked her teeth. "A lot of folks around here do, and it does seem that Joe's family has had more than their share of tragedies."

"W—" Kate caught herself then continued. "Ah, someone once said that their problems were more about greed than bad luck."

"I've heard about that, too, starting with the first Joseph cheating his brother out of his inheritance and down to your Joe's grandfather almost losing the farm."

"What happened?"

Doris tugged on her lip. "Something about making bad investments. I recall my mother talking about 'no such thing as easy money' in reference to the grandfather."

"But you don't know what those were?"

"No. You could ask Rose. She knows a lot about your husband's family."

Kate gave a short laugh. "That's not going to happen anytime soon. The woman hates me."

"No, she doesn't." Doris smirked. "I've got to admit, she's ticked at Joe right now and she sure doesn't like Trudy, but knowing Rose, once you two become acquainted, she'd like you."

Doris suddenly sobered. "There's something else I should tell you." She exhaled slowly. "Again, this isn't my business, but as your friend—you need to get Trudy to move."

Kate arched an eyebrow. "No *kidding*," she exclaimed. "Joe's a different person when she's not around. We actually have fun."

"There's a vacancy in the retirement apartments."

"I figured as much. I'm not stupid—I caught what you *almost* said at the barbecue."

"Then why haven't you got her skinny butt out of *your* house?"

"It's not that easy," Kate said with a sigh. "I've already told you that the subject of Trudy is taboo. It's been easier to let it slide." Reaching across the table, she squeezed Doris's hand. "It'll be okay. Once I get settled in this job and things even out, I'll give it another shot."

"Don't wait too long," Doris warned.

"Why do you say that?"

"Trudy's church group."

"What about them?"

"Let's just say that they're talking more about you than they are God," she answered sarcastically.

Kate's eyes flew wide. "They're gossiping about *me*? But I haven't done—"

"Of course you haven't, but it's not stopping Trudy from dishing a load of crap."

"Such as?"

Doris began counting off on her fingers. "You come from trailer trash and you married Joe for his money. You're not a proper wife and couldn't boil water without burning it." She stopped. "Personally, that's my favorite—who else besides those old biddies would care. And," she said, holding up a third finger, "you're so sloppy that Trudy has to clean up after you."

Kate wadded up a napkin and threw it on her plate. "That's so untrue." She picked the napkin up and began to shred it. "Well, maybe not the boiling water part, but the rest of it is a lie." She tilted her head and gave Doris a shrewd look. "Do you suppose Trudy's lies are why Mr. Forsyth gave me the fish eye when he came in for his checkup?"

"Probably. His wife is in Trudy's group."

"What does she hope to gain by trashing me?"

Doris settled back and crossed her arms. "It's obvious. She wants to turn people against you so—"

Kate felt sick to her stomach. "So Doc starts losing patients because of me and has to let me go," she finished for Doris. "That's disgusting."

"Look, sweetie, she won't succeed. People in town like you. You're not like the rest of them."

"Huh?"

"The rest of the women who've married into that family. Except for Trudy, who's been a bitch since the day she was born, the others jumped at their own shadows. You've got spunk."

"Me?" Kate was shocked. "No, I don't."

She thought back to all the things her grandmother had said about her over the years, and the word *spunk* had never been included. *Screw-up*, yes. *Spunk*, no.

"One more thing." Doris moved her empty plate to the side and leaned close to the edge of the table. "I don't think this is common knowledge, but someone has said that they saw you in Flint Rapids with Will Krause."

Kate's breath hitched in her throat and she felt the blood drain from her face. "It's not like what it sounds . . . it was completely innocent . . . I swear," she stumbled. "Will helped me pick out my Jeep. Joe didn't want me to have a car."

"Humph, I'm sure he didn't," Doris said with a frown, then switched to a tight smile. "It's okay. I believe you. Will's a good guy. He wouldn't take advantage of anyone." She sobered. "But you might have a problem convincing Trudy and Joe of that."

Chapter 18

Fall 2012, the Clement family farm

After work, Kate was still worried about her conversation with Doris, and the last place she wanted to go was home. She rested her forehead on the steering wheel. If she went home, she'd have to hold her temper and she didn't know if that would be possible once she saw Trudy. Over the summer, she'd seen how vindictive Trudy was, but to smear her own daughter-in-law ... *Why?*

And the tales about her and Will. Kate gnawed on her bottom lip. She had two choices—tell Joe about her trip to Flint Rapids with Will before he heard the rumors, or keep her mouth shut and pray it all died down without Joe ever finding out.

Turning the key, Kate started the Jeep and slowly backed out of her parking space. Neither one of her choices had much appeal. She made a left onto Main Street and headed out of town, but at the stop sign, she turned right. Might as well drive around a bit. It would give her a chance to compose herself before facing Joe and his mother.

Scattered farmsteads marked by clusters of trees dotted the flat landscape, while fields of corn and soybeans stretched to the horizon. Kate thought back to the comment Joe had made about these roads in the winter. Without groves of trees and hills to block the wind and snow, this area would be desolate in the winter. She could imagine the cold gusts blowing across the flatlands and she shivered. Would her marriage survive until winter?

Kate glanced down at her hands. Her simple wedding band didn't gleam as brightly as it once had. Neither did her dreams.

Returning her attention to the road, she spied a piece of heavy equipment parked near the edge of the road on her left. A large square out of the middle of the field had been stripped of its crops. A wide path led from the square to the machinery. Kate had a sinking feeling. She'd found the location of Joe's project with David Turner.

After stopping and turning off the ignition, Kate got out and walked across the road to the entrance of the field. She rotated slowly, and her attention swept the landscape. A farmstead to the east, a couple more to the west, and one to the north. She paused, looking toward the house to the north. It was closer than the other three.

"It's going to stink to high heaven every time the wind's out of the south," a voice next to her said.

Kate's hand flew to her chest. "I didn't see you."

"I know," Rose Clement replied, pointing to the machinery

with the large stick she carried in her hand. "I was over there."
She caught Kate focused on the stick and chuckled. "I wasn't
bashing in the windows with this, if that's what you're thinking.
But," she continued, her face sober, "I *was* trespassing, if you
want to run home and tell your husband."

"I don't think that's necessary," Kate mumbled.

Rose turned her attention to the fields surrounding them.
"I've lived on this land for sixty years, and I never once thought
I'd be driven from my home."

"I'm sorry, Mrs. Clement," Kate said in a hushed voice.

Looking over at Kate, Rose appraised her slowly. "Yes, I believe you are." She strode past Kate, moving toward the Jeep.
"Instead of standing here jawing on the side of the road, we
might as well finish this conversation at my house. You will give
me a ride, won't you?" she called over her shoulder.

With a shake of her head, Kate met her at the Jeep, then drove
down to the Clement place. A few minutes later she found herself sitting in Rose's kitchen.

Vintage 1960s, she thought to herself. White appliances,
low-pile kitchen carpet, and avocado green walls—it looked like
something out of an old *Better Homes and Gardens*.

"Have a seat," Rose said, waving toward the Formica and
chrome table in the center of the room. "Would you like coffee
or a beer? Personally, this time of day, I prefer a beer."

"I'd better have coffee," Kate replied.

Rose raised her brow. "Afraid Trudy might smell it on you
and think you've been hitting the bars?" she challenged.

"Okay," Kate shot back defiantly, "make it a beer."

She was rewarded with a wink. "Good girl. Don't let that old cow buffalo you." After getting the beer from the refrigerator, Rose sat in front of Kate.

"Do you want a glass?" she asked.

"This is fine."

Rose popped the top on her can and took a long drink, then placed it on the table. "I'll say this for you, young lady, you're not afraid to sleep with the enemy."

Thinking of the rumor about her and Will, Kate's face blanched. "Ah—"

Rose flapped her hand, stopping Kate. "I meant it figuratively not literally. First, you sashay into Krause Hardware bold as brass, then have a beer in my kitchen." Her eyes sparkled. "Trudy would *not* approve."

"Look," Kate said and began to rise, "if you've invited me in to cause tr—"

"Oh, sit down," Rose exclaimed. "I'm not going to tell her or anyone else about your visit. As far as I'm concerned, there's too much gossip as it is, and I don't intend to add to it. I learned a long time ago how to keep my mouth shut."

The talk about gossip made Kate uncomfortable, so she sought to change the conversation. "You've always lived here?"

"Like I said, sixty years." Her attention traveled the kitchen. "I came here as a bride with my first husband, then after he died and I married my second husband, he moved in and took over the farming." She gave a wide grin. "And contrary to what Trudy might have said, I'm not interested in a third."

"Do you have any children?"

"A son down in Des Moines and a daughter and her family over in Flint Rapids," she answered. "My daughter's close enough that I can see her whenever I want, but far enough away for me to stay out of her business."

Kate chuckled, then sipped her beer. For an old lady, Rose wasn't bad. Why couldn't Trudy and her grandmother be more like Rose? She grew thoughtful and pulled on her bottom lip.

"I'm sorry about the disagreement between you and Joe."

"You don't have to keep apologizing for your husband, young lady," Rose replied sternly. "Besides the battle's not over yet. Hasn't he told you that the project's been halted?"

"No."

Rose's lip curled. "That doesn't surprise me." She took a deep breath. "We formed a neighborhood action group, and so far, we've been able to tie up the approval on their building permits."

"So it might not go through?"

"Too early to tell, but we're not giving up without a fight."

Kate drained her beer and debated about her next question, then plunged ahead. "I know this hog confinement thing is the latest thing, but I've been told you've never cared for Joe's family. Why?"

Rose examined her with open curiosity. "How much do you know of his family's history?"

"*Please,*" Kate exclaimed with exasperation, "you're not going to trot out the story about ghosts and family curses, are you?"

"You don't believe in that?" Rose asked in a shrewd voice.

"No. Do you?"

"I believe that wickedness can live on."

"How so?"

"Greed and violence can be passed down from one generation to the next."

"But you're friends with Will, and he has the same great-great-grandfather as Joe."

"But Will's great-grandfather broke the cycle. With Jacob's death, he grew up without Jacob's influence."

"So you do believe in the family curse?"

"I would say that in some ways, Joseph, Jacob's son, was cursed. He buried four daughters and a wife during the Spanish flu epidemic. Only two sons were left—Joe's grandfather and his brother. Then the brother was killed in a farming accident." She sat back in her chair. "Joseph remarried to a much younger woman, who presented him with twin boys. By all accounts, he adored them to the point he neglected Joe's grandfather."

"Were they the great-uncles killed in World War Two?"

Rose nodded. "Yes, and it broke what little heart he had. He died a year later, leaving the farm to your husband's grandfather."

"Then Joe's grandfather lost a son in Vietnam," Kate said carefully.

"Right, Joe's Uncle Fred." She halted. "So whether it's simply a trick of fate or not, in each generation, there's only been one surviving son to take over the farm."

"And Joe's the last."

"That's right. All the deaths combined with some shaky business dealings have fed the legend of a family curse and given your husband's family their reputation."

"I mean no disrespect, but I think that's silly. A person shouldn't be judged by the way their great-great-grandfather, or even their grandfather, acted." Kate grimaced. "We all have a choice as to what kind of person we want to be."

"Yes, we do. But those choices are governed by what we see growing up."

"By what we learn from our parents?"

"Yes."

"Then, I'm mean and stingy," Kate muttered under her breath.

"What did you say?"

Kate looked chagrined. "Nothing . . . ahh." She played with her empty beer can, then shrugged. "My grandmother . . . she tends to be selfish."

"I see." Rose gave Kate a kindly smile. "I don't think you'll be like your grandmother."

"But if what you said is true—that we become like our parents—that's exactly the way I'll be."

"I said we're influenced by them. Your grandmother's influence pushed you in the opposite direction. From what I've heard about you, you're a fixer, a people-pleaser." Her eyes narrowed and she looked at Kate wisely. "In fact, maybe in your desire not to be like her, you've carried it too far and let people take advantage of you."

Kate thought about her marriage and the way she'd tried so hard to please both Joe and Trudy. "Do you have a degree in psychology?"

Rose answered her with a laugh. "No, child, I don't, but I've lived a long life. I would've been stupid not to have learned a few things by now."

Kate grinned. "I doubt anyone's ever accused you of being stupid." Her grin faded. "So you and Trudy . . ." Her voice trailed away.

"Don't care for one another because she's a Krause and all

that folderol about my grandfather and his investigation of Jacob's death?"

"Yeah."

She rolled her eyes. "A bunch of nonsense. Jacob's death did have a big impact on my family, but not in the way everyone thinks."

"How so?"

"Oh, we'll leave that story for another day, but back to the trouble with Trudy. Do you want the truth?"

Kate nodded emphatically.

"You're going to be disappointed. It's not as dramatic as stories of ruined lives . . . Joe's dad liked the ladies and it didn't matter that he was married. After my first husband died, he offered to *help* me out."

Kate's mouth dropped.

"That's right . . . he wanted an affair. Even though he was several years younger, I guess he thought as a widow, I'd be an easy mark." She laughed. "He thought differently after he'd come sniffing around, and I ran him off with my late husband's shotgun."

"I can't believe it," Kate responded in a shocked voice.

"Why? I didn't always look like this you know," Rose huffed, straightening in her chair. "At one time, I was considered quite pretty." She softened her words with a smile. "Trudy has always blamed me for her husband, shall we say, trying to jump the fence."

"She didn't hold him responsible?"

"Of course not. Joe's father did what he wanted, when he wanted. And Trudy either put up with it or paid the price."

Kate looked at the clock and jumped to her feet. "Oh no! I had no idea it was this late."

As Kate passed, Rose laid a hand on her arm. "I like you. If you ever need anything, call me." Her face was somber. "Even if you just want to talk. I'm good at keeping secrets."

Kate patted Rose's hand. "Thanks, Rose." She glanced at the clock again nervously. "I'd better get home before I get in trouble."

Chapter 19

Fall 2012, Braxton County, Iowa

The stones cast long shadows over the newly mown grass by the time Rose made it to the cemetery. As she made her way, she noticed the headstones bearing the names of people she'd known over the years—once the last date was blank, now chiseled in. Her neighbors from down the road; they'd been a devoted couple who died within months of one another. The headstone of the young man who'd shown such promise in school, but whose life had ended in a car accident thirty years ago. He'd rested alone for so long, but his parents had finally joined him last year.

She walked past the older stones and tried not to notice the number of markers that featured angels and lambs. Too many children back then died before they had a chance to live, and it always saddened her thinking of them. Rose kept moving until she'd reached a plot in the back of the cemetery, sheltered by pine trees.

She paused before the stone bearing the names of Dr. William Krause and his wife of sixty-four years, Clara. They had been a wonderful couple, and she had fond memories of the good doctor. He'd been close to her great-grandpa Gus Winter, and had visited him often when Great-Grandpa lived with her grandmother, Essie. When she was a child, the two men had allowed her to play cards with them. She smiled. Thanks to them, she still played a mean game of pinochle. After Great-Grandpa's passing, William's visits continued, and her whole family felt the loss when William died.

Rose patted the top of the stone, then moved to an unpretentious stone to the left of Dr. William and Clara's. Carved in gray granite, the stone bore only the name—HANNAH KRAUSE, and an epitaph. Using the stone for balance, Rose slowly lowered herself to her knees. After brushing away the grass clippings from the base of the stone, she placed a small pot of mums in its center. The dark bronze flowers looked nice against the gray granite.

"I think you'd like her, Hannah, even though she is married to Joseph's kin," Rose murmured, moving the pot a couple of inches to the left. "Trudy wants her gone, but if she'd quit her meddling, I think that girl could break the cycle." She gave a long sigh. "I'd appreciate it if you kept an eye on her."

As Rose walked away from the grave, she felt a soft whisper brush against her face and she smiled.

Chapter 20

Fall 2012, the Krause family farm

When Kate pulled in the driveway, Trudy was waiting for her on the porch.

"Where have you been?" she called down to Kate as she exited the car.

Flashes of her conversation zipped through Kate's mind and her temper spiked. "None of your business," she answered, moving around her.

Trudy grabbed her arm and Kate yanked back. "Don't touch me," Kate warned.

The screen door opened and Joe stepped out between the two women. "Where have you been?"

Trudy shot Kate a smirk. "You may not have to answer me, but you do your husband." She spun and slammed back into the house.

"You've been off work for hours. Where did you go?"

She couldn't tell him she'd been at Rose's. "Please, Joe, not now. I'm tired," she said, trying to put off his questioning.

"Maybe if you'd come straight home, you wouldn't be so tired."

There was no getting around it. "I did. I was working late," she lied.

"That's not true," he said, his face flushing. "When you didn't come home, I drove into town to check on you. Your Jeep was gone and the office was closed."

"It's not a big deal," she said in a tired voice. "I went for a drive."

"With Will," he spit out.

Great, she thought, rubbing her eyes with her fingertips. It didn't take the rumors long to circulate.

"No, I wasn't with Will Krause," she replied. "Can't we talk about this later?"

"No, we'll talk about it now." He towered over her. "How long have you been sneaking around with Will?"

"I'm not," she cried.

"You were in Flint Rapids with him."

"To get a car," she exclaimed, pointing to her Jeep. "You weren't any help. Will introduced me to his friend who fixes up old cars and sells them. That's all."

His eyes became slits as he glanced over at the Jeep. "You bought that from a friend of his? Get rid of it," he said, not waiting for her answer.

"How am I supposed to get to work?"

"You won't. You're going to call Doc Adams and give him your two-week notice."

"No," Kate replied in a hushed voice.

He came forward. "What did you say?"

"I said 'no.'" She shoved her hands on her hips. "I like my job. I like having my own money."

"And *I* said you're quitting. I'm not having my wife catting around and stirring up gossip."

"Listen, Will is a friend, nothing more. And," she said with a jerk of her head toward the house, "if anyone's stirring up gossip, you have your mother to thank. Her and her friends have had a grand time trashing me."

A vein began to throb on Joe's forehead. "That's not true."

"Oh yes, it is," she declared, "and I'm sick of it. You make a choice. Either you get your mother out of this house, or I'm gone." Kate got in his face. "And don't bother lying about the apartments. One has been vacant for months." She stepped back and turned, reaching for the screen door, but her hand never made contact. Joe grabbed her shoulders and spun her around.

"You are not leaving me," he said, giving her a shake. "Who do you think you are?" He gave her another shake. "You don't tell me what to do. My mother can stay here as long as she wants."

From the back of the house, she heard the music box begin to play.

"I'm your wife," Kate yelled. "I'm not living in the same house with her."

He shook her harder, jarring her head back and forth. "You will if I say so."

Kate stood, stunned, the discordant notes of "When Johnny Comes Marching Home" seemed to surround her. She struggled, but she couldn't loosen his grip on her shoulders. And the harder she tried, the more forcefully his fingers dug into her shoulders. She winced in pain.

"Joe," she gasped.

He stopped, then released her. Holding his hands in front of him, he stared at them as if they were foreign objects.

The music suddenly stopped, and Kate pressed her fist to her mouth and fled. Once in the bedroom, she slammed the door and locked it. Breathing hard, she threw her back against the door and wrapped her arms around her waist.

When would she learn? Shame ran through her. She should've never given him an ultimatum. Bucking away from the door, her eyes widened. No. He'd lied about Trudy living with them from the beginning and she'd put up with it. Looked the other way. Tried to avoid touchy subjects with him in order to keep the peace. She'd worked hard to please him and received blessed little in return.

Enough. She'd told Rose that everyone made a choice and it was time to make hers.

She started toward the closet, then stopped when her grandmother's voice echoed in her head. *You'll screw it up. You can't do anything right.*

"Shut up," she muttered to herself and returned to the door. After unlocking it, she opened it and ran down the hall to the spare room. She grabbed her suitcase from the corner and returned to the bedroom to begin emptying the closet.

When she'd finished that task, she started on the dresser, tossing things into the suitcase in no particular order. Suddenly she stopped.

Where did she think she was going? Not back to her grandmother's. She'd rather live in a ditch. She could ask Doris to take her in, but with three adolescent boys, Doris had enough to do.

A motel? She had a little money and would be able to afford a few nights, but the money wouldn't last long. A sob escaped as her vision blurred with tears. She placed both hands on top of the dresser, leaning against it. Hot blood flooded her face and she bowed her head, letting the tears plop on its surface.

What was she going to do?

A brush of air cooled her cheeks and she raised her head. Staring in the mirror, she noticed a shadow by the door, but when she pivoted, the shadow had disappeared.

Kate inhaled slowly. She didn't know if it had been Joe or Trudy spying on her, but she was relieved they'd left. The thought of being watched spurred her on. With her arms full of her things, she crossed to the bed and dumped them in the suitcase. Ten minutes later, she hauled the suitcase out of the room and down the stairs.

Joe waited at the bottom.

"Kate—wait—let's talk," he pleaded.

She skirted around him and headed for the front door.

"I suppose you're going to Will's?" he asked in a tight voice.

She shot him a withering glance over her shoulder and kept walking.

Kate sat at the crossroads trying to figure out which way to turn. Right, left, or straight ahead? Turning around and going back was not an option. Thoughts of Rose popped into her head unexpectedly, and as if with a will of their own, her hands turned the Jeep to the left.

As she approached Rose's house, she saw the porch light shining like a beacon in the distance. And when she pulled in the drive, Rose was standing on the porch, waiting, as if she'd expected her. After Kate rolled to a stop, she came to the Jeep and opened Kate's door.

"You look done in, child," she said, drawing Kate out. Placing an arm around her shoulders, she began to guide her to the house. "I wondered if you wouldn't be back."

Kate, too emotionally exhausted to respond, looked at her, perplexed.

"Have you eaten?" she asked, guiding her into the house.

"No, but I'm not hungry."

"You need to eat. I'll make you a sandwich."

Once in the kitchen, Rose steered her toward the chair, then busied herself making a ham sandwich while Kate gave her the short version of her fight with Joe. Rose's face flooded with anger when Kate related the part about Joe shaking her.

"Do you need to see Doc?"

"No, the muscles in the back of my neck are stiff, but I don't have a headache. I'll be okay."

After placing the food and a cup of hot tea in front of Kate, Rose took her own seat and waited silently as Kate tried to choke down the sandwich. Finally, Kate pushed her plate away.

"I'm sorry. I can't finish it."

"That's okay. Drink your tea. I'll make you a big breakfast in the morning."

Aghast, Kate stared at her. "I can't stay here."

"Why not? I've four big bedrooms upstairs."

"It would be an imposition."

"Nonsense. I told you if you needed anything—"

"Bet you didn't expect it to be this soon," Kate broke in, blinking hard to keep the tears at bay.

"Do you want to know the truth?" Rose hooked her arm over the back of her chair. "I knew trouble was coming. I heard about you and Will."

Kate covered her face with her hands. "Nothing—"

Rose reached over and drew her hands away. "I know it's nothing more than a lot of talk. Will's not going to go chasing after another man's wife, and from what I've heard, you're not the type to *let* yourself be chased." Leaning back, she grimaced. "I knew it wouldn't be long until Trudy got wind of the rumor and went running to Joe with it. And I'm sure she added her own spin." She tugged on her bottom lip. "You know you didn't deserve the way he treated you, don't you."

"I guess."

Rose smacked the table, startling Kate. "There's no guessing about it, and I hope to hell you're not planning on going back."

"I'm not," she answered with a brittle smile. "I'm tired of the lying, the heartfelt apologies that only last until the next time I make him angry, and Trudy."

"Are you moving back to your home?"

"I don't have a home—just my grandmother's."

"The stingy one?" Rose asked with a faint smile.

"Yeah. I lived on her charity for eighteen years."

"And she never let you forget it."

"No, she didn't and I'm not living with her again. She's almost as bad as Trudy, only sneakier."

Rose stood and picked up the plate. After carrying it to the counter, she placed it in the sink, then turned to Kate. "Stay here tonight. You can decide what you want to do tomorrow."

"That's very generous of you," Kate said in an astonished voice. "You've only met me twice."

Rose chuckled. "I'm a very good judge of character. Essie—"

"Essie?" Kate interrupted.

"My grandmother, Esther Winter Lloyd, but everyone called her Essie. She always said that I had eyes and ears too big for a child." She lifted a shoulder. "Great-Grandpa Winter had said the same about her, so I took it as a compliment."

"So it's a family trait?"

"One of them, I guess."

"There are others?"

"I'd like to think so, but that's a long story. It's off to bed with you."

Rose helped Kate to her feet and gave her a quick hug. "I know you feel pretty bleak right now, but it'll get better. I promise."

Chapter 21

Fall 2012, the Clement family farm

The next morning Kate woke up disoriented. Where was she? This wasn't her bedroom. It all came crashing back . . . Joe . . . the fight . . . the accusations. The confusion was followed by a clutch of fear. She sat up in bed and rubbed her sore shoulders. She had to come up with a plan and dawdling here in bed wasn't the way to accomplish it. After dressing in jeans, a cotton shirt, and loafers, she left to find Rose.

The smell of fresh coffee guided her. The table was set for two, and Rose stood at the stove scrambling eggs. She looked over her shoulder as Kate entered.

"Hungry?"

Kate began to deny it, but her stomach gurgled loudly, giving her away.

Rose chuckled. "Help yourself to the coffee and the eggs will be ready in a minute."

"Thanks. Is there anything I can do to help?" Kate asked as she grabbed a cup and poured her coffee.

"Nope. Sit and we'll eat."

They were silent for a few moments while they both dug into the plates of scrambled eggs, sausage, and toast. Rose was the first to break it.

"Did you sleep well?"

Kate lifted one shoulder. "All things considered . . . yes, I did. And I can't thank you enough for putting me up last night. I'll be out of your hair today."

"I told you last night that you're not an imposition," she said with a steely look, then smiled. "You're welcome to stay as long as you like."

"I can't sponge off you, Rose."

"Who said anything about sponging? Everyone needs a hand now and again."

"Yeah, but I prefer to pay my own way. I'm going to ask Doc for more hours, but if he can't, then I'll look for a second job."

"Okay, then stay here and pay room and board."

"I don't have much. I think I'd be better off staying at a cheap motel."

Rose's eyebrows shot up. "Sharing a room with roaches and living on Ramen noodles? I don't call that better off." She extended her hand across the table. "Look, I really don't need extra money right now, but I could use a little help around here—" The expression on Kate's face stopped her. "Oh, don't worry. I wouldn't work you half to death like Trudy did."

Kate flushed with embarrassment. "I don't think that—I—um."

"Stop," Rose said and laughed. "It's okay if you suspect my

motives after the way you've been treated. You really don't have much reason to trust me." She paused. "Yet."

"Essie was right. You do have big eyes."

"Yes, she was, and I'll say this before the thought pops into your head. I'm not like your grandmother. I don't want you to feel beholden to me for helping you."

Grateful for Rose's insightfulness, Kate smiled. "You're an amazing woman, Rose."

Rose's cheeks colored. "I don't know about that," she replied self-consciously. "But I did have a wonderful example in my grandmother. She was insistent about the need for women to help each other instead of turning a blind eye."

"She sounds like a wonderful person."

"That she was. Helping you isn't totally unselfish of me. I get something out of it, too. I get to feel useful and so many people my age don't. Instead of getting out there and doing for others, they're sitting around waiting to die." She tapped her chest. "Not me. I'm going out kicking and screaming."

Kate laughed.

"See," she said, wagging a finger at Kate, "I made you laugh and *that* makes me happy. Don't think this is a one-way street. I benefit from you staying here, too, and those benefits don't have to be monetary."

Kate thought for a moment. Staying with Rose would be a great help. She wouldn't be rushed into making a decision that she might later regret. She'd have the time to think about what direction she wanted to take in her life.

"Okay, you've got a deal. Will your daughter mind if I live here for a while?"

Rose's expression turned cagey. "My children learned not

to dictate to me a long time ago. They know they'd be wasting their breath. Besides," she said with pride, "my daughter, Annie, looks at things the same way I do. She'll be fine with the idea."

Her face grew serious. "I do have errands today. You're welcome to go with me, but I'll understand if you don't want to."

Kate sniffed. "As long as it doesn't have anything to do with Trudy and her church ladies, I'll welcome the distraction."

"It doesn't, but it still might be difficult for you."

"Why?"

"I do volunteer work in Flint Rapids on Tuesdays."

"Even better. I'll get out of Dutton for the day."

"At a women's shelter."

"Oh."

"See what I mean?" Rose asked kindly. "Given what happened to you yesterday, I understand if visiting a shelter is the last thing you want to do."

Kate picked up her coffee and sipped it slowly. She felt torn. On the one hand, Rose had been so kind and gracious and driving her to Flint Rapids would be one small way to begin to repay her. But did she want to face other women in situations similar to hers? Setting her cup down, she pursed her lips and looked across at Rose's blank expression. She was letting Kate make up her own mind without pushing one way or the other.

Kate stood. "I'll clean the kitchen then drive you to the shelter."

Following Rose's directions, Kate turned onto a quiet street in a residential section, then stopped in front of a large Victorian house. A brick walkway led across the yard, past two large maple trees, to the wraparound porch. White with blue trim, the house looked well cared for and spacious. Kate helped Rose out of the Jeep and walked around to the back, popping the rear door. As she grabbed two sacks of groceries, the sound of children's laughter caught her attention.

"We have a small daycare out back in the old coach house," Rose explained, picking up a third sack of food. "Come on. I'll introduce you to the staff and we can get the boxes of clothes and toys later."

Kate followed Rose up the brick path to the front porch and stood on the top step while Rose rang the bell. The door opened and Rose motioned her forward.

"Hello, Rebecca," she said cheerfully as a young woman with laughing eyes took the sack.

"Hey, Rose," she responded, sneaking a peek at Kate.

"Rebecca." Rose placed her hand on Kate's upper arm. "This is my friend Kate. She's visiting me for a bit and kindly drove me today."

"How's it going, Kate?" Rebecca said. "Come on in," she continued without waiting for a response. "We're back here in the kitchen."

Together they proceeded down a wide hall to a room at the back of the house. Two women sat at the table, chopping vegetables. Obviously pleased to see Rose, their expressions became more guarded when introduced to Kate. During the introduction, one of them quickly turned her face to the side, but not before Kate noticed a yellowing bruise on her left cheek.

"Rose," Rebecca said, "why don't you help Pam and Sharon with the vegetables while Kate and I bring in the rest of the boxes."

A few moments later, Rebecca and Kate were hauling the boxes out of the back end of the Jeep and stacking them in the entryway. With the last box in her arms, Rebecca glanced at Kate.

"I'm sorry for your troubles," she said quietly.

Surprised, Kate almost dropped the box she carried. "Excuse me?"

Rebecca gave a little shake of her head. "Rose didn't say anything, if that's what you're thinking." She scrutinized Kate. "You have that shell-shocked look around your eyes."

Kate balanced the box with one arm while her hand flew to her face.

"Don't worry about it," she said dismissing Kate's stricken expression. "We've all had it."

"You? I thought you were on the staff?"

"I am now, but I wasn't two years ago when I first came here. Thanks to Rose and Dr. Mike, I received the help I needed and ended it with my loser boyfriend. After my head got screwed on straight, they offered me a position and I took it." She smiled over at Kate. "Coming here was the best thing I could've done."

"Wait a second—I thought Rose was just a volunteer."

"She does work as a volunteer, but she's also the founder of Essie's House and still serves on the board."

"No kidding?"

"Umm-hmm. Her daughter, Annie, is on the board, too."

Kate looked up at the big house. "So Rose started this?"

"Yup, with a bequest from her grandmother, Esther Winter Lloyd." Rebecca tilted her head and watched Kate. "You don't know who she was, do you?"

"Ah, I know she was Rose's grandmother," Kate replied sheepishly as she entered the house.

"The kids are going to love this," Rebecca said, placing her box next to the others and eyeing all the toys. She faced Kate. "I take it Rose didn't say much about Essie?"

"Not really—she's talked about what an amazing woman she was, and I assumed she was a wife and mother like the other women of her time."

Rebecca smiled broadly. "She was, but there's more to her story than that. She was also one of the first women to practice law in the state, later serving as a judge. She was an early suffragette *and* a well-known author in her later years."

"Wow," Kate exclaimed.

Rebecca gave a knowing nod. "She knew the President and Mrs. Roosevelt, too. Eleanor even once quoted Essie in a speech."

"That's impressive."

"Darn right it is." Rebecca made a slow turn. "This house is just one of her legacies. We have some of her books in the reading room if you'd like to take a look at them?"

"I would. Thank you."

A woman's laugh echoed from the kitchen.

"Come on," Rebecca said with a nod toward the back, "we'd better help with lunch."

After they'd finished eating and cleaning up, Kate excused herself and wandered off to the reading room. The women had been pleasant during lunch, but Kate noticed their unease at having a stranger in their midst. Leaving them alone with Rose would give them time to chat freely.

The reading room was one of the largest in the house. The oak-paneled walls gleamed golden in the light spilling in from the high casement windows. Tall bookcases climbed toward the ceiling, their shelves packed with books and games.

As Kate browsed those shelves, she found works by everyone from Nora Roberts to Jane Austen. One section was devoted to women's history, and it was there she found Essie's books. After removing one from the shelf, she flipped it open. The first page was an acknowledgment:

To my mentor, Johan Bennett

Another unfamiliar name, Kate thought as she browsed through the pages. Evidently, she needed to take a crash course on women's literature of the early twentieth century.

"I see you found one of Essie's books," Rose said, coming to stand beside her.

"Why didn't you mention that Essie was famous?"

Rose chuckled. "I don't think she was ever considered famous. More likely, the men of her era saw her as a pain in the backside. Something that, I might add, gave her no small pleasure."

"She was an attorney and a judge?"

"Yes," Rose replied, the pride shining in her eyes. "Compared to her, I'm an underachiever."

"I doubt that."

"May I?" she asked, holding out her hand. After taking the book from Kate, she thumbed to its back pages, then gave it back to Kate. "Here's her picture."

The photograph was a side view showing a woman with a strong profile. Her hair was brushed back in waves away from her face and a pair of rimless glasses sat perched on her nose. Her lips were curved in a half-smile as if she had a secret no one else knew.

"She looks determined."

"That she was," Rose declared, "but it was her voice that captured everyone's attention. Very soft, but at the same time strong. I never saw her in court, but my mother had. She said Essie was a marvelous orator and could make a jury hang on her every word."

"It must have been difficult for her."

"It was. After attending Iowa Wesleyan College, she studied law at the University of Iowa. Women back then had to fight to get an education."

"Why the law?"

"She was always close to her father. In fact he lived with her and my grandfather during the last years of his life." Rose looked thoughtful. "I suppose she received her strong sense of justice from him."

"Not Johan Bennett?"

Rose smiled slyly and took the book from Kate, opening it to the acknowledgment. "Ah yes, her mentor. I'm afraid that's a story—"

"Let me guess," Kate asked with an arch of her eyebrow. " 'A story for another day'?"

"You catch on quick, my girl."

Chapter 22

Kate panicked as she pulled in Rose's driveway. Joe was waiting for her. Rose caught the expression on her face.

"Easy," she said in a soothing voice. "He's not going to be foolish enough to cause trouble here. Listen to what he has to say, but don't let him talk you into leaving with him."

Taking a deep breath and exhaling it slowly, she stopped and both women got out.

Rose was the first to speak. "I don't expect any problems here, Joe," she said sternly.

His attention focused on a spot by his foot. "There won't be," he said. "I just want to talk to Kate."

She walked up and stood right in front of him, her small elderly body dwarfed by his. She drilled him with a steely expression. "That's good, because I'm going to be watching out that front window. I'll have my cell phone in one hand and my shotgun in the other. If you so much as touch her, we'll see which one I use first."

"I understand," he mumbled as Rose breezed past him and disappeared into the house.

Kate leaned against the front of the Jeep. "How did you know I was here?"

"Someone saw you driving through Dutton with Rose."

"That 'someone' sure sees a lot," she replied sarcastically.

Joe jerked his head toward the house. "I didn't know you two were friendly."

"It's a recent friendship."

"She always did like sticking her nose in other people's business," he said with a frown. "And—"

"Hold it right there. I won't stand here and listen to you trash her. If that's what you intend to do, this conversation is over." Kate pushed away from the Jeep.

"Wait," he called, holding up a hand. "Not another word about Rose." He shoved his hands in his pockets. "I want you to come home."

Kate snorted in disbelief. "You've got to be kidding me—after last night? No way."

"But you're my wife and home is where you belong," he argued.

"I am your wife, but I'm not a prisoner, a whipping post, a doormat, or your mother's servant." She ran out of breath and inhaled sharply, then continued. "I'm done with all of it."

"But Ma—"

She sliced the air with her hand. "Stop. I don't want to hear any more excuses about your mother. And," she said, moving forward, "I won't be touched in anger."

"I'm sorry."

"That's what you said the last time. So what?" she asked, crossing her arms over her chest. "This time you really mean it?"

"I do . . . I do mean it," he insisted. "Please come home."

He looked so humbled that a portion of Kate's resolve weakened, then she remembered the woman at Essie's House. The one with the yellowing bruise on the side of her face. Next time she could look like that. Maybe it would be a busted lip or a broken bone.

"I'm sorry, Joe, I can't. Not until I'm sure that you have your temper under control."

"But how will you know if we aren't living together?"

She thought of an idea that should have occurred to her a long time ago.

"I'll continue to stay here, but we'll go to counseling together."

"*No*," he exclaimed, "I'm not spilling my private life to some shrink."

"Okay," she said as she moved by him, "this discussion is over."

His hand shot out to grab her wrist, but stopped short of touching her.

"Good," she said, glancing down at his hand still extended toward her, "you remembered the shotgun."

"Kate. Please."

With a shake of her head, she kept moving and didn't respond. Once inside the house, she shut the door with a sigh and collapsed against it, her knees shaking.

From the window, she saw him pacing back and forth across the yard. Why wasn't he leaving? Finally, he stopped and shoved his hands on his hips.

"Okay," he yelled at the house. "I'll go. You set it up then let me know." He whirled, jumped in his truck, and a minute later took off down the road.

Rose stepped out of the living room, and true to her word, she had her cell phone and a shotgun.

"You wouldn't have shot him, would you?" Kate asked, her eyes focused on the gun.

"If necessary," Rose replied, opening the gun and taking out the shells, then held one up. "Rock salt—I'd have peppered his butt with it." She grinned slightly. "It doesn't kill, but it stings like hell."

A few weeks later, Kate sat in her Jeep, staring at the door to their therapist's office. Joe had kept his word and was attending weekly sessions with Dr. Mike, the therapist from Essie's House, but he'd always sidestepped the doctor's questions. Would today be different?

Her own life had fallen into an easy rhythm. Doc had come through for her and given her additional hours, but she had Tuesdays off. Those days she spent with Rose at Essie's House. At Rose's suggestion, she was using her knowledge about money to help the women there with budgeting, learning how to save, and getting out and staying out of debt. She was amazed at their determination to make a better life. It made Kate feel good to help these women learn how to secure a stable financial future for themselves and their families once they left Essie's.

The sudden ringing of her cell phone broke into her thoughts. She picked it up and saw Doris's number flashing on the screen.

"Hey," she answered.

"Hey yourself," Doris said. "What are you doing?"

A small sigh escaped Kate's lips. "Waiting for Joe."

"At Dr. Mike's?"

"Yeah."

"You sound discouraged."

"I am . . . in a way."

"But last week you said you thought the therapy was helping."

Kate ran a hand over the steering wheel as she framed her words. "It *is* working for me. Dr. Mike's very good at forcing me to face things about myself and my life that I'd rather forget." She shook her head. "His approach reminds me of root canal—painful but necessary."

Doris chuckled. "But that's a good thing, right?"

"Yeah. Until these sessions, I never realized how I'd let my grandmother's opinions color my world. Somewhere deep inside, I felt abandoned, so I bought into every negative thing she said about me, my parents, my friends. I was so desperate for her approval that I let her words control me."

"And then along comes Trudy and you do the same thing."

"Exactly," Kate exclaimed. "And I'm done living my life to please others. I'm done trying to fit in and make others like me."

"So why are you discouraged?"

"I may be feeling better about myself, but I'm not about my marriage," she replied softly. "Joe hasn't once taken responsibility for any of his actions."

"Oh, sweetie, I'm sorry." Her voice brightened. "But give it time. Joe's old school and it's hard for a man like him to talk about his emotions. I know he loves you."

"Unless things change . . ." Kate's voice trailed away. "It's not going to be enough."

The sound of a truck pulling into the parking lot caught her attention.

"I've got to go," she said quickly. "Joe's here."

"Okay. Good luck."

"Thanks."

Kate threw her cell phone in her purse, and with heavy steps joined Joe, waiting at the door to the office building.

Kate sat silently and listened to Dr. Mike pepper Joe with questions.

"What was the relationship between your parents?" Dr. Mike asked.

"Normal," Joe answered with a shrug. "Ma stayed home like she was supposed to do and Pa farmed."

"Who defined what your mother's role would be?"

"Pa."

"Was your mother allowed to make any decisions?"

"Not really. Her job was to raise me and take care of the house."

"Your relationship with your father . . . did he take you fishing, to baseball games, or engage in any father-son activities?"

"Nope. You have a cushy office job, Doctor. Strictly nine to five," he answered with a superior grin. "My job is twenty-four/seven. We don't have time for a lot of pointless pleasures."

"Did he attend your school functions such as your football games?"

"Like I said, we didn't have time for stuff like that," Joe replied with a glimmer of resentment.

"So no going to the movies, taking family vacations, anything like that?"

"I went over to eastern Iowa once with Pa to buy a new bull."

"Did you have fun with your father on that trip?"

Joe shrugged. "It was okay."

"Did your father ever show any affection?"

"What do you mean?"

"Did he ever hug you? Did he ever praise you?"

"Pa didn't believe in all that mushy stuff." Joe shifted his weight on the couch. "He wanted me to grow up to be a man, not a wimp."

"You equate affection with weakness?"

Joe's face reddened. "Of course not, but there's a time and a place for it."

"Did you see affection between your father and mother?"

"I guess," he replied, his hands clenching and unclenching.

"Can you tell me of an instance where you witnessed your parents showing their love for one another?"

"I was a kid. I didn't pay attention to stuff like that."

"How did they resolve their differences?"

Joe's eyes narrowed. "What do you mean?"

"Arguments. Did your parents argue?"

"Not that I recall," Joe answered, staring at a spot over Dr. Mike's shoulder.

"I find that hard to believe. All couples have disagreements."

Sitting next to Joe, Kate felt the tension pouring off of him in waves.

"What's all this stuff about my parents? It doesn't have anything to do with my marriage."

"Yes, it does. Our parents set an example that can carry over into our adult relationships. We often subconsciously choose to mimic that example. Or we deny what we've seen and choose something completely different." Dr. Mike tapped a pen on his desk. "I'm trying to figure out which course you picked, Joe."

"That's a bunch of *bullshit*," Joe exclaimed.

"What happened when your father became angry?"

"Nothing," Joe spit out.

"I don't believe you," Dr. Mike replied in a steady voice.

Kate jumped as Joe exploded and shot to his feet. He began to pace the room.

"You want to know what happened?" he yelled. "He beat the shit out of whoever was handy! There—satisfied?" He marched over to the window and looked out with his back to the room. "Ma got the worst of it. She was always trying to protect me and took the beatings that I earned." He braced a hand against the wall. "Once, after I'd done something stupid, he came at me with his belt, but Ma got in his way." His head dipped. "He whipped her so bad that it almost put her in the hospital."

After Joe's outburst, the room echoed with silence, and Kate dared not break it.

"What did you do?" Dr. Mike finally asked in a quiet voice.

"I tried to help her . . . went at the old man kicking and hitting . . . but he brushed me away like I was no more than a fly. Hell, I was just a kid." He took a ragged breath. "Then he beat Ma all the harder." His shoulders began to shake. "I hated that bastard and was glad when he died. Now I'm becoming just like him."

Kate saw the scene in her mind—an angry man, a cowering woman, and a little boy trying to help his mother. Her heart ached and she made a move to go to her husband, but Dr. Mike waved her back.

The minutes ticked by and the only sound in the room was Joe's muffled sobs. Finally, Dr. Mike spoke.

"It made you feel powerless, didn't it?"

Joe nodded.

Dr. Mike waited for Joe to compose himself. When Joe had turned to face them, he continued. "We do have a choice, Joe. We can take responsibility for our feelings and for our actions, then change them. You don't have to repeat the mistakes of the past. Do you understand?"

Joe wiped his face and nodded again. He crossed the room and knelt before Kate.

"I'm sorry," he said, tears still shimmering in his eyes.

This time she believed him.

Chapter 23

Kate sat on Rose's front porch watching the storm clouds roll across the distant horizon, and the air was thick with moisture. They'd have rain by noon, she thought as she sipped her coffee. At one point during the day, she needed to go into the office and finish a few last-minute statements, but for now, she wanted to sit and enjoy the quiet.

Her thoughts drifted to Joe. She'd had no contact with him since their last appointment with Dr. Mike. No phone calls, no text messages, nothing but silence. Was he ashamed of the way he'd broken down after admitting to the violence he'd witnessed as a child? She hoped that wasn't the case. If anything, it made him more of a man in her eyes.

Her cell phone rang. *Joe.* He wasn't avoiding her after all.

She hit the Answer button. "Hi, Joe."

"Kate," he said without preamble, "I saw Dr. Mike again after our last appointment . . ." His voice trailed away.

She was stunned. "And?"

"And we had a long talk about why I get angry and what I can do about it. Well . . . I . . ." He cleared his throat. "I wanted you to know that I'm not going to press you about moving home again. Dr. Mike helped me see that I need to work some things out before I can ask that of you. I think it's good if you stay with Rose for now. Ah, I do have one question."

She heard him draw a deep breath.

"After all that's happened, do you still love me?" he asked quietly.

Kate hesitated. Did she? She knew the man underneath all the anger was worth saving, and that was the man she loved. But Joe needed to find that part of himself on his own. She couldn't do it for him.

"Yes, I do," she finally said, "but I don't know if I can trust you again."

"That's okay." His voice sounded relieved. "I understand. I'm not the man you need right now, but I'm going to work very hard to become him. Dr. Mike's given me a prescription for antidepressants and I'm taking them. Ma and I also need to fix some things about our relationship."

He'd shocked her again. "You're going to persuade Trudy to go to counseling with you?"

A warm laugh sounded in her ear. "Come on, we're talking about my mother. She's not going to change, but I can."

"If it's important to you, I know you can do it."

"It is. Dr. Mike helped me see that growing up, it was always me and Ma against a common enemy."

"Your father."

"Yeah, and I've always felt guilty that I couldn't protect her, but I was a kid. It wasn't my job to keep her safe."

"Maybe your mother felt she had to stay with him. Maybe she thought she had no other choice."

"You might be right but, damn it, Kate," he said, his frustration apparent, "I grew up feeling like I owed her. That somehow I had to make it up to her for all the beatings he gave her."

"What are you going to do?"

"Get her into her own place."

"Do you think she'll agree?"

"It might take some talking, but I think she'll come around. We'd both be happier. And with her out of here, I'll have a better shot at working on *my* problems."

"Your plan sounds good, Joe."

"You think so?" His voice sounded excited, like a little kid's. "If I carry through with all of this, do you think our marriage has a chance?"

"I hope so. It's what I want, too, Joe."

"God, Kate," he exclaimed, "there's so many things that I want to say to you, things that I should've said weeks ago. Is there any chance you'd agree to see me this afternoon? I swear, it's just to talk."

"Where? It's not a good idea to come here."

"Right," he replied, then chuckled. "Rose standing over me with a shotgun makes me nervous. Could you come to the farm?"

"I wouldn't want to run into your mother."

"You wouldn't have to. You could pull in the back drive and meet me in my office." He paused. "Tell you what—if it doesn't rain, we could have a picnic in the apple orchard."

Kate thought for a moment. She didn't know if she felt comfortable being alone with him, or that Trudy wouldn't spot them and confront her.

Joe caught her hesitancy and broke in before she could answer. "I don't blame you for saying no." He sounded disheartened. "I haven't given you any reason to trust me. Maybe we can do it some other time."

"A picnic sounds fine. When do you want me to meet you?"

"You'll come?"

"Yes, I'll come."

"I've got to take care of some business first so would one o'clock work?"

"I'll be there."

"Thanks, Kate . . . I love you and I'm going to prove it. See you then," he said, ending the conversation.

Kate stared at the now-silent cell phone in her hand. "I hope this isn't a mistake," she muttered to herself.

"What's a mistake?" Rose asked, suddenly standing next to her.

"I didn't see you. Did you hear my side of the conversation?"

"No. I noticed you were on the phone and didn't step out until I saw you were finished." She pointed to the phone. "Was it something important?"

Kate placed the phone on the porch railing and ran her fingers through her hair. "It was Joe. I'm meeting him at the farm this afternoon."

Rose touched her arm, alarm written on her face. "Do you think that's wise?"

"I don't know." Kate tilted her head back and sighed. "He had an appointment with Dr. Mike—"

"He went without any prodding?"

"Yeah," Kate replied, facing Rose. "He's also started on antidepressants."

"That's a good sign."

"I thought so, too, and here's the real zinger—he intends to move Trudy *out*."

"Humph, that'll be the day," Rose snorted.

Kate shook her head. "I don't know. He sounded pretty determined. He sounded like the man I fell in love with."

"Do you think he's trying to manipulate you into coming back to him?"

"Maybe I'm being stupid, but I don't think that's the case. In fact, he's promised not to force the issue and even said it's good that I'm staying here."

"And you believe him?"

"Yeah . . . yeah, I do."

"For your sake, I hope it works." She looked thoughtful. "I guess for his sake, too. When he was a boy, he always struck me as different from the rest of them. He always seemed kinder, more sensitive than his grandfather or his father."

"So you think this is a good idea?"

"I guess you'll find out." Rose brushed a strand of hair away from Kate's face. "Just be careful. I don't want to see you hurt."

Kate decided to leave for Joe's early so she could stop by the office and finish the billing. She parked in the rear lot and slipped in the back door. Able to work uninterrupted, it didn't take her long to complete the last of the bills. In a way, she wished it had taken more time. As the minutes ticked by, her nerves accelerated. So much had happened and so much had changed since she'd first come to Braxton County. She sighed. One thing hadn't changed: she still loved her husband.

Kate shut off her computer and straightened the papers on her desk. It was only a quarter after twelve. Catching up on the billing didn't take as long as she'd expected. If she left now, she'd be too early and there'd be a greater chance of running into Trudy.

For the next thirty minutes, she futzed around the office. She watered the plants, dumped the wastebaskets, and dusted off her shelves. Finally, she realized that she'd wasted enough time and headed out the door. Looking up, she noticed the sky had darkened. The storm that had threatened all morning was moving in. No picnic in the apple orchard today. She hoped Joe had a Plan B.

A few minutes later, Kate pulled in the back driveway by Joe's office and saw his pickup. After parking behind it, she got out and glanced up as thunder sounded in the distance. Not wanting to get caught in a sudden downpour, she hurried into the building.

"Hey, Joe," she called out as she came through the door. "I don't think we're going on a—"

The room was empty and the lights were on. She crossed over to his desk. His computer was on, too. Strange. Joe usually didn't go off and leave it running. She picked through the papers on his desk, checking for a note indicating where he'd gone. Nothing, then a paper with an envelope attached to it caught her eye. Kate picked it up and started reading.

It was a lawsuit naming the plaintiff as Joseph J. Krause and the defendant as Edward A. Rodman. Rodman? The name sounded familiar, then Kate remembered. He was the farmer whose fence line encroached on Krause land. A notation on the document stated when the papers had been filed at the clerk of court's office. Joe was carrying out his threat and suing him. She wondered if the business Joe had mentioned this morning had anything to do with this lawsuit. She looked at the envelope. It was addressed to Ed.

A flash of fear overcome her. Had Ed showed up with his letter and confronted Joe? After the last meeting Joe had with Ed Rodman, he'd struck her. Her attention darted to the door. She should leave.

She had taken a step toward the door when a rustling sound came from over by the filing cabinet. Rats? Kate moved another step away from the desk. Then she heard a pitiful mewling. Rats didn't sound like that. Cautiously, she rounded the desk.

An animal carrier sat next to the cabinet, and Kate watched as a tiny yellow paw with soft pink pads came out from between the bars. She went to the carrier and crouched down. Two amber eyes peered back at her. The carrier held a kitten with a big red bow attached to its collar.

As Kate watched, the kitten began twisting its head back and forth while tiny white teeth tried to gain purchase on the red bow. It was so intent on getting at the bow that it lost its balance and tumbled over. Not giving up, the kitten continued its wrestling match, rolling from side to side.

Kate laughed. "Poor thing. You really don't like that bow."

After unlatching the door, she scooped up the kitten, and holding it close, removed the bow. Then she saw the note attached to the ribbon.

"Hi, Kate. My name is Topaz."

Joe had got her a cat. She clutched the kitten gently to her chest and rubbed her chin on its head. The kitten began to purr and snuggled closer to Kate's body.

Touched and amazed by his thoughtfulness, Kate prayed Rose liked cats. She wanted to thank him for his gift. *Where is Joe?*

She grabbed her cell phone and quickly dialed his number. "Country Boy," Joe's ring tone, sounded from the top of the desk. *He went off without it. Another oddity.* He usually had it clipped to his belt. He had to be returning soon.

For the next twenty minutes, she amused herself by playing with her new pet, then she began to worry. Should she go or should she stay?

A boom of thunder made her decision for her. The storm was getting closer and she needed to leave before it hit. Kate placed the kitten in the carrier, securely fastening the door. With the carrier in hand, she swiftly crossed the room but paused at the window. Too late. The rain came pouring down, pinging against the metal roof and sheeting across the windows. Wind rattled against the door while lightning flashed.

Kate watched the branches of the apples trees whip back and forth until a bright flash made her draw back, away from the window. She rubbed her eyes. Right before the burst of light, she thought she had seen a shape standing under one of the old trees. Drawing closer to the window, she peered out. Whatever had been there was gone now.

The lights flickered twice, then went out. Kate stood in the darkened building, clutching the cat carrier while a shiver prickled the hair on the back of her neck. This was a bad idea.

Her cell phone rang and showed Rose's name on the display.

"Hello," she answered quickly.

"Kate," Rose exclaimed, "where are you?"

Kate could barely hear her above the raging storm. "I'm still at the farm," she said loudly.

There was no response.

"Rose? Rose? Are you there?" The phone crackled in her ear.

" . . . hospital . . . Joe . . ."

Kate felt a rush of panic. "What? You're breaking up."

"I said Joe's in the hospital in Flint Rapids."

Kate ended the call and rushed into the storm.

As Kate drove into the parking lot of the hospital, she spotted Trudy's car. She pulled up next to it, parked, then ran through the rain to the entrance for the emergency room. Once inside, she tore up to the counter, her loafers squishing across the floor. Wiping the rainwater out of her eyes, she searched for someone to help.

"Excuse me," she said, taking the arm of the first nurse she found. "I'm Kate Krause. Is my husband, Joe, here?"

"This way," she replied, motioning for Kate to follow.

The nurse led Kate down the long hallway, then stopped in front of a door marked Family Waiting Room.

"In here," she said gently as she opened the door.

As Kate stepped inside, the faces turned toward her. Trudy sat on a couch with a handkerchief held tightly to her mouth while a man dressed in a sheriff's uniform knelt before her. Another man, also in a uniform, stood next to them. The man standing stepped forward.

"You must be Kate?"

She nodded, her eyes traveling from one face to the next.

"Why don't you take a seat, Kate? I'm Sheriff Tom Shaw and this is Detective Mark Shepherd."

"Joe?"

"I'm sorry, Kate. Joe passed away."

At the sheriff's words, Trudy bent at the waist and sobbed into the handkerchief. A sense of unreality settled over Kate and she sank into the nearest chair. The sheriff sat in the chair next to hers.

"Kate, do you understand what I said?"

"Yes," she answered in a monotone. "My husband's dead."

The sheriff and the detective exchanged a look.

"We've been trying to reach you. Can you tell us where you've been?"

"The farm."

"We understand that you and Joe are separated?"

Kate nodded.

"Why did you go to the farm?"

"Joe wanted to talk."

"Was he there when you arrived?"

Kate shook her head. "I—I didn't see him." She looked down at her hands clasped in her lap. "I saw the kitten." Lifting her face, she stared at the sheriff with stricken eyes. "*The kitten!*" she cried and shot to her feet.

Spots danced in the corners of her vision and her eyes rolled back. Her knees gave way as the blackness folded in on her.

Chapter 24

Summer 1890, the Krause homestead

A low early-morning mist drifted over the fields while the rising sun colored the sky with threads of pink and gold. The damp clung to the hem of Hannah's black cotton dress. Unconsciously, she smoothed the gathers at her waist as she watched the sun rise. Thank God Ida had thought to bring her two day dresses for her mourning. Without them, she would have been forced to wear the silk dress that she had worn two days ago at Jacob's funeral. Life on a farm doesn't stop because the master is dead. The silk dress wouldn't have withstood Hannah's chores.

At least she wasn't expected to wear the heavy crepe veil. A small smile played across her face as the ridiculous image of gathering eggs while encased in the veil came to mind. The frightening sight would have been enough to make the chickens quit laying. She let out a long, steady breath. The stench of the dyed veil had clogged her nose and throat during the funeral. She'd gladly stay out of the public eye for the next year if it meant never wearing it again.

A hand on her shoulder startled her out of her thoughts. Glimpsing Ida out of the corner of her eye, she reached up and clasped her sister's hand. In their teens, they'd been the lovely Dunlap sisters, but Hannah knew the years hadn't been as kind to her as they had Ida. Only eighteen months separated them, but she now looked at least five years older than her elder sister.

"Are you upset about the article in *The Braxton County Journal?*" Ida asked with a slight squeeze.

Hannah stepped away with a slight shrug. Louis had brought home a copy yesterday, and though Ida had insisted she not read it, she had. Fannie had been right about Harry Rosenthal. The article was peppered with his quotes. He'd started out by stating what a heavy duty it had been for him to sit at the inquest investigating the death of such a dear friend, then continued to almost deify Jacob. He'd ended by promising that the community would not rest until this heinous crime was solved.

"Harry sounded like he would be the one to solve Jacob's murder."

Ida gave an unladylike snort. "I imagine Sheriff Winter would have something to say about that, and he wasn't quoted." She eyed Hannah. "How do you feel about the way the article portrayed you?"

"A lot of half-truths and misrepresentations." Hannah rubbed her temple. "Their veiled references to our 'problems' were correct, but I've never been involved in the Women's Christian

Temperance Union or the National Women's Suffrage Association. Jacob wouldn't allow it."

Ida's lips twisted in a frown. "They insinuated that you weren't a proper wife."

"The neighbors have been saying that for years," Hannah replied, her tone short.

Ida settled her hands on her hips. "Humph. They were one step away from declaring that Jacob's treatment of you was justified."

"I can't help what they write."

"Well, it's not fair," Ida shot back with a toss of her head.

Hannah twirled to face her sister. "What *is* fair?"

"Stop," Ida said, holding up her hand. "You may not have been involved with those organizations, but I know you agree with some of their principles."

"And you don't."

"A woman's sphere is in the home," Ida replied with a sniff.

Hannah stifled a groan. Ida might claim to believe that, but her life said differently. Thanks to a childless marriage, she'd always been involved in Louis's mercantile business. She had a voice that so many women didn't.

"At least no one repeated my remark to Joseph," she said in a grim voice.

"That was unwise."

Hannah looked to the horizon. "I know, but when he brought up separating me from Willie, my tongue ran away with me."

Ida came up to her and placed both hands on Hannah's shoulders, turning her around. She studied Hannah for a moment, then shook her head. "That's always been your problem, but you must . . . *must*," she emphasized, "quit. If they question you again, think before you speak."

Hannah lifted an eyebrow. "That's easier said than done."

"That may be, but think of Willie."

"I know." She rubbed her upper arms, suddenly chilled. "I won't allow Jacob to reach from beyond the grave and ruin Willie's life. Joseph can't be appointed Willie's guardian."

Ida put her arm around Hannah's shoulders. "I don't believe there is a will. I think Joseph was trying to trick you." She released Hannah and stepped away. "Louis thinks that you stand to inherit the biggest portion of this," she said with a sweep of her arm.

"Joseph wouldn't like that."

"No, he won't and we'll fight him in court if necessary," she answered with a smirk. "We'll let things settle a bit, then I'll have Louis send a telegram to Andrew Lubinus."

"Who?"

"Andrew Lubinus. He's a brilliant young attorney and has already handled several difficult cases. Louis knows his father," she said in a satisfied voice. "Andrew has never lost, and they're already predicting that he'll be an important man someday." She crossed her arms over her chest. "We'll see how someone as backward as Joseph likes coming up against Andrew."

"Don't underestimate Joseph," Hannah warned.

"Nonsense," Ida replied with a wave of her hand. "Andrew will make Joseph wish he'd never—" She stopped at the sight of a buggy coming up the road. "Who can that be?" she asked, shading her eyes.

Hannah gave a small gasp as she recognized Sheriff Winter driving the buggy.

Both women watched silently while the sheriff came to a stop in front of the house. He dismounted and approached them with a stone-faced expression.

Hannah's hand flew to her throat. "You have news about Jacob's murder?"

With weary eyes, he looked directly at Hannah and shifted uncomfortably. "Hannah Krause, I have a warrant arresting you for the murder of Jacob Krause."

Black spots danced in Hannah's vision and she heard a roaring in her ears. *No . . . no . . . this can't be.* She felt her knees weaken as Ida reached out to steady her. The sudden slam of the screen door made Hannah stiffen.

"Hello, Sheriff Winter," Willie called out brightly as he skipped down the porch steps. He ran to his mother, and looking up, his eyebrows drew together. "What's the matter?" he asked, his small hand stealing into Hannah's.

Hannah exhaled slowly and forced a smile. She knelt and brushed the hair from his forehead. Glancing at her sister who stood with her hand clamped tightly to her lips, Hannah gave a slight shake of her head. She returned her attention to Willie and broadened her smile.

"There's been a mistake and—"

"What kind of a mistake?" Willie asked, cocking his head.

"It's one that can't be straightened out here, so I need to go with Sheriff Winter."

"But you're comin' back, right?"

Hannah stood and tousled his hair. "Of course I am." She motioned to her sister. "I want you to go with your aunt Ida now," she said, bending to place a kiss on the top of his head.

Ida took Willie's hand, then leaned in and hugged Hannah.

"Take care of him," Hannah whispered in Ida's ear. "And have Louis send the telegram today."

Sheriff Winter slowed the buggy as they approached a white two-story house with a small stone building attached to its side. Hannah gulped as she noticed the barred windows of the smaller building.

After coming to a halt, the sheriff dismounted and hitched the buggy to the post. At the same time, the front door of the house opened and a slight woman, dressed in a simple day dress with her hair pulled into a neat bun atop her head, stepped out. The sheriff's wife, Nora, hesitated, then crossed the porch and came down the steps to the buggy.

Two small faces pressed against one of the front windows caught Hannah's attention—the oldest of the Winters' four young children. Pain stabbed at her as she remembered the questioning look on Willie's face as Ida led him away. She lowered her head and swallowed hard. She couldn't bear the sight of those children.

Sheriff Winter gently took her arm and guided her toward the stone building. With a shudder, Hannah stepped inside.

Four stone walls surrounded her. The center of the room was open but had two cells running down the north and south side of the building, each containing a small barred window. In the center sat a cast-iron potbellied stove and a small desk. To her right and next to the door, a set of keys hung from a nail. Sheriff Winter removed the keys and unlocked one of the cell doors. After stepping back, he motioned for Hannah to enter the cell.

Hannah faltered as unshed tears threatened to gag her. *How could this be happening?* With misery written on her face, she turned to the sheriff.

"Why? Why am I being charged?" she choked.

Ill at ease, he rocked back on his heels and refused to meet her stare. "The warrant was issued last night at the insistence of the county attorney." He looked up. "I'm sorry, Hannah—I'm only doing my job."

"I'm innocent," Hannah cried.

He turned his head. "That's something for the court to decide," he replied. "Please step inside."

Hannah felt as if every muscle had turned soft and she stumbled forward. Catching herself, she stiffened her spine. She survived years of her husband's abuse and—damn it—she'd survive this, too. With a deep breath, she entered the cell and didn't turn until the door clanged shut behind her.

He held out his arm to his wife. "Nora will be taking care of your needs," he said abruptly, then strode from the room, leaving his wife and Hannah staring at each other through the bars of the cell.

Nora cleared her throat. "The cot's not much, but the sheets and blanket are clean," she said, not masking the pity in her voice.

Hannah gathered her shattered pride and began a slow walk around the cell.

Nora continued. "There's fresh water and a tin cup in the pail. Breakfast is at seven; dinner at noon; and supper at six." She pivoted to leave. "Oh," she said over her shoulder in a low voice, "the chamber pot is under the cot."

"Will I be able to see my family?" Hannah asked softly.

"Probably not today."

Hannah nodded. "Thank you."

Nora inclined her head in response then quickly crossed to the door leading out of the jail. After opening it, she stepped over the threshold and shut the door firmly behind her.

At the sound of the lock clicking into place, Hannah's control fell away in tattered pieces. She sank to the cot and buried her face in the pillow while sobs wracked her shoulders. She had to find a way to save her son.

Chapter 25

Fall 1890, the Braxton County Jail

Hannah's days stretched into an endless, boring routine. Due to the "heinous" nature of the crime, the judge had refused to grant bail. Now finally, after weeks of waiting, the trial was set to begin in a couple of days.

Hannah agreed with Ida's assessment of Andrew Lubinus. Tall, dark haired, and with dancing brown eyes, charm graced his every move. And his voice—smooth, yet at the same time commanding. Hannah had no trouble imagining him standing before a jury and delivering an impassioned summation. She was also aware of his ambition. It sparked beneath the surface of his captivating demeanor and flared whenever Louis questioned him on points of her defense.

The only bright spot of her days had been her growing relationship with Sheriff Winter's young daughter, Essie, who was close to Willie's age. The child helped her mother by doing chores around the jail. Hannah discovered that Essie possessed a sharp, curious mind and loved to read, so together, they'd spent afternoons reading *Aesop's Fables*, *The Prince and the Pauper*, and Hannah's best-loved book, *Pride and Prejudice*. Essie's excitement over the unfolding tale of the Bennet sisters made Hannah feel as if she, too, were experiencing the book for the first time. Still, Essie's companionship did little to heal the yawning hole in her heart caused by her separation from Willie.

Each time Ida had been allowed to visit, the conversation had centered on him. She had been relieved to learn that Joseph was steering clear of both the house and Willie. According to Ida, the boy was confused by the rumors he'd overheard about his mother, but well.

Hannah absentmindedly smoothed the skirt of her black dress. Andrew had instructed her to wear the black silk during the trial, but no widow's veil. She'd still wear the hat, but thankfully the veil would not be covering her face. Andrew had stressed the importance of the jury looking at her as a person, not a lump of black sitting at the table for the defense. Ida was bringing the dress today, and it would be their last meeting before the trial started. Today was her only chance to persuade Ida and Louis to agree to her demands.

After crossing to the cot, Hannah picked up the document Andrew had prepared at her request. She clutched it tightly. Could she go through with it?

The sound of voices drifting through the open window suddenly caught her attention. The sheriff and Nora. She moved closer to the window.

"This is a travesty, Gus," Nora declared.

"Nora, you're letting yourself be swayed by Hannah's kindness to Essie."

"No, I'm not. Do you think if I really felt she was guilty I would have allowed Essie to spend time with her?"

"No."

"There is no harm in that woman," she insisted.

"Sweetheart . . . that's for the courts to decide," he replied softly.

"And will those courts be fair? Everyone overlooked Jacob's 'spells' for years, and the poor woman was crucified in the papers after her arrest," she cried vehemently. "What if it happens again? What if public sentiment is against her again? Do you really think she'll receive justice?"

"I don't know," he answered softly.

Hannah's eyes widened in surprise at Nora's fervent support and the sheriff's reaction. An argument like this with Jacob would never have included gentle words. A slap across the face was more likely.

"Well, you're the sheriff. Do *something* about it," she exclaimed.

"My hands are tied. Charles Walker is convinced she's guilty."

"And will do whatever it takes to prove it," Nora shot back.

"Now, Nora—"

"What about Peter Ziegler?" she asked, cutting him off. "He hated Jacob. How do you know he didn't slip in and kill Jacob while Hannah was with Willie?"

"His sister, Minnie, swears he was at her place all day, putting up hay, then he spent the night."

"She could be lying," Nora insisted. "He could've slipped out during the night."

"Maybe, but there's no way to prove it."

"What about the knife? Hannah swore she'd never seen it before."

"I don't know, Nora . . ." His voice trailed away. "We checked and it's a Sheffield knife. Hannah doesn't have any knives like that. That pattern is still manufactured, but not that style of knife. And it's old and used—there are scratches along the blade." He hesitated. "Abe said that the knife reminded him of one his father had. His old man had taken it off a dead Confederate soldier down in Atlanta."

"Honestly, Gus! How would Hannah get her hands on a knife dating back to the Civil War?"

He sighed. "I don't know . . . maybe it was Jacob's. Hannah found it and used it."

"Ha," she snorted. "If that knife is a valuable war trophy . . . As much as Jacob liked to brag, don't you think he would've showed it off to visitors? He wasn't in the war, was he?"

"No. In fact his wife was a Southerner. The story goes, he met her while she was up North visiting a cousin."

"Gus, you have to fix this."

"How do you suggest I do that?"

"Go back out to the house—see if there's something you might have missed."

"It's been weeks, sweetheart. If we had overlooked something, it's long gone by now. Besides," he insisted, "I'm confident that we didn't make a slip investigating the scene."

"Gus—"

Silence grew and Hannah peeked over the edge of the window. Gus had his arms around Nora and appeared to be murmuring in her ear while he stroked her back.

Hannah stepped away at the sight of such tenderness between a husband and wife and felt a spark of jealousy. Why hadn't her father married her off to a man like the sheriff? One who would've cared and respected her. She looked at the gray walls surrounding her. Her life would've been so different.

She glanced down at the papers still gripped in her hand. If Jacob had never come into her life, she'd never have known the joy of raising her son.

Her mouth tensed with determination. Willie was all that mattered now.

It was late afternoon when Hannah gathered with Ida and Louis around the jail's small desk. Since her arrest, only her visits with Andrew had been private. Either Abe or the sheriff monitored the rest. The sheriff now stood leaning against the wall near the door.

Ida's hand stole across the desk and clasped Hannah's tightly. "This will soon be over," she said bravely. "Andrew is confident in winning an acquittal."

Hannah forced a smile. "I hope he's right." Her smile fell away as she withdrew the papers from the pocket of her dress. Unable to meet Ida's eyes, she smoothed the papers out on the desk. "There's something," she said hesitantly, "that I need to discuss with you."

Ida released Hannah's hand and peered at the document in alarm. "What's that?"

Taking a deep breath, Hannah then launched into her explanation. "Guardianship papers—"

Ida shot to her feet. "What? No—"

Hannah held up a hand, stopping her. "Wait . . . listen to me," she pleaded. "Andrew may be confident over the outcome of this trial, but I can't take any chances. No matter what happens, I have to make sure Willie is protected." She frowned. "I don't trust Joseph and I have to make sure Willie stays out of his control."

"I understand. I don't trust him either, but," Ida argued, "is this necessary?"

"Yes, it is," Hannah said as she pulled Ida back into her chair. "I know taking in someone else's child is a big responsibility—" Her voice caught. "But Willie's a good boy . . . and won't be any trouble, I swear."

Ida leaned over and put her arm around Hannah's shoulders. "Of course, Willie's a good boy and we love him, but I can't take him away from you."

Hannah gave a bitter laugh. "If I'm convicted, the court will separate us." She picked up the papers and handed them to Ida. "Joseph wants control of the farm, Ida, and if that means taking Willie to get it, he'll do it." She looked at Louis for support.

"She's right," he answered, stroking his chin. "As the boy's brother, he could petition for custody. He's closer kin than we are, so the court might grant it."

Ida withdrew her arm from Hannah's shoulders and sat back in her chair. "But—" she began.

"Please," Hannah cried. "I don't have a choice. I won't have the strength to face the trial unless I know that Willie's safe from Joseph."

Ida and Louis exchanged a long look, then finally nodded in agreement.

Hannah breathed a sigh of relief and turned to the sheriff. "Andrew said this agreement must be witnessed and notarized."

With a pained expression on his face, Sheriff Winter pushed off against the wall. "Ben Hutchinson is a notary. I'll send Essie to fetch him." He jerked his head toward the house. "Abe's here, so we both can serve as witnesses."

He opened the door and called to Essie. When she appeared, he gave her his instructions, then turned toward Hannah.

"Are you sure?" he questioned.

"Yes," she replied slowly, "but I'd appreciate if everyone kept silent about this. I don't want Joseph to know."

Twenty minutes later, Sheriff Winter, Abe, and Ben Hutchinson gathered with Hannah, Ida, and Louis around the small desk. In a moment it was finished. Hannah had given away her son.

Chapter 26

Fall 2012, Braxton County Hospital

The sound of voices pulled Kate out of a deep sleep. Her first emotion was one of relief. A nightmare—it was only a nightmare.

Bits and pieces of it glided through her head . . . a storm, a rain-slick highway, the thump of the windshield wipers as they fought against a torrential downpour. She remembered the urgency she felt. In the dream, she had to reach her destination, but now what that had been, eluded her.

Her mouth felt dry and her tongue thick. She wanted a glass of water, but didn't have the strength to open her eyes let alone get out of bed to fetch one.

Words spoken as if in a tunnel began to penetrate her brain.

". . . and her reaction was off," one voice said.

"The doctor blamed it on shock," another voice replied.

"The sooner we question her, the better."

"I know, but you can't right now. The doctors want her to wake up from the sedative on her own." Kate heard the speaker exhale slowly.

"Where's the mother?"

"At the farm. She refused to have anyone drive her home, but a friend was coming to stay with her."

"The team's there, too, right?"

"Yeah, but I don't expect they'll find much after that heavy rain. Damn it," the voice exclaimed. "We need to talk to her."

"As soon as she wakes up, we will."

A memory niggled at the corners of Kate's brain, trying to eat its way into her consciousness. The voice that had just spoken sounded familiar, but she couldn't place where she'd heard it.

"When will we get the autopsy results back?" the first voice continued.

"Soon, but based on the initial examination, the emergency room doc is convinced his death was caused by internal bleeding."

His poor family, Kate thought dimly. Wait, what were two men doing having a conversation outside her bedroom at Rose's? Was the TV on in Rose's room? She brushed her face with her hand and felt something cool touch her skin. She struggled to open her eyes, then jerked to a sitting position.

A clear bag of liquid was strung from an IV pole to the bed and a thin plastic tube ran from the bag into her right arm. Kate stared in terror at the liquid drip . . . dripping into the tube.

Reality crashed in, chasing away the fogginess from her mind. It wasn't a nightmare.

"No . . . no," she gasped. Grief clawed its way into her mind and heart.

"God, no," she cried.

"Nurse," one of the voices called out, "I think she's awake."

The door swung open and a nurse, along with two men, entered the room. The men were Sheriff Tom Shaw and the other man who'd been with him last night. Kate's head began to pound. What was the other man's name?

Both men hung back as the nurse checked Kate's vitals. When she had finished, she patted Kate's arm. "Everything looks fine. We'll be back later to take out the IV, then you should be able to go home."

After the nurse left, the men approached her bed.

"Joe's dead, isn't he?" she asked bleakly as the tears ran down her face.

The sheriff nodded. "Do you remember Detective Shepherd?" he asked, handing Kate a tissue from a box on the nightstand.

"Yes," she answered in a thick voice.

Sheriff Shaw noticed a glass of water and handed it to her.

Kate took a sip. "How long have I been here?"

"Since last night. Dr. Adams said that you were in shock, and he wanted to keep you overnight for observation. Mrs. Clement and Will Krause were here for part of the night, but Will took Mrs. Clement home so she could rest. They'll be back later when you're released." He exchanged a look with Detective Shepherd, then with a nod, moved to the window.

Detective Shepherd pulled a chair over to the bed. "I need you to answer a few questions. Are you feeling up to it?"

She wiped her eyes, took a deep breath, then nodded.

"When was the last time you spoke with Joe?" Detective Shepherd asked.

"Yesterday morning," she replied, clearing her throat.

"Did you call him?"

"No, he called me."

"Why?"

Kate took another drink of water, stalling in order to gather her thoughts. Somehow telling these strangers about their marital problems seemed disloyal to Joe. He couldn't tell his side of the story.

"Kate," Detective Shepherd said quietly, "we know you were separated."

She had a dim memory of someone mentioning it last night, but did they know the reason why she had left Joe? Joe's reputation was all he'd left behind, and she wanted to protect it.

"We were separated, but were working on mending our marriage. Joe wanted to talk to me in person."

"You agreed?"

"Yes. I debated—" *No, that will open a line of questions that I don't want to answer. Better keep my responses short.* "Yes."

Detective Shepherd flipped opened a notebook and quickly scanned it. "You're staying with Rose Clement?"

"Yes."

"What time did you leave Rose's?"

Kate rubbed her forehead. "About eleven thirty."

"What time did you arrive at the farm?"

"I didn't go straight to the farm. I'm a receptionist for Doc Adams, and I stopped by the office to finish some last-minute billings."

Detective Shepherd scribbled on his notepad. "Is it normal for you to go in on a Saturday?"

"No, but I hadn't finished the statements and wanted to get them done."

"Did you see anyone?"

"No, the office was closed." Kate's eyes narrowed. "Why?"

"No reason. We're just trying to establish exactly what happened yesterday. How long were you at Doc's office?"

"I left at twelve forty-six."

Detective Shepherd cocked his head. "Not twelve forty-five or twelve fifty?"

"No, I glanced at the clock on my way out the door."

He made another note on his pad. "What did you do next?"

"I drove out to the farm."

"Did you see anyone on your way out there?"

"What do you mean?"

"Did you notice any other vehicles on the road on your way to the farm?"

"No."

"What time did you arrive?"

"A little after one."

"Were any other vehicles parked in the driveway?"

"I parked out by Joe's office, so I don't know."

"Why did you park there instead of in the main driveway, then walk over from the house?"

"I didn't—" She stopped herself again. *Another thing that they don't need to know—my conflict with Trudy.* "I—ah—well—there was a storm moving in," she said quickly as she picked at the wadded-up tissue in her palm, "and I didn't want to get caught in the rain."

"I see," Detective Shepherd said in a neutral voice as he wrote again on his pad. "What happened next?"

"I went inside Joe's office."

"Did you notice anything unusual?"

She thought about the notice of the lawsuit lying on Joe's desk. "Not really," she hedged. "The lights were on and so was his computer. His cell phone was on his desk. I assumed he'd be coming right back."

"But you didn't go looking for him?"

"No. No, I didn't."

"How long did you wait?"

Kate rubbed her temples, trying to ease the throbbing of her skull. "I don't know . . . I found the kitten—" She drew a sharp breath. "*The kitten!* . . . It's out—"

Detective Shepherd held up a hand. "You mentioned the cat last night," he said brusquely. "Mrs. Clement took it home with her when she left."

Kate teared up again. "Joe was giving me the kitten as a present . . . he killed the other one . . ." she began to babble, wiping her eyes with the shredded tissue.

"The cat's okay," Detective Shepherd said, his tone short. "Back to your actions yesterday—"

"I already told you. I waited for Joe and played with the cat," she cut in, tired of answering all the questions. Why couldn't they leave her alone and let her grieve?

She exhaled slowly, then continued. "After Rose called and said Joe was in the hospital, I drove here. You know the rest."

"Did your husband have any enemies?"

Kate frowned. "What do you mean?"

"Was there anyone he felt had a reason to harm him?"

She shook her head in confusion.

Detective Shepherd shut his notebook and stood. "Mrs. Krause," he said, looking down at her. "You haven't asked how your husband died."

He was right. She hadn't. It was all such a shock, she couldn't think straight. God, she wished they'd go away.

"I assumed it was a farm accident," she said halfheartedly.

"Your husband died as a result of a knife wound in his back. Someone stabbed him."

When Rose arrived to drive Kate and her Jeep back to the farm that afternoon, she appeared to have aged over the past twenty-four hours. Her skin had a gray pallor to it and her eyes had lost some of their sparkle.

"Are you okay?" Kate asked once Rose had settled her into the car and they were on their way back to her farm.

"Joe's death has shocked everyone, but don't worry about us. You're the one who's lost her husband. What did the sheriff say?"

"I didn't talk much to Tom. A Detective Shepherd asked most of the questions."

"Did they say what happened?"

Kate drew a shaky hand across her forehead. "Trudy wasn't very coherent, but from what they can piece together, Joe came stumbling into the house, wounded, and Trudy rushed him to the hospital." Her breath hitched. "He died before they got there."

"They don't know where it happened?"

"No, he was somewhere on the farm."

"And he didn't say anything to Trudy about who'd hurt him?"

"If he did, Detective Shepherd didn't share it with me."

"Kate, I'm so sorry. What an *awful* thing," Rose exclaimed.

"I should go out to the farm and check on Trudy. Joe would want that," Kate said, staring out the window.

"Don't think about Trudy now. Right now you're worn out.

You can visit her tomorrow," Rose replied in a tone that brooked no opposition. "And she's not alone. Agnes Forsyth is staying with her."

Kate faced Rose. "What do I do now?" she asked, her voice despondent.

"I don't have an answer for you," Rose replied, her brow crinkling. "It's never easy losing a loved one, but to lose Joe like this . . ." Her voice trailed away and she shook her head. "I can't imagine what you're feeling."

Kate traced a line on her jeans. "That's just it—I don't feel anything right now. I'm numb. I suppose I'll need to think about the funeral."

"Not today, you don't," Rose said sternly. "Today you rest. You can start making arrangements once we know when the body will be released."

He'd gone from being Joe to being "the body." Gut-wrenching sorrow pushed the numbness aside, and Kate's eyes welled with tears. How did she have enough moisture still left in her body to cry?

Rose lightly touched her leg. "Life hasn't been very kind to you since you came to Braxton County, has it?"

She dashed away the tears. "I feel like I'm at the bottom of a big black hole and it keeps getting deeper," she said in a dismal voice. "Who hated Joe enough to kill him?"

Rose let out a long breath. "That's for the sheriff to find out." Her mouth twisted in a frown. "But it's a question a lot of people are asking. The snoops came out in droves this morning. I got so many calls this morning that I finally shut my phone off."

"I'm sorry, Rose."

"You don't have to apologize," she huffed. "They ought to know enough to mind their own business at a time like this."

"But—" Her cell phone rang, cutting her off. She answered without glancing at the screen. "Hello."

"Didn't I tell you that no good would come of this?" her grandmother's voice sounded in Kate's ear. "Now your husband's been murdered. Murdered," she exclaimed, continuing her tirade. "We've *never* had anything like this happen in our family. It's all over the news. Why, I can hardly step outside my own door without someone asking me about it, and what do I tell them? You never even thought to call me."

Cold replaced the sorrow in Kate's heart. Such cold, she began to shiver.

"As soon as this is all over," she huffed, "you're moving home. You can live with me."

Kate thought of her sessions with Dr. Mike and the shivering suddenly stopped. She took a deep breath.

"Thanks for asking about me, Gran," she said, her voice hard, "your concern is positively underwhelming."

"There's no need to get spiteful with me, young lady. I—"

Kate broke in. "Believe it or not, this is one time it isn't about you, and if you can't see that, I don't want to continue this conversation." She went to push End, but her grandmother's voice stopped her.

"Wait. I'm sorry." Her tone had changed from forceful to whimpering in a flash. "It's such a shock, and for a person my age . . . of course I was going to ask about you. I've been so worried."

Yeah right, Kate thought, but kept silent

"You poor thing," her grandmother continued. "You need your grandmother."

"No—w-wait," Kate stammered.

"I've already made the arrangements. You'll need to reimburse her for the gas, but Mrs. Cutter is driving me out there tomorrow."

"You *can't*," Kate cried into the phone, but her grandmother had ended the call.

Chapter 27

Fall 2012, the Clement family farm

The next morning, Kate braced her hands against the bathroom counter and stared at her reflection. Her eyes were swollen and her hair hung in clumps. She should take a shower, but she didn't have the energy. She had to see Trudy today and also steel her nerves in preparation for her grandmother's visit. Hanging her head, she took a deep breath. The idea of the two of them in the same room boggled her mind.

An hour later she was dressed and, with Rose along, pulling into the driveway at the farm. Agnes Forsyth greeted them at the door with a sour expression.

"How's Trudy?" Kate asked as Agnes stood aside and let them enter.

"Not well," she replied with a haughty look toward Rose. "I wanted to take her in to see Doc Adams, but she refused."

"Is she awake?"

"Yes, can't you hear the TV in her room?" Agnes answered with a sniff as she turned and led them back to the kitchen. "I don't know what you're going to do. She can't be left alone and I need to get home. Albert missed his supper last night because I wasn't there."

Kate heard Rose mutter something from behind her that sounded like, "Maybe Albert should learn how to use a stove." She shot Rose a look over her shoulder and shook her head.

Once in the kitchen, Rose smiled sweetly at Agnes. "I'll stay here and help Agnes."

Rolling her eyes, Kate went out the back door and found Trudy sitting in an old rocking chair. She was dressed much the same way she'd been the first day Kate had met her—in an old housedress and stockings rolled to her knees—but her skin looked blanched and her hair straggled around her face. Slowly, she turned her head; eyes that were once sharp and assessing were now dull and empty.

"Trudy?" Kate said as she knelt in front of her.

"My son's dead," she said in a flat voice.

"I know."

"Parents aren't supposed to bury their children," she continued, her gaze traveling over Kate's head and toward the apple orchard. "The farm was the only thing that mattered until he met you." Her attention returned to Kate and anger flashed in her eyes. "It's your fault. You brought the curse down on us."

"Trudy, you're not well. I think we should let Doc Adams take a look at you."

Her lips twisted in a bitter line. "No. You want to get rid of me." She wagged a bony finger in Kate's face. "You were going to make Joe send me away."

"Trudy—"

"Only Joe was the one who went away," she cried and clutched at the front of her dress. "I've lost my son and now I'm going to lose my home."

Kate sighed and bowed her head. She'd never seen a person so distraught. Raising her head, she looked at Trudy, and the woman seemed to shrink before her eyes.

"I'm tired now. I want to go lie down," she said, hoisting her body out of the rocking chair. "Will you take me back to my room?"

Kate gently took Trudy's arm and began to guide her across the porch. Trudy abruptly slid to a stop.

"They're all gone now," she whispered, "all of Joseph's sons. But the land's still here and so is she. Be careful, girl, that you're not the next."

She tugged away and shuffled into the house, leaving Kate bewildered. By the time Kate followed, Trudy had disappeared into her bedroom.

Rose handed her a cup of coffee. "How did it go?"

"Badly," Kate answered with a shake of her head. "She's really confused. I wonder if she hasn't had a minor stroke." Kate looked over at Agnes. "What do you think? How did she act last night?"

"She spent most of the evening in her bedroom while I was on the phone with Albert."

"Why? Was Albert having problems finding the bathroom?" Rose asked in a snarky voice.

"Rose—please," Kate said. "I'm going to call Doc."

A few minutes later, Kate returned. "Doc wants us to take her in to the emergency room. He said someone should have called him last night."

Rose looked pointedly at Agnes, who in return glared at Rose.

Agnes then switched her attention to Kate. "I'll have you know I barely slept last night," she said with a lift of her chin. "In case you've forgotten, there's been a murder here. How did I know they wouldn't come back and kill us in our beds?"

"No, I haven't forgotten," Kate replied coldly, "but I hardly think you were in any danger."

"You don't know. There could be a crazed homeless person out there right now, waiting to strike again," she said, waving an arm toward the window.

Rose rolled her eyes. "I haven't seen a homeless person in Dutton since Vivian Patton threw Wally out after one too many trips to the Silver Goose. They found him sleeping it off on the park bench."

Agnes ignored Rose. "What about drug dealers? We don't know. Maybe Joe wound up mixed up with them. Everyone knows he had money—"

"Agnes Forsyth," Rose said, cutting her off, "I always knew you were an idiot, but—"

Agnes shoved her hands on her hips. "It wouldn't be the first time someone saw it as an easy way out of their problems."

"Of all the callous things to say," Rose exclaimed. "Kate—"

Kate held up a hand, stopping her. "I'll take it from here," she said, turning on Agnes. "You're supposed to be Trudy's friend and you're trashing her son's memory by spreading rumors about him?"

"I'm not spreading rumors. They're going around like wildfire," Agnes huffed.

Kate gave her a steely glare. "And instead of putting the fire out, I bet you're fanning the flames." Kate walked over and picked up a purse and a bag sitting by the back door. She held them out to Agnes. "You know, I'll take over from here. Thanks for your help."

Kate and Rose remained silent as Agnes stomped out of the room and didn't speak until they heard her car go down the drive.

Rose arched an eyebrow. "Well, at least you didn't say, 'Don't let the door hit you in the ass on your way out.'"

Kate leaned against the counter and exhaled slowly. "I didn't handle that well."

"You sure did."

"No, it's going to be all over town that I kicked her out."

Rose gave her a sneaky grin. "I've lived around here longer than Agnes, and I know how to play the gossip game. A few well-chosen words in the right ears and everyone's going to be talking about her. Most people don't take kindly to a person insulting a recently bereaved family. Not speaking ill of the dead still means something in these parts."

They managed to convince Trudy to go the emergency room, where Doc Adams met up with them. The fact that Trudy hadn't shot daggers at Rose on the way to the hospital only proved to Kate how confused she was.

As Kate sat waiting, her foot tapped a nervous rhythm on the polished floor. Rose touched her knee, quieting her.

"It's okay, Kate."

"I don't like being here."

"Too soon after Joe?"

She nodded and covered her face with her hands. "How am I going to get through this, Rose?"

"You just do," she said putting an arm around Kate's shoulders. "I'm not saying it's easy, and you're going to feel like you've shoveled a lot of crap before it's done. But you'll get through."

Kate dropped her hands. "I'm not good at dealing with difficult situations."

"Who said?"

"My grandmother," Kate answered wryly. "She said I was helpless and hopeless."

"Why?"

Kate shrugged. "I suppose it had something to do with the way I acted when my mother died." She looked at a spot near the ceiling. "After Mom died, we were cleaning out the house we'd lived in and Gran was tossing everything she didn't think she could sell at a garage sale, including the bear I'd had since I was a toddler." Her gaze traveled back to Rose. "I pitched such a fit, she let me keep it. She said I cried more over that bear than I did my mother."

"I imagine the bear represented security," Rose responded quietly.

"Yeah, I guess. It was something I had left from my life with my mother." Kate frowned. "When Mom died, I went all numb inside . . . just like I am now."

"It's shock, my dear."

"I know, but back then Gran said my reaction was unnatural."

"I thought you were learning to ignore what your grandmother said."

"I'm trying, but it's hard to overcome years of conditioning. It wasn't just the way I acted when Mom died. No matter what I did for Gran, it was always wrong."

Rose gave an indignant snort. "In her opinion. I bet she never complained when you made sure the utility bills were paid, did she?"

Kate's lips twisted into a bitter smile. "No."

"I thought not. No offense intended, but the woman's a fool—telling a teenager who'd just lost her mother that she's unnatural." Rose huffed. "Since I've known you, I've seen you make some hard decisions. Decisions that took courage."

"I'm not courageous."

"Yes, you are. You could have shut up. Let Trudy and Joe run your life, but you didn't."

Grief wrung her heart. "Maybe if I had, Joe wouldn't have died."

Rose grasped her arm and gave it a shake. "You wipe that thought out of your mind right now," she scolded. "We don't know what happened. That's for the sheriff to figure out."

"Two murders have happened on this farm," Kate said in a low voice. "Do you think Trudy's right? That history does repeat itself?"

Rose looked at Kate, her expression deadly serious. "I hope not."

Trudy's diagnosis was a transient ischemic attack or mini stroke to the right hemisphere of her brain. Short-term memory loss, paranoia, and changes in Trudy's behavior could be expected, but would eventually dissipate. Doc had assured Rose and Kate that it wasn't as severe as a major stroke, but her attack might indicate one in her future. It was important that Trudy change her lifestyle—more exercise, less fat in her diet—and start taking a low dose of aspirin daily.

Once back at the farm, Trudy retired to her room while a steady stream of neighbors showed up bearing casseroles and Jell-O salads. Kate accepted their condolences and pretended to be brave. Many were sincere in their sympathy, but she caught the whispers and stares of others. Those so-called friends had come to ferret out the latest story and report it back to the gossip mill. Rose picked up on her growing tension and sent her outside.

Walking toward the apple orchard, Kate concentrated on relaxing the tight muscles in her shoulders and taking deep cleansing breaths. She stopped and leaned against one of the old trees as she replayed the afternoon of Joe's death in her mind.

She thought about the envelope addressed to Ed Rodman. Should she have told Detective Shepherd about it? Then she remembered looking out the window during the storm and the figure she'd seen standing beneath one of these trees. She hadn't mentioned that either.

Tilting her head up, she looked at the branches of the old tree. It had been a long time since these trees had borne fruit. They were barren—just like her life. No husband, no children, no parents. Loneliness pressed down on her. She'd spend the rest of her life mourning what might have been. The leaves above her gently rustled, and she felt a touch on her shoulder. Startled, she whirled away from the tree.

No one was there.

Goose pimples prickled her arms. Grasping her upper arms, she rubbed at her skin, trying to make them go away. She was as bad as Trudy.

"Hey, kiddo."

Kate faced the house in time to see Doris crossing toward her.

When she reached Kate, Doris drew her into a big hug. "I'm so sorry," she murmured in Kate's ear.

"Thanks," Kate replied, stepping out of Doris's embrace.

"Do you know what happened?"

"No—we don't even know when Joe's body will be released."

"They'll catch the person who did this," Doris said with a firm jerk of her head. "What can I do to help you?"

"Nothing . . . just be my friend. I have so many decisions to make that I don't know where to start. I know nothing of Joe's farming operation. I'm sure that there are bills to be paid, loans that might be coming due. The livestock has to be cared for. And the harvest?" Kate looked at Doris in panic. "What am I going to do about that? I don't even know how to drive a tractor, much less Joe's combine."

"First of all, don't worry about the livestock. Greg McCarthy down the road has volunteered to see to that. Second—I imagine Joe's attorney and his CPA will be contacting you about the business." Doris took a deep breath before she continued. "And last but not least, the harvest. Let Rose help you manage that. She's been handling her own farm for sixty years and I'm sure she'll find a way to get your crops in."

"It's all so overwhelming," Kate said with dismay.

"Quit worrying about everything all at once. Take one step at a time and you'll get through this."

Kate hesitated for a moment. "Do you know Ed Rodman?"

"Everyone knows Ed. Why?"

"Is he a violent person?"

Doris raised her brow. "He's a hothead, that's for sure." She studied Kate. "Do you think he's involved in Joe's death?"

"I witnessed a fight between him and Joe. It was heated, and for a minute, I thought it might come to blows."

"Was it about the fence line?"

"Yeah. Joe was suing him." Kate tugged on her lip. "I think Ed might have been at the farm on the day Joe was killed. I found a letter addressed to Ed laying on Joe's desk."

Doris grabbed Kate's arm. "You told the sheriff, right?"

"No."

Doris looked dumbstruck for a moment. "Why the hell not?"

"I don't *know*," she exclaimed. "I didn't want to make false accusations. And," Kate added, running a hand through her hair, "stupidity, I guess. My brain felt scrambled the whole time they were questioning me."

"Hey," Rose called out from the porch, "are you ready for round two? Your grandmother's in the parlor."

With a groan, Kate rolled her eyes and started toward the house. Doris followed behind.

They proceeded through the house into the parlor where a woman Kate didn't recognize sat stiffly on the couch—her grandmother, ensconced in one of the high-backed arm chairs. She reminded Kate of a queen waiting impatiently to receive her subjects. Upon spotting Kate, she shot to her feet and scurried toward her.

"My little girl," she cried out and threw her arms around her, sobbing, burying her face in Kate's shoulder.

Kate stood with her arms hanging stiffly at her sides and let her cry. When she'd determined that her grandmother had put on enough of a show, she drew back, disengaging her grandmother's arms.

Her grandmother backed away a few steps and, after withdrawing a handkerchief from her pocket, began to mop her eyes.

"Gran," Kate said brusquely, "it wasn't necessary for you to come all this way."

Her grandmother sniffed sharply. "Yes, it is—when my little girl is in trouble."

Part of Kate felt like applauding at her grandmother's performance. She'd been her grandmother's burden, *never* her little girl. The woman didn't have an empathetic bone in her body. Kate eyed the number of suitcases stacked at the end of the couch.

"I see you have your luggage. Why didn't you drop it off at the motel?"

Her grandmother's eyes opened wide in surprise. "Kate, darling, at a time like this you need your family." Her attention shifted as she scanned the parlor. "I'm staying here."

Chapter 28

Fall 1890, the Krause homestead

Soft light from the house's kerosene lamps cast shadows across the front porch. From where Joseph sat at the cabin's rough-hewn table, he saw occasional indistinct forms pass by the windows. He'd been exiled from his own home by the bitch's sister and her weak-kneed husband, and they'd turned him into nothing more than a hired man. Hell, even a hired man would be receiving better treatment than he was. Since they took over the house, he'd been forced to fix his own meals and do his own laundry. At least when Hannah was here, she waited on him.

Bitterness swamped him. Every day he sat in the courtroom, which seemed to be filled with women, and had to listen to Charles Walker yammer on about Hannah's life with his pa. At first, the press had been against her, going so far as to brand her as unnatural, to comment on her sinister appearance and label her a troublemaker.

But Charles then made a tactical error. He allowed a witness to insinuate that Hannah had been connected to the Women's Temperance Union and the National Women's Suffrage Association. Suddenly the reports of the trial took on a subtle shift. Hannah became the victim instead of the attacker. The attitude was apparent in the courtroom, too. While Hannah's fancy attorney twisted Reverend Green into knots over his lack of compassion toward Hannah and her marriage, several of the men on the jury shuffled uncomfortably in their seats. Their attention never once roamed toward Hannah, who sat ramrod straight with her chin up. Later, he'd overheard people in the lobby praising Hannah for her courage.

Joseph slammed his hand on the table and rose, then crossed to the window. If Hannah was found innocent, she'd be in a position to control the farm. He knew she'd figured out that he lied about the will. He snorted. *Pa acted like he intended on living forever.* Joseph doubted the thought of death ever crossed his mind. Now he would pay the price for his father's thoughtlessness.

Not fair! he wanted to scream. The land belonged to him; his mother's money and blood had paid for the place, not Hannah's. *Pa had nothing until he married my mother.*

Joseph's mother was a lady, and not made for the harsh life with his father. She treasured her lovely things and even as a boy, Joseph hated seeing Hannah touch them. How many had Hannah destroyed with her careless and sloppy ways? He hated watching her neglect the home that had brought his mother such pride. All Hannah ever cared about was that squealing brat.

His nails bit into his palms. He had to do something and ran across the room, then climbed to the loft. The box he sought was in the corner, hidden under a blanket. He knelt and rummaged through it until he found what he sought.

Holding the battered case up to the light, he smiled. This would do the trick.

Chapter 29

Fall 2012, the Krause family farm

After three and a half days with her grandmother, Kate was ready to move back to Rose's. The pick, pick, pick was driving her insane, and she felt all the progress she'd made in counseling slowly eroding. She had installed her grandmother in the small bedroom on the west side of the house and taken the back bedroom for herself. Too many memories haunted the bedroom she'd shared with Joe.

Topaz also shared Kate's room and had the run of the house, much to her grandmother's disapproval. The kitten seemed to sense Gran's attitude and took delight in tormenting her. Her favorite game was stalk, pounce, and run, preferably when Gran least expected it. Ankles, arms, feet, shoulders, Gran's head— nothing was out of bounds as far as the kitten was concerned;

and the more Gran protested, the more the kitten pursued her. Watching their daily battles was the only thing that made Kate laugh.

Kate functioned, but grief never left her—it was there buried beneath the daily tasks. A snatch of a special song or the discovery of something Joe had carelessly left lying about would bring it raging to the surface. She caught herself absentmindedly thinking of things she wanted to tell him, only to have the realization that she'd never talk to him again flood her with pain.

Thank God for Rose. Once the body was finally released, she'd accompanied Kate and Trudy to the funeral home to make Joe's final arrangements. The funeral was set for Monday at ten o'clock, followed by burial in the Krause family plot.

Now they sat at the dining room table with Larry Wood, Joe's accountant, ready to go over Joe's financials. His bony fingers carefully spread the documents over the table, and one by one, he handed them to Kate.

First he gave her the lists of debts, and as she read through them, her hands began to tremble. No wonder Joe was concerned. He owed over two million dollars: loans for operating costs, equipment, his new pickup, livestock purchases, all adding up to the staggering amount. Kate's eyes widened when she caught sight of what he'd spent on his new combine. Two hundred thousand dollars. The tractor had cost almost as much.

Mr. Wood saw her expression of dismay. "I cautioned him about overextending, but Joe never bought something unless it was the newest and the best." He paused and handed her another document. "These figures show his losses over the past couple of years. Quite a sum was lost not only speculating on hog futures, but also investing in high-risk stocks."

Kate returned her attention to the first document. "Many of these loans are coming due by the end of the year," she said breathlessly.

"Right. Joe had fallen behind on some of the payments, but was able to catch them up shortly after your marriage."

Now she knew where her savings had gone.

He continued. "It was reaching the point where he might have had to liquidate some of his assets, like acreage, in order to meet these obligations." He glanced quickly at Rose, then returned his attention to Kate. "It was his hope that the deal with David Turner and Turner Farms would prevent taking that step."

"But that's on hold, correct?" Kate asked.

"Yes."

"Some of the land will have to be sold, then?"

Mr. Wood thumbed through another set of papers. "Joe's attorney will be going over this with you, but Joe did have a will. I helped him set it up right before your marriage. He left the farm and all its assets to you and any offspring." He handed her another document. "Then there's the life insurance policy. He had it for a number of years, but changed it to name you as the beneficiary." He smiled condescendingly. "If you so choose, you may use it to pay off the debts and the farm can stay intact."

Kate tapped her temple nervously as she studied the list of debts. "But he owes over two million," she said in a subdued voice.

He flipped his hand toward the paper. "The policy is for four."

Kate's mouth dropped. *"Four million?"*

"Yes, and there's another policy for five hundred thousand

with Trudy as the beneficiary. He wanted to ensure that you were both secure financially."

Kate's brain was reeling, and she gripped Rose's hand from beneath the table. "I can pay off the loans, keep the farm, and still have two million left over?"

"Right. As far as the assets, we'd have to do an inventory using current prices and depreciation, but based on this year's appraisals, the land alone is worth eight."

"Eight?"

"Eight million. Of course if you do decide to sell there's capital gains, taxes, etc., to consider, but you'd still be comfortable financially."

Standing, he gathered up the papers, put them in a large envelope, and handed it to Kate. "I'll leave these with you. Take your time, study them. You don't have to make any decisions right away, and if you have any questions, please call."

Rose escorted Mr. Wood out, and when she returned, Kate was still standing there, looking down at the envelope. With a shake of her head, she tossed it onto the buffet and sank into a chair.

"Are you okay?" she asked, sitting across from Kate.

"I'm shocked. I had no idea that farming took this kind of money."

"It's big business, sweetie," Rose replied with a chuckle.

"And you've been handling this kind of stuff for sixty years?"

"Well, both first and second husbands were involved, but I always did the books." She folded her hands on the table. "It's always a gamble. Will it rain? Are grain and livestock prices headed up or down? Should I sell now or later? I've made a lot of money and I've lost a lot of money."

Kate leaned back in her chair. "The life insurance policy came as a big shock, too."

Rose lifted one shoulder. "It's not unusual. Using a life insurance policy to pay off outstanding debts at the time of death is one way to ensure that farms stay in the family. The heirs aren't forced to sell in order to meet expenses."

"What do you think I should do, Rose?"

"I think you should sit tight. Get through the next few days, the next few months. You've got time before the bank's going to be knocking at the door."

"I've made one decision," Kate said with determination. "One way or the other, I'm backing out of the deal with Turner Farms."

Rose gave her a questioning look, and started to open her mouth, but Kate spoke first. "I would've wanted to pull the plug even if you weren't my friend."

Rose dropped her gaze for a moment, then looked back up at Kate.

"What's wrong? Aren't you pleased that I want to stop the hog confinement operation?"

"Yes—yes, of course I am, but there's something else." She took a deep breath. "Kate, you didn't know about the life insurance, right?"

"No. I just told you how shocked I was when Mr. Wood explained it to me." Kate was puzzled. "Why?" She thought for a moment. "Wait a second, you don't think—"

"That the sheriff might think it's a good motive for murder?" She stretched her hand across the table and clasped Kate's. "I believe in you completely, but I don't count. The sheriff does. It's a lot of money, Kate, and people have been killed for less." She gave her hand a squeeze. "To be on the safe side—I want you to hire an attorney."

It was ridiculous, Kate thought later, but Rose's words were almost prophetic. Detective Shepherd called and asked to stop by the farm. Reluctantly, Kate agreed.

After she'd greeted the detective, she led him into the parlor. She tried to gauge by his manner if he suspected her in any way, but he seemed friendly and pleasant. Much more so than when he was drilling her with questions at the hospital.

"I won't stay long," he said amiably. "I wanted to stop by and let you know that the investigation is ongoing, and ask you to sign a few forms."

He handed her a stack of papers.

"What kind of forms?"

"It's routine. They're for the release of information. You know—bank records, phone records—that type of thing. We need to get a good picture of what was going on in your husband's life right before his death."

Kate hesitated, staring at the papers in her hand, and the detective gave her a sharp look.

"Is there a problem?" he asked.

"I don't know—I hate the idea of people, even your department, digging around in our personal lives."

"You want your husband's murderer brought to justice, don't you?"

"Of course I do," she replied, flipping through the papers, stopping at the last one. It was for Dr. Mike.

"Why do you want to know about our marriage counseling?"

"Joe might have indicated during one of the sessions that he was concerned for his safety. If he did, we need to know."

Kate shook her head. "Any concerns that he might have had were never discussed."

Detective Shepherd removed the notebook from his pocket and scanned through it. "Joe had an individual appointment last week. You weren't there. You don't know what he told the doctor."

Staring down at the papers, Kate remembered how hard it had been for Joe to discuss his childhood. It had been intensely private and personal, and the last thing he'd want would be for strangers to learn of it.

Kate grabbed a pen and, placing the forms on an end table, signed all but the one for Dr. Mike.

"Here," she said, handing them back. "I signed everything but the last one. I'm not giving permission for our therapist. Joe never once mentioned any danger to me, and I doubt that he said anything to Dr. Mike."

Detective Shepherd took the forms. "We can get a warrant you know."

With a wave of her hand, Kate pointed him toward the front door. "Then I guess that's what you'll do."

After Detective Shepherd left, Kate felt as if the house was crowding in on her. Trudy was in her room, and who knew or cared where Gran was. She grabbed Topaz and headed to the apple orchard.

While sitting under one of the trees, she played with the kitten.

She'd made a mistake. She realized that now. She should've

told them about the letter and the person she'd thought she'd seen in the orchard that day. It was too late now. She wasn't stupid. She knew the victim's family were the prime suspects. Why hadn't she considered they would take a long, hard look at her?

"Guess I wasn't thinking," she muttered to the kitten.

If she spoke up now about Ed and the figure in the orchard, it would look like she was trying to cast suspicion on someone else.

She picked up the kitten and nuzzled it with her cheek. "If you could only talk, Topaz," she whispered, "you'd tell them I was with you the whole time."

"Why are you worried about an alibi?"

Startled, Kate looked up to see Will standing over her. She jumped to her feet.

"You frightened me."

"I'm sorry," he said, with a glance toward the house. "I came around the side. I didn't want to upset Trudy." He did a slow turn. "So this is where Willie was born?"

"You've never seen the place?"

"No. No one from my side of the family has set foot on this land since Willie left after Jacob's death."

"What happened to him?"

"He grew up, became a doctor—practiced medicine over by Montgomery—married, had kids." Will smiled. "And by all accounts, he had a very long, happy life. He's buried out in the cemetery here."

"In the Krause plot?"

"Ah no. Our family has a plot in a different part of the cemetery."

"What happened to his mother?"

"Hannah?" Will picked up a dried leaf and crumbled it. "Not too much was ever said about her." He dropped the shredded pieces. "Enough about ancient history. I'm sorry for your loss, Kate."

"Thanks."

"I won't lie—I didn't always agree with Joe, but I've always believed that underneath all that Krause bluster, he was a good man," he said in a somber voice. "And I know he was proud of you."

"Me?"

"You sound surprised, but I know he'd bragged about you around town. Always telling people about how pretty and smart you are."

"He stopped saying those things to me after we were married," Kate said with regret.

"It was the way he was raised, Kate. I doubt he heard many compliments growing up."

"No, he didn't." Kate's voice thickened. "You know we were separated, don't you?" She gave a brittle laugh. "What am I saying? Sure you did—everyone in town's been talking about it."

"I also heard that Joe was determined to get you back."

"We were trying to work things out." She swallowed hard. "I thought we were making progress, but I'll never know now."

"I'm sorry."

Kate sniffed. "You don't know a good criminal lawyer, do you?"

"Hey, what I said about an alibi was inappropriate and I apologize. You surely don't need a lawyer," he said vehemently.

"I might. They haven't come out and accused me yet, but I think they consider me a 'person of interest.' And after today, I feel like I'm shooting up their list fast."

Will scuffed the ground with the toe of his boot. "I had heard they've been asking questions about you and Joe. I know they've talked to Doc."

"Great," Kate declared. "Now I'm going to lose my job."

"No, you won't. Doc didn't appreciate the questions and gave them an earful. He told them that you were the best thing that had ever happened to Joe."

She clutched Topaz. "I was at the office, but I was alone and can't prove what time I left."

"Listen—they've been asking questions about Ed Rodman, too. The story's going around that he doesn't have an alibi either."

"Do you think he might have killed Joe?" she asked in a hushed voice.

"I'd hate to think someone I know might be a killer, but Ed does have a temper and he doesn't like to be pushed."

"And Joe was determined to make him move his fence."

Will shook his head. "They might have argued and things got out of hand." He looked at her intently. "If you do feel like you're the focus of their investigation, maybe you should get a lawyer."

She'd worked so hard to gain everyone's respect and now they were beginning to turn against her. Talking about her behind her back, suspecting her of a terrible thing. The strength she'd tried to muster since Joe's death leached out of her.

"That's what Rose advised." Kate looked away in dismay. "But I don't know if it matters what happens to me."

Will stepped toward her. "You don't mean that."

"Look at this, Will." She swept an arm toward the fields that lay beyond the orchard. "Supposedly, this might be mine, but it's only land. I'd rather have my husband."

"I'm sure you would and I know the future seems bleak without him, but you'll get through this."

"That's what everyone keeps telling me, but I don't know if I can."

"I'm disappointed in you, Kate," he said harshly. "I thought you had more guts than that."

"I don't care what you think," she shot back.

"Yes, you do. I've watched you and you care what everyone thinks . . . too much so. You've worked overtime trying to please everyone but yourself."

"That's not true," she said, the anger showing in her voice.

"It has been. You did whatever you were told and now you're ready to give up and let the sheriff think you killed your husband."

"*That's* not fair," she exclaimed.

Will glared at her. "But it *would* be fair to go to prison for something that you didn't do?"

"What do you want me to do? Take out an ad proclaiming my innocence?" she asked sarcastically.

"No!" he cried. "I expect you to fight back, be smart, and hire the best damn attorney you can find!"

He spun on his heel and marched away.

Holding the kitten, Kate paced back and forth underneath the apple tree. Every nerve in her body tingled as panic tore at her. *It's too much.* Dropping to her knees, she felt as if she were breaking into a thousand little pieces and could never glue them back together.

She closed her eyes and a picture of Essie's House and the women who'd sought refuge there flashed in her mind. Several of them had shown up with only their kids and the clothes on their backs, yet they were determined to make a new and better life for themselves.

She heard a rustling above her, and a shower of red and gold leaves spread in a blanket over and around her. A soft breeze lifted her hair as if in a silent benediction, and suddenly, she felt surrounded by a warm presence. Peace flowed through her.

Staring aimlessly at the horizon, she thought of those who were standing with her. They had faith in her, yet she persisted in believing she was weak, accepting that she was worthless.

Holding Topaz tightly to her chest, Kate scrambled to her feet.

No more. If the women at Essie's House could fight for a new life, then so can I.

Chapter 30

Fall 2012, Braxton County, Iowa

Another fifteen minutes and it would be finished. Kate stared at Joe's polished oak casket. She couldn't believe that the wax-like figure lying inside it was Joe. The family visitation last night had been an emotional wringer, and now she sat stiffly at his graveside waiting for the minister to say his last words. The air around her was heavy with the mixed scents of all the floral memorials—and the roses on Joe's casket. There had been an arrangement of them on her mother's casket, too. She would never see red roses again without thinking of death.

She turned her attention to the bright sky above them. It was wrong. The heavens should be boiling with storm clouds. Nature should be as indignant as Kate was over the loss of this man.

The sound of shuffling brought Kate's focus back as the minister bent to murmur his final words of comfort, then he moved on to Trudy, sitting next to her. She waited, dry-eyed and detached, as Joe's neighbors and friends followed him. Finally, the last of the condolences had been expressed and it was time to return to the farm and the luncheon that Trudy's church ladies had prepared.

When they arrived in the limousine provided by the funeral home, Agnes and two other women Kate didn't recognize rushed the car. They hustled Trudy out, patting and cooing over her as they escorted her to the house. Agnes paused in her comforting long enough to shoot Kate a disgruntled look over her shoulder.

Kate walked past the rows of tables and chairs they'd set up in the yard, and by the time she'd reached the house, they'd propped Trudy up like a life-sized doll in an armchair in the parlor. Kate left Gran with her and proceeded to the kitchen. As she entered, ten pairs of eyes turned toward her and all chatting ceased.

She lifted her chin a notch and returned their stares. "Is there anything I can do to help?"

They resumed their bustling about the kitchen, ignoring her.

This was her house, and she was standing her ground. She cleared her throat and repeated her question. "*Do* you need help?"

One of the women separated from the group and shoved a plate of sandwiches into Kate's hands. "Put these in the dining room."

Kate did as she was told, and was amazed to see the amount of food the women had laid out. Sandwiches, pickles, desserts, and salads of every kind and description covered the table. At a loss for what to do, she wandered between the dining room and parlor, accepting more condolences, until she felt the crowded house pressing in on her. She fled to the back bedroom upstairs.

Kicking off her shoes, she sat on the bed and gazed around the room. With her hands dangling at her sides, she tapped one foot on the floor and wondered what to do with herself now. She hadn't worried about filling her time during the last few days—just getting out of bed and dealing with all the arrangements had been enough of a challenge. But now, with the funeral over, she needed to do *something*. Trudy couldn't live out here alone, and for now, out of respect for Joe's memory, Kate had to stay.

She rose and walked to the window. Men stood over by the barn chatting. Fallen leaves covered the ground beneath the old apple trees. A few short months ago, she'd come to this place with such dreams and plans. Gone now, she thought, fingering one of the lace curtains. Bitterness began to creep into her heart, but she tamped it down. No, she'd sworn to make a new life, and maybe it wouldn't be the one she'd planned, but it could still be worthwhile.

One thing at a time, she thought, turning away from the window and looking about the room again.

She'd always liked this room. Even with all its clutter, there was a sense of peace here that the other rooms lacked. She'd start her new life with a small step: make this room her own. And the first thing would be to clear out all these boxes.

Kate crossed the room and, as she bent to rummage through one of them, a sudden noise came from behind her, made her twirl around. One of the large boxes had tipped over.

"What are you doing hiding out up here?" Doris said, appearing in the doorway.

Kate looked from the box to Doris. "I needed a little time alone." She gave a rueful smile. "And I was tired of the church ladies giving me dirty looks."

Doris walked over to the books scattered across the floor. "Don't worry about them," she said, picking up one of the books. "If it makes you feel better, Agnes isn't much ahead of you in popularity." Her lips twisted in a sneer. "Somehow her unkind speculations about Joe got around. So she's been working her butt off to get back in their good graces."

Kate allowed herself a small smirk. "That would be thanks to Rose."

"Hey, these are old photo albums," Doris said as she flipped open the book in her hand.

"Let me see," Kate said, joining her.

Doris held out the album to her and, kneeling on the floor, picked up another one.

Kate opened the album and began to carefully turn the heavy black pages. Her nose wrinkled at the musty smell they emanated. Sitting down next to Doris, she showed her one of the pages.

"This looks like it was taken here," she said, pointing to one of the pictures.

The picture was of an old man standing on the front porch. Flanking him were two young boys and a teenager.

Doris took the album and studied the picture. "Those two boys are twins." Her eyes widened. "Joe's grandfather had half brothers, so if that's who this is, then the teenager is his grandfather." She lightly tapped the picture. "And I'd bet anything that this old man scowling at the camera is Joseph."

"That's the one who accused Rose's great-grandfather of mishandling his father's murder, right?"

"Yeah." Doris shuddered. "He doesn't look like someone I'd want to cross."

Kate pulled the box closer and began removing the rest of its contents. "I wonder how far back these go?" she asked, browsing through them, then stacking them in a pile next to her. "From the background, I'm assuming that a lot of these pictures were taken here. No names, though."

"Look at this," Doris said, removing a shoe box from the bottom—the last of the carton's contents. "Wonder what's in here?" She opened it and found more pictures. These were in plastic sleeves and appeared to be printed on heavy cardstock. Turning one over, she read the back, "'From the Photographic Studio of R. G. Strauss and Son, Flint Rapids, Iowa.'" She reversed the photo. "Look at the way they're dressed. Late 1800s, I'd say."

Kate fished another sleeved photograph out of the box.

It showed a couple—a man and a woman—seated in high-backed chairs. A younger man stood next to the seated man, and a small child, clothed in a short dress and holding a box, leaned against the woman's leg. She had one arm protectively wrapped around the child's shoulders. The woman wore a pained expression and looked as if she'd rather be somewhere else.

Kate's attention shifted to the seated man and was caught by his eyes. Two dark orbs set in a glowering face seemed to reach out to her from across space and time. The peace she'd always felt in this room dissipated, and she felt an oppressiveness descend on her as a shudder rippled her shoulders. She dropped the picture and unconsciously rubbed her palms on her dress.

Doris gave her a quizzical look, picked up the photograph. "Pretty grim, aren't they?"

"I don't like the old man," Kate said uneasily. "Something about him creeps me out. Do you feel it, too?"

"No." Doris held up the picture and studied it closely. "There is something about his eyes, though. It's probably due to the lighting that they used back then."

"What about the child? Is it a boy or a girl?"

"I think it's a boy. Small children were dressed alike back then no matter what the sex."

Doris squinted. "Did you notice the younger man?"

"Not really."

Doris grabbed the first album and opened it to the first picture they'd seen—the old man with the three boys. She laid the second photograph next to it.

"Look at this picture," she said, tapping the plastic-sleeved photograph. "Then this one," she continued, pointing to the album. "Do you see the resemblance?"

Kate's focus traveled from one face to the other, then back again. Same nose, same mouth. "Could be that they're related."

"I think they're the same man. I think it's Joseph," Doris said, her voice excited. "And if it is, then the adults in this older photo are Jacob and Hannah."

"And the little boy is Willie—Will's great-great-grandfather." Kate gave the picture closer attention. "The box he's holding—it must be the music box from the parlor. I recognize the clasp."

Doris started to hand the picture back to Kate, but she shook her head. "Go ahead and put it back in the shoe box," Kate said without touching it. "I'll look at it later."

Doris returned it and replaced the lid. Once the picture was out of sight, Kate felt her anxiety vanish.

"You know," Doris said, rising to her feet, "Trudy has all these old family photographs displayed downstairs. I wonder why they've never framed that one? It's got to be one of the earliest Krause family portraits."

"Maybe Trudy found it disturbing, too," Kate said, standing.

"I guess," Doris answered thoughtfully. "All that family curse stuff does revolve around Jacob."

Kate shook her head. "I've heard the stories about that and about the hauntings, but no one has ever mentioned how Jacob was killed."

Doris shifted uncomfortably and kept her gaze on the floor. "He was stabbed."

Chapter 31

Fall 2012, the Krause family farm

By the time Doris and Kate came back down the stairs, the crowd was beginning to thin. For the next thirty minutes, Kate stood at the door, thanking everyone for their attendance and their show of sympathy.

Once the last of the guests had left, Kate found Rose in the dining room. She crossed to the older woman and hugged her.

"Thanks," she said, moving a step back. "I couldn't have gotten through this without you."

Rose blushed. "I'm glad I was here to help," she replied, brushing a strand of hair from Kate's face. "How are you holding up?"

"I'm okay for now. I have my moments, but I need to keep busy until I go back to work."

"When's that?" Rose asked, picking up the last of the empty dishes and heading for the kitchen.

"Next week," Kate answered, following her.

"Has Detective Shepherd talked to you again?"

"No."

Rose grimaced. "I saw him lurking toward the back of the crowd at the cemetery. You are going to talk to an attorney, right?"

"I guess." She hesitated. "Don't you think it'll appear that I have something to hide?"

"No," Rose said vehemently. "You need someone who understands the system."

Kate lifted an eyebrow. "What happened to 'let the sheriff handle it'?"

Rose shoved her hands on her hips. "That was before we learned about the life insurance policy."

"Okay, I'll see an attorney, but I'm not going to spend my days looking over my shoulder." Kate tossed her head. "I don't know how or why this happened, but I'm going to trust that the truth will come out."

A strange look crossed Rose's face. "Not always," she murmured, then swiftly changed the subject. "What are your plans for tomorrow?"

Kate tugged on her bottom lip. "I'm not ready to go through Joe's things, so I thought I'd clean out the back bedroom to give me more space." Her expression grew uneasy. "Did Doris tell you that we think we found a picture of Jacob Krause in a box full of old photo albums?"

"You must be mistaken," Rose said quickly.

"Doris is convinced. It's a picture of a man and a woman with a teenage boy and a small child."

Rose muttered something, but Kate failed to catch it.

"What?"

"Nothing," Rose answered with a shake of her head.

"Would you like to see the picture?" Kate asked with an uncertain note in her voice. "To tell you the truth, I found the picture disconcerting."

Rose suddenly turned her back to Kate and began wiping off the already clean counters. "In what way?" she asked, her voice tense.

Baffled by Rose's reaction, Kate shrugged. "Something about the man in the picture gave me the chills." She gave a nervous smile. "I'm being silly. It's just an old photograph, and as Doris pointed out, people in them always look unhappy."

Rose faced Kate. "I have an idea. Why don't I take the box home with me? I can go through them and figure out who some of the people are."

"That's okay," Kate said. "Let me get them organized first, then we can go through them."

Abruptly, Doris appeared in the doorway. "You'd better get in here," she called, then spun on her heel.

Rose and Kate followed her through the dining room into the parlor.

The sight that met them had Kate stumbling to a stop.

Gone was the catatonic woman they'd witnessed over the past few days. Trudy was spitting mad and stood facing off with her grandmother in the center of the room. She held the old music box clutched tightly to her chest.

"Don't you touch my things," Trudy hissed.

"What's going on?" Kate asked as she rushed to Trudy's side.

"That woman," Trudy replied through clenched jaws, "was walking around handling my treasures."

Kate shot her grandmother an angry look over her shoulder and received one of feigned innocence in return.

"I don't know what she's talking about," her grandmother replied blandly.

"Here," Kate began as she touched the music box, "let's put this back on—"

"No," Trudy cried, stepping out of Kate's reach. "I don't trust her." She held the music box tighter. "I'm going to my room."

Kate motioned Rose and Doris over.

"Come on, Trudy," Doris said gently, "I'll help you." Taking Trudy's arm, she guided her out of the parlor. Rose followed, leaving Kate alone with her grandmother.

"What were you doing?" Kate asked, not trying to hide her indignation.

"Nothing," her grandmother replied, strolling nonchalantly over to an armchair. With a sigh, she plopped into the chair. "This place is full of antiques, you know."

Kate rolled her eyes as she sank onto the couch. "To Trudy, they're family heirlooms."

An avaricious light came into her grandmother's eyes. "Family heirlooms that would bring a nice tidy sum at an estate sale." She eyed Kate with speculation. "You *are* having a sale, aren't you?"

"Really, Gran?" she asked, not hiding the disgust in her voice. "The funeral was only a few hours ago. Do you think now is the time to talk about money?"

Her grandmother ignored her question and settled back in the chair. "You're going to have a hard time ahead of you," she said with a click of her tongue. "A lot of decisions to be made, and obviously Trudy is in no shape to be of help." Her fingers tapped the arm of the chair. "I think it would be best if I stayed here to advise you."

Kate's face twisted with dismay. "I don't think that's a good idea."

"*I* do," her grandmother argued. "If I lived here, then I wouldn't have to pay those worthless girls to come in every week. Think of the money I'd save."

"We've been over this," Kate said in a weary voice. "You're not moving in here."

Her grandmother gave an indignant sniff. "I don't see why not. This is a big house. There's plenty of room for me."

Kate shot to her feet and began to pace. "No. You have a life in Des Moines. You'd be leaving your friends—"

Her grandmother cut her off with a wave of her hand. "I can make new friends." Her attention roamed the room. "This is a nice place—far nicer than the cracker box I live in. We'll have to clean out some of this clutter to make room for my things."

A vision of plastic Elvis statues lining the mantel made Kate shudder.

"The sale I mentioned," she continued, "would be a good way to do it. *And* it could bring in thousands."

Kate came to a halt in front of her grandmother. "It's not mine to sell."

"Yes, it is. You inherit everything," her grandmother replied quickly.

Kate stared down at her. "What makes you say that?"

Her grandmother shifted in the chair. "Oh, um, I think I overheard something this afternoon at the luncheon."

"At the luncheon?" Kate asked, crossing her arms.

"Yes." She nodded her head swiftly, her eyes not meeting

Kate's. "In the kitchen. That's right . . . the kitchen. Some of Trudy's friends were talking about how Joe left everything to you."

Kate dropped her arms. "Cut the crap, Gran," she said, her temper rising. "The only time any sort of an inheritance was mentioned was the day the accountant was here. You were eavesdropping weren't you?"

Her grandmother jerked her chin in the air. "Is it my fault you were talking loud enough for me to hear you?" Her expression shifted and she leaned forward. "You're going to be so much better off than your mother was when your father died. Kate, you're going to be wealthy," she said, awestruck. "Millions. My granddaughter is going to be a millionaire."

The greed on her grandmother's face sickened her.

"And you want to help me spend those millions, don't you?" she asked in a deadly calm voice.

"It's only fair," she said, dropping her voice. "I took you in when your mother died—"

"And reminded me of it every day of my life," Kate cried, her anger erupting. "Before I met Joe, I spent ninety percent of my free time stepping and fetching for you. I didn't like it, but I did it because I thought I owed you."

"You do owe me," her grandmother insisted.

"No—no, I don't. Since moving here, I received more kindness from strangers than I ever received from you. I've realized that what you did for me should've been done out of love and not with some price tag attached." Kate took a sharp breath. "But that wasn't the way it was, and as far as I'm concerned, that bill was paid in full a long time ago."

"The very idea," her grandmother huffed, "that my only grandchild would talk to me like this." She rose to her feet. "I don't intend to stay here and listen."

"Good." Kate glanced at the grandfather clock. "How long will it take you to pack? There's a nice motel in Flint Rapids. While you're getting your suitcases, I'll call and make a reservation."

Her grandmother whirled on her, sputtering.

Kate held up a hand before she could get the words out. "I'll pay for two nights. That will give you time to call Mrs. Cutter and for her drive out to get you." Turning on her heel, she began to march from the room. "After you pack your suitcases, I'll find you a ride to the motel," she called over her shoulder.

For the first time in Kate's life, her grandmother was speechless.

Chapter 32

Fall 2012, the Clement family farm

The car turned into the drive as Rose was pulling the last of the dead annual flowers from her front flower bed. Rising to her feet, she smiled at the sight of Will Krause striding across her yard.

"You're out early," she said, stripping off her gloves.

Will gave her a cheeky grin. "I was in the neighborhood." He looked at the pile of pulled flowers, then at Rose. "Shouldn't you have someone do that for you?"

Rose grimaced. "I'm not so old that I can't take care of a few flower beds, young man." She softened her words with a smile. "Though I will admit, it's not as easy getting up and down as it used to be." Her smile faded. "Seriously, Will, what brings you out this way?"

He picked up one of the dried stems and plucked at the brown leaves. "I'm concerned about Kate. I don't like the direction the investigation is taking. From what I hear, they seem to be zeroing in on her."

Rose pursed her lips. "I agree. Detective Shepherd was at the cemetery yesterday, and he's been asking a lot of questions about Kate." She glanced over to the porch. "Come on, let's sit a spell," she said, waving toward the house and two wicker chairs sitting by the front door. "Would you like coffee?" she asked, moving toward the house.

"No, thank you," he replied, settling into one of the chairs and stretching out his long legs.

Rose eased herself into the chair next to him. "I've already talked to Annie about a lawyer for Kate, and she recommended Brown and Brown over in Flint Rapids. Darwin's a fine man." She squinted, looking off into the distance. "Kate's had one shock after another recently, so I'm going to let things calm down a bit, then encourage her to go talk to him."

"I wouldn't wait too long."

Rose turned her attention to Will. "What do you think happened?"

"I don't know." He rubbed his chin. "Joe always had more than his share of enemies, and people can carry grudges for a long time. Maybe a fight with one of them that got out of hand?"

"Ed Rodman?"

"I'd say they're looking at him just as hard as they are Kate. He doesn't have an alibi either." Will drew in his legs and leaned forward, dangling his hands over his knees. "One thing that puzzles me . . . What did Joe tell Trudy when he stumbled into the house that afternoon?"

"From what Kate said—it all happened so fast, and Trudy was incoherent at the hospital." Rose held out her hands helplessly.

"Since then, due to the stroke, she's barely been with it. I don't know if they've even questioned her again."

Will sat back. "Doc did say that Detective Shepherd asked him about Trudy's condition, but that's it."

"Did he offer any more information than that?"

Will shook his head.

"The past repeating itself," Rose murmured softly.

He snorted in disgust. "Come on—don't start with that crap."

She gave him a sharp look. "Kate found a box of old albums and individual photographs yesterday."

"So?"

"I didn't see it, but from the way she described it, one was of Jacob, Joseph, Hannah, and Willie." Rose plucked a piece of dried grass off the knee of her jeans. "She's already asked a few questions, and now with this picture showing up . . ." Her voice trailed away as she focused on Will. "How much do you want her to know?"

He stood and walked over to the porch railing and was silent for a moment. He leaned against the railing, looking out, then turned toward Rose. "Kate's already heard enough about family curses and ghosts, and things are tough enough for her right now. Have you considered what it will mean to Kate if they don't solve this case?"

"I guess not." Rose tugged on her bottom lip. "I've been too worried about the present to think about the future."

"Right—and everyone knows that Kate is under suspicion, so if the killer is never found—"

"She'll live the rest of her life with that hanging over her," Rose said, cutting in.

Will moved over to her. "Exactly. She could start drawing crazy comparisons about what happened then and now. It would only add fear and anxiety."

"So if she asks—" Rose began thoughtfully.

He laid a hand on her shoulder, interrupting her. "Let the secrets stay buried."

Chapter 33

Fall 2012, the Krause family farm

When Kate entered the kitchen the next morning, she found Trudy awake and cooking at the stove. She was wearing one of her housedresses, her hair pulled back in a bun, and she appeared alert.

Surprised at the change, Kate crossed to the counter. "How are you feeling?"

"Fine," Trudy spit out. "I wondered if you were going to spend the whole day lollygagging around in bed."

Kate ignored the remark and poured a cup of coffee. She eyed the table. Three places were laid out.

"Are you expecting someone for breakfast?" she asked, pointing at the table.

Trudy rolled her eyes as she flipped a pancake. "Of course not."

"Umm—there are three places set," Kate replied cautiously.

"You, me, and—" Her hand stilled and she braced herself on the counter. "Joe's not coming back," she said, her voice desolate.

Kate reached out to lay a hand on her shoulder, but she shied away. "Do you remember yesterday?" Kate asked gently.

She nodded, then stiffened her spine. "I don't want to talk about it. Breakfast is getting cold."

As Trudy filled the serving dishes, Kate placed them on the table. Neither woman made a move to put away the third place setting. While Kate picked at her food, the silence in the kitchen grew. Finally, she moved her plate to the side and said, "I'm sleeping in the back bedroom and I'd like to move the boxes to the attic, if you don't mind."

"I don't care what you do," Trudy answered with eyes downcast.

"One of the boxes contains photo albums. I, of course, don't recognize anyone in the pictures," Kate said, attempting to lighten the mood. "Would you like to go through them? Maybe make a list of where they were taken and who's in the photos?"

Trudy's fork clattered to her plate. "What's the point? Who's going to care now?" Her expression hardened. "Joe's gone and there are no children to carry on his legacy."

Her words were a direct hit to Kate's heart and she drew a sharp breath. If only she hadn't lost the baby. Regret flooded her. She clasped her hands tightly in her lap.

"Your family has played an important role in this county's history," she said in a controlled voice. "The historical society might be interested in the pictures."

Trudy rose to her feet and picked up her plate. After carrying it to the counter, she dropped it into the sink. "Do what you want. I'm going to my room."

Moments later Kate heard the TV come on.

After cleaning up the kitchen, Kate retrieved the envelope containing Joe's financial records. She spread them out on the dining room table and turned on her laptop. With Topaz curled up on her lap, she began to go through all the debts and assets, creating a spreadsheet as she went.

Joe's folly became clear. In the pursuit of quick money, he'd failed to diversify. If he had invested in more secure stocks, his returns would have come at a slower rate, but in the long run, his assets would have grown.

Once Kate understood the financial mistakes Joe had made, she began making notes on a legal pad. She read online articles about market trends, yield projections, and the impact of weather over the past few years. She entered the operating costs that the farm had incurred versus the profits onto her spreadsheets. Several questions came to her as she entered the numbers. She wrote those down on her pad, too, and soon she'd filled three pages.

Leaning back in her chair, she absentmindedly stroked the cat as she looked over the notes. A plan began to form in her mind, and she picked up her pen and began to chart it out. A knock on the front door interrupted her.

Opening the door, she found Rose waiting patiently on the porch. Rose handed her a plate, and the scent of hot cinnamon rolls drifted toward her.

"I thought you might be getting tired of Jell-O salads and casseroles," Rose said with a laugh.

"Bless you," Kate said with a grin. "I'll grab a couple of plates and some coffee." She jerked her head toward the dining room table as Rose followed her into the house. "I've been going over Joe's financial records and I have a few questions for you, if you have the time."

Rose crossed to the table and picked up Kate's notes. "Sure," she said, seating herself.

Two hours and a couple of cinnamon rolls later, Kate had carefully outlined the farm's situation and what she thought could be done to improve it.

When she'd finished, Rose hooked her arm over the back of her chair and shook her head.

"It won't work, will it?" Kate asked, disappointed at Rose's reaction.

Rose leaned forward. "I'm sorry. I didn't mean to give you that impression," she said quickly and picked up the outline of Kate's plan. "Actually, I'm astounded. You've no experience at running a farm, yet you've an excellent grasp of Joe's operation. You're a quick study."

Kate felt her cheeks turn pink. "You really think so?" she asked, pleased.

"Yes," Rose replied, thumbing through the papers. "You have the bottom line laid out concisely and your ideas of ways to increase your profit margins are excellent." She winked. "I might steal some of them. Have you always been this good at money management?"

"I had to be," Kate answered ruefully. "If Gran has a dime, she'll spend a quarter. I started taking care of the money as a teenager." She grimaced. "It was the only way to keep the lights on and the water running."

Rose placed the notes on the table and folded her hands. "There's no doubt in my mind that you could manage this place if you so choose."

Kate felt a rush of pride and pleasure.

"My next question," Rose began, her tone serious, "is . . . Do you want to do this?"

Kate hesitated. "I've always enjoyed working with money." She gave a dry chuckle. "But it always belonged to someone else. It might be kind of fun if it's my own. I would be the one who stood to gain or lose. A definite challenge."

Rose smiled. "If you want a challenge, running a farm will certainly give you that."

Kate's face became somber. "There's another reason." She paused. "Trudy said something this morning that's been eating away at me. Joe was the last in his family, and—" Her throat tightened and she swallowed hard before continuing. "There's no children to inherit his heritage—no one to remember him."

Rose reached across the table and gave Kate's hand a sympathetic squeeze.

"I have a little idea. If I can make this work, I'd like to start a scholarship in his name for kids that are interested in farming." She chewed on her bottom lip. "I thought about contacting the agribusiness department at the junior college in Flint Rapids to see if they might be interested in using part of the farm for hands-on training programs. I think it would benefit their students."

"That's wonderful, Kate!"

"You don't think it's dumb?"

"No. You'd be enabling young people to achieve their dreams, and at the same time, remembering Joe in a positive way." She stopped and scrutinized Kate. "But you don't have to do this. Once the will is probated, you could walk away from all of this a very wealthy woman. You'd still have the challenge of managing your funds, but without so much risk."

"I've never been wealthy." Kate shrugged. "I wouldn't know how to spend that much money."

"Your grandmother sounded like she'd be happy to help," Rose said, arching an eyebrow.

Kate's lips curled in distaste. "I'd give away every last dollar before I let that woman touch a penny of it," she declared emphatically. "My grandmother likes to pretend otherwise, but she has more than enough to live on. I've invested for her over the years, and she has a decent annuity in addition to her Social Security."

"Is she going back to Des Moines?"

"I assume so. She called and left a garbled message on my voice mail about how sorry she was that I misunderstood her intentions." Kate gave a brittle laugh. "No matter what happens, it's never her fault. It's always mine."

"It isn't. I heard part of the conversation. Her plans were clear."

"They were. She intended to make sure she profited from Joe's death." Kate picked up her papers, straightening them. "That's the way she's lived her entire life. It's always been about her and how she can benefit." She looked at Rose, her gaze intent. "Do you remember our conversation about my grandmother's influence in my life?"

Rose smiled slightly. "I do. You said that you didn't want to be like her."

"I don't, and I'm not," she insisted. "I'm not going to be that woman." She reached across the table and clasped Rose's hand. "I've learned a lot over the past few months. Working with the women at Essie's House made me feel useful. It gave me a purpose and built my confidence. And so will these plans that I've made. By helping others, I can survive Joe's death."

After Rose left, Kate filed away her papers and turned off the laptop. It would be easier if she'd set up in Joe's office, instead of dragging everything out all the time. But she wasn't ready to face that yet; the office could wait along with their bedroom.

She heard Trudy moving around in the kitchen and went to check on her.

"Do you need anything?" Kate asked, leaning against the door frame.

"No," Trudy replied in a curt voice. "I heard you and that Rose Clement talking." She grabbed a knife and began hacking away at a head of lettuce. "I don't like that woman in my house." She whirled with the knife still in her hand. Her eyes filled with tears. "But I guess it's not mine, it's yours."

Kate took a step forward, but Trudy turned back to chopping the lettuce.

She sighed. "Trudy, I'm sorry you feel that way. Rose has been good to me and she's welcome here. I hope you'll accept that."

"Guess I'll have to, won't I?" she muttered. "I suppose I should just be grateful that you haven't kicked me to the curb."

"Trudy—" Kate began, then stopped herself.

This conversation was pointless. After the will was read and she had the farming operation straightened out, she was going to have to address the situation with Trudy. As far as she was concerned, she didn't care if she lived in this house or not. Trudy could have it, but at this point, Kate wasn't convinced she could stay on the farm by herself. Kate took a deep breath. One step at a time, she told herself.

"I'll be upstairs if you need anything," she called, leaving Trudy alone.

Once in the bedroom, Kate stared helplessly at the stacked boxes. Where did she start? *The air is stifling . . .*

First, she thought, crossing the room, she'd open a window, but a hissing sound from behind her made her stop and turn. Topaz was standing stiff-legged in front of the boxes. Her ears were laid flat and her fur formed a ridge down her back.

"You silly cat," Kate said, moving toward Topaz. She picked her up and tried to calm her. "Did you see a mouse?" she asked as she nudged the boxes with her foot.

The top box tumbled and once again photo albums and pictures spilled across the floor. The picture of Jacob and his family lay on top of the pile.

She placed Topaz on the floor and barely noticed as the cat took off out of the room and down the hallway.

"Funny," she muttered to herself. "I could've sworn Doris put it back in the shoe box. The lid must've come off."

She knelt, and after retrieving the smaller box, placed the photograph inside. This time she made sure the lid was on tightly. Kate placed the box to the side and went to open the window. Immediately, a cool autumn breeze filled the room, chasing away the stale air.

Sitting cross-legged on the floor, Kate gazed around the room. Until the situation was resolved with Trudy, she'd make this her sanctuary. With a new coat of paint, new curtains, and a TV, this room would do nicely as her personal space.

She picked up the first album and, thumbing through it, tried to determine its age. From the way people were dressed, she assumed the pictures were from the 1930s. After placing it beside her, Kate went on to the next album and used the same process. She decided to separate them by decades, and as the piles grew, it became apparent that most of the albums covered the time period prior to the 1950s, with the majority from the 1940s. The deeper she dug in the box, the older the albums became, and in a way, Kate felt as if she were traveling back through time.

Finally, she reached the last one. As she hauled it out of the box, a piece of yellowed newsprint fluttered to the floor. She picked it up and carefully unfolded it. It was an old newspaper article that, from the date, came from the 1890s. Pleased with her find, Kate settled back and started to read:

> *The wife of Jacob Krause was arrested yesterday on the charge of stabbing her husband to death while he slept. The brutality of this heinous crime has rocked the small northern Iowa community of Dutton.*
>
> *Small of stature and approximately thirty-five years of age, it is hard to believe that a woman of her size had the strength to drive a knife into the sleeping man. However, Braxton County Attorney Charles Walker is convinced Mrs. Krause is indeed responsible, alluding to years of strife in the Krause household as her motive.*
>
> *Harry Rosenthal, a good friend and neighbor to the late Mr. Krause, has confirmed Mr. Walker's statement concerning the atmosphere in the Krause household. He stated that his friend had long been dissatisfied with his wife's lack of submission and displays of temper. Mr. Rosenthal also pointed to Mrs. Krause's lack of*

*attendance at regular church services and went so far as
to call her a "fair weather Christian."*

*Other neighbors have attested to Mrs. Krause's slovenly
ways and her inability to maintain a proper home for her
husband and children. According to them, it was a great
burden that the late Mr. Krause bore stoically.*

The matter will come to trial later on this year.

The clipping slipped from Kate's finger while her mind raced.
Will's great-great-grandmother had killed her husband, but everyone said that the murderer was never found guilty. Had she
been vindicated?

Kate flipped through the album, looking for an answer, but
came up empty.

The coincidence was too much to contemplate. She had
buried her husband, also a victim of a stabbing, yesterday. Then
today she found this article.

Kate hugged herself tightly as she rocked back and forth. A
sense of dread slowly grew. Trudy had warned her.

History might repeat itself.

Chapter 34

Kate scrubbed her face with her hands as she got out of bed. She hadn't slept well last night. It seemed that she had spent most of the night drifting in and out. At one point, she was so groggy that she could've sworn she heard the distinctive sound of the antique music box drifting up through the floor grate. She had to get moving. Joe's attorney was coming to the house later on in the afternoon to go over the will.

After Kate showered and dressed in jeans and a cotton shirt, she felt better. The curiosity generated by the old newspaper article nagged at her, but it was a perfect fall day with crisp air and bright sunshine—too nice a day to dwell on the past and a good one to finish cleaning out her new bedroom. But first she needed to purchase plastic storage bins.

She hurried to the kitchen and grabbed her purse. Looking out the window, she spied Trudy working in the garden, pulling dead plants.

"I'm headed into town. Do you need anything?" Kate asked as she joined her.

Trudy tossed a handful of the plants into the waiting wheelbarrow. "This garden needs to be tilled before a hard freeze," she said, ignoring Kate's question. "Joe always took care of it . . ." Her voice trailed off. Then, clearing her throat, she continued. "You'll need to get someone over here to do it."

Kate scanned the garden. Amid what was left of Trudy's garden, she spied this year's crop of pumpkins. Their bright orange stood out against the black dirt and brown vines. Fond memories of carving jack-o'-lanterns, trick-or-treating, and, when she was older, soaping windows and hanging toilet paper from tree branches, flitted through her mind.

"Bet this is a popular place to steal pumpkins," she said, waving a hand toward the splotches of orange.

Trudy yanked at one of the plants and snorted. "They wouldn't dare," she exclaimed. "The bigger ones are headed to the farmers' market and we'll can the rest."

Kate thought of the part she liked least about carving pumpkins—pulling out the stringy, slimy seeds—and shuddered. Maybe she'd suggest that Trudy and her church ladies have a canning party, hopefully after she went back to work for Doc.

Turning her attention back to Trudy, she noticed her glaring at her.

"Did you hear what I said?" Trudy asked gruffly. "I need this garden tilled."

Kate gave an exasperated sigh. "Okay. Do we have a tiller?"

"Yes."

"Then I'll take care of it tomorrow," Kate replied, pivoting on her heel.

"You're a woman. You can't run a tiller," Trudy scoffed.

Kate turned back. "I don't see why not. I can give it try," she said defiantly.

With a shake of her head, Trudy resumed pulling the plants.

Fifteen minutes later, Kate strode into Krause Hardware, still fuming over her conversation with Trudy. She was tired of hearing the words *you can't*. It seemed like people had been telling her that her entire life.

As she passed the counter, Will paused in waiting on a customer and smiled at her. She returned his smile and headed toward the shelf containing plastic containers. While she was making up her mind what sizes to buy, Will greeted her.

"What's up?" he asked.

"I'm cleaning out the back bedroom and I need containers to store all the stuff." She pulled out one of the larger storage boxes. "This should do for all of Trudy's material."

"What else are you packing up?"

"Christmas decorations, photo albums—" She stopped. "I found something you might like to see."

Will's face remained expressionless. "What would that be?"

"An old photo. Doris thinks the child in it is your great-grandfather, which means the couple would be your great-great-grandparents."

Will grabbed a smaller container off the shelf. "Would this one be big enough for the Christmas decorations?"

Kate gave him a puzzled look. "Aren't you interested in the photograph?"

"I've seen pictures of Willie."

"But what about Jacob? Doris didn't think there were many photographs of him."

"Kate—" he began.

She interrupted. "And what about Hannah? Everyone seems reluctant to talk about her." She gave him a speculative look. "Was it because she was arrested for Jacob's murder?"

Will's face flushed. "How did you find out about that?"

"I found an old newspaper article written about her arrest. Was she convicted?"

"No," he spit out.

"Then what happened to her? What's the big secret?" she persisted.

"You're talking about an event that occurred over a century ago, and it's one that some have never let go. Maybe if they had, lives would have been different."

"If it happened so long ago, then why can't you tell me?" she asked. "I could ask Trudy if you won't."

"I wouldn't. You won't like her reaction." His voice dropped. "It will only upset her. Do you want to risk another stroke?"

"Of course not."

"Forget about Jacob and Hannah." Noting the defiance in her face, he exhaled slowly. "Look, Willie was only a child when Jacob died, and he adored his mother. Her arrest changed the course of his life, and as an adult, he never spoke of it. My family has always respected that."

"You're telling me that in all this time, your family has never discussed Hannah?" she asked, amazed.

"There's no point. The past can't be changed." He gave her a careful look. "I think *you'd* be better off focusing on today and what might happen tomorrow."

* * *

Will's words echoed as Kate sat down with Trudy and Joe's attorney, Mr. Tolliver. Eyeing him from across the table, Kate was reminded of a partridge. He was plump and brown. He had thinning brown hair and brown eyes. His suit was brown—he even wore a shirt that was tan.

After reading all the conditions of the will, he sat back, looked first at Kate, then Trudy. "Do you understand everything we've gone over thus far?"

Trudy gave Kate a sour look. "Sure. She gets everything."

"Now, Trudy, that's not true," he answered in a condescending voice. "You're the beneficiary of one of his life insurance policies. Then there's the money he paid you for your share of the farm when your husband died." He smiled. "You've been taken care of quite handsomely." He focused on Kate. "Do you have any questions?"

"What happens next?"

"Well," he said slowly as he gathered up the papers spread across the table. "First we have to file the will, then we'll need to do an inventory of all the assets." He smiled again. "Once the will has finished probate, you'll be ready to start liquidating."

Trudy's attention traveled around the room, settling on one heirloom at a time. Mr. Tolliver noticed.

He reached across the table and patted her hand. "I'm sure Kate will be willing to give you those things that have a special sentimental value, Trudy. She won't sell them."

"Excuse me?" Kate asked.

"Once the probate is finished, we'll start making arrangements for the farm and estate sale."

"I didn't mention selling out," Kate replied.

He appeared flustered. "Managing a farm is a big responsibil-

ity and you have no experience. I assumed you'd want to liquidate and return to your family . . . Des Moines, isn't it?"

"Rose Clement manages her operation."

"But Rose has been farming all of her life," he said with a
patronizing smile.

"And she's willing to help me. We've already discussed it."

Mr. Tolliver made a tut-tutting noise. "Really, Kate, I think
that would be very foolish. As it stands now, you can walk away
financially secure for the rest of your life. If you persist in this,
you will be risking your future."

"Isn't that true of anyone who runs a business?"

"Yes." He shoved the papers back in his briefcase and stood.
"If you really want to become a businesswoman, why don't you
open . . . say, a craft shop? You'd have more success in a venture
like that than running a farm."

Kate's eyes narrowed. "I don't want to run a craft shop. I want
to run this farm, and I've already made a detailed business plan."

He shook his head slowly. "It's highly unlikely that you'll succeed," he said.

Kate handed him his briefcase. "I appreciate your concern,
but I believe according to the terms of the will, this is my decision to make and I've made it." She shook his hand and steered
him toward the front door. "Start the probate and we'll go from
there."

When she returned after escorting Mr. Tolliver out the door,
she found Trudy wandering around the parlor, straightening
pillows and fussing over the framed photographs of long-dead
Krauses.

She wiped one of the photos with the corner of her apron.
"What are you going to do about me?"

"I'm not going to do anything about you," Kate replied, leaning against the door frame. "Let's be honest. The only thing that tied us together was Joe and he's gone now."

Trudy swiveled toward her. "I *knew* it," she exclaimed. "You're going to kick me out of my home."

"No, I'm not. I have to live in this house until everything is settled, but after that?" She shrugged. "As far as I'm concerned, you can stay here as long as you want. I'll find a place in town, or build a small house for myself."

She saw the doubt in Trudy's face. "You can believe me. I don't know if it's a good idea, considering your health, if you live alone, but that's your choice. You do have enough money to hire help now."

"Well," Trudy said, crossing her arms over her chest, "I don't believe you. You married Joe to get this farm."

Kate rolled her eyes. "That's absurd. The first time I ever set foot on this place was the day after our wedding." She looked toward the window. The sun was sinking lower, but she still had enough daylight to till the garden. That sounded like a better plan than standing here and listening to Trudy.

Without a word, Kate ran upstairs and changed into a pair of old jeans, a sweatshirt, and a pair of old shoes. Fifteen minutes later, she'd pulled the tiller out of the machine shed and was trying to figure out how to start it. Once she did, the machine bucked to life, startling her, and she lost her grip on the power bar.

She pulled her hand through her hair. "Okay," she muttered, "I can do this."

Adjusting her grip and tightening her grasp, she tried again. This time the tiller's tines dug into the black earth, churning it up. Slowly, she pushed the tiller ahead until she reached the other side of the garden. Stopping, she pivoted the machine and began to till a second strip across the garden.

Forty-five minutes later she'd finished. A fine layer of grit covered her face, her shoes were filled with dirt, and her clothes were filthy. The tracks she'd made in the turned-over soil weren't straight; they waved from side to side. But the garden *was* tilled.

Pleased with herself, she pushed the tiller back to the garage. She'd shown Trudy and she'd show Mr. Tolliver.

After Kate's shower, supper with Trudy had been a dull affair. They'd eaten in stony silence, and Kate had been relieved when Trudy had retreated to her bedroom. Trudy hadn't commented on her newly tilled garden.

Now Kate sat with an afghan wrapped snugly around her, moving slowly back and forth on the front-porch swing. Mr. Tolliver's warning had made her all the more determined to succeed. She thought about the coming months. She had challenges ahead and things to look forward to with anticipation— her job at Doc's, managing the farm, volunteering at Essie's House. It might not be the life she had planned, but it could be fulfilling.

A sliver of pain lifted from her heart.

A set of headlights coming down the road drew her attention. She watched it pull into the driveway and was surprised when she recognized the driver.

Will.

Joining her on the porch, he eyed the front door. "Is Trudy around?" he asked warily.

"She's in her room," Kate replied with a small chuckle.

"Whew." Will made a big show of wiping imaginary sweat off his forehead. "I wouldn't want to find myself staring down the barrel of a shotgun."

Kate jerked her head toward one of the wicker chairs. "Have a seat and tell me what brings you out here."

"I'd like to apologize," he answered earnestly as he sat. "I know I was short-tempered at the store today."

Kate thought for a moment. "I should be the one to apologize. Hannah is your ancestor, not Joe's, and I shouldn't pry into your family's past."

Will gave her a small nod of acknowledgment. "Friends again?"

Kate smiled. "Friends."

Will propped one leg on his knee. "I heard a rumor today—"

"*No*," Kate exclaimed with mock surprise.

He chuckled. "I heard you weren't selling out and had plans to stick around."

"You must've talked to Rose."

"Nope—chatter at the Four Corners."

"What do you know?" Kate said, slapping her knee. "For once they got it right."

"You're staying?"

She nodded. "I have a business plan started, but I don't think there's much I can do until the estate is settled."

"You're going to run the farm."

"I'm going to try." Kate leaned forward. "Do you think it's a bad idea?"

"No. I think you're smart and can do anything that you set your mind to."

"I bet that wasn't the opinion at the café."

"Ahh—no." Will gave her a rueful smile. "Albert Forsyth gave you two years before you lost everything."

"He sounds like Mr. Tolliver," she said, leaning her head against the back of the swing. "He wasn't very supportive either."

"Why do you want to do this, Kate?"

She lifted her head and looked at him while tucking the blanket around her legs. "Various reasons, but I guess I need to prove something."

"To your grandmother?"

Kate jerked forward. "Hell no," she declared, "to myself. All my life, I've been told I couldn't and now I want to prove I can." She spread her hands wide. "If I fail, at least I gave it a shot. Does that make sense?"

"Yeah." Will rubbed the arms of the chair. "When I got out of college, I didn't think I wanted to join Dad at the hardware store. The economy's tough for small retailers, so I decided to play it safe and work for a chain store." He frowned. "Hated every minute of it."

"Why?"

"I found it to be all about the hustle and how the store could stay ahead of the competition." He lifted one shoulder. "I like a slower lifestyle and giving customers the personal touch. The store is never going to turn a huge profit, but that's okay. I'd rather enjoy my life than make a lot of money."

"Ahh, so you don't want to be the 'Hardware King of Northwest Iowa'?" Kate teased.

"Nope," he answered easily. "At one time, I might have had that grand ambition, but things change." He looked at Kate with a solemn expression. "I don't have to point that out to you."

"No, you don't," she answered softly.

They were both silent as they listened to the rhythmic creak of the porch swing.

Kate was the first to speak. "Your life changing doesn't mean it's over, does it? Happiness can still be found, can't it?"

"I think so. It might be different, feel different, than what you expected, but it's still a form of happiness."

Kate sighed and let the night and a sense of peace wrap around her.

Chapter 35

Kate bolted up in bed. The sense of peace she'd felt as she'd fallen asleep had vanished. A scream? Had she heard a scream? Grabbing her robe, she threw it on as she shoved her feet into her slippers and ran to the window. She pulled back the curtains and stared out into the darkness.

A harvest moon hung in the sky like a huge golden ball, illuminating the landscape. A figure moved between the apple orchard and the old cabin. Were kids stealing pumpkins? Kate ran from the room to check on Trudy.

The door to her room was closed as usual, and Kate flung it open. A wave of cold air slapped her in the face. Rubbing her arms, then turning on the light, she checked the bed. Empty. She crossed to the window. Shut. On her way through the kitchen, she snatched a flashlight from the counter then headed out the door. The figure still moved through the apple orchard. Kate flicked on the light and shone it toward the figure.

Like a deer caught in the headlights, Trudy froze. She was

dressed in an old robe, with her thin hair straggling over her shoulders.

With a shake of her head, Kate went to her.

"It's too late to be wandering out here in the dark," Kate said, reaching out for Trudy's arm.

She skittered away, her feet shuffling in the fallen leaves. "I can't find it," she muttered.

"Find what?"

"The music box," she said as she bent and brushed away the leaves at her feet. "I think she took it."

Oh God, she's got it in her head Gran stole it.

Kate laid a hand on her shoulder. "Gran didn't take your music box," Kate said in a calm voice. "Remember you took it back to your bedroom."

Trudy straightened and gave her a sneer. "Not her," she answered in a voice that hinted at Kate's stupidity. "Hannah. The music box was Willie's and she doesn't want me to have it."

In the light of the moon, Kate saw Trudy's lips tighten in a mutinous line.

"But it's mine. Joe's grandfather gave it to me. He said he couldn't trust that worthless man I married to hold the secret."

Kate felt like slapping her forehead in frustration. "Trudy," she said, trying to cut through the fog in Trudy's mind, "Hannah's been dead a long time."

"You never have understood, have you?" Trudy asked with a sneer.

"Understand what? That you're convinced the family's cursed? Yeah," Kate said sternly, "I do . . . Heaven knows you've told me about it often enough. I get it about Jacob roaming the earth, too."

"Ha," Trudy exclaimed, wagging a finger in Kate's face.

"Shows how much you know. It's not Jacob, it's her. It's Hannah. She cursed this family and won't rest until we've all paid."

Kate took a deep breath and tried to gentle her voice. "Come on. Let's go inside. It's late and you should be in bed."

Trudy moved farther away. "I want my music box." Suddenly she whirled toward Kate with her eyes wide. "It's you," she cried. "'The sins of the father.' You brought this down on us. I told Joe you were like her, but he wouldn't listen." Her face crumpled. "Now he's dead just like Jacob."

"Trudy . . . please."

She seemed to shrink before Kate's eyes as she began to shuffle toward the house. "Hannah's won," she said, defeated.

Kate followed her into the house, but instead of heading for her bedroom, Trudy made for the parlor.

"I think you should go to bed now," Kate called after her.

"I'm not sleeping in there—not tonight."

"But you like your room."

"I'm not sleeping with a dead man."

Kate ran her fingers through her hair. "There's no a dead man in your room."

"Yes, there is," she replied, casting a wild look at Kate over her shoulder. "Jacob—that's where she stabbed him."

With a groan, Kate returned to the kitchen and called Doc Adams.

While taking her shower the next morning, Kate let the hot water pound onto her tense shoulders. The episode with Trudy worried her.

Doc had been concerned, but not overly. In his opinion, Trudy was beginning to show signs of dementia. He'd suggested taking her to the hospital, but Trudy refused to go. By the time he'd finished his examination, she was no longer acting odd. He had warned Kate that these episodes might continue, and if she was determined to keep Trudy here, alarms should be installed on all the doors.

What should I do? Kate turned and let the water cascade over her face. It wasn't a problem to install the alarms; she'd pick them up today at the hardware store. But she didn't know how to handle Trudy's fixation with Hannah. Trudy had insisted Hannah had murdered Jacob, but everyone claimed that the killer had never been convicted. Did Trudy's obsession stem from what she felt was a miscarriage of justice?

"Stop it," Kate muttered to herself as she shut off the faucets. Will was right. She grabbed a towel and furiously dried off her body. She had enough to worry about without dwelling on the past.

Wrapping the towel around her, Kate stepped out of the shower and crossed to the sink. She picked up a hand towel to wipe the steam off the mirror, then stopped, the towel slipping from her fingers.

One word . . . *DANGER* . . . was written on the foggy mirror.

Kate cleaned the mirror in two angry swipes. She was beginning to suspect that Trudy was playing tricks on her. The confusion, the preoccupation with the music box and with Hannah—Trudy could be putting on an act in order to drive Kate out of the house.

"Humph," she grumbled as she pulled a comb through her wet hair. "We'll see about that."

◆ ◆ ◆

She hadn't given Trudy the satisfaction of acknowledging the stunt pulled with the mirror. Kate dressed and left for the hardware store without engaging in a conversation.

It did trouble her, and she was not concentrating on her driving. She hit the brakes as a car turned in front of her, throwing everything in the backseat of the Jeep to the floor. Then as she approached the four-way stop at the edge of Dutton, she failed to come to a complete stop and rolled through the intersection. The next thing she knew, she heard the wail of a siren and saw the flash of lights in her rearview mirror.

Kate felt like pounding her head on the steering wheel as she pulled off onto the shoulder and came to a stop. Great—now she'd have a ticket. After turning off the ignition, Kate fumbled in her purse for her driver's license, then removed her proof of insurance and her registration from the glove compartment. She couldn't understand what was taking the officer so long to approach her car, and glanced up into the rearview mirror. When he finally did walk toward her, she noticed his right hand lingered in the vicinity of his weapon.

When he reached the Jeep, she rolled down the window and smiled. "Sorry, officer," she said politely and began to reach for her license and documents.

"Hands on the wheel," he said brusquely.

Perplexed, Kate did as he said and waited.

"You failed to stop."

"I know . . . I wasn't thinking."

The officer peered into the backseat. "What's that on the floor?"

Kate looked over her shoulder. "My jacket."

"Would you step out of the car please."

Again Kate did what he requested, standing nervously next to the Jeep.

"Do I have your verbal consent to search your car?" he asked, studying her reaction closely.

Kate's temper rose. "Are you kidding me? On a traffic stop?"

"No, I'm not kidding, ma'am." The sun glinted off his dark sunglasses, and Kate couldn't read his expression.

"Sure," she said with an angry wave of her hand. "Why not?"

"So I have your permission?"

Kate grudgingly nodded. "Yes."

"Would you step to the front of the vehicle?" He opened the driver's door and removed the keys, then moved to the left rear passenger door and opened it.

Kate leaned against the front of the Jeep and crossed her arms. This was ridiculous, she thought as she heard him rummaging around.

After a moment, she saw him remove a handkerchief from his pocket and, using it, he picked something up off the floor. He straightened, talked into the radio attached to his shoulder, and began to walk toward her. In one hand, he carried the handkerchief, while his other lingered on his sidearm.

After motioning her to stand in front of the Jeep, he placed the handkerchief on the hood, then unfolded it.

The silver blade of a long knife glimmered in the sunshine.

Kate's mouth dropped open.

"I found this under the front seat."

She snapped her jaws shut as the blood drained from her face. *"I've never seen that before,"* she cried.

"It's not yours?"

"No!"

"You don't know how it came to be in your car?"

"Absolutely not."

"Did you know that a knife over five and a half inches long is considered a weapon?" he asked, rewrapping the knife.

"A w-weapon?" Kate stammered.

"Yes, and you had it concealed under the front seat." His hand gripped his gun. "Please turn around and place your hands on the hood."

"What?"

His hand tightened on the gun. "Do as I say, ma'am."

Wordlessly, Kate turned and placed her hands on the hood. From behind her, using his foot, the officer nudged her feet apart.

Oh my God— He was going to pat her down and arrest her. Kate's knees trembled.

"Do you have any other weapons on your person?" he asked as his hands moved up and down her sides.

She shook her head mutely.

"Place your hands behind your back," he said, keeping one hand on her shoulder.

Hot tears stung her eyes as she felt the handcuffs snap into place and the officer repeated the Miranda warning.

The drive to Flint Rapids and the county jail was the longest in Kate's life. Her mind numbly refused to accept what was happening to her. Arrested and her car impounded. She swallowed hard.

Once they reached the jail, a garage door opened and the patrol car pulled in. It closed and the officer exited, then opened the door for Kate. He escorted her to another door. After it buzzed loudly, he opened it and they entered a hallway with another door at the end. The first door clanged shut, then the buzzer on the second went off. The procedure happened four more times as the officer led Kate deeper into the bowels of the jail.

With each buzz, with each clanging shut of the door, Kate's nerves stretched, until she felt like a quivering mass of jelly. When they reached a room with a high counter, he unlocked a small cell in the corner and motioned her inside. After removing the handcuffs, he shut the door and locked it. Kate stared up at him blankly.

"There's the phone," he said, pointing to the wall.

Sinking down on the small bench, Kate wrapped her arms around herself and bent forward. Nausea swirled through her belly as she heard the officer say "aggravated weapons charge" to the man standing behind the counter.

Oh my God, oh my God, rolled through her brain as she sat there trembling. With a shaky hand, she picked up the phone and dialed Rose's number.

"Please answer . . . please answer," she prayed softly as she listened to the phone ring.

"Hello," sounded Rose's voice in her ear.

"Rose," she cried while tears spilled down her face. "I've been arrested—"

"What!" Rose shouted over the phone.

"They pulled me over—they found a knife—it's not mine. I—I . . ." Kate stammered, words continuing to rush out of her mouth.

"Kate, Kate, slow down. Tell me what happened."

Quickly, Kate related the events leading up to her arrest.

"You're at the jail in Flint Rapids?"

"Y-Y-Yes."

"Have they booked you yet?"

"No."

"Don't worry, sweetie," Rose said gently. "We'll get this straightened out. I'll call an attorney and we'll get him over there as soon as possible."

"What should I do?"

"Hang in there. Cooperate, but don't volunteer any information until you have a chance to speak with the attorney, okay?"

"Okay." Kate wiped her face. "Rose, I'm scared," she said in a hushed voice.

"Don't worry. There's been a mistake and we'll fix it," Rose assured her. "I'm going to hang up now, so I can call the attorney."

Reluctantly, Kate replaced the receiver.

A few minutes later, another officer unlocked the cell and handed Kate a bundle of orange clothing.

"You can change in there," he said, indicating a small room next to the cell.

Once inside, Kate's fingers trembled as she tried to unbutton her shirt. Finally, she managed to dress in the jail clothing, then she was returned to the waiting cell. Time crawled by until they were ready to fingerprint her and take her photograph. She went through the process as if she were sleepwalking. Part of her brain accepted the reality, but another part refused.

When one of the officers started to lead her down the hall, every fiber of her being screamed *Run!* but she knew there was no escape. He led her to a small room instead of a jail cell, and Kate's eyes widened in surprise when she saw Detective Shepherd waiting for her.

"Come on in, Kate," he said pleasantly. "Have a seat." He pointed to one of the two chairs sitting next to a small table.

An evidence bag containing the knife lay on the table.

"You don't mind answering a few questions, do you?" he asked after she sat in the chair.

She shook her head.

"Good," he said, sitting across from her. He slid the bag across the table until it was right in front of her. "Do you recognize this?"

"No."

"You've never seen it before?"

Kate bowed her head. "No."

"Do you know how it came to be in your car?"

"No."

As Detective Shepherd scooted his chair closer to the table, Kate raised her head.

"We're not getting very far, are we, Kate?" He slid the knife away from her and removed papers from a folder. "Let's go over your statement concerning Joe's murder, shall we? Would you start at the beginning?"

Swallowing hard, Kate retold the events leading up to her arrival at the hospital the day Joe was killed.

"You left the office at twelve forty-five, right?"

"No." She cleared her throat. "Twelve forty-six. I glanced at the clock."

He withdrew another paper from the folder and placed it in front of her. "Can you explain these?" he asked, tapping some highlighted lines on the paper.

Kate picked up the document. It was a copy of her bank statement, and the lines he'd indicated were the checks she'd written to Will for the down payment on her Jeep.

"I'd borrowed money from Will Krause and these are the payments on the loan."

"Why did you borrow money from him? Why didn't you ask Joe for the money?"

"Joe led me to believe that he was having financial problems, so I didn't want to ask him. Will offered and I accepted."

He leaned forward. "That's kind of odd, isn't it, Kate? Everyone knows that Will and Joe never got along—that there was a grudge between the two families."

"The grudge was one-sided. Joe's family were the ones who resented Will's."

"Since Will is so good at helping you out, did he go with you that day to see Joe?"

Kate's chin shot up. "Of course not," she declared.

"We, also, found this," he said, handing her another paper.

It was a copy of Joe's life insurance policy.

"Looks like once this is paid out, you won't have to borrow money again from Will Krause."

"If you talked to Larry Wood, I'm sure he told you that I knew nothing about this policy," she said.

He took the paper back and picked up the evidence bag. Holding it up to the light, he studied it. "Do you see this?" he asked as he pointed to the knife's handle. "See those little brown specks? Kind of looks like dried blood, doesn't it?" He dropped the bag in front of her. "Once we send this in, we'll know if it's the murder weapon," he said softly and folded his hands on the table.

Kate met his gaze as she moved the bag toward him, saying nothing.

"Kate, we know Joe was physically abusive, so why don't you tell me what really happened that afternoon? If it was self-defense, we can work out a deal with the county attorney."

She studied the detective as intently as he was looking at her. She was in over her head. Time to keep her mouth shut.

"I'm sorry, Detective. I've told you everything about the afternoon Joe died. I've never seen that knife before, and I have no explanation as to how or why it wound up in my vehicle." She watched him without blinking. "I'm not going to answer any more questions without my attorney being present."

He shrugged. "Okay—guess we'll wait for the fingerprints and the DNA results to come back." He stood and gathered the papers. "We're still holding you on the weapons charge." He nodded to an officer standing outside the room.

The officer led Kate out of the room and down a hallway. He stopped in front of a door, unlocked it, then swung it open to reveal a small area with another door—one with bars. Opening it, he motioned for Kate to step inside.

She took a few steps forward, crossing the cell's threshold. With her back to the door, she tried not to jump as she heard both doors bang shut and the locks turn. Looking up, she noticed a camera pointed down toward the cell. Underneath it and out of its range was a stainless steel toilet with a sink attached to the top. A cot was along one of the walls, well within the range of the camera's all-seeing eye.

No privacy. No freedom of any kind. Kate began to pace the confines of her cell. How long had the knife been in her Jeep and who could have placed it there? She never locked it, even when she parked it in Dutton. Anyone could've planted that knife. She had no doubt that the knife was the murder weapon, and she wasn't stupid—someone was setting her up.

Kate had never felt so alone and so hopeless. Her insides cramped. Running to the toilet, Kate threw herself on her knees as her stomach emptied into the toilet. She heaved until nothing was left except the bitter taste of bile. After wiping her mouth, she curled on her side and laid her head down on the cold, hard floor. She hadn't the strength to walk to the cot.

Chapter 36

Fall 1890, the Braxton County Jail

A cool breeze blew in through the open window, bringing with it the taste of autumn. Soon Hannah's trial would be over. Each day Andrew seemed to grow more and more confident of an acquittal. If his prediction came true, she'd finally be reunited with her son. For the first time since this nightmare began, Hannah felt a glimmer of hope. She could make a new life for herself and Willie.

Hannah tugged at her lip. That meant dealing with Joseph. She'd noticed him out of the corner of her eye as he sat scowling at Andrew and any witness who dared to speak out in her favor.

She stretched her arms over her head and smiled. The high point for her had been Andrew's hard cross-examination of Reverend Green. He had the pompous twit stammering on the witness stand before he'd finished with him. Hannah gave a small chuckle thinking of the way Reverend Green's jaws had come unhinged when Andrew had made his final point. He had asked if he, the good Reverend, would tolerate the beating of a junkyard dog. Reverend Green had responded with a heated *"No!"* Andrew pressed the point home by asking, "Then why did you turn your back on Mrs. Krause? Did a member of the gentler sex deserve less consideration than a dog?"

From behind her, Hannah had heard the wave of twitters floating over the courtroom, and she'd had to fight the desire to turn and look at the spectators.

"Hannah, are you ready?"

She spun to see Sheriff Winter standing by the door. "Good morning," she answered pleasantly.

"Mornin'," he mumbled.

Hannah started, watched him, and was perplexed. As the trial had progressed, his demeanor had brightened, but today he seemed grim.

"Is something wrong?" she asked as he unlocked the cell door.

"No," he replied in a curt voice. "Mr. Lubinus is waiting for you at the courthouse. He'd like to meet with you before today's testimony begins."

Hannah accompanied the sheriff on the short walk to the courthouse. On the way, confusion swept through her. Then she noticed a change in the people that they passed. Lately, she had witnessed a growing sympathy on their faces, but today everyone turned away, refusing to look at her.

Once inside the courthouse, they found Andrew waiting in one of the courtroom's small adjacent rooms. Immaculate as always, he stood at the window with his hands clasped tightly behind his back. He turned when they entered and motioned for her to take a seat at the table.

"Hannah, we need to talk before the trial convenes." He glanced toward the sheriff.

"I'll be waiting in the hallway if you need me," the sheriff said then left, quietly shutting the door.

"Andrew, you're frightening me! Has something happened to Willie?"

"No, Hannah . . . It's about the trial." He took a chair next to her and leaned forward. "I'll be direct. They've found additional evidence."

She shook her head in disbelief. "What kind of evidence?"

"Cutlery."

"Cutlery," she repeated like a parrot.

"Knives, Hannah . . ." He paused. "Knives with a pattern that matches the one used to kill Jacob."

Hannah gripped her hands tightly. "I don't understand."

Andrew sighed loudly. "Abe Engel returned to the farm to see if anything had been missed and found the set of cutlery wrapped in an old dish towel."

"But . . . I've never owned a set like that."

"Really?" One eyebrow shot up. "They were found hidden in the bottom of Willie's dresser."

Hannah's hand flew to her throat. "Wait—you don't think— h-he's a child," she stammered.

"Simmer down," he said sternly. "No one is suggesting that Willie is in any way involved in his father's death."

Hannah gave a gasp of relief and dropped her hand.

"Charles Walker believes you were the one to hide them there." His eyes drilled into Hannah's. "I want you to tell me the truth. Did you kill your husband?"

The flash of hope Hannah had felt earlier died. Andrew had lost faith in her. She bowed her head. "No."

"You still claim never to have seen the knife used to murder Jacob?"

"Yes."

"Can you explain then how they came to be in your house?"

She rose abruptly. "Isn't it obvious? . . . Someone planted them there to make me appear guilty."

Andrew sat back in his chair and stared at her. Gone was his charming demeanor. "How?"

"I don't know," she replied, pacing around the table. "Ida and Louis have been in the courtroom every day while Fannie Thompson watches Willie at her home. Anyone could've entered the empty house and planted them there."

"I don't know if a jury is going to swallow that one," he replied skeptically.

Hannah came to an abrupt halt beside his chair. "Why not?" she asked in an angry voice. "Abe and Sheriff Winter didn't find them the first time they searched the house. How can Charles Walker explain the sudden appearance of this new evidence now?"

"Willie's room was never searched."

Hannah sank onto a chair and bowed her head while a cold sweat trickled down her back. If her lawyer didn't believe her, how could she expect a jury of twelve men, men who had known Jacob and considered him a friend, to find her innocent?

Andrew stood and helped Hannah to her feet. "The knives are circumstantial at best—just like the rest of the evidence. We can still win this." He guided her toward the door. "Are you ready to take the stand?"

Hannah walked back and forth across her cell, her dress swishing around her ankles. She didn't need Andrew to tell her that she'd failed to make her case on the witness stand. Instead of concentrating on Charles Walker as he grilled her unmercifully, she worried that regardless of Andrew's assurances, suspicion might somehow fall on Willie. Rubbing her forehead, she remembered an incident only last year where an eleven-year-old boy in northern Iowa was found guilty of killing his stepmother. No doubt Charles Walker was familiar with that case, and if he failed to convict her, he could set his sights on Willie.

As she hemmed and hawed on the witness stand, she saw the faces of the jury and those in the courtroom change. Gone were the twitters and the compassionate nods. Their eyes watched her with open hostility.

It was a never-ending nightmare.

"Hannah, there's someone here to see you," Sheriff Winter suddenly called from the now open door.

Hannah groaned. She couldn't bear facing Ida right now.

She turned and was shocked to see Joseph follow the sheriff into the jail. Her body stiffened. "I don't want to see him," she said, giving them her back.

"Oh, I think you do, Hannah," Joseph said softly as he sauntered into the room.

"Hannah?" Sheriff Winter called.

Pivoting, Hannah nodded while a smug grin spread across Joseph's face.

"If you don't mind, Sheriff," Joseph said, "I'd like to speak to my stepmother alone."

The sheriff gave Hannah a questioning look, and she nodded again. Frowning, he grabbed the ring of keys and stepped outside, closing the door behind him.

"What do you want?" Hannah asked, crossing her arms over her chest.

Joseph strolled over to her cell until he faced her through the bars. "Things didn't go too well in court today, did they?"

Hannah glowered at him without answering.

He stuck his hands in his pockets and rocked back on his heels. "In fact, I'd say the outcome is pretty iffy right now."

"I didn't kill your father."

"Well, someone sure as hell *did*," he exclaimed, grabbing the bars to her cell, "*didn't they?*"

Hannah dropped her arms and jerked back. "What do you want?" she asked in a weary voice.

"The farm."

"It's always about the land, isn't it?" she asked, then gave a brittle laugh.

His face flushed. "It's all I have left," he shot back as he withdrew a sheaf of papers from the inner pocket of his jacket. "You're going to sign this quit-claim deed, giving me the farm."

"The estate isn't settled."

"It doesn't make a difference. Once it is, this deed will give it all to me."

"Not Willie's share."

"You're his guardian—it signs over his share, too."

"No, I'm not."

Hannah watched with satisfaction as Joseph's eyes widened in shock. "I signed over guardianship to Ida and Louis."

His lips twisted in a nasty sneer. "You think you've found a way out of this, don't you?" He studied her carefully. "If you're found guilty, which you will be after today, there's nothing stopping me from taking your sister and her sissified husband into court and suing for custody . . ." He paused and let his words soak in. "I'm a member of this community and they're nothing more than a couple of outsiders. Who do you think the judge is going to side with?"

Hannah thought back to her time on the witness stand and the faces of her neighbors. They were against her now. Would those feelings spill over onto Ida and Louis? And would those feelings be enough to influence a judge?

She walked to the window and saw Essie and her brothers playing in the yard. The peals of their laughter stabbed her heart. If Joseph ever got his hand on Willie, her son would never know laughter again. If she was found innocent, Ida and Louis would help her until she found a way to support herself and Willie. She wouldn't like relying on their charity, but it was better than risking Willie's happiness on the outcome of the trial.

Her decision was made. "I'll sign."

Joseph hurried over to the desk and grabbed a pen.

"Wait," Hannah called out. "Not tonight—tomorrow. That will give you enough time to draw up a second document stating that you will never . . . *never*," she insisted, "fight Ida and Louis's guardianship."

Shortly after Joseph had left in a huff, Nora brought in Hannah's supper.

"Nora, may I have a pen and a piece of paper?"

"Of course," she said, taking both from the desk and handing them to Hannah. "Are you writing a note to your son?"

"No . . . to my sister," she replied, sitting on the cot. "And when I'm finished, would you have Abe or your husband deliver it?" She glanced up at Nora and tried to hide the grief threatening to overcome her. "It's important that she receives it tonight."

Hannah ignored Nora's frown and tried to organize her words. This really was for the best, she thought as she began to write:

My Dearest Sister,

With heavy heart, I compose this missive. Today's events have convinced me that this community is no longer safe for my son. I have done all that I can to protect him from the machinations of others, but fear for his future if he remains here.

Therefore, I must most earnestly beg you to take my darling boy and return to your home. Only then will I feel at ease, once he is safely away from those who have no care for his interests.

If you have ever loved me, dear sister, please do this last thing for me. And do not think that you are abandoning me in my time of need. No one could have asked for a better companion than the one I have always found in you. I know that although the dis-

tance between us will be great, I will always be in your thoughts and prayers as you are in mine.

I am entrusting you with my most precious posses-sion, my son, and I know you will not fail me.

Ever, your loving sister,
Hannah

Chapter 37

Hannah could barely stand attending the trial every day. The stares and the whispers had grown during Charles Walker's summation, and even Andrew had watched her with angry eyes. The only blessing was that Joseph no longer sat with the spectators. He'd gotten what he wanted. Her only relief the past couple of days had been her conversations with Essie. At least the sheriff and his family hadn't turned against her, but she saw the worry in Nora's face each time she brought Hannah her meals or took a moment to visit. Andrew would present his closing argument tomorrow and then the ordeal would be over.

And Willie was safe. She'd received the telegram from Ida yesterday. That knowledge had given her the strength to face her accusers.

Now she waited impatiently to meet with Andrew. He said he had an important matter to discuss with her, and she prayed it wasn't more bogus evidence.

Finally he arrived, and Hannah was shocked to see him accompanied by Charles Walker. She waited silently until she'd been released from her cell, and the sheriff had left.

After taking a seat at the desk, she looked up at both men. "What's this about?"

"Hannah," Andrew began in a condescending voice, "Mr. Walker has a proposition that I believe has merit and I'd like you to hear him out." He turned expectantly to Charles.

Charles cleared his throat and, hooking his thumbs under his suspenders, studied her. "Mrs. Krause, the events of July second have torn this community apart, but I believe Andrew and I have come up with a solution to heal the rift." His attention stole toward Andrew and he nodded for Charles to continue. "After much consideration and a lengthy discussion between myself, Andrew, and Judge Preston, we are dropping the charge of murder in the first degree—"

Hannah's breath caught in her throat.

"Instead," he went on, "Mr. Lubinus will enter a plea of 'irresistible impulse.'"

"In other words, I plead guilty even though I'm not?"

Andrew and Charles exchanged a look. "Not really," Andrew said smoothly, "it means that you weren't in your right mind therefore not responsible for your actions."

Hannah shot to her feet, tipping over her chair. "In other words, say I lost my mind and killed Jacob?"

"Now, Hannah, calm down," Andrew said in a soothing voice. "Mr. Walker is being quite reasonable. There's every chance that you'll lose."

Hannah noticed that he didn't mention it would also be his defeat.

"This whole sordid mess can be put behind us and—"

"Don't you mean buried?" she broke in.

"Not at all," he insisted. "Testimony has shown that Jacob had driven you to your breaking point. You had sought help and were refused. And in a fit of rage, or maybe as an act of self-defense, you killed him." He lifted one shoulder. "The community will be much more comfortable and sympathetic to that scenario versus one in which you're a cold-blooded killer."

"And we must make sure everyone is comfortable," she said in a voice dripping with bitterness.

Charles ignored her statement. "Are you really sure that isn't what might have happened? Isn't it possible that you suffered a blackout? After all, Joseph testified that you were acting strangely that night."

Unbelievable. "I had just found my husband *murdered* in his bed," she cried. "*How* is one supposed to act under those circumstances?"

"Hannah, think of your son," Andrew said, trying a different approach. "Do you want him to grow up believing that his mother is a murderess?"

"He knows I'm innocent."

"What about others? If you're convicted, it will be a blot on your son's entire life. When he's of age, no self-respecting family would welcome his courtship of their daughter. No employer would consider his application. His life would be ruined."

"And if his mother was declared insane? That would be better?"

Charles quickly jumped in. "Irresistible impulse only means a momentary loss of reason."

She eyed both men shrewdly. "And if I agree, I'd go free?"

"Umm . . . well . . . not exactly," Andrew began, but Charles cut him off.

"What Andrew is trying to explain . . . You would have to be admitted to a hospital and evaluated by a doctor. It has to be ascertained that you're not a danger to yourself or society, but," he said quickly, "I'm sure if you were reasonable and cooperated, you'd be released in no time at all."

Hannah's eyes narrowed as she looked first at Charles, then Andrew. They were lying. Hospital be damned—they were talking about an insane asylum. They were both unsure about what the verdict might be and were trying to save their reputations.

Folding her hands at her waist, she kept her expression calm, belying the terror she felt inside. "No. I won't do it. I'll take my chances with the jury."

Both men stood simultaneously. Andrew went to the door and called for the sheriff.

"I'm sorry, Mrs. Krause," Charles said as he moved toward the door. "This visit was really just a courtesy. Mr. Lubinus as your attorney of record has already entered your plea."

Hannah's knees gave way and she grabbed the desk for support.

"Transportation to the Mt. Pleasant Asylum has already been arranged. You will leave later this evening." He paused at the door. "If you do ever expect to be released, I suggest you try being more cooperative than you have today."

Numbly, Hannah allowed the sheriff to escort her back to her cell. Anger warred with terror. An insane asylum—she'd heard stories . . . suddenly the sound of voices coming from the open window cut through her misery.

"I think that went well," she heard Andrew say.

Charles snorted. "No, it didn't. If she continues to act this way, she'll die in that asylum."

"Oh," Andrew replied, disappointment evident in his voice. "I really thought that—"

"Don't worry about it, son," Charles answered companionably, "you gave your client the best representation possible under the circumstances."

"But maybe it would have—"

"Now, now, this isn't the time for second thoughts," Charles interjected. "What were you telling me about your plans to run for state representative? I do believe an old classmate of mine, Senator Baldwin, might be of assistance . . ." His voice trailed away as they moved from the window.

Rage drove her to the cot. Sold out. If they couldn't shut her up, they'd lock her up. She wouldn't allow it. Willie was safe, so all she had to worry about was herself. She kicked at the bed. They thought to silence her, did they? She didn't know how, but someday she'd beat them. She'd figure out a way to win. And before they carted her off, there was one score she could settle.

She wasn't sure if he'd come when she'd asked Sheriff Winter to send for him, but here he was, enjoying his last opportunity to gloat.

"Good evening, Joseph," she said calmly.

"I don't think it so good for you, Hannah," he answered with a smirk. "Talk's all over town that they've decided you're crazy."

She allowed herself a slight grin. "There's only one crazy person in this room, Joseph, and it isn't me."

His face paled, but he replied with bravado. "I hope you enjoy life in the insane asylum."

Hannah moved slowly to the cell door, her eyes never leaving Joseph's face. "Your father tried to break me for years and failed. I won't be silenced, Joseph," she said softly. "Someday, I'll be free and then—"

"Then what?" he blustered. "Are you threatening me?"

"No," she replied in an even voice. "It's not necessary—" she paused. "I know what you did," she continued in a whisper.

"I didn't have *nothing* to do with any of this," he declared loudly.

Her eyes glinted. "Oh, yes, you did. You've been working behind the scene the whole time, pulling strings. Where did you get the knives you used to frame me, Joseph? Did you order them from a catalog? The sheriff said one could still buy them."

"I don't know what you're talking about."

"I think you do."

He puffed out his chest. "Say what you want—no one's going to believe the talk of a crazy woman."

"Maybe, maybe not," she replied with a shrug. "I guess you really don't care. You got what you wanted."

"Damn right," he cried, spittle flying from his lips.

She crossed her arms over her chest and stared him down. He looked away.

"You have the farm now, but that's all you'll ever have," she said in a strong voice. "Violence begets violence and your father was a violent man." She studied him closely, gauging the effect of her words. "So are you. Oh, you'll put on the façade of a successful man, but you'll never know peace. You can never escape your heritage. It will haunt you and yours forever."

His eyes darted toward the door. "I don't have to listen to this," he said as he started backing away.

"That's right, Joseph, run. Run back to the land you wanted so desperately—but remember one thing. 'The sins of the father . . .'"

He bolted out the door with the sound of her laughter ringing in his ears.

Chapter 38

Fall 2012, the Braxton County Jail

Sometime during the night, Kate's fear shut off. It was the oddest sensation. She was aware of the danger she faced. Once the forensics lab finished their tests, there was a good chance she'd be arrested for Joe's murder; and unless her attorney was able to convince the jury of her innocence, she *would* go to prison.

Yet she felt clearheaded and detached.

Sitting on her cot, she shook her head—amazed at the way she felt. Perhaps her mind and body could only take the rush of adrenaline that her fear had caused for a short period of time. Did Hannah experience this same feeling all those years ago?

Shortly after Kate had finished her breakfast in her cell, one of the deputies came to escort her across the street to the courthouse. He handcuffed her and shackled her ankles. Once outside in the frosty morning air, Kate kept her head up and her attention focused straight ahead. She noticed the passersby out of the corner of her eye. She knew they were there watching, but she had no desire to meet their stares with one of her own.

When they reached the courthouse, a man was waiting inside the door for them. With a nod to the deputy, he approached Kate.

"Kate, I'm Darwin Brown. Rose Clement hired me to represent you. Do you agree?" he asked.

Kate observed the man standing before her. He was dressed immaculately in a tailored suit and possessed a full head of snow white hair, worn a little longer in the back. He reminded her of a lion.

"I trust Rose's judgment, Mr. Brown," she replied softly.

"Good," he said in a cultured voice. He glanced over to the deputy. "May I have a room to talk with my client?"

Mr. Brown followed Kate and the deputy as he led them to a small room on the second floor.

"Have a seat," Mr. Brown said, motioning toward a conference table with chairs place around it. "How are you doing?"

"I'm okay," Kate replied briefly.

"Rose filled me in on what has been happening as far as the investigation into your husband's murder, but I'd like to hear it in your own words."

With a sigh, Kate told her story for what seemed to be the hundredth time. Mr. Brown took notes.

When she finished, he tapped his pen on the table and read quickly over what he'd written.

"Can you think of anything else?"

"No."

"Right now all they have is an aggravated weapons charge. The minimum penalty for that is a fine of two hundred fifty dollars and probation. The maximum is one thousand five hundred and two years."

Kate's breath caught.

"I'm not very worried about that charge. *But*," he stressed, "the county attorney is going to push to hold you until the DNA tests come back."

"How long?"

"Well," he said with a slight smile, "it doesn't play out in real life like it does on television, so a week, maybe ten days."

Her heart thumped. "I'd have to stay in jail that long?"

"Not if we can help it. They did get a search warrant and are executing it this morning." He peeked at his watch. "Probably as we speak."

"Mr. Brown—"

"Please," he broke in, "call me Darwin."

"Darwin—you didn't ask me if I'm innocent."

He smiled compassionately. "Rose thinks you are and that's good enough for me." He collected his notes and stood. "Ready? Let's see if we can get you out of that ugly orange outfit."

A few minutes later, Kate found herself sitting before the magistrate with Mr. Brown at her side. She listened as he went back and forth with the county attorney concerning her bail and release. She had the same sense of aloofness as she had experienced sitting in her cell. Her thoughts returned to Hannah.

Hannah had been torn from her child. Kate couldn't imagine the pain that had caused her. She remembered the vow she'd made to Trudy—history wouldn't repeat itself. But here she was, just like Hannah. A need to learn what really happened between Hannah and Jacob took root.

Mr. Brown's light touch on her arm drew her away from her thoughts. He gave a slight nod toward the magistrate.

Kate forced herself to focus.

"We keep going over the same ground," the magistrate said impatiently, directing his words to the county attorney. "Are you charging her with first-degree murder or not?"

"Not at this time."

"Then all I have before me at this time is a weapons charge. Not a gun or a switchblade. A common kitchen knife, is that correct?"

"Yes, but—"

"No 'buts.' Given that this could be part of a larger investigation, I'll take that into consideration in setting bail. The defendant is released on a five-thousand-dollar bond."

A couple hours later, dressed in her own clothes, Kate was free. When she saw Will and Rose waiting for her outside the jail, she collapsed with relief into Rose's arms.

"Rose, I can't thank you enough," Kate said, taking a step back.

Rose draped her arm over Kate's shoulder. "It's okay. Will's car is parked over here. Let's get you home."

After Will had Kate settled in the backseat, they started toward Dutton.

"What happened?" Will asked with a quick glance at Kate in the rearview mirror.

Kate quickly explained.

"What did the knife look like?" Will asked.

"A kitchen knife. A long thin blade with a black handle."

Rose turned in her seat to face Kate. "A boning knife?"

"I guess," Kate said with a shake of her head. "All I know is that I've never seen it before and have no idea how it got in the Jeep."

Will glanced in the mirror again. "They're easily acquired. The store probably carries five different brands of cutlery that would match that description. Did it have any distinguishing marks?"

"It was just a knife," Kate answered disjointedly. "Either someone is playing a cruel trick, or they're trying to implicate me in Joe's death. I guess I'll know which when the DNA results are in."

Rose turned her attention to Will. "Who would do something like this?" she asked, aghast.

"If we knew that, Rose," Will answered gently, "we'd know who killed Joe."

Kate leaned her head against the window. "I do know this—my fingerprints aren't on it."

"Then the only thing they have linking you to the knife is where it was found," Will reasoned.

"Right, and all Mr. Brown has to do is convince a jury that I'm telling the truth and knew nothing about it."

Kate thought back to the article about Hannah. Not only had Hannah been tried in front of a jury, she'd also been tried in the court of public opinion. Gazing out the window at the passing scenery, Kate wondered if the same fate awaited her. Of course it did. The parallels between now and then were frightening. She leaned forward.

"Rose, I have to know what happened to Hannah," Kate pleaded.

Slowly, Rose began to shake her head. Kate jerked forward and placed her hand on the back of the front seat.

"Wait before you answer," Kate begged. "Don't you see? History is repeating itself."

"No, it's not," Will interjected. "Hannah's story has no relationship to what's happening to you."

Kate fell back against the seat. "How do you know?"

She caught Will looking at her in the mirror.

"It can't, Kate," he said in a soft voice. "Your stress is making you grasp at straws."

"I don't care what you think," she shot back defiantly. "There's some kind of connection. It's too big of a coincidence."

Will sighed. "Becoming obsessed with an old murder can't be healthy for you."

"I'm not crazy," she mumbled.

She caught the look Rose gave to Will, but let it pass.

"Let it go," Will said after a moment. "Let's concentrate on clearing your name."

Chapter 39

Fall 2012, the Krause family farm

As soon as Will's car pulled in the driveway, Agnes Forsyth came running out of the house and headed toward her car.

Kate caught the fearful glance Agnes had cast toward Will's vehicle. *Wonderful.* Agnes would have the gossip mill churning before nightfall, and she'd be judged just as Hannah had been.

"I'd better not go in," Will said over his shoulder as Kate exited the car. "I don't want to upset Trudy."

"No. According to Joe's will, the house is mine, at least for now. And I'm tired of worrying about who's allowed in and who isn't. We're friends and Trudy needs to learn how to deal with it," Kate insisted.

Reluctantly, Will followed Kate and Rose into the house. Inside, Trudy took one look at him and, waving a finger in his direction, whirled on Kate.

"*What's* he doing here?" she bellowed.

"As of today, the feud is over," Kate said wearily. "Will is a friend and as long as I live here, he's welcome."

Trudy's lips thinned into a straight line. "Joseph Krause is rolling in his grave," she declared, then flew over to the music box and grasped it in her hands. "If you've come for this, you can't have it. Joe's grandfather gave it to me. It stays here."

"I don't want your music box," Will said calmly. "I don't want anything that belongs to you."

"Liar," she cried out. "Hannah gave Joseph the farm and your family has never gotten over it."

Will shook his head. "Not true. I think we've been better off without it. I can't see where all this land has brought your family much happiness."

Rose placed a hand on Will's arm. "Maybe you were right, Will. We're upsetting Trudy. We'd better go." She walked over to Kate and gave her a hug. "You get some rest. And if you need anything, call."

"I will," she replied with a hesitant nod.

Saddened, Kate watched Will's car slowly pull out of the drive, leaving her alone with Trudy. She heard her come up behind her.

"The sheriff was here," she said brusquely.

"I know," Kate replied, continuing to watch out the window.

"They searched the house."

"Know that, too, Trudy."

"They think you killed Joe," she said with a malicious note in her voice.

Kate whirled and faced her. "Well, I didn't," she said, moving past her. As she headed for the stairs, she heard Trudy muttering.

"Just like Hannah."

• • •

Unwilling to tolerate Trudy's glaring presence or listen to any of her nonsense about curses or Will and Rose, or how Kate might be a murder suspect, she hid out in the back bedroom. She tried to rest as Rose had recommended, but Hannah's story kept buzzing through her mind.

What happened in this house? she thought as she stared up at the ceiling. Will was right—owning this land hadn't brought Joe's family much happiness. Their history was littered with tragedy—almost as if a judgment had been rendered against them.

Sounds from downstairs caught her attention. Trudy was playing that stupid music box again. Her son was dead, but it seemed that all she cared about was that music box.

Kate swung her legs over the side of the bed and tried to ignore the music. The way the tune skipped a note was driving her insane. If it weren't so valuable, she'd steal it away from Trudy and smash the damn thing. *At least have it fixed so it plays properly.*

She stood and paced to the window. Pulling back the curtain, she stared out over the farm. Whether or not she'd be arrested again was out of her hands. She'd told the truth and it was going to be up to Mr. Brown to build her defense.

Turning away, she looked at the boxes stacked in the corner and the empty storage containers sitting next to them. She couldn't do anything about the present, but she could try and make sense of the past.

She picked up a nail file lying on the dresser, then knelt

beside the box containing the photo albums. Carefully, she went through each album, running the file under each picture. She hoped to discover another article or maybe a note—something that would shed light on Hannah's mystery.

Finally, she'd finished the last of the albums and found nothing. Only the shoe box containing the portrait of Jacob and Hannah remained. Reluctantly, she picked it up, took off the lid, and began to remove the pictures.

Once that box was empty and all the portraits were stacked on the floor, she noticed something. The one of Jacob and Hannah had disappeared. She peeked into the larger box. It was empty, too.

When she'd entered the room earlier, she'd noticed that the room had been searched and had assumed her bedroom was listed on the warrant, but that picture wouldn't be considered evidence in a murder trial. She sat back and looked around the room but didn't see it lying about.

She hated that picture. Handling it spooked her, so she should be relieved it was missing.

What next? Her attention wandered the room. The attic. She'd never been up there.

Once she'd climbed the narrow stairs and stood in the dust-covered room, she wondered about the wisdom of her idea. The area was packed with *stuff*. Boxes were stacked haphazardly in the corners; old trunks sat in the middle of the room. She spied a moth-eaten dressmaker's dummy leaning precariously against a chair, its stuffing sticking out in puffs.

With a sigh, she crossed to the first trunk and began her quest.

Two hours later, all she had to show for her trouble was a lot of sweat and a lot of dirt.

The Krause family had thrown nothing away in the 140 years that they had lived in this house. The trunks and boxes were full of nothing but junk—broken dishes and toys; books with the covers gnawed by mice; pieces of material that fell apart when touched.

Kate stood and shoved her hands on her hips while she thought about where she could search next. She snapped her fingers. The old cabin.

After washing the dirt from her face, Kate went to the kitchen. Trudy stood at the sink peeling potatoes.

Kate walked over to the key rack and began to thumb through the various key rings hanging there.

"Which one is the key to the padlock on the old cabin?" Kate asked.

"It's empty," Trudy replied, tossing a potato into a pan. "Nobody ever goes in there."

"Which key?" Kate repeated.

"The one with the red tag," she answered in a disgruntled voice.

Kate grabbed it and headed out of the house. When she reached the cabin, she inserted the key and unlocked the padlock. She pushed the door open and stepped inside.

The pale light shining through dirty windows revealed an empty room. Cobwebs hung in swaths from the beamed ceiling while dust obscured the wide plank floor. A fireplace was at one end and a long work counter at the other. Stairs to the left of the fireplace led to a loft. The air was cold yet at the same time musty, and if Kate wasn't mistaken, it also smelled of dead rodents.

Wrinkling her nose, Kate eyed the stairs. While she was there, she might as well check out the loft. Mindful of any skittering creatures that lurked in the corners, Kate crept toward the stairs and gingerly tried the first step. It stayed solid under her weight. Step by step, she climbed until she was in the loft.

Because it was chillier here than the floor below, Kate shivered as she swatted at cobwebs in front of her. Squinting, she spied a tarp covering something in the corner. Again she tested the strength of the old boards, and once she was convinced that she wouldn't tumble through the floor, she crossed to the tarp. She grabbed it and tossed it to the side.

Another trunk—much older than the ones in the attic. A name had been scrawled on the side, but the spidery handwriting was too faint for Kate to read.

She knelt and opened the lid. A blackened set of cutlery lay on top. Next she found a stack of books. She opened a cover and, holding it up to the light, saw the copyright listed as 1850. With a shake of her head she carefully laid the book on the dusty floor. One by one, she gently removed the objects from the old trunk and placed them next to the book. She discovered a graceful figure of a shepherdess, a fragile blue vase, a box of buttons. These things really should be in a museum.

When she'd reached the bottom of the trunk, only one more item remained. Another book—only it was in sad condition. Kate ran her fingers over the cover. Deep gouges obliterated the title and its author. Flipping it open, she saw that both the title page and copyright page had been ripped out. She slowly turned the pages, scanning them as she went. The book was a series of essays, but without the two missing pages, she couldn't tell when it had been written. She abruptly stopped when one chapter title caught her eye.

"The Sins of the Father."

Kate quickly read the first paragraph. The author was making a point about how, in families, violence can perpetuate violence. Immediately her thoughts flew to Joe and the revelations he had made about his childhood. She anxiously turned the page.

Nothing.

The rest of the chapter had been ripped from the book. She could still see the ragged edges sticking out from the binding.

Wanting to make a closer examination of the book, she quickly replaced the rest of the objects back in the trunk and stood. She had taken one step when she heard a noise from the main room of the cabin. Not the scraping of mice running across the floor, but the clump of heavy boots.

Alarmed, she clasped the book to her chest and held her breath. When she heard the sound of the door slamming shut, a lungful of air came out in a whoosh. She tore out of the loft and down the stairs, still clinging to the book. She pushed at the door.

It didn't budge. She was trapped in the old cabin.

Chapter 40

Kate ran over to the window and tried to force it open. It was stuck tight. Outside the cabin, the shadows of the trees were creeping across the ground. Soon it'd be nightfall, and the last thing she wanted was to spend the night locked in this old cabin. She placed the book on the floor and pushed at the window frame with both hands. It still wouldn't move. *If I could just pry it open.* She remembered the box of cutlery.

She went to the loft, then returned with a couple of the old knives. Taking one, she carefully jammed its blade between the sill and the frame and ran it along the width of the window, cutting through the layers of paint. She repeated the procedure on each side and along the top. Placing both hands at the top of the frame, she pushed again.

The window moved a centimeter. She repeated the procedure again. The window frame raised a little more. She scraped again and again as the shadows grew longer and the room colder. The hair on the back of her neck prickled, and a thin sheen of sweat gathered on her top lip. She felt a rising sense of panic and urgency.

She gave the window another try, and if it didn't work this time, she'd break the glass. She had to get out of the cabin. Finally, the window slid far enough for her to wedge her body through and to toss a leg over the sill. Then she lost her balance and tumbled to the ground, landing flat on her back. Winded, she stared up at the sky and let relief flow through her. She was free.

The book. After scrambling to her feet, she went to the door. The latch had fallen back into place, but the padlock still lay on the ground where she'd left it. She pulled hard, expecting it to be stuck, then stumbled backward as the door opened easily. Perplexed, she propped it open with a nearby rock and went to retrieve the book.

Kate returned to the house and heard Trudy's TV playing loudly as she went up to her room, where she set the book down. She showered quickly, then dressed in a pair of sweats and sat cross-legged on the bed, skimming the book's pages one by one.

It was a series of essays, specifically about family life and the role of women. Based on the way the subject matter was discussed, Kate deduced that the book had to have been written before women had the right to vote.

As she read, she thought of the things she had always taken for granted. She could vote, run for a political office, receive an education, hold a job outside of the home. She had choices that the women of the early 1900s were never given. This was the world Hannah had lived in?

She closed the book and stared at it thoughtfully. If this book was published in the early 1900s, as she suspected, the author must have caused quite a stir. Running her hands over the front of the book, Kate began thinking—whichever Krause had acquired this hadn't been a fan, as witnessed by the gouged cover and the torn-out pages. Without a publication date or a title, she had no way of discovering who had been the author, and she knew nothing of twentieth-century women's literature.

But Rose did.

After shoving her feet into a pair of tennis shoes, she grabbed the book and headed out of the house.

Rose answered her door with a look of surprise. "You're supposed to be home resting," she said as she motioned Kate into the house.

"I know, and if it's too late to talk, I can come back tomorrow," Kate answered in a rush.

"It's fine." She eyed the book in Kate's hand. "What have you been up to?" she asked with a note of suspicion in her voice.

"I went through the attic and the old cabin," Kate said, following Rose into the kitchen.

Rose shot a look over her shoulder. "You're not still focused on Hannah, are you?"

Kate pulled out a chair and plopped down at the table, placing the book in front of her. "Can't you see the similarities?" she asked. "Both men were stabbed and their wives were arrested."

"Not yet," Rose pointed out. "No charges have been brought against you."

"No, but that's where it's headed as soon as the tests come back." She tapped the book nervously. "And there's nothing I can do about it. Either they're going to arrest me or not. But I can try and figure out what happened one hundred and twenty-two years ago."

"Kate," Rose began in an exasperated voice, "you can't solve a murder that happened over a century ago."

"Maybe not solve, but I can find some answers." She leaned forward. "You were close to your great-grandfather. Who did he think killed Jacob?"

Rose rolled her eyes, but answered. "He didn't speak of it often, but as I recall I overheard him tell Essie that he suspected one of Jacob's neighbors, but his suspicions weren't proof. The man's sister gave him an alibi."

"Anyone else?"

"There were the same kind of rumors floating around then as now: an indigent—someone passing through the area."

"Other than the fact Hannah was his wife, why did suspicion fall on her?"

Rose pursed her lips. "Jacob was abusive and everyone had turned a blind eye." Her face grew grim. "Women didn't have a lot of choices back then. Divorce caused a scandal, and there were the children to consider. They belonged to the husband, and it was within his rights to deprive his ex-wife of any contact with them." She shook her head sadly. "It's only been in the recent past that we've created women's shelters. Back then, they had nowhere to go if their families weren't in a position to help them."

"So Hannah allegedly killed out of either revenge or self-defense?"

"Yes," she answered with hesitation.

"Your great-grandfather didn't buy into that?"

"No, and neither did Essie." An angry light flared in Rose's eyes. "You're picking scabs off some very old wounds—of both my family's and Will's."

"Why is looking for the truth reopening old hurts?"

"Not solving Jacob's murder was the biggest regret of my great-grandfather's life, and we've always let it be." She gave a tired sigh. "Then there's Will's family. His great-grandfather, Willie, lost not only his birthright, but his mother."

"Will said Hannah's arrest changed his great-grandfather's life, but I assumed it was because she was arrested." Confusion was written on Kate's face. "Will said she wasn't convicted."

Rose leaned back in her chair and studied Kate. "You're not going to let this go, are you?"

"No, I'm not."

"You want the truth?" she asked, leaning forward abruptly. "Her attorney and the county attorney made a deal without Hannah's knowledge. It was determined that she was not guilty due to 'uncontrollable impulse.'"

Kate's eyebrows shot up. "An insanity plea?"

"Yes, and they confined her to an insane asylum. Willie was taken away and raised by her sister and brother-in-law."

Kate's mouth had dropped open and she snapped it shut before speaking. "Those were terrible places," she declared.

Some of the anger seemed to leave Rose. "Yes, they were. Inmates often lived in substandard conditions. Some were beaten. They were isolated and not allowed any contact with family or friends." Her lips tightened. "If a body wasn't crazy going in, they would be shortly after living under those circumstances."

Kate remembered how she'd felt last night locked up in the jail cell. Sympathy for Hannah flooded her. The woman had lost everything, her home, her child, and never received a reprieve.

"How did Willie ever survive the trauma?"

"He had a good home with his aunt and uncle and went on to become a doctor." Rose traced a line across the table. "But I don't think he ever got over the way his mother had been treated. He seldom spoke of her."

"Is that why Will won't talk about her?"

"Yes. We've come a long way since then, when it comes to the treatment of mental illness. But even now, it carries a stigma." She tugged on her lip. "Even today, there are those who view it as a genetic defect and one that can be passed on to children."

" 'The sins of the father,' " Kate murmured.

Rose looked at her sharply. "What did you say?"

"It's in this book." She handed it to Rose. "There's an essay in here entitled that, but it's talking about violence not insanity. At least I think it is. Most of the chapter's been ripped out."

Rose's eyes narrowed as she stared at the book. "Where did you get this?"

"I found it in a trunk out in the old cabin." A realization dawned in Kate's mind. "You recognize this book, don't you? Do you know who the author is?"

"I don't know what you're talking about," Rose said quickly and handed the book back to Kate. "I'm not familiar with this at all."

"But, Rose, your grandmother was an early-twentieth-century writer, so was this person. Take a look at it and maybe you will recognize it." She pushed the book toward her.

Rose's attention darted away. "No, I won't. I'm too old to re-member such things."

Bullshit. There wasn't a thing wrong with Rose's mind or her memory.

"Rose," she said painfully, "I don't believe you."

Rose abruptly stood. "I'm sorry to hear you say that." She glanced at the clock. "It's getting late and you don't want to leave Trudy for too long."

Dismissed, Kate picked up her book and left, but on the way home her mind spun with questions.

Hannah had been unjustly locked away, and according to Trudy, this cursed their branch of the family. If Trudy was correct, then logically Hannah must've held her stepson Joseph responsible for what happened to her. Why?

And Willie's birthright—how did it manage to fall to his brother? She understood why Hannah hadn't inherited a portion of the farm, but it didn't explain Willie not receiving his share.

Will had minimized the bad blood between his side of the family and Joe's, but both he and Rose clammed up whenever she brought up Hannah. She'd heard the pride in his voice when he'd spoken of his great-grandfather Willie. Did he harbor more resentment over Willie's fate than he let on?

A terrible thought occurred to her.

Was it deep enough to seek revenge?

Chapter 41

Fall 2012, the Clement family farm

As Rose watched Kate pull out of the driveway, her heart ached for her young friend. She wanted to help her, but old loyalties superseded new friendships. She picked up her cell phone and dialed Will's number.

He answered on the second ring.

"Kate was here and she found a book in the old cabin," she said without preamble.

"Okay—"

She cut him off. "A book containing essays. One is titled 'The Sins of the Father.'"

"Oh." Will was silent for a moment. "Did you tell her?"

"No. There's no time limit on promises, Will." She paused. "I did tell her about the verdict and Hannah's incarceration."

"That's it?"

"Yes."

"She's not going to give up, is she?"

"No. She doesn't want to face what might come about over the next few days, and she's using this quest of hers as a distraction." Rose began to pace back and forth in front of the window. "She's truly convinced that if she learns the truth about Jacob and Hannah, it will help her out of her situation."

"What can we do?"

"You've tried to get her to drop it?"

"Yes, and it didn't work. Can you think of anything else she might find?"

"How would I know?" Rose replied in a frustrated voice. "Who would've suspected that she'd find that old newspaper article or that book? It's been out of print for decades."

"How do you suppose a Krause wound up with a copy?"

"I imagine it was sent to them. And from the looks of it, they didn't appreciate the gift—the cover was obliterated and the essay was ripped out."

Will snickered.

"It's not funny," she declared. "Not if you want to protect your secrets. I'd hate to see reputations that have stood for a long time destroyed."

"I wonder which one of the mighty Krauses received the book? Joseph or his son?"

"Joseph, I would think. No one else would get the connection."

"Hmm," his voice grew thoughtful. "Maybe I should pay Kate a visit tomorrow. Offer to help her look for clues."

"Then lead her in a different direction?"

"It's worth a try."

Chapter 42

Fall 2012, the Krause family farm

Kate was upset by her conversation with Rose. She could try pumping Trudy for information, but she'd have to get past all of her mutterings about curses and ghosts.

She found her sitting on the back porch, watching the sun climb higher in the morning sky.

"I'm sorry if Will upset you yesterday," she said.

A steely look from Trudy was her only response. She tried another topic.

"I found an old trunk out in the cabin."

"That would be the one that belonged to Joseph's mother, Suzanne," she replied, rocking back and forth. "She was a Southerner."

"No one ever mentions her. She must've died young."

"She did."

"How?"

"She fell down the cellar steps and broke her neck."

Kate looked out over the farm. A cool morning breeze stirred the autumn leaves, and in the distance, she heard birds singing. She shivered. One would never know that three tragic deaths had occurred in such a peaceful setting.

"How old was Joseph when his mother died?"

"About eight or nine, I guess," she answered with a shrug.

"Then Jacob married Hannah?"

Trudy's lip curled. "He'd have been better leaving that one alone."

"I know she was confined to a mental institution," Kate said quietly.

"They should've hanged her." Trudy rocked a little faster.

If Kate wanted to avoid one of her tirades, she needed to proceed carefully.

"So the family's always believed she was guilty?"

Trudy faced her with eyes blazing. "Of course she was guilty. Her and that boy were the only ones in the house that night."

"Not Joseph?"

"No, he didn't get along with Hannah, so he stayed in the old cabin."

"What about Willie? Did Joseph get along with Willie?"

"That boy was a pampered brat. He didn't deserve this place."

"He signed it over to his brother?"

"No. Hannah did." Her eyes narrowed. "Why are you asking all these questions?"

"Just curious. So Hannah signed it over to Joseph before the trial?"

"Yes, and contrary to what that Will Krause's family has always claimed, it was legal." She frowned. "Always made me sick listening to people rattle on about 'the good doctor' and how we cheated him."

"You mean Willie?"

"His mother was a crazy murderer." She gave Kate a sly look. "I'm not too sure that he wasn't just like her. Bet you've never heard anything about him attending Charles Walker's death bed?"

"Who's Charles Walker?"

"Humph, that's what I thought. No one ever talks about that." She settled back in the chair. "Charles Walker was the county attorney who charged Hannah. I always thought it was kind of funny that Willie was present for the death of the man who locked up his ma."

"You think he killed him?" Kate asked in a shocked voice.

"Not saying he did, but that family's not as lily white as they'd like everyone to think." She smiled with satisfaction. "Joe knew, and one of these days, he was going to let it out." She turned her attention to Kate. "You're asking a lot of questions about the past when you've got worries of your own right now. They think you killed my son."

The directness of her words shocked Kate.

"You know I wasn't here until after you drove Joe to the hospital." She leaned forward. "What happened that day?"

"I already told the sheriff," she answered in a bitter voice.

"Did Joe say anything? Did he tell you who'd hurt him?"

Trudy rubbed her forehead with a trembling hand. "I don't remember—it all happened so fast—Joe's shirt turning red with blood—" She stopped, her face stricken. "Why are you trying to make me remember? I tried to save him. I didn't want my son to die."

Kate reached out to her. "Trudy—"

She pushed herself to her feet and glared down at Kate. "You—you brought this on us. If you never came here, this wouldn't have happened."

Doing an about-face, Trudy scurried into the house. The door slammed, and a moment later, Kate heard the music box begin to play.

Questioning Trudy hadn't brought Kate any closer to the truth. She never got the chance to ask her about the book she'd found in the cabin. Rose and Will weren't going to tell her anything. The only place left was to check at the library. They might recognize the essays.

As Kate walked into the library, she felt eyes watching her, but she ignored them. However, it was hard to disregard the librarian's look of disapproval when she approached the counter.

"May I help you?" the librarian asked in a grim voice.

"I found this book," Kate replied, placing it on the counter, "and I wondered if you might know the title and the author. As you can see it's in bad shape."

With a shake of her head, the woman opened it and flipped through the pages. "No, sorry," she said. "This isn't familiar."

"Do you have any suggestions as to how I might discover the title and the author?"

The librarian's gaze slid to her left. "Well," she said with reluctance as she studied the chapter titles. "You could try an Internet search . . . using twentieth-century authors and women's issues."

Kate received the distinct impression that the woman would prefer it be done somewhere other than *her* library.

The woman handed her the book and Kate gave her a broad

smile. "Thanks," she said brightly, "I'll use that computer over there."

Once seated at the computer, she typed in the librarian's suggestions, and thirty minutes later had decided it was hopeless.

Stretching her arms overhead, she squinted at the screen. At first, she'd wondered if Essie, Rose's grandmother, was the author, so she followed several links about her, but found nothing about any essays. The name of Johan Bennett had popped up in conjunction with Essie, which didn't surprise her. Rose had mentioned that Johan had been Essie's mentor.

She typed in Johan's name and followed those links. Not much was out there even though he'd been a prolific writer and staunch supporter of the suffragette movement. His opinions had caused a quite a stir. One article had credited his work as being the driving force behind changes in the child-labor laws.

But as for the man himself, Kate found a reference calling him "reclusive," and that was it. No formal biography or photographs—and nothing that would indicate a connection to Iowa, much less the Krauses.

Next she tried "Iowa mental institutions in 1890." Forcing herself to skim through those, she was appalled at the conditions in which the patients lived. Her horror grew as she uncovered articles mentioning the use of lobotomies for the treatment of the mentally ill.

While she was reading one of the articles, a familiar name popped out at her, "Dr. William Krause." Further searching led to a biography of Dr. Krause.

He wasn't the simple country doctor Kate had assumed. He had been active as a mental-health advocate and had fought until his death in 1970 for the abolishment of lobotomies.

Kate leaned in. His work wasn't surprising, considering the fate of his mother. Had Hannah still been living then? Had, in the course of his work, he seen his mother?

"Hey," a voice whispered in her ear, startling her.

She turned to find Will standing behind her.

Leaning in, he squinted at the screen. "I see you're reading about Willie."

Kate closed the screen and looked up at him. "How did you know I was here?"

He pulled a chair over and sat. "I saw your Jeep parked out front." He paused. "Why were you looking up my great-grandfather?"

"I—well." Kate squirmed in her chair. "It wasn't my intent. Rose told me about Hannah."

"And you discovered Willie's name by looking up mental institutions?"

"Yeah. I thought he was a small-town doctor. You never mentioned his work for the mentally ill."

Will shrugged. "It's no big secret. I don't understand why you feel the need to dig up all this old history."

"Does it bother you?" she asked, remembering what Trudy had said about his family possessing secrets.

"I think you should be concentrating on building your defense, so that you're ready in case it comes to that."

"That's not really an answer."

"The truth? I don't appreciate it," he said, his eyes narrowing. "What happened to Hannah was a miscarriage of justice, and I think it only fair that the poor woman should be allowed to rest in peace."

She tried another tack. "What about Joseph? How do you

think he played into what happened to her? Did he testify against her?"

"I can't stop you, can I?"

Kate shook her head.

"We believe he set her up."

"How?"

"He might have tampered with the evidence. Maybe he orchestrated the deal between the county attorney and Hannah's attorney. It's all supposition and we'll never know for sure."

"About the county attorney—Trudy said Willie was the attending physician at his death."

Will's face grew stony. "What are you suggesting?"

"Nothing," she said, looking back at the computer screen. "I just thought it was a funny coincidence—to be present at the death of the man who railroaded his mother."

"There's nothing coincidental about it," he said in a low voice. "Willie was the only doctor in this area."

"He was an advocate for mental health. Why? If he was uncomfortable about his past and wanted to hide it?"

"There's a difference between hiding your past and talking about it." Will leaned in. "He never tried to hide anything. For God's sake—he came back here to practice medicine, but he did avoid reliving the painful memory of what happened to Hannah. Nothing sinister in that."

"I didn't say that there was," she replied defensively. "How did he feel about losing the farm to Joseph?"

"He didn't care. He was never cut out to be a farmer."

"Did he resent his brother?"

"My family is none of your business, Kate," he declared in an angry voice. "And I don't appreciate some of your insinuations about my great-grandfather. He was a fine man and his memory is well-respected in this community."

Kate shrank away from him.

"The same can't be said for Joe's side of the family. No one ever respected them half as much as they did Willie."

"Is that why you're afraid? You think I'll uncover something that will hurt Willie's reputation?"

Will stood and, placing a hand on the back of her chair, leaned toward her until his face was close to hers. "I thought we were friends," he whispered, his breath brushing her ear, "but I'm warning you—you have nothing to gain by nosing around in my family's past."

Chapter 43

Fall 2012, Dutton

As Kate left the library, she was so upset by Will's reaction that she almost missed Doris calling to her from down the block.

"Hey, how are you?" Doris asked, running up to her and giving her a hug. "I tried calling you."

Kate glanced past Doris and down the street. She noticed two of Trudy's friends standing on the corner, looking their way and whispering.

"You're not afraid to be seen talking to me?"

Doris followed Kate's gaze, then turned toward her and took her arm. "Bunch of narrow-minded people," she muttered. "Let's really give them something to gossip about." She tugged on Kate. "We're going to the Four Corners Café for coffee."

Kate pulled back. "I don't know if that's a good idea," she said with hesitation.

"Sure it is," Doris answered with a wink. "You're not going to let those old busybodies scare you, are you?"

Kate took a deep breath and fell into step next to Doris. When they entered the café, all conversation ceased and all eyes turned toward them. She lifted her chin a notch and, following Doris, breezed past them to a booth in the back.

"That was fun," Kate muttered after taking a seat, and the hum of conversation resumed.

After placing their order, Doris leaned forward. "Tell me everything."

Kate related the events of her arrest, and when she'd finished, Doris nodded.

"Rose did good. Darwin Brown has a statewide reputation."

"I don't know." She paused for a moment. "I might regret it."

She explained her disagreement with Rose and how threatened she'd felt by Will.

"I don't understand it, Doris. On the one hand, they talk like the past doesn't matter—yet at the same time, they won't talk about it."

Doris dumped creamer and two packets of sugar into her coffee. "People have long memories, and Will was right—his great-grandfather worked hard to establish his reputation." She slowly stirred her coffee. "Because of his mother, he had to overcome a lot of prejudice. Joe's murder has everyone riled up, and they've begun to rehash Jacob's. Willie's reputation might lose some of its glimmer in the process."

"You know Will's family. Did you know that they've always believed Joseph might have somehow engineered what happened to Hannah?"

"It doesn't surprise me. It's my guess that there's been a lot of closed-door discussions lately. Will has always acted like the past isn't a big deal, but I don't know if I believe it."

"But his family's done well."

Doris chortled. "You bet they have. They could buy and sell Joe's side of the family ten times over."

"No kidding?" Kate's eyes widened in surprise. "I never would've suspected that from the way Will acts."

"They've always kept it on the down low, and his family's never bragged or lorded it over people. They've been more concerned about carrying on the legacy they feel they inherited from Willie."

"Philanthropy and social activism."

"Exactly. They've been involved in Essie's House from the beginning. The money for the new mental health clinic at Braxton County Hospital came from them."

"And Will's afraid that *this* could hurt his family's reputation?" Kate shook her head. "I'm not buying it. There has to be more to it than that."

Doris laid a hand on the table. "No—listen—they've dedicated decades to preserving the way this community sees them. If it were you, how far would you go to protect that? Any scandal—even an old one—might damage it."

"Trudy hinted that there might be a few skeletons rattling around."

"Did she say what?"

"No, she talked about the night Jacob was killed—said only Hannah and Willie were in the house that night." She thought for a moment. "She made a vague reference to Willie being present when the county attorney died." Kate lifted an eyebrow. "Which made Will mad when I brought it up."

Doris leaned forward, her face animated. "You don't suppose? Nah." She waved a hand. "That's impossible."

"What?"

"Suppose Willie killed Jacob?" she asked in a whisper.

"That's a terrible thought," Kate said in a stunned voice. "He was a child."

"A child who'd witnessed his mother's abuse at the hands of his father."

"That's crazy," Kate answered with a shake of her head.

Doris sat back deflated. "I suppose you're right. By all accounts, Willie grew to be a peaceful, gentle man. Not someone you'd suspect of committing patricide."

A strange thought popped into Kate's mind, but she failed to share it with Doris.

What if Willie's life hadn't been driven by selflessness, but by a need for redemption?

All the talk with Doris had planted suspicion in Kate's mind. No matter how she tried to convince herself otherwise, their reaction to her interest in Hannah had been abnormal. They were desperate to keep the past buried. She'd been a fool to blindly trust people she barely knew. Not only did the friendship between Rose and Will go back for years, Will was connected to Rose's pride and joy—Essie's House.

After pulling into the driveway, Kate sat in the Jeep, her mind racing. It was as if her doubts opened a floodgate of crazy ideas and she couldn't move.

Joe had been jealous of Will and he knew something damaging about Will's family.

Joe was in financial trouble. Will's family had money.

No, she thought, trying to shove her theories away.

She failed. She'd already started to wonder if Will was bitter over his lost heritage and had argued with Joe. What had Doris said? How far would you go to protect a reputation that had taken years to build? Kate couldn't stop the idea forming in her mind.

Had Joe attempted to blackmail Will? Had Will killed him to protect his secrets?

There—the questions were asked, and they made her sick.

Rose had hired Darwin Brown. They were setting her up, just like Hannah had been.

Discouraged, Kate dragged herself into the house and the first thing she heard was that damn music box with its skipping tune.

"That's it," she muttered, striding over to the box and slamming the lid.

She looked around quickly and didn't spot Trudy. After tucking the box under her arm, she hurried from the house and crossed the yard to Joe's office. After opening the door, she paused. The last day she entered this room had been the day Joe died. The memories of the hope she'd felt that day turned her mouth sour.

Squaring her shoulders, she moved to Joe's desk and started to rummage for a small screwdriver. She finally found one small enough.

She sat in the chair and studied the box, screwdriver in hand. In a way, she hated dismantling the antique, but the constant missed note was driving her crazy. There wasn't much in her life that she could fix at this point, but at least she could do something about this.

Carefully, she removed the movement from inside the box and placed the box on the floor. Leaning over, she studied it. One of the prongs responsible for playing the tune was missing.

She bent over in the chair and lifted the lid of the box. The missing prong lay in its corner—right next to words someone had roughly carved into the bottom.

THE SINS OF THE FATHER

Chapter 44

Fall 2012, the Krause family farm

Kate was shocked, and sat staring inside the box. The same words she found in the old book were carved in Willie's music box. The lettering was crude and it was hard to tell if a child or an adult had done the carving.

She thought for a moment, wishing she could remember the quote. Did the rest of it say something about visiting the sins of the father onto the children? If she could only make the connection between the book and the music box, she knew it would lead to the truth.

She opened the desk and started to rummage through the drawers. The sheriff had no doubt been through it, but a piece of paper or note that seemed innocuous to them might mean something to her.

She found nothing in the first drawer, then opened the

second. Pictures of ocean liners sailing across turquoise seas lay on top. With tears filling her eyes, Kate removed the brochures and spread them across the desk.

Joe had talked about a cruise the night they'd had their picnic in the apple orchard. He'd remembered and had planned to carry through.

Kate traced a finger across one of the brochures. This was the surprise he'd mentioned on the morning of his death. She sniffed and dashed the tears from her cheeks.

Returning to the drawer, she dug deeper. With a gasp, she pressed her fingers to her lips. She was wrong—here was the *real* surprise: a rental agreement for the retirement apartments, made out in Trudy's name. It was dated for the first of next month.

She leaned back in the chair as regret overtook her. Joe had been serious about changing. Glancing down at the brochures, she thought of how the whole community had been comparing him to Jacob. They were wrong. Joe was nothing like Jacob. He was facing his mistakes and trying to mend them.

And she was nothing like Hannah. The past held no secrets that would help her with the present.

She was scooping up the brochures when a sound in the doorway caught her attention. She froze as Will strolled over to the desk.

"What are you doing here?" she asked, trying to keep her voice even.

"I came out to apologize . . . again . . . saw the door open and figured I'd find you in here." He looked down at the scattered paper. "Looking for more clues?"

She shuffled the papers around, intent on returning them to the drawer. "No—no—I'm just cleaning things out," she replied, sounding lame to her own ears.

Will picked up one of the cruise brochures and gave her a quizzical look. "Planning on a trip?"

She snatched it out of his hand. "No. Joe had mentioned it once and evidently was pursing the idea."

"I thought he had financial problems?" he asked as his eyes narrowed.

Kate dropped the brochures into the open drawer and slammed it shut. "That's none of your business." She folded the rental agreement and stuck it in her pocket.

He placed both hands on the desk and leaned forward. "Did he tell you where he planned on getting the money?"

Kate scooted the chair away from the edge of the desk. "You know how closemouthed he was when it came to his finances."

"Didn't he talk about money in your counseling sessions? That's one of the things that most couples fight about, isn't it?"

She looked up at the man staring at her with eyes just like Joe's. She really didn't know this man at all. A thin trickle of sweat snaked down her spine as Will sat on the corner of the desk.

Before she could respond to his question, he picked up the movement from inside the music box.

"What's this?" he asked.

Kate nudged the box with her foot. "Parts to the music box."

His face flushed. "You dismantled an antique?"

"Um—yeah. I wanted to know why it kept skipping that one note. A piece is broken off." She slowly rose to her feet and edged to the corner of the desk. "I'll have it repaired." Her gaze flitted toward the door as she began to slide in that direction.

His hand on her arm stopped her. "Where's the rest of it?"

"Rest of it?" she repeated with a blank face.

"Yeah. The case, the box?" He dropped his hand and went behind the desk. He spotted it, then picked it up.

Kate backed toward the door as Will lifted the lid. "What in the hell is this?" His attention zeroed in on Kate, and she froze. "Did you do this?" he asked, the anger building in his face.

"No."

Will placed the music box on the desk and came toward her. "Do you know what it means?"

"No." She took a step back. "Do you?"

"I've got a pretty good idea, and I think you do, too." He continued to advance toward her. "The next question would be . . . what do you intend to do with that information?"

"N-Nothing—I don't know anything," she stammered.

He stopped and put his hands on his hips. "What in the hell's wrong with you?"

Kate darted toward the door. "*Get out* and leave me alone," she cried, fleeing to the house.

Once inside the house, Kate pulled the paper out of her pocket and tossed it onto the counter before heading to her bedroom. Anger and fear warred inside her.

What next? Will thought she knew something and she didn't. She was clueless as she had been from the beginning. She had no idea how the carving inside the box connected with the old book. But Will did. Had Joe seen the carving and figured it out?

Was he blackmailing Will? Did Will kill him? She kicked the storage container holding the pictures. Those damn things had started all of this.

The only one who might have a glimmer of what was going on was Trudy. Returning downstairs Kate found her flitting around the parlor with a crumpled piece of paper in her hand.

When she noticed Kate, she faced her. "Did you take my music box?"

"Yes," Kate said as she crossed her arms.

"How dare you!" Trudy's face turned crimson and she looked as if she were ready to spring at Kate.

Kate held up her hands. "You said it held a secret. Did you know the words 'the sins of the father' were carved into the bottom?"

"You destroyed my music box," she cried.

"It can be fixed." She watched her intently. "I want to know what the words mean and why they were carved in the box."

Trudy sank into one of the armchairs and started picking at the crumpled paper in her hand. "I don't know," she answered, all the fight gone out of her.

Kate believed her.

"What did Joe know about Will's family? Was he blackmailing Will?"

Trudy stopped shredding the paper. "I don't know, but I know my son wasn't a criminal."

"Did Willie kill Jacob?"

A confused expression crossed her face. "Hannah killed Jacob," she said slowly, letting the pieces of paper fall around her feet like confetti. "Hannah cursed our family."

She raised her eyes and looked past Kate. An uneasy sensation settled between her shoulder blades, and she fought the desire to whirl around.

"It's over," Trudy mumbled. "I've failed. All these years . . . all the work . . . all for nothing. The last of Joseph's sons is dead." She rose to her feet, dropping the paper from her hand.

Without a glance toward Kate, she walked from the room with her head down and her shoulders slumped.

Kate thought about following her, but she looked so beaten, to engage in further questioning would only make it worse. It had been futile. She heard the door to Trudy's room close; a moment later, the TV began to blare again.

With a sigh, Kate knelt and picked up the scraps of paper littering the rug.

One, with the printing still readable, caught her eye.

It was the rental agreement.

Chapter 45

Kate opened a can of soup for supper and heated it on the stove. After it was warmed through, she knocked on Trudy's door, but there was no response. She opened it and peeked inside.

Trudy lay on her side with her back toward the door while the TV still blasted away.

Lacking the strength for another go-around with Trudy, she quietly shut the door and left her alone. After she'd completed her solitary meal, she checked all the windows and doors, then trudged up to her bedroom. Today's drama with Will and Trudy had left her exhausted.

As she entered the bedroom, she glanced at her laptop. She could do more research, but her brain felt fried. All she had were scattered threads of ideas and none of them connected.

"Probably never will," she muttered to Topaz, who lay curled up in the center of the bed.

The cat raised her head and blinked her amber eyes slowly.

After staring at Kate for a moment, she laid her head on her paws and went back to sleep. There's a definite advantage to being a cat, Kate thought as she changed into a pair of sweatpants and a T-shirt. She wished she could shut her mind off as easily.

Kate lay on her back and cradled the back of her head with her hands. The first thing she intended to do tomorrow was take Trudy to see Doc Adams and set up a full battery of tests. One minute the woman seemed normal, then the next deluded. She needed to know if Trudy's issue was, as Doc suspected, dementia.

Kate frowned into the darkness. The second thing she'd do was fire Darwin Brown and hire a new attorney. She no longer trusted Will and Rose, and Will had frightened her twice in one day.

The house creaked and settled around her as Kate curled on her side and stroked Topaz.

"You've the right idea, don't you, cat," she whispered, "go to sleep and forget about it for now."

Kate must have drifted off. The next time she opened her eyes, the clock said almost midnight. Groaning she pounded her pillow and tried to find a comfortable spot. She shivered and pulled the quilt up to her shoulders.

The strains of "When Johnny Comes Marching Home" wafted up through the floor vent.

Son of a bitch! Kate bolted upright in bed. That crazy woman had found the music box and somehow put it back together. After turning on the light, she jumped out of bed and shoved her feet into a pair of slippers.

From the behind her, Topaz hissed. Looking over her shoulder, Kate saw the cat standing in the center of the bed with her back arched and her ears laid back. Before Kate could grab her, Topaz leapt off the bed and headed out of the room.

Kate followed, but when she reached the bottom of the stairs, she stopped and sniffed the air. *Gasoline.* She rounded the corner of the hallway into the parlor and noticed a soft glow coming from the kitchen.

Oh my God . . . was the house on fire? She had to wake Trudy and get them both out of there.

In her rush through the parlor, she struck her thigh on one of the end tables, sending its antiques flying. She heard the crash of fragile glass but didn't slow her speed.

She jerked to a stop when she reached the kitchen. The smell was stronger there and it made her light-headed.

The light above the stove was on and Trudy was awake. She stood in the doorway between the kitchen and her bedroom with her back toward Kate, staring into the room. Her gray hair straggled down her back, and she appeared weighted down by something in her arms. She slowly turned.

In one hand, Trudy had a large red plastic jug that Kate recognized as containing gasoline, and clutched in her other hand was a box of matches. The front of her nightgown was wet.

A low growl from the kitchen table caught Kate's attention momentarily. Topaz was crouched on the table, watching Trudy.

"Come on," Kate said, trying to keep her voice calm. "Let's go outside."

Trudy shook her head and, before Kate could grab her, she dropped the can and opened the box of matches, then held one aloft.

"Only fire will cleanse this house," she said, her eyes wild.

Kate held up her hands. "Wait—don't you want to tell me why?"

"You know why," she replied petulantly. "But you weren't supposed to wake up. Why did you wake up?"

"I heard your music box."

Trudy smiled. "No, you didn't. You took it away from me. You shouldn't have taken it away. Now the secret's out."

"You still haven't told me why." Kate slid one foot forward.

"We have to die, of course," she answered in a childlike voice. "Joe's lonely without us." She held the match against the strike plate on the side of the box.

"Joe wouldn't want this," Kate insisted, trying to draw Trudy's attention away from the match.

"Yes, he would." Her face twisted. "We both have to pay for our sins. The sins of the father," she finished in a singsong voice.

"What sins?"

"You were a bad wife. You brought the curse down on Joe."

Out of the corner of her eye, Kate noticed a flicker of movement at the kitchen door, followed a second later by Will's face appearing in the window. Kate gave a slight shake of her head, and he disappeared.

She had to keep Trudy focused on her, not the box of matches or the kitchen window.

"You told me *my* sins—what are yours, Trudy? Why don't you explain it to me?"

"Don't you try and fool me," she exclaimed with a wave of the box. "You knew what he was going to do—pack me off. He came in that day, gushing about you, how happy the two of you were going to be." A tear slid down her wrinkled cheek. "He didn't care about my happiness." She gasped for breath as if saying the words physically hurt.

"But you said he'd been stabbed when he came into the kitchen."

"No, no, no. It happened when we argued—about you," she

spit out, "I was so mad that I forgot the knife in my hand and when I whirled around, the knife stabbed Joe."

Kate forgot her fear and took a couple of steps toward Trudy. *"You stabbed your own son!"*

Trudy began to tremble. "The knife gouged him. It was an accident. I tried to save him."

"Why didn't you tell anyone what had happened?" Kate took another step.

Trudy backed away from her. "I—I couldn't think." Suddenly her trembling stopped. "See, if we both die, then it will be fine. My hand killed my son, but you made it happen."

Trudy held the match next to the box and cocked her head as if she was listening to a voice that only she could hear.

The grandfather clock striking midnight suddenly brought her out of her daze, and before Kate could grab her, she struck the match and tossed it into the bedroom.

As flames whooshed across the floor and engulfed the bed, the back door flew open and Will rushed into the room.

"Get out of here!" he yelled as he yanked Trudy away from the flames rushing toward her. The room began to fill with smoke, but not before Kate saw Topaz dash out the open door. Covering her mouth with the bottom of her T-shirt, Kate looked for Will and Trudy.

He'd slung her over his shoulder and, as he came by, gave Kate a push in the direction of the door. Together, they fled into the night.

Standing in the yard, Kate watched as flames danced in the windows of Trudy's bedroom. And over the distant howl of sirens, she heard a woman's scream.

◆ ◆ ◆

"Drink this tea," Rose said, shoving the warm cup into Kate's hands.

She took a sip, then sputtered. "This isn't tea."

Rose shrugged. "Well, it might have a shot or two of whiskey in it. Drink it down. It'll be good for you."

Kate did as she was told and let the warm liquid ease the tightness in her throat. Sitting in Rose's recliner, she looked out the window as she pulled the afghan tighter around her shoulders.

Topaz, not taking kindly to being disturbed, stood, kneaded Kate's lap, then settled down again.

"Has Will called?" she asked Rose.

"Not since you asked me five minutes ago." Rose took a seat on the couch across from Kate. "He'll call as soon as he can. He wanted to stay until the fire was out."

"I wish I knew how Trudy was."

"She's probably at the hospital by now."

"Rose, I'm sorry I doubted you," Kate said.

"You've apologized about ten times now, and you needn't again," Rose replied kindly. "I understand why you questioned our motives."

Kate placed the cup on a table next to her chair and massaged her tired eyes with her fingertips. "I can't grasp what happened tonight."

"None of us can, sweetie." Rose was silent for a moment. "Did you make much sense out of what Trudy said?"

"Just that they were fighting about her moving into town.

Somehow, she whirled without thinking and accidentally caught Joe with the knife." Kate dropped her hands away from her face. "I suppose she was so shaken by what happened that she carried it to the car with her."

"Then threw the knife in your Jeep as she was leaving the hospital." Rose frowned. "Do you think she was trying to frame you?"

"Honestly?" Kate asked with a lift of her eyebrow. "I think when Trudy saw Joe die on the way to the hospital, all sense of reality broke for her. You saw how she acted until after the funeral. Her mind had shut off."

Before Rose could respond, Kate jumped to her feet. "Someone just pulled in."

She hurried to the door, expecting Will, but it was a sheriff's car. Kate stifled a groan as Detective Shepherd got out and walked to the house.

"Let me guess . . . you have some questions?" she asked sarcastically.

"I will, but not tonight. I've already got Will's statement." He glanced down at his feet. "I just wanted to stop by and let you know that your mother-in-law died on her way to the hospital. Doc Adams thinks it might have been a massive stroke."

Trudy had joined her son. As the detective walked away, Kate prayed that at last she had found peace.

Chapter 46

Fall 1890, the Krause homestead

Joseph wove across the barnyard, a lantern clutched tightly in one hand and a bottle in the other. His, all his. He'd won. No more Pa . . . No more Hannah. He didn't care what that bitch said. Crazy talk, that's all it was. He snorted. "The sins of the father." He took a long pull from his bottle. He'd never allow his woman to back talk him like she did tonight. His woman. He did a little dance in the hot evening air. He owned property now. He could have his pick of any woman he wanted. He stopped and thought for a moment, squinting his eyes up at the moon. *Better pick a stupid one.* He gave a drunken nod. *Yup, stupid and pretty, that was the way to go.*

That had been the trouble with Hannah. She was too smart. He chuckled. *Smarter than Pa.* And he'd tried to beat it out of her. Not him, better to start out with stupid—less trouble. And whoever the lucky woman was, she'd be so grateful for his at-

tention that he'd never hear a sharp word out of her mouth.
She'd raise his kids and wait on him. He threw out his chest.
And he'd make sure those kids grew up tough like him. Just like
his father had done for him.

"Sins of the father"? He felt a niggle of fear. Ahh, he waved his
hand at nothing, bullshit, nothing but a load of bullshit.

Feeling better, he started back toward the house, then stopped.
What was that claptrap about not being silenced? Apprehension
seized him. She didn't know, couldn't know. He kicked a rock
across the yard and almost fell. Righting himself, he took two
staggering steps.

She was the one responsible for what happened. She hadn't
been where she was supposed to be.

He covered his face with his hands and began to sob. "I'm
sorry, Pa, I'm sorry." He dropped to his knees. "Her—it was supposed to be her. Why didn't you fall asleep on your side of the
bed instead of hers?"

Wiping his nose, he staggered to his feet. He was safe. No one
remembered his mother's fancy cutlery set, but he had. They'd
been long hidden in the loft. Closing his eyes, he could still see
his mother polishing those knives in the aftermath of Pa's spells.
He'd always wondered if she'd get the gumption to use one on
Pa, but she never had the chance. She'd "fallen" down the cellar
steps and died from her injuries. The knives hadn't helped her
any more than they had Hannah.

He cocked his head and the world tilted. In a way, it was
rough justice—his father had killed his mother and his mother's
knife had killed him. After stumbling up the steps, he crossed
the floor to the kitchen table. He blew out the lantern and fell
into one of the chairs.

Yup, rough justice, he thought as his eyes closed and the room spun. He could live with that.

His hand stole over the polished wood of Willie's music box, and he lifted the lid. A drunken grin spread over his face as he clapped along, one beat off, to the music of "When Johnny Comes Marching Home." Rocking back and forth he chuckled. The brat's never going to come marching home again. And neither is she.

When the tune had finished, Joseph grabbed the long knife lying on the table. So happy that Charles Walker had seen fit to give him back the knife. A Civil War side knife like this one was worth a lot of money and it had belonged to his ma's father. He took the tip, and using it as a screwdriver, dismantled the music box, then with one eye shut and using the same knife, began to carve words into the bottom of the box.

When he finished, he studied his handiwork. THE SINS OF THE FATHER. He choked out a sob and wove his way back to Pa's bedroom. Falling across the bed facedown, he buried his face in the pillow.

"I'm sorry, Pa. I'm sorry," he muttered to the empty house.

He was unconscious a moment later and never heard the faint scream drifting across his land.

Chapter 47

Fall 2012, the Krause family farm

The next day, Kate stood in the apple orchard and surveyed the damage to the house. Thanks to Will arriving when he did and his 911 call before Trudy had tossed the match, the destruction was minimal compared to what it might have been. The kitchen and Trudy's bedroom had fared the worst, and the rest of the house had water and smoke damage.

Kate shook her head at the irony. The room where Jacob had been murdered was now nothing more than charred timbers.

"What are you going to do now?" Will asked from where he stood next to her.

"I spent most of the night thinking about it," she replied, kicking at the leaves at her feet. "A crew's coming in today to rip out the burned areas, then they'll board it up. I guess after that I'll start cleaning it out. Most of the antiques were saved, so I'll get them ready for the estate sale."

"Are you sure you want to sell them all?"

"Yes, I am." She stuck her hands in her pockets as her attention roamed over what was left of the old house. "Then the house will be torn down."

"No more Krause family home?"

She turned to face him. "This never was a home. From what I've learned, the families who spent their lives here knew nothing but misery." She glanced back at the house and the blackened shell of Jacob's bedroom. "If Trudy was right, and fire does cleanse, maybe now those restless spirits will be free."

"You finally believe in all the stuff about curses and ghosts?"

Kate thought for a moment. "I don't know. Last night, I could've sworn I heard the music box." She shook her head. "But that's impossible. I checked this morning, and it's still lying in pieces on Joe's desk."

"Maybe Hannah was looking out for you."

"If so, then I owe her my life. Hearing the music box was what got me out of bed." She smiled up at him. "I also owe you a debt of gratitude. What made you drive out here so late last night?"

"I couldn't sleep. I kept replaying our conversations over and over in my mind, and I wasn't proud of the way I acted." He rocked back on his heels. "I wanted to set things straight, so I took the chance you'd still be up and drove out here. That was when I saw the light in the kitchen and went around to the back—"

"And saw Trudy with her can of gasoline and box of matches," she finished for him with a shiver.

"Where are you going to live?"

"Not out here—I'm not going to rebuild. I still plan on managing the farm, but I'm going to get a place in town. And I want to keep working at Doc's and serving as a volunteer at Essie's House. In fact, the proceeds from the estate sale are going there."

"You're not keeping it?"

"No, I don't need the money." She gazed back at the house. "After the violence that Hannah must've suffered, there's a certain amount of justice in giving the proceeds from the Krause family heirlooms to Essie's House. The money will help other abused women." She gave him a half-smile. "I think Hannah would've approved."

"Hey," Will said abruptly, "you want to go for a ride? I want to show you something."

"Now?" she asked with a lift of her eyebrow.

"Yeah, come on," he said, grabbing her hand and leading her to his car.

Once in the car, Kate turned to him. "I have a confession to make." She picked at the hem of her shirt. "I . . . well . . . I thought you might have killed Joe."

The car swerved toward the shoulder. "What?" he asked as he regained control.

"Yeah. Look, I know you and Rose are hiding something—"

"But—" he interrupted.

She held up her hand, stopping him. "I know it's crazy, but I got the wild idea that maybe Willie had killed Jacob, that Joe knew about it, and you were trying to protect Willie's reputation. I even wondered if Joe had tried to blackmail you over it." She finished with a nervous laugh.

"You were right about one thing—"

"Not Joe?" she blurted out.

"No, not that or," he said, shooting her a sideways glance,

"about Willie killing Jacob. But we were protecting someone's reputation." He paused. "Johan Bennett."

"Essie's mentor? I looked that name up yesterday while I was at the library."

"Then you must have noticed that there isn't much written about Johan."

"Right. The articles referred to him as reclusive."

"That's true. Johan lived in Chicago and worked hard to improve conditions for families, specifically women."

"I read where his writing contributed to changes in the child-labor laws."

"They did. That book of essays? It's one of Johan's earliest works and not as well-known as his later writings."

"How did a Krause get a copy?"

"My guess is that someone mailed it to Joseph. You saw that the essay, 'The Sins of the Father,' had been ripped out?"

"Yes," Kate answered slowly.

"That essay is about how violence in families can be perpetuating and passed down to the children."

"The victim grows up to become the abuser."

"Yeah."

Kate stared out the window before returning her attention to Will. "That was true in Joe's family. I don't know about his grandfather, but his father abused Trudy throughout their marriage. Joe talked about it in counseling."

"By all accounts he was an abuser and so was Joseph."

Kate counted on her fingers. "Four generations. That's where the 'sins of the father' comes in."

Will nodded.

"So who carved those words in the music box?"

"My guess is Joseph. We've always believed he was the one who really killed Jacob."

"Why?"

"We'll never know. My grandfather once mentioned rumors concerning the death of Jacob's first wife and Joseph's mother. She died under mysterious circumstances, but nothing was ever proved."

"Revenge?"

"Maybe, or maybe he got tired of waiting around for his inheritance. I figure that carving is the closest thing to a confession that Joseph ever made."

"Johan knew the Krauses?"

"Yeah. Here we are," he said, turning into the cemetery.

Kate's eyes widened. "You brought me to the cemetery?"

"I told you that I wanted to show you something."

Will drove past the rows of headstones, their polished surface gleaming in the morning light. When he reached a corner of the cemetery, he stopped and got out, motioning for Kate to follow.

A slight breeze whispered through the pines and stirred the leaves littering the graves. Artificial wreaths and flowers marked a few of them. Some had bright banners waving next to them that seemed out of place in such a somber space.

Finally, Will stopped at a headstone made of gray granite.

Smiling, Will pointed to it. "Kate, meet Johan Bennett."

Kate's chin dropped as she stared at Will. "Hannah? Hannah was Johan Bennett?" She shook her head. "But how? I don't understand—I thought Hannah spent her life in an insane asylum?"

"She spent ten years," he answered grimly. "Her sister and brother-in-law worked for her release, but it wasn't until Willie became an adult that they managed to get her out." He wiped a dead leaf off the top of the stone. "They both moved to Chicago where Willie went to medical school and Hannah found a job as a secretary."

"When did she start writing?"

"Right away, but she did it under her pen name." He chuckled. "When her essays started causing a stir, she quit and wrote full-time."

"No one ever made the connection?"

"No, not even when she became successful. She was always very careful to keep her past, and the fact that she was a woman, secret. She didn't believe that she'd be taken seriously if it got out she'd spent ten years in an insane asylum."

"She was probably right. I take it Rose and her family knew?"

"Yeah, in fact Hannah helped Essie get established."

"And both families have kept her secret all these years?"

A look of sadness crossed his face. "Hannah went through hell and back, first with Jacob then in the asylum. We've always felt that the least we could do was respect her wish for anonymity, even after she'd passed away."

Kate knelt by the granite stone and traced the lettering of Hannah's epitaph.

A VOICE NOT SILENCED

Acknowledgments

I've often been asked where I find the inspiration for various stories. In this case, this book was inspired by a real event that happened in Iowa in the early 1900s, and by the intriguing book *Midnight Assassin* by Patricia Bryan and Thomas Wolf. I'd like to thank them for creating such an interesting book and for whetting my desire to learn more about women's issues during that time period. (Thank goodness I live in this age!)

Another big thanks to my editor, Emily! You not only spot the holes in the story, but give me specific ideas on what I need to do to fill them! The story is better and stronger thanks to your input and I can't tell you how much I value your comments!

My agent, Stacey—for the past seven years, you've guided my steps down this crazy path, and I never would have made it without you! Always patient and kind, you have been a joy to work with!

To Alexx Miller, my beta reader. Thanks for being there with the praise and/or swift kick in the keister, and for knowing which I needed the most at any given point in time!

To my friend and fellow author, Tamara Siler Jones—thanks so much for being the "voice of reason" during the process of this book and for the endless brainstorming! I knew that I could always count on you to give it to me straight!

Mark Shepherd, Dallas County Deputy Sheriff and Medical Examiner Investigator—thanks, Mark, for all of the valuable information about law enforcement procedures and ideas on how to set up my poor characters! *And* thanks for the tour of the Dallas County Jail! So happy that you didn't make me stay, and I pray I never have to enjoy your hospitality!

And, as always, a heartfelt thanks to my family and friends. You've been on this journey with me since the beginning and I know it hasn't always been an easy one, but your love and support has never wavered.

To all the readers who've spent their time and their money on these tales I spin—without your interest, my stories would be just another file on my hard drive. As you can see a lot of people had input into this story, but all errors and mistakes are mine alone! Hopefully you, the reader, will forgive those oversights and enjoy the story!

About the author

About the book

Insights,
Interviews
& More...

Read on

Meet Jess McConkey

Expressions Photography by Valerie Allen

JESS MCCONKEY, aka Shirley Damsgaard, is an award-winning writer of short fiction and the author of the Ophelia and Abby mysteries and *Love Lies Bleeding*. She lives in a small Iowa town, where she served as postmaster for more than twenty years. ༼

The Story Behind *The Widows of Braxton County*

EVERY AUTHOR is asked the question "What inspired you to write this book?"

Personally, my inspiration never comes from the same place: TV, news articles, a book of nonfiction, a tale told by a friend. Often a story or pieces of a story will be influenced by more than one thing. At other times I might not even be aware of what exactly started my brain churning.

However, in the case of *The Widows of Braxton County*, it's easy for me to pinpoint the source of my inspiration. Several years ago, I attended a book signing at a semilocal independent bookstore (which sadly is no longer in business) and listened as the two authors explained how they came to write a book detailing a murder that happened here in Iowa over a hundred years ago. I bought the book, read it, and found it to be much more than a story about a murder and its aftermath. *Midnight Assassin* by Patricia Bryan and Thomas Wolf not only deals with the Hossack family's tragedy but goes into detail concerning women's lives at the turn of the twentieth century.

I knew life was hard back then— farming is backbreaking work—but until I read this book, I had never stopped and thought about how difficult it could be for a woman living during that period. In 1890, women had little control over their lives. First they were under the ▶

3

The Story Behind *The Widows of Braxton County* (continued)

jurisdiction of their fathers, and then after they married, as was expected, under that of their husbands. In some of the situations written about in *Midnight Assassin*, women were little better than slaves, with no recourse when situations were bad. There were no women's shelters, divorce was considered extremely shameful, and not only was family counseling unheard of, it wasn't the "done thing" to air your dirty laundry in public. Some of these women were truly trapped in a life not of their own making.

Reading *Midnight Assassin* made me want to learn more. I learned about the Cult of True Womanhood, a middle-class value system that arose during the 1820s and flourished for the rest of the nineteenth century. It promoted the idea that a woman's place was in the home. A woman's role in life was to provide a refuge for her husband; she was thought too fragile to face the hustle and bustle of the outside world. The watchwords of the Cult of True Womanhood were piety, purity, submission, and domesticity, and these ideals were advocated in popular literature and from the pulpit. A true woman devoted her time to unpaid domestic labor. In 1890 only 4.5 percent of married women were employed outside of the home. Some states even had laws legally limiting a woman's working hours so work wouldn't affect her duties to her family. Needless to say, under conditions such as these, a widow whose husband hadn't provided for her would have been devastated financially, left with little means to care for herself and her children.

I'm a child of the 1960s and '70s, so some of these ideals seemed very foreign to me. Also, my father died when I was an infant, and until Mom remarried five years later, I watched my mother do everything! She worked her entire life, slowing down only when she was in her late sixties. She could drive anything with wheels, be it tractor, truck, or car; can vegetables; hang wallpaper; plow a field; tend pigs. And the same hands that were strong enough to help my stepfather butcher an animal were gentle enough to dry all my childhood tears. Oh sure, she had definite ideas about what being ladylike meant and I heard the words "act like a lady" plenty of times growing up, but being a lady never stopped her from doing a job that needed to be done.

And after reading more about society's expectations of women in the late 1890s, I realized that back then women like my mother had helped change those views about what a woman could or couldn't do. They lobbied for the right to vote, the ability to receive a higher education, the opportunity to work outside of the home and earn their own wage.

But it wasn't just women who sought change. In 1869, John Allen Campbell, the first governor of the Wyoming Territory, approved the first law in ▶

The Story Behind *The Widows of Braxton County* (continued)

U.S. history explicitly giving women the right to vote. In 1848 at the Seneca Falls Convention, Frederick Douglass signed the Declaration of Sentiments, which urged passage of national suffrage. Although when women's suffrage came to a vote before the House of Representatives in 1918, the proposed amendment eventually failed in the Senate, many congressmen went to great lengths to cast their votes in favor of it. One congressman, at his wife's request, left her side as she lay dying so he could support the bill's passage. All of these people made a difference. These stories got my mind spinning. Who were these people? Where did they find their courage? What day-to-day challenges did they face that we can't conceive of?

When I began creating the characters and plotline for *The Widows of Braxton County*, all this material was fermenting in my mind—the problems faced by women in the 1890s, the expectations placed on them by society, the example my mother set for me growing up, how the world has changed for young women today, and how some things *haven't* changed. I wanted my character Hannah, who in my opinion is expected to achieve an unattainable level of perfection, to rail against the status quo and have the strength to fight against all odds. At the same time, I wanted Kate to be the opposite: a woman who has many more advantages and privileges than Hannah had in the 1890s but who, at the beginning of the story, is determined to play by the rules and do what is expected of her. It's only through learning from her mistakes and dealing with tragedy that Kate is able to find her inner strength and become an instrument of change to help others, just as Hannah did in her time.

I hope that you, the reader, enjoyed Hannah's and Kate's journeys, and that you too will have a new appreciation of the real-life battles fought by the women and men who've gone before us. Their fight earned us many of the freedoms we now have, and personally I'm grateful that each of them chose to be "a voice not silenced." ∾

A Reading Group Guide

1. *The Widows of Braxton County* focuses on two central characters. In what ways do you think Kate's life runs parallel to Hannah's? How do their lives differ?

2. What is your first impression of Kate? Does it change by the end of the book? What impact do Doris and Rose have on your perception of Kate?

3. What is your impression of Hannah? Was there anything she could have done to change her life? Do you think that she ever loved her husband?

4. Do you believe the Krause family was cursed? If so, where did the curse originate? Discuss the difference between a curse and a haunting. Was the Krause home haunted, and if so, by whom? How much do you think that Trudy knew about her family's history?

5. Did Trudy deliberately place the knife instrumental in Joe's death in Kate's vehicle? Did she want Kate blamed for his death?

6. Joe is incredibly attached to his mother. Was Joe's attachment to Trudy justified? How do such strong attachments form?

7. In the beginning, Kate struggles to be the "perfect wife." Why do you think it was so important to her to please both Joe and Trudy?

8. How does Kate's relationship with her grandmother shape the other relationships in her life?

9. How does the quote "The Sins of the Father" resonate throughout the story?

10. Does Hannah's stepson Joseph have any redeeming qualities? How was his personality shaped by growing up in an abusive household? Was there justice for the crimes that Joseph committed?

11. One act of violence, the murder of Jacob, has shaped many lives throughout the generations. How did it affect Hannah? Willie? Joseph? Essie? Rose?

12. In the end, did Hannah triumph over her adversaries? If she did, is it important for the townspeople to know? ᕲ

More from Jess McConkey

A NOVEL

LOVE LIES BLEEDING

To what lengths would you go to keep a past buried?

Samantha Moore is a golden girl—with a perfect job, a perfect man, a perfect life—until a random act of violence changes everything. Unconscious for two months, Sam awakens from her coma a different person—bitter, in constant pain, and forced to endure medications that leave her nauseated and paranoid, struggling to keep a grip on reality.

Furious with her family for sending her away to a small, remote town to recuperate—placed completely under a physical therapist's care and robbed of what little freedom she has left—Sam lashes out at the "nice people" all around her who claim to have only her best interests in mind. But are her violent outbursts the by-product of her condition . . . or something else entirely? Strange things are happening here—and either Samantha Moore is losing her mind or her friendly new neighbors are far more dangerous than they appear to be. . . .

"Haunting, mysterious, and subtly romantic, this debut under Shirley Damsgaard's pseudonym is inspirational and full of hope."

—RTBookReviews.com

More from
Shirley Damsgaard

WITCH WAY TO MURDER

Thirtysomething Ophelia Jensen
wants to live a quiet life as a small-town
librarian. She's created a comfortable
existence with her kooky, colorful
grandmother Abby, and if it had been
up to her, they could have lived out
their days—along with Ophelia's dog,
Lady, and cat, Queenie—in peace and
quiet. But to Ophelia's dismay, she and
Abby aren't a typical grandmother/
granddaughter duo. She possesses
psychic powers, and Abby is a kindly
witch. And while Ophelia would do
anything to dismiss her gift—harboring
terrible guilt after her best friend was
killed and she was unable to stop it—
threatening events keep occurring,
forcing her to tap into her powers of
intuition. To make matters worse,
a strange yet devastatingly attractive
man is hanging around Ophelia's library,
and no matter how many times she tells
him she has sworn off men forever, he
persists. Soon this handsome newcomer
reveals he's following a lead on a local
drug ring, and then a dead body shows
up right in Abby's backyard. And much
as Ophelia would like to put away her
spells forever, she and Abby must use
their special powers to keep themselves
and others out of harm's way.

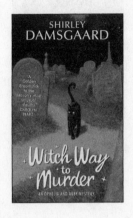

CHARMED TO DEATH

Ophelia Jensen's good witch granny Abigail revels in her paranormal powers. But Ophelia never asked for her bothersome psychic abilities— especially since they proved worthless when the thirtysomething librarian's best friend Brian was murdered by a still-unknown assailant.

Now, five years later, another friend is gone, killed in almost identical fashion. Even dear old Abby isn't safe, distracted as she is by her fight to prevent a massive mega-polluting pig-farming operation from invading their small Iowa town. And Ophelia can't count on her snarling, scoffing nemesis, police detective Henry Comacho, to get the job done, so she'll have to take matters into her own hands. Because a common thread to the crimes and a possible next victim are suddenly becoming troublingly apparent . . . Ophelia Jensen herself!

Ophelia has always considered her psychic abilities an imposition, except for those times she's been able to put her paranormal talents to good use— as when a friend asks her to help find a missing teenager. Unfortunately it means she and Abby, her kindly, canny sorceress granny, will be taking to the road to pursue the vanished girl in the wilds of Minnesota.

The signs are pointing toward the secluded new age research facility of Jason and Juliet Finch, who live with their troubled—and possibly matricidal—thirteen-year-old niece. A bizarre local murder that follows their arrival—along with the appearance of a mysterious Native American shaman— only emphasizes the urgency of Ophelia and Abby's hunt, drawing them into a web of dark secrets and to the last place they'd ever wish to be: a cottage in the woods where true evil quite possibly resides.

WITCH HUNT

Small-town librarian Ophelia Jensen is finally starting to embrace her lot as one of the "chosen"—a psychic and folk magick practitioner, aka a witch. Expert loving guidance from her magickally adept grandmother Abby helps—and adopting Tink, an exceptionally talented teenage medium, has given Ophelia's life new purpose . . . until a brutal murder clouds the sunshine of their days.

Ophelia's coworker and best friend Darci is distraught when her cousin is implicated in the small Iowa town of Summerset's most recent murder—the violent death of a biker. Unfortunately for Darci's cousin, her fingerprints are all over the murder weapon. She claims she's innocent, but it'll take Ophelia and Abby more than a good incantation or two to get to the bottom of this crime— what with ghosts, crooked cops, secret identities, and a small army of outlaw bikers thrown into this devil's brew.

THE WITCH IS DEAD

Life is busier than ever for witch Ophelia Jensen. In addition to her day job at the library, she—with the help of her grandmother Abby—is preparing to officially adopt Tink, the young medium she has taken under her wing. So when Ophelia's elderly Aunt Dot, eager for adventure, wants to investigate the murder of a funeral director in the neighboring town, Ophelia tries to say no. But then Tink's dog pulls a skull out

of the woods—a skull that may belong to a murder victim.

Finding mysterious bones in the woods isn't the only strange thing that has happened to Tink lately. She's been having visions of ghastly ghosts imploring her for help. But before Ophelia can connect the apparitions with the murder, Tink is kidnapped! Ophelia and Abby will have to battle a creepy crematorium owner and an invasion from some modern-day body snatchers to find their protégé . . . or else they'll have to hold a séance just to speak to her again.

THE WITCH'S GRAVE

Cupid has cast his spell on good witch Ophelia Jensen. The practical, pragmatic, law-abiding librarian has just begun letting down her hair with Stephen Larsen, the author of some of the most scandalous crime exposés ever written. It's a match made in the stacks—until the would-be lovers take a quiet countryside stroll and shots ring out.

A murderer, not magick, made Stephen disappear—and Ophelia might be next. The sheriff warns her and her grandmother Abby not to meddle, but after another shooting leaves them shaken, the women can't help but get involved. A sinister stalker is trailing Ophelia, and she'll have to summon all her powers to prevent herself from ending up six feet under.

More from Shirley Damsgaard *(continued)*

THE SEVENTH WITCH

Small-town librarian and psychic Ophelia Jensen hails from a long line of wise and wonderfully gifted women. There's her grandmother Abby, a talented witch, along with her great-aunt Mary, who's about to celebrate her hundredth birthday. But as Ophelia learns, when she and Abby travel to North Carolina for the centennial celebration, their family secrets aren't just magickal—they're murderous as well.

Someone in the sweet Southern town wants Abby dead. Could it be a rogue witch in Ophelia's own family? A vengeful local witch desperate to settle a bitter feud decades in the making? Ophelia must use all her talents to save her loved ones—before the witching hour comes upon them, and bad blood turns deadly.

Don't miss the next book by your favorite author. Sign up now for AuthorTracker by visiting www.AuthorTracker.com.